P9-BZZ-264

She's with the band . . .

Tension filled the room. Emmie looked uncomfortable, like she needed to do something. But there was nothing she—or anyone—could do. It took time. Violet wasn't worried. She watched as the guys tore open the pizza boxes, twisted the caps off the beers, and dug into their dinner.

"Are you as cool inside as you look on the outside?" Derek reached for a slice of pizza. "Because nothing seems to faze you. Not even Pete's stanky dreads."

Emmie nearly snorted lemonade out her nose. Everyone laughed.

Violet noticed the look of affection in Pete's gaze as he regarded Emmie. A pang of envy struck her— these guys were so tight. No matter their troubles, they really liked each other. They were better than a family because they'd chosen each other.

She looked at Derek, who was laughing. That night in the bowling alley? She'd wanted so badly to let him in. Feel the stroke of his tongue in her mouth. Have him pour that energy, that passion into her. She wanted to know what it would feel like to have his possessive hands all over her body.

Titles by Erika Kelly

YOU REALLY GOT ME
I WANT YOU TO WANT ME

I WANT YOU
TO WANT ME

Erika Kelly

BERKLEY SENSATION, NEW YORK

**BERKLEY
SENSATION**

**Published by the Berkley Publishing Group
An imprint of Penguin Random House LLC
375 Hudson Street, New York, New York 10014**

A Berkley Book / published by arrangement with EK Publishing LLC

Copyright © 2015 by Erika Kelly.
Excerpt from *You Really Got Me* copyright © 2015 by Erika Kelly.
Penguin supports copyright. Copyright fuels creativity, encourages diverse voices,
promotes free speech, and creates a vibrant culture. Thank you for buying an authorized
edition of this book and for complying with copyright laws by not reproducing, scanning, or
distributing any part of it in any form without permission. You are supporting writers and
allowing Penguin to continue to publish books for every reader.

BERKLEY SENSATION® is a registered trademark of Penguin Group (USA) LLC.
The "B" design is a trademark of Penguin Group (USA) LLC.
For more information about the Penguin Group, visit penguin.com.

ISBN: 978-0-425-27729-4

PUBLISHING HISTORY
Berkley Sensation mass-market edition / July 2015

PRINTED IN THE UNITED STATES OF AMERICA

10 9 8 7 6 5 4 3 2 1

Cover photograph of lead guitarist copyright © indigo lotos / Shutterstock.
Cover design by Rita Frangie.
Interior text design by Kelly Lipovich.

This is a work of fiction. Names, characters, places, and incidents either are the product of
the author's imagination or are used fictitiously, and any resemblance to actual persons,
living or dead, business establishments, events, or locales is entirely coincidental.

If you purchased this book without a cover, you should be aware that this book is stolen
property. It was reported as "unsold and destroyed" to the publisher, and neither the author
nor the publisher has received any payment for this "stripped book."

Penguin
Random
House

This book is dedicated to Tom,
who filled the second half of my life
with all that was missing from the first.

ACKNOWLEDGMENTS

♪ All my love goes to you, Superman, for your boundless love, support, and dedication.

♪ There's no denying it. I wouldn't be published without you, Sharon. Yes, for your insightful critiques, but also for keeping me sane.

♪ My angel, Olivia, my most ardent supporter, thank you for being with me every step of the way.

♪ Joshua, your support and music industry expertise have been invaluable to me. You, sir, are awesome.

♪ I am wildly grateful to my publishing team. Thank you Leis Pedersen, Courtney Wilhelm, Bethany Blair, Courtney Landi, and Rita Frangie and the art department (I love my gorgeous covers!).

♪ Kevan Lyon, you're the best agent. Thank you for all you do for me.

♪ The romance community is filled with the most generous people I've ever known. My writer friends in CTRWA, WRW, CoLoNY, and COFW have lit the path for me, and I can't thank you all enough for your help.

♪ Thank you to the wonderfully supportive blog-gers who shared my first book with their readers. You all made my debut a joy.

ONE

"You're gonna give a girl a complex."

Derek Valencia looked up from his phone to take in the woman coming out of his hotel bathroom. Licking her glossy lips, she cupped her big tits and leaned forward, giving him a view of lush cleavage. His pulse quickened, and he got hard.

He probably shouldn't be fucking the woman who did publicity for the band, but it was rare to find a woman like her. One who genuinely wanted exactly what he did—the occasional night of hot, freaky sex, no strings attached. And when it ended, they'd both move on, neither letting it affect their business relationship. Careers came first.

And whichever role she played, Genevieve Babineaux played it balls-to-the-wall, whether she was in business, social, or sex kitten mode. He just happened to be the lucky bastard currently starring in her sex life.

Unfortunately, though, sex would have to wait. "You look gorgeous, sweetheart. But you gotta get dressed. Ray Montalbano's on his way up."

"Ray?" The seductiveness dropped right out of her tone, and her arms fell to her sides.

"Yep."

"How'd that happen?" She didn't look happy, but then she hadn't been the one to set up the interview.

"Ran into him in the green room tonight. Said if I had a few minutes, he'd like to ask a few questions."

Music blasted through the walls of the adjoining suite, and he checked the time on his laptop. He hated to shut the party down so early, but with the most revered music critic in the country on his way up to the room, he couldn't risk any problems.

Especially after the gig they'd just played. Only ten days into their tour to promote their first album, and they were killing it. He had no doubt they'd go gold by the end of summer.

They *had* to go gold. Not only would it be a reward for all the hard work they'd put in the last several years, but it'd ensure the tour would continue beyond the summer.

And, of course, it would shut his dad up. Irrefutable proof his son had talent.

"I love it." Another thing he liked about her. No issues, no tantrums. Just business. She turned back into the bathroom, flipped the light on. "I'll get dressed."

Just as he got up to talk to the guys, he heard the knock at the door. *That was fast.*

No time to shut down the party, he pulled out his phone, and shot Ben and Cooper a text. Didn't bother including Pete. He'd be too wasted to check his phone.

Shut it down. Ray Montalbano's in my room right now.

A while back, when the partying had started getting out of control, the band had signed a contract with each other. Sure, they wanted the rock star lifestyle, but they wanted longevity in the business even more. So they'd made a line they wouldn't cross—no drugs, no trashing hotel rooms . . . basically, nothing destructive.

The guys got it. He could trust them. Besides, Ray had said he'd only be there a few minutes. It couldn't get too out of control.

On his way to the door, he leaned into the bathroom. "He's here. You good?"

She smiled. "I'll be better when he leaves and we can have some time to ourselves. It's been too long, and I'm *desperate* for you."

Fuckin' A. He had a hot woman in his bed, they were taking the festival circuit by storm, and Ray Montalbano was here to interview him.

Life couldn't get any sweeter.

Unlocking the security latch, he took a moment to get his head on right. He needed to be sharp for interviews, especially with the bombs his dad kept dropping all over the press. No matter how down and dirty his dad got, Derek would not respond. He'd stay focused on the band, the tour, on the *music*. The stuff that mattered.

He opened the door, and Ray gave him a chin nod.

"Hey, thanks for seeing me on such short notice." With his scraggly dark hair and ill-fitting clothes, the guy came up to Derek's shoulders. Seemed crazy a guy so unremarkable could wield such power in the music industry.

"Happy to do it." He shook the guy's hand, noticing the old Snatch T-shirt he wore. "Come on in." He gestured to the shirt. "We're gonna have to get you a new one."

"I want this one. It'll be a collector's item one day."

First order of business with Irwin had been changing the band name to Blue Fire. Derek had to smile at the original image of a beaver they'd come up with nearly ten years ago. They'd come a long way since then.

Leading the critic to the desk, he pulled out the chair. "Have a seat." Derek sat on the edge of the bed.

"Awesome." The guy flopped into the chair, took out his phone, and set it on the desk. He played with it for a moment. "You mind if I record this?" He touched the phone.

"Not at all."

"Fuckin' great show, man."

"Yeah, thanks. It was pretty incredible."

"How the hell'd you get those guys onstage with you? Was it planned?"

Pretty much everything Derek did was planned. Sure, they had a great label, they had Irwin Ledger, the best A&R guy in the business, and everything that came with it but, bottom line, it was *his* band. No one cared about his success or failure as much as he did. He couldn't just hope things worked out. "Sure. We had a list of celebrities in town for the festival, so we invited the guys we knew played in bands to jam with us."

"Brilliant idea—especially for a new band. Talk about generating buzz. That was fuckin' awesome." He shook his head, smiling, as though still in the audience, watching the jam. "You seen any reviews yet?"

"Just got back to the room, so no. You post yours already?" After a show, he and Slater had to do press, spend some time in the green room shaking hands. It ate up a lot of time.

Ray nodded. "You should check it out."

"I definitely will."

"No, I mean now. Read it now."

An uneasy feeling crept down his spine. *This* was why he always took that moment to get his head on right. The look in Ray's eyes . . . the guy was up to something, and it wasn't good.

At that moment, the bathroom door opened, and Gen's expensive scent came billowing out. She sashayed over to them, always the seductress, even in business mode. "Ray." She reached for him, but the critic didn't even get up to greet her, just stared, jaw hanging.

Gen did that to people.

She pushed right through the awkwardness, air kissing the guy on each cheek. "Was that a spectacular show tonight or what?"

Ray swallowed.

"Honestly, Irwin's convinced these guys are the next U2."

That snapped him out of it. "They are. Huge potential. That's why I wanted to talk to you tonight." He homed in on Derek. "Go on and read the review."

Derek reached for his laptop on the desk and dragged it closer. Once he logged onto the Beatz website, his pulse kicked up a notch in anticipation. *Let it be good.* It was one thing for his dad to fuck with *him*, but he couldn't let it hurt the band.

He had to be careful. Ray wouldn't want him reading the review right then if Derek's reaction didn't mean something. He had to stay cool and manage the situation. By tomorrow morning, everyone in the industry would have read this article.

Gen leaned around his shoulder. "So?"

A thrill shot through him seeing his band's name in the headline.

BLUE FIRE ROCKS MIAMI JAM, STEALS THE WHOLE DAMN FESTIVAL

"Oh, Ray, that's just wonderful." Gen's voice sounded sultry.

Derek gulped whole sections of the article, basically skimming all the praise—fuck yes, only good shit about Slater and the guys—and then his gaze slammed into his father's name. An electrical charge rocked his body.

> When asked how it feels to watch his son onstage performing with the likes of Russell Crowe, Jared Leto, and Johnny Depp, just like he used to do twenty years ago when Fusion Stream filled arenas, Eddie Valencia said, "I suppose the comparisons are inevitable. But I really think you're dealing with apples and oranges." He laughed. "Not sure you can compare 'the jazz virtuoso' to the 'sex god,' but okay. Let's just say I'm glad to see him achieving the kind of fame he craves."

"When did you talk to Eddie?" Gen spoke in the brisk tone she used for damage control. "He wasn't at the show tonight."

"I called him," Ray said. "He's been in the press a lot lately, right? It seems weird. He's been out of the scene for years, and the minute his son breaks out, suddenly Eddie's back? So I was curious. Wanted to find out his game."

Derek really needed to say something, but the loud music from next door merged with the noise in his head, making it difficult to think.

The kind of fame he craves.

Fucker. What was his dad's problem? *Jesus, I'm his son.* But he had to pull himself together. He couldn't lose his shit in front of the press. Which was exactly what Ray wanted.

"Oh, it's not a game," Gen said. "He's genuinely proud of his son. Tells him all the time."

Ray's gaze slid to Derek. With every bit of restraint he could marshal, he kept his features impassive. He would not give the critic a poisoned arrow to fling back out into cyberspace.

Think of the band. Think of your brothers.

"So they're not digs?" Ray asked. "The sex god remark? Not a dig?"

"Well, come on, just look at him." Gen practically purred. "Nicknames are given for a reason. Just ask his last two girl-friends."

Why the hell had she brought that up? Like he'd dated them because they were supermodels. *Give me a break.* He'd worked with Adriana on a music video, for Christ's sake.

Okay, this was bullshit. He wasn't going to just sit there and let this guy try to provoke a reaction out of him.

Determination rose like a motherfucker inside him. He would not let his dad get to him. Would not let him into his head. Derek had left home at seventeen and never looked back for this very reason. His dad was toxic.

"You have to know my dad's sense of humor. He's just giving me shit because I play bass, where he played sax. He was the boss, and I'm in the background. He likes to joke around that I use the tats and girlfriends to make up for the fact that I stand behind Slater onstage."

The taste of his father's words on his tongue made him sick. But he knew he sounded convincing, and he hoped Ray printed it word for word.

"I guess I can see that." But no, Ray *didn't* look convinced.

Smart guy.

Glass shattered in the adjoining room. *Shit.*

"Are you coming to any more shows?" Gen reached out to touch Ray's arm. Her silky dark hair spilled over her shoulders, drawing the guy's attention to her plump cleavage.

Great distraction. *Thanks, babe.*

"I'll be at Madison Square Garden, of course." He paused, shifting in the chair. "Your dad's invited me into his studio, wants me to check out some new stuff he's working on."

"Yeah? Cool. It's great. You'll love it." What new stuff? The old bastard hadn't played a note in years.

"You got all those celebrities onstage with you tonight," Ray said. "Ever think about jamming with your dad?"

"Apples and oranges, remember?" Gen laughed. "Trust me, Eddie's brilliance would get lost on the stage with these five rockers."

Derek blocked out the implied cut in her comment. Had to. "My dad can open his own show on any stage in the city. He doesn't need to get up on mine."

Ray enlivened. "I think he wants to. How would you feel about that? You and Eddie Valencia, jamming at MSG?"

A body thumped against the wall, the voices growing louder. *Dammit*. Derek got up. Fortunately, Gen continued the conversation with the guy, giving Derek a chance to go over there. He'd kill the party and, at the same time, grab a minute to calm his shit down. "Excuse me." He headed for the door to the adjoining room.

His father wanted to *get up onstage with him*? After shutting him out of everything—every jam session, every road trip, every fucking meal or cup of coffee he'd ever had with his musician friends. And ten days into his son's first headlining tour, his dad wanted in? What a prick.

An image flashed in his mind. Him, the little boy, standing outside his dad's basement studio—the sound of laughter, deep voices, an instrument being tuned—peering in to see the greatest jazz musicians in the world preparing to jam. To this day, that feeling of desperation lingered within him. Talk about *craving* something? He'd craved being a part of his dad's world. Nothing hurt worse than seeing his dad's features harden at the sight of him. Watching the legendary sax player storm over and slam the door in his son's face.

The boy's whole body vibrating with the sound of it.

Why *the fuck* did that still hurt?

It didn't.

Unlocking the door, he pushed into the suite.

And froze. What had started out as a couple dozen people had turned into a full-on rave. His skin chilled. What if paparazzi had gotten in? They didn't need any bad press.

Quickly, he made his way through the large room, scanning faces, looking for his friends. Finding Cooper in the kitchen, he grabbed him by the back of his shirt. "Shut this down right now. Didn't you get my text? I've got Ray Montalbano interviewing me next door."

Cooper's eyes looked glassy, and he swayed.

"Snap out of it, Coop. I'm serious. You have to get everyone out of here."

He had to get back to his interview. The last thing he needed was for Ray to come looking for him and find his bandmates getting fucked up.

Trusting Coop to get it done, he wove his way back into his room to see Gen at the door with Ray.

Thank Christ.

"Hey, thanks for coming by, man." He shook Ray's hand. The noises coming from next door grew louder, something else hitting the wall. Something heavy. Was furniture being thrown? He was going to kick some asses.

"Yeah, sure. Appreciate the time. Listen, hit me up when you get to the city. I'd like to sit down with—"

A piercing scream cut through the thumping bass.

Adrenaline punched through his system. He shot Gen a look, making sure she understood to get rid of Ray. Not a chance could that guy see what was going on in there.

Another shriek drove Derek to the connecting door of the suite. Once inside, he bolted the lock to keep Ray out. Gen could come in the other door with her key card.

It took him a few seconds to size up the situation. The sea of bodies seemed to be moving toward the balcony.

Derek pushed and shoved, fighting his way through the packed crowd. Once on the balcony, he found Pete greedily sucking on a girl's tit, then lifting her naked ass and hauling her to the railing. Derek lunged, grabbing the girl around the waist and pulling her out of Pete's hold.

"Hey." Pete reeled, completely spaced out. "Give her back."

Cooper slammed into him from behind, laughing hysterically, completely drunk. "Dude, toss her."

Disappointment slammed him. *Not Cooper.* "Are you out of your fucking mind?"

Derek glanced over the railing, saw naked women treading water in the turquoise blue pool two stories below. "I told you to shut it down. Jesus, Coop. Look down there."

It took a moment for Cooper to get it, but Derek saw the moment his friend sobered up. "It was just fun."

He cuffed the back of his head. "What if one of them cracks her head on the side of the pool? Breaks her neck on the bottom? What's the matter with you?"

A wash of color spread over his friend's features. "Fuck, I don't know."

"Help me out, man. We gotta get everyone out of here."

Cooper sucked in a breath, then made his way through the throng into the hotel room.

Derek set the naked girl down. She reeked of booze. "You okay, sweetheart?"

Eyes glazed, she nodded, reaching for the railing to steady herself.

"Where are your clothes?" He dropped to a crouch, looking on the ground, when a hand squeezed his ass.

"Oh, my God, you're Derek Valencia," a girl said.

"Hey, I saw him first." This one pulled at his hair.

Derek got up, forcing the girls back.

The music shut off, and he heard Cooper shouting for everyone to clear out.

Someone moaned, and Derek swung around to find Ben sitting in the corner, his back against the railing. One girl kneeled between his legs, swallowing his dick; another straddled him, naked, her pussy in his face, his hands clamping her ass.

Jesus Christ. Derek snatched a T-shirt and some jeans off the ground and handed them to the girl. "These yours? Can you put them on?"

And then he turned to the crowd. "Everyone out. Right now. Party over." Arms opened wide, he swept them off the balcony. Shooting Pete a hard look, he realized the keyboard player was too far gone to help. With an arm slung around a girl for support, his friend's legs barely held him upright.

"Ben," Derek shouted. "Get up and help us clear the room." When the drummer didn't immediately move, he snapped. "Get your fucking dick out of her mouth and get dressed. I need your help now."

Ben jumped to action, wobbling before righting himself and throwing on a T-shirt.

Derek fished his phone out of his back pocket, texting Abe, the bus driver, to bring the bus around to the back of the hotel. He sent another to Vince, their trusted roadie, asking him to make a quick check around the pool to make sure no one was hurt. And a final one to Slater, letting him know the plan.

Finally, he gathered up all the clothing on the balcony and dropped it onto the patio below, so the women could get dressed.

Now, he just had to get the guys packed and on the road before the paparazzi got hold of the story. Heading back into the main room, he watched the stream of partiers making their way out the door. Gen stood among them, herding them out. When she saw him, she hustled over. "What the hell's the matter with these guys?"

"They're having fun. It was a big night."

She planted her hands on her hips. "I thought you guys had some deal about how many they could take home with them."

"How many of them?" Sometimes her detachment creeped the shit out of him. "Jesus, Gen. It's not a *deal*. We're just careful about it."

"Well, obviously not. Can you imagine if Ray had seen what went on in here? Bad enough he heard it. Maybe I should set something up with him in New York—something with you and your dad—to buy his discretion."

"Not a chance." She had no idea what she was asking of him, but he didn't care. At the moment, he had to get the band safely on the road. He checked the bedroom on the other side of the suite, found it cleared. Bathroom, too.

Fortunately, things hadn't gotten too out of hand. Now, he just had to hope no one had recorded anything with their phones. Irwin wouldn't stand for this shit.

"Okay, it's cool." Cooper met him in the living area. "Everyone's gone."

"Great, pack up. We're heading out."

"What?" Cooper said. "No. I'm too tired to hit the road. Let's crash here."

Ben joined them. "We're not supposed to leave until tomorrow."

"Yeah, that was before you tossed naked girls off the balcony. Let's go."

Pete slumped on the couch, head rolling back. "I didn't get laid."

"Guys." He said it so sharply Pete's head snapped up.

He didn't need to give them a lecture, didn't need to chastise. He simply held out his forearm, displaying the tattoo they'd all gotten last year. The Hand of Eris. It was a permanent reminder of the contract, of their promise to one another not to wade too deeply into the chaos of this industry.

When all of them looked away, Derek knew they got it. "Listen, the hotel's swarming with press from the festival, so we're getting out now. Pack up your shit."

He needed to take one more look over the balcony, double-check no one had gotten hurt. But it should be all right. It was all under control.

They'd wake up in a new town, with a fresh slate. He'd talk to the guys, remind them what they were about.

He peered over the railing, and it took a minute to make sense of what he was seeing. The naked women formed a chain in the pool, arms wrapped around one another's shoulders. Smiling for . . .

Oh, shit. For Ray Montalbano. Who aimed his phone right at them. Someone noticed Derek, and the girls looked up to the balcony. A minute later Ray swung the phone up, trained it on him.

With a chin nod, the critic said, "Smile."

TWO

So . . . this is awkward.

Standing at the back of the restaurant, Violet Davis watched her former client tap his knife against his wineglass, quieting his friends, family, and colleagues.

He rose, resting a hand on the back of his fiancée's chair, and addressed the room. "Thank you all for coming tonight."

In his six-thousand-dollar custom-made Brioni suit, Joe looked nothing like the man she'd known three months ago. Back then, he'd worn soiled clothes, a greasy beard, and bruises. He'd also smelled like a man who'd been locked up in a hotel room with prostitutes on a three-day binge.

Probably because he had been.

This man? The one lifting a champagne flute, smiling with warmth and humility? This man was healthy, clean, and reunited with his former fiancée.

"I can't begin to express what it means to stand here before all of you and announce my engagement to the love of my life," he continued. "Yes, for the second time." Some in the audience laughed. "But this time, I'm not letting her go."

His future bride, a stunning blonde in a sparkling blue cocktail dress, wiped tears from her eyes. She reached a hand up to his. He clasped it, brought it to his mouth, and pressed a kiss on her palm.

The dissolute partier had regained his life, his company, and his soul mate. Violet could not have been prouder of him.

And now it was time for her to go and leave him to the people in his life who mattered.

"Am I the only one who thinks this is freakishly awkward?"

At the sound of the familiar male voice, Violet quickly shoved her foot back into the stiletto she'd kicked off.

Breathing in Randall Oppenheimer's very masculine and expensive scent, she laughed. "Oh, no. Believe me, by the looks I've been getting all night, you're in good company."

Besides board members and Joe himself, of course, everyone in the room thought she was his ex-girlfriend. They'd "broken up" less than a week ago. All night long people had given her furtive and pitying glances. But she didn't mind. She'd likely never see any of them again.

Randall tipped his champagne flute back, looking effortlessly sophisticated and cultured. With his khakis and light blue button-down, his short-cropped hair and boyish features, he could've been the poster boy for Yale frat life.

"You want to get out of here?"

I'd love to. Fortunately, she caught the words before they flew out of her mouth. "I'd better not."

"Oh, come on. You don't seriously want to hang around your former boyfriend's engagement party, do you? Come on, we'll get on my hog and ride like the wind."

One eyebrow rose in disbelief. "You have a motorcycle?"

He looked away, half his mouth curling. "Nope. But it sounded pretty badass."

More likely he'd arrived in his family's limo. With his parents. The Oppenheimers' law firm did a lot of work for Joe's company, so she'd run into them often during the course of her "relationship" with Joe.

"Can't really see myself straddling a hog in this dress anyway." She'd chosen the sleek Armani sheath to fit in with the wealthy crowd but not stand out. In her line of work, invisibility worked in everyone's favor.

"Oh, I can." Still looking away, the other half of his mouth joined the first.

"Someone's frisky tonight." The worst part of her job? The lies. "You better go easy on me. I just got my heart broken." But then, after tonight, she'd never see Randall again. They didn't exactly move in the same circles.

"Come on." He leaned in, so close she could see the ghost of his beard. "You don't really think I'm buying the whole you-and-Joe thing."

A jolt of fear shot down her spine. Did he know? Nothing mattered more to her business than client confidentiality. Her reputation was her bond. "Now, why would you say that?" She tried to play it cool, but his answer mattered.

"Because he's old. And you're . . ." His gaze took a slow ride from her mouth to the stiletto she was glad she'd put back on. "You're . . . *you*."

Oh, thank God. He didn't know anything about her job. He just couldn't picture her with Joe. Well, he was right about that. At forty-eight, nearly twice her age, Joe Capriano was definitely not her type.

"Well, thank you. But Joe's a great guy, and I enjoyed my time with him very much." Once he'd stopped fighting her anyway.

"You *enjoyed your time* with the guy? Doesn't sound like he got anywhere near your heart." He said it with a cute smile, but she couldn't tell if he knew the truth or not.

He was a lawyer and worked closely with the board of Joe's company. He could have found out. "Your point?"

"Date me."

"Date *you*?"

He nearly spit out his champagne. "So you'll date a man twice your age with a comb-over, but not me?"

What did she say to that? She couldn't date anyone she met through clients. "That's not a *comb-over*. That's a side part. Just ask Donald Trump." She smiled, hoping he'd drop it. Because he certainly wouldn't be asking her out if he knew her real identity.

But then his gaze sharpened, the teasing tone gone. "I really would like to date you. I've watched you for three months, waiting for this moment."

Her heart skipped, sending her pulse skittering. She almost lost her composure. *Randall Oppenheimer* had waited three months for *her*?

Well, of course, he didn't know the real her. Her pulse settled down. He thought she was a twenty-five-year-old "consultant" who'd graduated from Williams, came from an "important" family, wore designer clothes, and had tamed major partier Joe Capriano back into a polished and sober CEO of a billion-dollar company.

That was the woman he'd waited three months to ask out. Not her.

"Well, thank you, Randall. That's lovely of you to say, but I'm not really looking to date at the moment." No way could she start a relationship based on a lie.

"I'll tell you a secret." He shoved a hand deep into his pocket, his cheeks turning rosy, and she could not believe how vulnerable this sophisticated, confident man had become. "I knew the moment I laid eyes on you that . . ." He blew out a breath. "Well, that you were special. And that I wanted to go out with you. And, come on, anyone could see there's no fire between you and Joe. So I'm not going to give up."

Her inner teenage girl gave a little sigh. That was about the sweetest thing a guy had ever said to her.

And he wasn't just some guy. He was a really good one. Not just his education, but his family. Sure, his dad ran the biggest law firm in the city and they had unbelievable wealth, but they were known for their down-to-earth kindness and generosity.

Okay, just stop it.

"Remember that night I dropped you at your apartment?"

She barely nodded. Of course she remembered that night. Seated in the back of a town car jockeying along Sixth Avenue with a gorgeous man she couldn't have—sure, she remembered.

"I wanted to kiss you."

She did *not* need to hear this. She couldn't date a guy like Randall. And not just because of client confidentiality, but because everything he knew about her was a lie.

First off, he knew her as Scarlet. Not Violet Davis. But

worse? She didn't live in a Fifth Avenue penthouse. She lived on a farm. And this outfit? All the others he'd seen her in? Purchased for jobs, thanks to a lucrative salary.

If he saw her on the farm, dressed in her shorts and tank top, wearing no makeup, would he still get all shy about asking her out? She didn't think so. "I should get going."

His look turned intense. "Let me give you a ride home. Please?"

Gazing into those intelligent blue eyes, she allowed herself just a moment to imagine going with him. Tossing aside everything—her job, her responsibilities, her history, and just letting herself be a *woman*. A reckless, fun-loving woman who threw herself into passionate relationships.

But then the memory of the social worker's words jarred her.

She'll likely never be able to trust or fully experience love.

Well, hell. So much for giving her imagination the run of the place. She simply wasn't that woman.

And yet . . . a tiny ember glowed deep inside her, the hint of hope that the worker could've been wrong. What if she *could* love? She'd had her grandma for four years, so maybe a seed had been planted. No, she hadn't loved anyone yet, but maybe she hadn't met the right man. She got that she'd never love like a normal person. But maybe she could feel *something*.

She'd never know unless she gave someone a chance. She looked at Randall. What if she gave him a chance?

Her phone chimed in her clutch. "I'm so sorry. It's my work phone." She gave him an apologetic smile. "It's the nature of my business." Well, no, it wasn't, but she needed a reprieve from considering what she couldn't have.

"Sure." He gave her a warm smile.

Pulling out her cell, she saw Emmie Valencia's name on the caller ID. "Please excuse me, I have to take this." She strode around the periphery of the room, looking for the bathrooms. "Emmie?"

"Hey, V, how's it going?"

"I'm all right." Finding a long corridor, she made her way down it. "How about you?"

"Not so great. I've got a problem."

Seeing that no one was waiting for the bathroom, she stepped inside and locked the door. "What's up?"

"Are you interested in a job?"

"I am, actually." Violet took in the dark red wallpaper, crystal faucet handles, and gold accents of the spacious bathroom. The rich scent of roses made her wonder at the source, and she noticed the bowl of potpourri on the counter. Ah—potpourri. What a great idea for her wildflowers. As soon as she got off the phone, she'd text herself a reminder.

"Oh, good. You did such an amazing job with Caroline, you're the first person I thought of."

Uh-oh. "Go on." Emmie managed a rock band. Violet hoped very much she wasn't offering her a job in *that* industry.

"Yeah, so this one's pretty important to me. It involves my brother."

"Isn't your brother in a band?"

She hesitated. "He is."

Now she understood why Emmie seemed wary. Violet had made it clear she didn't work with rock stars. Businessmen could be decadent enough, but people in the music industry? She'd gotten only a glimpse of that world when she'd worked with Irwin Ledger's daughter, Caroline, but it had been enough for her to tell Emmie to lose her number when it came to rockers.

"You still there?" Emmie asked.

What should she do? "Yes. I hate to disappoint you, but I think you know I don't want to work with musicians."

"My brother's not a bad guy. He's not an addict or anything."

"Okay, but he *is* in that world. And it's just not for me." Although she shouldn't be so dismissive. She *did* need a job now that this one had ended.

"I know, I know. Believe me, no one knows better than I do. But my brother's not like that." She exhaled. "Okay, bottom line. The guys are partying too hard, getting too much attention in the media for their behavior and not their music, so Irwin's losing interest. They're good, V. And I'm not saying that because of my boyfriend and brother."

"Then again it *is* your boyfriend and your brother." She kept her tone light.

Fortunately, Emmie laughed. "I know. I know how it sounds. Look, this is so important. And I know I can find someone else, obviously, but I saw what you did with Caroline. It's the way you do it, you know? My brother's really stubborn." She sighed. "That's not the right word. God, I'm so worried you won't take the job that I can't even think. Okay, listen, our dad's always been really hard on him. Always putting him down and criticizing him. So Derek has a hard time taking suggestions. It has to be delivered in just the right way and, V, you do it just right."

"I want to help you out. I do. But I really don't want to work in the music industry." Did she need the money? Of course. Who didn't? But not at the cost of her sanity. Besides, she'd looked forward to spending some time this summer on the farm, developing new products. She closed her eyes, picturing acres of brightly colored flowers set against the stunning backdrop of ocean and clear blue sky. She lived on the most beautiful parcel of land in the world. And she rarely got to be there.

"I'm touring with them right now," Emmie said. "So you know if I can handle it, you can, too. Derek keeps the groupies off the bus. He's really respectful of me being there."

Leaning against the wall, she kicked off her shoe and rubbed her foot. "If Derek doesn't have a substance abuse problem, what exactly do you need me to do?"

"I need you to do just what you did with Caroline—give the guys something to do other than partying."

"So I'm working with four guys?"

Emmie hesitated. "Yes. But, of course, Amoeba will pay you for all four."

Holy cow. Four times her usual pay per month. "How long would you need me?"

"It's a summer tour, so they'll be on the road for three months. Well, two and a half now. Are you free?"

"Yes." She'd hoped to put off choosing the next job for a little while, but she couldn't turn down this kind of money. She had to at least consider it.

But four rockers . . . oh, boy.

"V, I know this is last minute, and I know you said no musicians, but I wouldn't ask you if it wasn't really important. Please. I'll be here the whole time to help you."

"Why don't you give me some information, and I'll do the research. Get back to you in a few days." When Emmie didn't respond immediately, she said, "Okay?"

"I kind of need you sooner than later."

"Which means?"

"Tonight."

Violet wheeled her suitcase to the elevator, listening as Francesca filled her in on the day's events.

"Cutlers says they can't keep the ice cubes in stock," Francesca said in her husky voice. "Customers are raving about them."

A gush of satisfaction flowed through her. Luckily for her, tea had become trendy, and people loved the idea of loose leaf. But the leaves lost their flavor pretty quickly, and some people didn't like the messiness of an infuser, so she'd had the idea to freeze the leaves—wrapped in pretty pink mesh—in ice cubes. Dropping one ice cube in six ounces of boiling water made a perfect cup of tea. They sold like crazy in the gourmet shops on Long Island.

She pushed the button for the elevator. Glancing down at her outfit, she wondered if the supershort shorts and thigh-high boots made her look more like a hooker than a groupie.

"Other than that . . ." Violet could hear her friend shuffling through papers. "Other than that, we've got a new order from Mirabelle's for the tins. They'd like to try ten tins of each flavor."

"Are you serious? Mirabelle's in East Hampton contacted us?"

The doors opened, and she wheeled her suitcase inside, then pressed the button for the lobby.

"Yes. I got a call this afternoon."

"Way to bury the lead." Violet smiled. "Francesca, that's huge. I can't believe you didn't call me as soon as you got off the phone with them. That's fantastic."

"You were at Joe's engagement party. Oh, and if it sells well, they might include us in their catalog."

"Are you kidding me? This is amazing. This could change our lives completely." She could close her company, live on the farm full-time.

Of course, she didn't own the farm yet. Doubt worked its way back into her consciousness. She tried hard not to worry about things out of her control, but come on. Hard not to worry when all she had to prove ownership was a paper napkin contract. If it came to it, she'd fight, of course, but the more money she earned, the sooner she could own the land outright and put her fears to rest.

"Okay, anything you need me to do before I go?" Violet asked.

"You'll need to transfer funds into the business account, but other than that we're all set."

"I can do that electronically, once I'm in the car."

"V, with all we've got going on, what about skipping this job and spending time on the farm?"

A little jolt of energy passed through her. She would love nothing more than to spend the summer out there. They'd gotten a firm handle on the wildflower tea products and were ready to launch the soap. She'd planned on developing stationery and honey next. Oh, and potpourri. She'd have to remember that one. Easy, simple to package.

"That sounds amazing, but I need the money."

"The sooner we get the products into the marketplace, the sooner you won't need to take jobs."

True. But she'd have no peace until she owned the farm outright, so she needed the income. "You could ask Mimi to come out and help you. Just until she finds a job." Francesca's twenty-four-year-old daughter had recently graduated and hadn't found a job yet. "Would she like to work on the stationery this summer?"

"I think she'd love it. But you know she's not going to give up her dream of working with her dad. So, no, I don't see her coming out here. Even if we both know it's where her heart is."

The elevator rocked to a stop. "Okay, I have to go."

"So you're going to take the job?"

She had to. Ever since Jedidiah Walker had died, Violet had waited for someone to show up and kick her off the land. She knew he had two adult children. One lived overseas—Tokyo, she thought. The other, in the city. Neither one had ever visited him on the farm in all the years she'd known him, so she clung to the possibility they simply didn't care about the little bit of land at the tip of Long Island.

But another part of her knew better. They—or their lawyer—would show up—any day now—wanting to put it on the market. Would they accept her handwritten contract?

Even so, at the rate she was going in the lease-to-own plan they'd agreed on, it'd take twenty years to finally own the land. So any chance at earning a big chunk of cash . . . "Probably. I have to meet them first."

The elevator doors parted.

"Okay. Let me know how it goes."

"Thanks, Francesca. Talk soon." She tucked the phone into her leather messenger bag, hitched the laptop case higher on her shoulder, and reached for the handle of her luggage. Moving forward, she walked smack into the hard wall of a body. "Oh, my God, I'm *so* sorry."

Randall stood before her, eyeing her oddly. He clearly didn't recognize her.

"Randall?"

He cocked his head, gaze narrowing. Once recognition hit, his eyes widened comically. "Scarlet?"

Violet's gaze shot to Louis. The doorman gave her a barely noticeable shake of his head. His expression said, *You're in trouble now.*

Well, hell. Should she tell Randall her real name?

No, of course not. Then she'd have to explain why her boyfriend of three months had called her Scarlet. Oh, brother. She turned back to Randall. "What're you doing here?"

And just like that his features shuttered. "You left so quickly, I was worried." Gone was the earnest man she'd left in the restaurant.

"I have to work."

"So you said." He gave her a long look, and she hated that he was seeing her in this outfit. "On a Saturday night?"

She couldn't even imagine what he was thinking about her,

standing in her Upper East Side lobby, wearing thigh-high boots and supershort shorts. How did she get out of this one?

"What kind of consulting do you do, exactly?"

She gave an uncomfortable laugh. Normally, she had an easy, professional answer for everything. But it was *Randall*. And an hour ago he'd surprised the heck out of her by wanting to date her. Now . . . God, now she stood before him in thigh-highs.

"I'm afraid I don't have time to explain, Randall. I'm heading to the airport."

Giving him a warm smile, she stepped around him, continuing across the marble-floored lobby. "Maybe when I'm back in town, we can grab a coffee and catch up."

"Scarlet." His commanding tone made her stop to face him. "Can you please tell me where you're going? I don't understand."

She flashed a look to Louis, but he just rocked back on his heels and pressed his lips together disapprovingly. "God. I hate what you're thinking right now." She blew out a breath. "I really am sorry, but I have to go."

Randall's nostrils flared, and she could see him fighting for self-control. "Go where, exactly?" He strode over to her, leaning down to her ear. "Please tell me right now what kind of consulting job requires you to dress like . . . like . . ."

"Like what? What do I look like?"

"Well, frankly, like a hooker."

"I look like a hooker?" Oh, hell. She *had* gotten it wrong. Did she have time to change? A lot of the groupies she'd Googled had worn jeans. Plain—but tight—jeans. She turned to Louis for help.

The fifty-eight-year-old father of two tipped his head, giving a jerk, indicating she should come closer. "What're you supposed to look like?" he asked quietly.

"A groupie."

Mouth in a tight line, he assessed her thoughtfully. "The boots."

"Too much? Okay." Resting a hand on his desk for support, she pulled the boots off.

"Scarlet," Randall snapped. "What the *hell* are you doing?"

"I don't want to look like a hooker."

"You . . . What are you talking about? What do you want to look like? None of this makes any sense."

Ignoring him, she laid her suitcase on the floor and dug through it until she pulled out a pair of wedges. She held them up to the doorman, who nodded with confidence.

"Okay." She slid her foot into the sandal. "Great. Is my car here?"

"Waiting out front."

She stuffed the thigh-highs into the suitcase, zipped it up, and gave Louis an appreciative smile. "Thanks so much." Swinging the messenger bag over her head, she turned to Randall.

He looked a mixture of worried, angry, and confused. "Wait. Tell me what kind of job requires you to dress like that. Can you just give me that?"

"Give the kid a break," Louis murmured.

Randall probably thought she'd been Joe's *escort* for three months. *God.* How humiliating.

Louis relieved her of the suitcase, holding the door open for her, while Randall followed them out. It was fairly chilly for June, and she wished she'd brought a wrap. She'd only thought of summer and outdoor concerts.

Louis loaded the suitcase in the trunk as the driver set her laptop case and messenger bag on the backseat. Just before she slid in, Randall appeared at her side.

"I'm sorry for saying you're dressed like a hooker. That was uncalled for." Frustration pulled on his features. "I just . . . I don't understand. Did you bail on the engagement party to go to a concert, is that it?"

"No, of course not. I really do have a job to get to. I wish I could explain. I do. But it's the nature of my work . . ." No, she couldn't talk to him about client confidentiality. He might put the pieces together and figure out the truth. That would be devastating for Joe.

"Go on."

"I don't want to leave you with terrible thoughts, but there's not much I can tell you. I really am dressed like this for a job." She smiled, because she knew that comment made it sound like she *was* a hooker. "But trust me when I say I don't do anything illegal, unethical, or immoral."

"I know that. Of course I know that. I'm sorry."

"No, *I'm* sorry, Randall."

"Can we talk later?"

"I'm not sure how long I'll be gone." She moved to get into the car, but he reached for her.

"Wait. Just . . . wait." He stood there confused. "I knew it didn't make sense for you to be invited to his engagement party. That's all kinds of messed up. And you just stood there, smiling, like you were proud of him or something."

"I *am* happy for him. She's the right woman for him."

"I don't understand . . . nothing rattles you. The whole time I've known you, you've never shown an ounce of emotion."

Way to hit a girl where she hurts. "Joe and I had a nice time together, but it wasn't a love affair. Not like what he has with Judy. I'm happy for him."

"Is that all you want out of a relationship? Something *nice*?" He jammed a hand through his short blond hair. "Do you remember that closing dinner? When you first started dating him? I was there, Scarlet, right behind you when he came out of the bathroom with another woman. You didn't yell or cry or anything. You didn't even look upset."

Well, of course she'd been upset. But jumping into the drama with her coked-out clients accomplished nothing. Her handling of each situation built the foundation of trust, cultivated an attitude of willingness with them. "Joe and I worked out our issues."

"Jesus, listen to you. Are you always this flat emotionally?"

He was really twisting the knife, wasn't he? No, she wasn't a passionate person—and she hated that about herself—but she certainly couldn't show emotion on a *job*.

But she couldn't explain any of this to him. "No, Randall, I'm not the most emotional person. So maybe it's best we don't date, after all."

He shook his head, looking frustrated. "But I want to get to the woman underneath."

Oh. Oh, that was so nice. Okay, enough. She really couldn't take any more of this. "I'm sorry, Randall. I have to go now."

"Jesus, do you feel anything? *Is* there a woman underneath?"

And just like that she flashed back to the social worker talking to her grandma.

I'm afraid children without touch or nurturing lose the ability to form attachments for the rest of their lives.

She'll likely never be able to trust or fully experience love.

I wish I could be more encouraging, but it's unlikely she'll ever have normal relationships.

The pain of those words still packed a wallop. "God, I hope so. Good-bye, Randall."

THREE

Did she have the right bus?

Violet peered through the tinted window of the door. She could see the driver locked in conversation with a figure that certainly looked like Emmie. Why weren't they letting her in?

She pulled out her phone and texted. Outside the bus.

Within seconds, the door whooshed open, and Emmie charged down the stairs. "Oh, my God, I'm so sorry. I didn't recognize you at all." Her hands covered her mouth. "I thought you were a groupie. A really determined one." In her pretty summer dress, she stepped back up. "Come on in."

The bus driver reached for her suitcase. "I got that."

"Oh, thank you." Violet held out her hand. "I'm Violet Davis."

"Abe, the driver." He motioned for her to go ahead.

Relieved to get out of the humid Florida air, Violet followed Emmie into a wood-paneled living area. Black couches on either side of the aisle, a long table, and a big flat-screen TV in the wall made up the space. She pulled off her messenger bag and set it and the laptop case on the table.

"Oh, my God, look at you." Emmie's eyes sparkled with mischief.

Gesturing to her outfit, she said, "Yeah, so hooker or groupie?"

"Can I say a cross between the two? Although, to be honest, you'd be amazed what some of the nymphs dress like."

Nymphs? "You should've seen me in the thigh-high boots."

Emmie's eyes widened. "I can't even imagine you dressed like that. You're always so elegant and polished."

"Yeah, well, my doorman made me take them off. But I brought them just in case."

"Where do you want this, Em?" Abe asked.

"How about the lounge until we figure things out?" Emmie looked to Violet for confirmation.

"Sounds good." She hadn't considered sleeping arrangements on a band's tour bus. Where *would* she sleep?

Abe edged around them, carrying the suitcase close to his chest, as he angled down the narrow hallway.

"What time will the guys get here?" Violet thought about changing her outfit, now that Emmie thought she looked like a hooker. The right presentation meant everything to a successful job. She needed to fit in seamlessly, so they didn't view her as an outsider.

"The show ended about fifteen minutes ago. Right now they're doing some press. So we have, maybe, ten minutes or so to talk privately."

"How long does it take them to run the gauntlet through the army of groupies?"

"Yeah, it's not easy dealing with them. You can't really run through the nymphs. The guys have to stop and sign autographs along the way. You want to keep the fans happy."

"Nymphs?" Violet smiled.

"Irwin doesn't like the word *groupies*. He prefers to call them nymphs."

"Got it. Okay, well, I guess I'll be learning all about it soon enough."

"You don't have to worry, though. Derek does a great job of managing everything. He gives the guys an hour or so to party on the bus, but then he kicks the girls off."

She'd seen throngs of groupies as the car had driven

through the festival grounds. They surrounded the artists, hovered outside the buses. How did Emmie do it? "I know tonight you're waiting here for me, but you usually stick with the band, right?"

"Not every night. I don't like all the chaos."

"You leave Slater with all those girls?"

It was interesting to see Emmie's features soften. "Oh, sure. He's . . . he's not into all that."

With her long, dark hair and lovely figure, Emmie Valencia was indisputably a beautiful woman. She stood out from the fans with her fresh-faced, girl-next-door beauty. Still, Violet wasn't sure she'd share Emmie's confidence. Not with all the temptation thrown at these guys.

Emmie motioned to the couches. "We've got a few minutes before they come on board, so let's talk. What can I do to convince you to take this job?"

Abe came back down the aisle. "She brought her entire wardrobe. I wouldn't worry too much about whether or not she's taking it." He gave her a wink.

Violet laughed. "Hey, I had to come ready to work." It wasn't like she could fly back to New York. The job would start immediately.

Abe went back to his seat, flicking on an overhead light to read his cell phone.

"Okay, so what happened exactly?" Violet asked. "Why am I here?"

"Well, things have been building. The guys are partying harder, which is a problem in itself, but it's worsened by the fact that my brother has developed a relationship with the media. He likes to tip them off when he thinks he can get some good press for the band. Unfortunately, when you get the press involved, they're not looking to post a nice, clean story. And last night was a perfect example. Derek invited some paparazzi to the show because we had some celebrities jamming with us at the Miami festival. Well, of course, they wanted more than just shots of Jared Leto rocking out with the guys. They followed us back to the hotel, hung around waiting, and . . ."

"And they got their shot." Violet had spent the car and plane ride looking up Blue Fire and Derek Valencia. She'd seen the shots of naked women in the pool, and Derek looking down at them.

Emmie cringed. "Yeah, but I have to tell you, Derek was only on that balcony to make sure no one had gotten hurt. He wasn't throwing girls into the pool. In fact, he's the one who shut the party down. Unfortunately, Irwin saw the picture of Derek and assumes he was the ring leader." She let out a breath. "It's not good. Irwin's not coming to the show tonight. He's going into the studio with another band instead. Which, in Irwin-speak, means he's losing interest."

"So he asked you to hire me?"

"Oh, believe me, he hasn't said a thing. No, I met with their publicist. We've been racking our brains trying to come up with a way to get Irwin's attention back on the guys before it's too late. And I thought of you. He trusts you. If you're involved, he'll believe the guys will get their heads on right."

"And what about the guys? What exactly do they know?"

"Slater, of course, knows everything. I don't keep any secrets from him. But you told me not to clue the others in yet, so I haven't."

"Okay, so let's start with Derek, since he seems to be the leader. How do you think he'll react to having a minder?" It never went well. And, in fact, it only worked if the client wanted to keep his job more than he wanted to party.

Emmie looked uneasy. "His initial reaction won't be good. But once he gets that it'll keep Irwin, he'll go along with it."

"Let me ask you something. What does it mean to him? Why is it so important to have Irwin, specifically, as his A&R guy?" The answer would determine the outcome of the job.

"Well, it's kind of personal."

"Everything about my involvement with him will be deeply personal. That's how I'll be able to help him."

"Right. I know. But . . ."

"He's your brother."

She smiled. "Yeah. But I know how much this means to him, so I'm going to tell you what I can because he absolutely won't get what he wants if you're not involved. Okay, so I told you about our dad, and the way he's constantly criticizing Derek. Well, as soon as Derek signed with Amoeba Records, my dad started nosing around the industry again. He tried to get me to come back and work for him. I mean, knowing I was Derek's manager, he still wanted me to quit my job and work for him. That sums him up right there. It's all about *him*. Total narcissist."

"I read some articles on the way here. Your father makes veiled remarks about modern-day musicians with their scandals and preoccupation with social media. He's obviously talking about his son. Is that why Irwin doesn't think Derek's taking his music seriously? Could Eddie Valencia, jazz virtuoso, have that kind of power over Irwin?"

Emmie sat back in her seat, looking a little stunned. "Uh, yeah. Wow. You're good, V. I mean, incredibly good. We haven't even gotten started yet. How can you be this insightful at twenty-five years old?"

She smiled. "I had to grow up fast."

"Well, as much as I'd like to say Irwin can't be influenced, I think it's hard to dismiss the opinion of someone who stayed on the Ledger List for ten years."

"The Ledger List?"

"Irwin puts out an annual list of the best rock and jazz musicians in the world. My dad stayed on the list for a decade."

"What would it mean to Derek to be on that list?"

Tears glistened in Emmie's eyes. Oh, Lord. She must've hit on something. She waited for Emmie to pull herself together.

"I don't even know what to say. You got it. You just friggin' nailed it." She wiped her eyes. "It would mean everything to him, V. I mean, he'd never say it out loud—I'm his sister and he's never actually said it to me—but I know it would mean the world to him. The whole thing about having Irwin as his A&R guy means he's made it. Something our dad told him would *never* happen. Losing Irwin's interest just confirms everything Dad ever said about him. But making the Ledger List? It would be proof that he's got true talent. On his own, outside of the band. It would make him believe in himself."

Violet couldn't help picturing the little boy, looking up

with adoring eyes at the dad he revered and seeing pure rejection reflected back. She could imagine the hard nut of pain in the little boy's heart. God, it made her sad for him. "Got it."

"So what do you think? Will you take the job?"

"Normally, I come in after rehab. Sure, I can see hiring me to get a handle on the situation before it gets so far that they *need* rehab, but if no one has a substance abuse issue, then I'm not sure what my role would be. Other than, obviously, winning over Irwin. And that doesn't feel right to me. This is my livelihood, you know? My reputation is my calling card. Not to mention, Irwin was nothing but good to me. As much as I want to help you out, I'm not sure I'm willing to spend my summer on tour with a bunch of hard-partying rockers just so they can keep their A&R guy." Of course, she needed the money, but she only got jobs on referrals. She couldn't ruin her reputation.

"Oh, no. I'm so sorry. I've given you the wrong impression. Everything's just happened so fast. The pictures went viral this morning, Irwin bailed on the show tonight, and I've just been going crazy trying to figure out how to get him back. Last night showed us—all of us—that the guys are out of control. So, yes, we want you because we believe it'll get Irwin back, but the guys *do* need your help in finding ways to manage life on the road without drugs and too much alcohol."

"That makes sense." And that she could definitely do.

"See, when they were opening for Piper Lee last fall, they started to go down the wrong path. That's why . . ." Emmie held out her wrist, revealing a small black tattoo. Two arrows pointing toward each other, their heads merged. "We all have these. It's basically a symbol for balancing opposing forces. The music industry is really chaotic, and we need to keep our heads on right and find our balance, so we can enjoy it without letting it destroy us."

"I like that. A lot." She wondered if Emmie knew how lucky she was to be part of this tight-knit band. She *belonged* to these guys.

Emmie's phone buzzed, and she picked it up off the table. A smile lit her features. "They're on their way." She turned a hopeful expression on Violet. "So what do you say? Please tell me you'll do it?"

The quadrupled fee would nearly buy the farm outright. And she couldn't resist the force of Emmie's passion for her guys. "I'll do it."

"Oh, thank you. Thank you so much." And then she drew in a breath. "What do you need from me?"

"First, when you say partying, I need you to be specific."

Emmie nodded. "Alcohol, for sure." With a troubled expression, she looked at her hands. "I know they're doing drugs. Pete, especially. Not Derek, and of course, not Slater. I'm pretty sure Cooper and Ben are doing stuff, too, but not nearly as much as Pete."

"Listen, I know we're talking about your boyfriend and your brother, but I'll need some time to observe. I hate to start off with deception, but I really do need to assess the situation. The moment they know I'm a minder, they'll hide their drugs and alcohol and their sources. Can you give me some time?"

"I can't keep anything from Slater but, then, he's not the problem. Lie to my brother?" Clearly, Emmie didn't like that. But she had to see how important it was not to tip anyone off until she figured out who was doing what and who was supplying. "How much time?"

"Twenty-four hours. Can you give me that?" Even that wouldn't be enough, not with the craziness of touring—the unfamiliarity with venues, the hangers-on. But she had to consider Emmie's relationship with her brother.

Deep male voices and shrieks of girlish laughter drew nearer.

"They're here," Abe said. The doors whooshed open.

Emmie slid out of the bench seat, her smile luminous. "Jonny wants a few minutes alone, okay? Just to meet you."

"Jonny?" Violet asked.

"Sorry, Slater. His real name's Jonny. That's what I call him."

Violet nodded, her attention turned to the big hand grasping the rail, pulling up a huge, muscled body. Slater Vaughn topped the stairs, latched his gaze on to his girl, and strode right to her. He scooped her up, arms banding around her waist, lifting her so her feet dangled. Angling his mouth, he kissed her like he'd just come back from war.

And then Emmie's legs wrapped around his waist, and he gripped her bottom, pushing her back against the wall.

A bolt of electricity shot from Violet's core right to her heart, making her scalp tingle. She had to look away from the insanely intimate moment.

She got that she couldn't love the way a normal person did, but could she feel *passion*? Were the two inextricably linked?

She hoped they were separate. She wanted that. She wanted that so much.

Murmurings pulled her from her thoughts. She turned to find Emmie unlocking her legs, gently stepping away from her boyfriend. "Sorry about that. The guys have a crazy amount of energy after a show." She reached for Slater's arm. "Jonny, this is Violet Davis. You remember Caroline's minder?"

With about the sexiest grin she'd ever seen, Slater nodded. "Of course. You really turned Caroline's life around."

"Oh, thank you, but she was ready to make some changes." She extended her hand. "It's nice to meet you."

Keeping one arm around Emmie's waist, he extended the other, grasping her hand in a firm shake. "What exactly are you going to do for the guys?"

Good question. "Keep the drugs and alcohol away, create alternatives for partying, and offer a healthy lifestyle that will make all of you more creative, more productive, and a closer community."

A dazzling smile appeared, and she felt the sizzle of it down to her toes. "Well, then, welcome aboard." He called to the driver. "Abe, you wanna let the guys on?"

"You got it, boss."

And just like that, the quiet bus exploded into mayhem.

FOUR

Derek watched Emmie and Slater head to their bedroom. They hadn't had a chance to talk about the pictures that had gone viral, since they'd been working all day and night. From sound check to interviews to the performance itself, they hadn't had a break.

He had no doubt Irwin had seen the pictures. *Oh, hell.* He hated letting Irwin down. Instead of spending time with Gen last night, he should've stayed with the guys. He'd watch them more carefully from now on.

Just then the bathroom door opened, and out stepped a woman he didn't recognize. Long legs, incredibly short jean shorts, and a stretchy tank top that hinted at big tits. But the silky shirt she wore unbuttoned over it mostly covered her chest, so he couldn't tell.

"Hi." She stood before him, eyes all bright and eager.

"Hey." His gaze slid past her to the other nymphs. Had she come in with them? He couldn't recall. He hadn't seen her in the green room, but maybe she'd joined them along the way. It'd been too dark outside to say for sure.

"You're Derek, right?"

He nodded. Something about her . . . no, she definitely wasn't with the others. First off, she was older. But it wasn't age that made him question her. It was the intelligence in her eyes. The sharpness.

Reporter?

"I'm Scarlet."

"Those your friends?"

She glanced to the other girls. "No, I don't know them. I met Slater after the show. I sorta followed him. He said he didn't want to party, but that I could hang out with you guys for a little while."

Legit answer. Okay, so maybe she *was* just a nymph. He relaxed a little. "You from Daytona?"

She shook her head with a soft smile. "Just visiting."

He liked her soft voice and the spark in her eyes. "So where're your friends, Scarlet? What're you doing alone on a bus with a bunch of horny rockers?"

"My friends are with ElectroRocket." She made a face, indicating she didn't like that band. "I hate electronic music. I like you guys much more."

"You like our music or you want to hang out with the band?"

"I'm down to party. It's just . . . I don't have a ride until my friends get kicked off ElectroRocket's bus, you know? I didn't want to party with them—they don't have the best reputation—and then I saw Slater, and I thought . . ." She hunched her shoulders. "I don't know. I'd see what was going on with you guys." She stepped closer to him, eyelids lowering just a little. "You don't want me here?" She got a little breathy.

He leaned a hip against the counter. What he wanted was to find out how Irwin had reacted to the pictures in the press, but Emmie and Slater probably wouldn't surface until morning, and Gen had spent half the day traveling back to the city.

"Tell you what. In forty minutes, we hit the road. So you want to hang with a rock band . . ." He gestured to the guys. "That's your best bet."

Meanwhile, he'd spend his forty minutes with Gen. Maybe get some phone sex.

"They've already got friends." Her pink tongue flicked out to moisten her lips.

A shock of lust hit him, making his dick hum. Okay, he

had no idea what-was-what with this chick, but her whole demeanor . . . she was just too fucking *elegant* to be a nymph. "That's kind of how it works, sweetheart. So just enjoy it while you can." He pushed away from the counter. "Coop?"

His friend had a girl on each knee; one had her hands shoved down his pants. Maybe he should send Scarlet to someone else.

"Ben?" The drummer was swallowed up in a three-pack. *"Ben?"*

Ben tore his attention away from the girls.

"You got room for one more?"

The drummer smiled, checking Scarlet out. "Fuck, yeah. Come on over, beautiful." One of the girls gripped his shoulder and forcibly returned him to the conversation.

"Did you just pass me off to someone else?" Scarlet didn't have even a hint of hurt in her. She just looked amused.

"That a problem? It's not like you had your heart set on me." Like nymphs cared who they fucked, as long as they could say they got with someone in a band.

"I wouldn't bring my *heart* into it, but the rest of me was looking forward to spending time with the bass player."

So she knew what he played. "You got a thing for bass players?"

"Oh, yeah. You guys are the coolest. I always think the front man's so . . . full of himself. I can't stand show-offs. All big and loud and look-at-me."

He liked this chick. "And yet you saw Slater and thought you'd get some of that."

She smiled. "Well, come on, Slater-fucking-Vaughn? Can't blame a girl for trying."

What the fuck?

"I'm just kidding. Seriously, everyone knows he's with that girl . . . I forget her name. I'm just messing with you. No, seriously, he's not my type." While her smile was sweet, it was also soft and surprisingly sensual.

"Okay, well, have fun. I've got shit to do."

If he were drunk, he wouldn't have noticed it. If he weren't already suspicious, he probably wouldn't have either. But he *did* notice the look of intensity—the rush of energy that suddenly galvanized her. "We could do shit together. We've got, what, thirty-five minutes?"

"I'm not the guy for you. Don't worry, they'll show you a good time."

If he stayed with her any longer, he probably would've caved. She had a soft, sexy femininity that stirred his blood. So he quickly turned and shut himself in the lounge. He only had one thing on his mind. Pulling out his phone, he called Gen.

"Hey, handsome."

Her sexy purr usually got him hard. Tonight, though, he just wanted information. "You back in the city?"

"Just got to my building." She snapped right back into business mode.

Sitting down on the couch, he tipped his head back against the wall and scraped a hand through his hair, still damp from a shower. "Talk to Irwin yet?"

"Not yet. He's not returning my calls."

"Shit. He's pissed."

"I'll take care of it."

He heard the message in her tone, and it pissed him off. He'd dropped the ball, and she had to clean up the mess. "It won't happen again."

"Oh, I know it won't."

"What does that mean?"

"It means you'll make sure you do everything you need to keep your band on track."

Okay, now she was really pissing him off. Like he needed her to tell him that? "I got it under control, Gen."

"Hang on," she said. "I just walked in the door." He heard some background noises, a door slamming. "Ah, home sweet home. Where I can strip off my dress and dip into my honeypot while I listen to your sexy voice. Mmm."

"I've been thinking about it all day," he said. "Talking to the guys doesn't work. Limiting their partying isn't working either. I'm thinking about imposing fines. I know they're not going to like it, but that's too bad. We can't afford another night like last night." When she didn't answer, he said, "Gen? You there?"

"Mm-hm."

"What're you doing?"

"Just checking mail." And then her tone turned seductive. "Now, I'm heading into my bedroom so you can take care of me."

"Christ."

"I'm sorry we didn't get to finish our business last night. Such a waste. We hardly ever get to be together. But you can make it up to me right now. Do you want to know what I'm wearing?"

"A black push-up bra and a thong." He felt restless, edgy. He wondered what Scarlet was doing. Wondered if he should check on her, make sure she wasn't too uncomfortable. No matter who she was, he knew this wasn't her scene.

"Guess what I'm doing right now?" she purred.

"Skinning a cat?"

"Okay, you're taking all the fun out of our evening. I'm trying to relax you."

"Gotta tell you, not feeling all that relaxed. I want to know what Irwin's thinking."

The door opened, and Scarlet peeked into the small room. She took in the *Rolling Stone* and *Guitar Player* magazines littering the table, the beer bottles and discarded clothing on the floor and counters. Her gaze followed the soles of his boots up his legs, hovering around his package before finishing its lazy appraisal of his body at his mouth.

And, *fuck*, if his dick didn't feel the love.

She smiled. "Hey."

"I'm not really in the mood tonight, babe," he said to Gen. "Got too much on my mind. Sorry."

"Ouch. Are you dismissing me? We haven't even had any sexy time yet."

"I've got to clear out the bus," he said. "Almost time to hit the road."

"Call me later."

"Count on it." He disconnected the call. Standing up, he pocketed the phone. "Problem?"

Scarlet came all the way in, leaving the door open. "I don't think there's room for me out there."

"Don't like competition, huh?"

She shook her head, releasing all that dark, silky hair. His senses hcightened, and he became aware of her scent. Light, floral . . . different. "I prefer one-on-one situations."

Desire kicked hard, heat spreading through him. "Yeah?"

"You got a beer or something?" Again, she looked around the room, reactivating his suspicions. She sure as shit wasn't looking for an unopened warm beer.

"In the refrigerator." He pointed behind her, toward the kitchen. He'd see what she did next.

"You don't keep anything in here?"

"By anything, I assume you're talking about things other than liquor?" He was right about her. Underneath all that eyeliner and those flirty clothes was a shark. And that scent? It was too elegant, too . . . unique.

This woman was a reporter. And she was out to dig up some dirt on him.

Had Irwin sent her?

No, of course not. Irwin wouldn't bother with petty shit like that. Reporters did it for their own gain.

He moved closer to her, watching her reaction carefully. How far would she go to get her story? "What exactly are you looking for? We've only got fifteen minutes left." Stopping inches from her, he peered down into her hazel eyes.

"What've you got?" She slid her hands into his back pockets, clutched the fabric—but not his ass. Now, that was interesting. Did she have limits?

He took her chin, forced her to look at him. "Look, sweetheart, let's get right down to it. What do you want?"

"I want to have fun with you."

"What kind of fun?"

"I just want to party."

"You bring anything?" He watched carefully for a reaction.

She shook her head. "I figured you guys would have something here."

"Oh, I've got something, all right." Pulling her hand out of his pocket, he brought it around to his cock.

She tensed, wrenching her wrist away.

Why did he like that so much? He didn't give a shit about a reporter out to fuck him over, but he liked that she had a line she wouldn't cross. She had some sense of decency. "This is how we have fun, sweetheart. You know that, right?"

With a mischievous look in her eyes, she licked her lips. "Oh, I know. I just thought we'd have another kind of fun first, you know?" And then she got on her toes, her breasts brushing his chest as she leaned into him, and whispered in his ear, "I get so wild when I'm high."

"Yeah?" One finger on her collarbone pushed her back on her heels. "We don't have time to get you high." Settling a hand on each shoulder, he pressed, urging her to her knees.

And here it was. Just how far would she take this game?

She stepped away. "Oh, come on, don't be like that. It's so much more fun when we're high. Come on."

He reached for her, tugged her toward him. "Your time with the band is almost up, sweetheart." He unzipped his jeans with one hand, while the other reached for her wrist. "You either get on your knees or you can get off the bus and go find your friends."

He was so sure he'd see fear in her eyes. So sure she'd freak out, that he wasn't prepared for her head tilting back as she let out a laugh loud enough to hurt his ears in the small room.

"That's it? That's all you got?" She shook her head, wiping her eyes. "Oh, my God, you're supposed to be the sex god."

Derek froze.

"I thought you'd make it really good for me. But pushing me on my knees? I can get that anywhere."

Every muscle in his body tightened. "Then get after it, sweetheart." He pushed past her, a dangerous energy coursing through him.

Striding to the front of the bus, he saw a girl writhing on Cooper's lap, his jeans down at his knees. Pete had two topless girls making out with each other, one perched on each thigh. "Jesus Christ, guys, I told you no fucking on the bus. My *sister's* here."

Ben looked up, his glazed eyes coming into focus as he pushed the girl between his knees away. "Dude, chill, no one's fucking." He looked completely wasted.

Fuck, what had they become? It was just over a year ago they'd written up a contract of acceptable behavior. And now, not two weeks into their first headlining tour, they were already spiraling out of control.

"Everyone off the bus. Now. Let's go." When no one moved, he smacked Cooper's shoulder. "Coop. We're hitting the road. Get the girls off the bus."

Ben and Cooper pulled their girls off reluctantly, but Pete was completely lost in the action on his lap as the groupies writhed against each other. Coop punched his arm. "Dude, let's go."

Pete's head wobbled, and he seemed completely out of it. Booze didn't do that to him, so Derek knew Pete was taking some serious shit. They didn't need a reporter catching them behaving like this.

Too much anger pulsed through him, so he grabbed Ben's shirt to get his attention, brought him right up to his face. "You've got five minutes to clear the bus."

He nodded, and Derek turned to the kitchen.

Fuck. He had this under control, right?

His eyes squeezed shut. Imposing fines? Like that would mean shit to these guys. He needed to figure something out. In the morning, he'd meet with Slater and Emmie. Between the three of them, they'd get a handle on the situation. It wasn't that far gone.

He'd grab a beer, head to his bunk, and get his shit together—but wait. Fuck. Where'd the reporter go? Had she gotten pictures of the guys just then? But when he turned around, he didn't see her.

His pulse kicked up and he charged back into the lounge, found her rooting through a drawer. "What the *fuck* are you doing?"

She stepped back. "I've always wondered what it was like on a tour bus. It must be so hard to have six people living here together."

"Game over, sweetheart. I know you're not a groupie." He stalked toward her. "Give me your phone."

"What?" The very first hint of fear in her eyes blew the roof off his anger.

So she *did* have pictures. But of what? He didn't have anything incriminating. "Hand it over. Now."

She softened, looking all sweet again. "I'm sorry. I didn't think you'd mind if I took a quick look around."

"Cut the shit. I know you're a reporter."

Genuine confusion tightened her features.

"Derek?" He heard Emmie, but he didn't take his eyes off the woman.

"Not now, Em. I'm trying to get everyone off the bus so we can get out of here."

"Derek." Emmie stood beside him, one hand on his shoulder blade. "She's not a reporter."

"You *know* her?"

"Very well."

He gave the woman a hard look. "Who are you?"

She gave him a gentle smile. "I'm Violet Davis. I'm—"

"Wait," Emmie said, stepping between them. "Let me explain."

He didn't care who did the talking, he just wanted answers. "Talk."

"Do you remember when Caroline got kicked off the plane in Dublin?" Emmie asked.

The noise of a thousand cymbals crashed in his head.

"Derek, man, let me talk to you." Slater came up behind Emmie.

"You're a fucking sober companion?"

"Don't shout at her," Emmie said. "None of this is her fault."

"Right. It's mine. I can't control my own fucking band so you hire a fucking *sober companion*?" Christ, Caroline Ledger popped Oxy like they were Skittles, forced planes to land from her batshit crazy behavior, got caught shoplifting a dozen times, trashed multiple hotel rooms—when she was nothing more than a student at NYU—and these people compared the band's behavior to *that*?

"No, that's not what this is about." Emmie looked on the verge of tears, but he didn't give a shit.

"Can you give us a minute?" Slater asked the women.

But the moment Slater made a move toward him, Violet stepped in his friend's path. She gave him one of her soft smiles and said, "Actually, I'd like to talk to him by myself, if that's all right."

Emmie nodded. Slater looked to Derek like he was asking if it was okay. Nothing about this situation was okay. Nothing.

And while it might not be Violet's fault—and even in his anger, he knew it wasn't—he still didn't want anything to do with her.

"You're throwing me under the fucking bus?" he said to his sister and Slater.

"It's not like that, man. It's not." Slater looked to Violet. "Let me just talk to him."

Derek didn't want to talk to Slater or Emmie, so he appreciated that Violet stood her ground. With a slight shake of her head, she ended the conversation. Slater stood there a moment longer, then exhaled roughly, and left them alone.

Violet, her subtle floral scent floating in the air around him, gazed at him sweetly. "Well, good to know you've got more game than that."

"What?" Not the comment he expected.

"You know, earlier. You were testing me."

The mischief in her eyes rubbed against the anger, diffusing it. "Yeah."

"That's good to know. Otherwise the whole sex god thing wouldn't make any sense."

What a fucking day. He collapsed onto the couch, covered his face in his hands. He couldn't believe his sister had hired a sober companion. Did she think he was a drunk? That the reason he couldn't control the guys was because he was partying as hard as they were?

The cushion shifted beside him. She tugged on his T-shirt to get his attention, acting like they'd known each other since third grade. "No one thinks you're an alcoholic. That's not why I'm here."

"Are you a sober companion?"

"Yes. But I'm not an addiction counselor. I'm a *minder*. There's a big difference. I'm here to look out for you guys, keep away the bad influences."

"So if you'd had more time, would you have gone through my bunk and checked for hidden bottles?" *Does Emmie really think I'm a drunk?*

"Yes and no. Yes, I would check your bunk—all of your

bunks. But, no, I'm not looking for bottles or flasks. Alcohol's easy to detect. I'd smell it on your breath and coming off your skin."

"Emmie and Slater knew you were gonna snoop through my shit?"

She nodded. "Not just you, all the guys. Like I said, I'm not here to be your sober companion. I'm here to help the band get a handle on the partying. Before I take a job, I have to do a basic assessment. I'm not actually digging through personal belongings. Just taking a quick glance under pillows, inside shoes. But if we told the guys what I do, they'd hide everything. They'd shut down all their sources. I have to get a handle on the situation first."

"Nice try, babe. Sweet touch, trying to make it sound like we're on the same team. But these guys? They're not just some assholes I'm stuck on a bus with. They're my brothers, and I don't fuck with their heads. If we've got a problem, we deal with it."

"My understanding is that you don't have time to get a handle on things. Hiring me now gets Irwin back, gaining you time to square things away."

Get Irwin back? "What're you talking about? What do you mean, get Irwin back?"

"He didn't come to the show tonight. Emmie seems to think that means he's losing interest."

"Fuck." He shot off the couch, ready to tear into his sister. And what about Gen? She had to have known. Why the hell hadn't she said anything? Christ, she was in on this, too?

"Derek?"

That fucking sweet voice. And then that scent swirled around him, letting him know she was there. She touched a hand to his shoulder blade. "Can we talk first? Before you go and yell at your sister?"

"You have nothing to do with this."

"Turn around and talk to me, please." Something in her voice—commanding, but soft, *caring*—made him listen. She had a strength, a steadiness. A determination that cut right through him.

"What?" he snapped.

"This isn't Emmie's fault. It isn't Slater's fault, and it

certainly isn't your fault. You've got a situation." She shrugged, as if to say it was as simple as that. "And I can help you. First, just hiring me gets Irwin's attention back on you. He trusts me. Secondly, though, let's put this into perspective. We don't have a huge problem here. I mean, it's all relative, isn't it?"

That warm, sexy smile again. He didn't want it to penetrate, but it did. He let her go on.

"Any other A&R guy would be partying with you. You just happened to get the one who doesn't work like that. Let me ask you something, do *you* think the guys are solid? Partying, sure, but everything's under control?"

His gaze shifted away. Fucking Pete. "Mostly."

She pulled a baggie filled with pills out of her back pocket. "I found this in that shoe over there."

In the corner of the lounge a scuffed Nike high-top lay on its side, as though it'd been hastily kicked off. Its companion sat upright a few feet away. Derek's pulse quickened as he recognized Pete's shoes. "What is it?" He didn't do drugs so he didn't recognize them.

With a fingernail, she pressed one pill into a corner of the baggie and held it up to him. "These green capsules? They're called greenies. Athletes use them to get more aggressive, more alert before a game." She shifted the pills, pushing a different one to the corner. "This pink one's Ambien. To get to sleep."

He closed his eyes. "It isn't easy, on the road. Every day's a new city, every night a different show. And after a show, you're too amped up to sleep. You have so much energy you don't know what to do with it. But you also have to get up the next day and do it all over again."

"I get that. But see this bag? This isn't one of your guys buying some weed or a couple ounces of coke from some random guy out there. This is deliberate. Someone's playing doctor with one of your guys. It's one person, one source."

He blew out a breath, giving a curt nod. He hated that he hadn't known what Pete was doing. Had to hear it from some stranger. "I'll handle it."

She reached for his forearm, lifted it, letting her fingernail trace his tattoo.

The shot of lust electrifying his nerves made no sense in this moment. She stood close to him, feeling so . . . *familiar*. And she smelled so fucking good. He wanted to yank his arm away, but for fuck's sake he didn't.

Her thumb kept circling his tattoo. "This whole notion of chaos? That's where I come in. Of course you can handle anything, but in order to focus on what the record label needs you to do, which is write amazing songs and perform them, you can hand the other stuff off to me. You wear a lot of hats. I wear one. So allow me to take care of the partying issue. Not only will it enable you to do your work, it'll preserve your relationship with your friends." She smiled like she was so sure she'd won him over. Like she was offering him relief, the answer to all his prayers.

"You can cut the shit." He pulled his arm away. "If it'll keep Irwin happy, then fine, have at it. I know I'm not going to win this one. But let's get one thing clear." He leaned into her, all his anger and frustration making his muscles rigid. "I'm twenty-eight years old, and I've done damn well for myself. I don't need a fucking babysitter."

FIVE

Derek Valencia had a fucking babysitter.

He hardly recognized her this morning, as she sat beside him in the little banquette. Wearing no makeup and a simple white T-shirt and black leggings, she looked younger, fresher. Other than the dainty antique-looking watch, she wore no jewelry.

Still, even with his eyes closed, he'd recognize her by her scent alone.

Emmie and Slater sat across the table from them. He knew they expected him to yell or give them shit. But he wasn't going to do that.

He didn't need more trouble. He needed to focus on selling out shows, getting the band's name out there, and making sure the album went gold. Everything else? He'd let the minder play hide and seek with Pete's stash. Let her find out who was supplying the guys. It would only help him in the long run.

"I've got good news and bad." His sister placed her hands palm-down on the table. She smiled at him. "I know you well enough to know you want the bad news first."

He nodded, unwilling to make nice just yet.

"Okay, the bad news is that Irwin's not coming to the next couple of shows. But the good news is that he's thrilled

Violet's with us, and he totally believes you had nothing to do with throwing the girls in the pool. Basically, he said, 'He's not a bloody muppet, for Christ's sake.' So that's good."

That *was* good news. He hated Irwin thinking he needed a babysitter.

"So, Violet, tell us the game plan." Slater leaned back on the bench seat, one arm slung on the back of the cushion, his other hand on Emmie's thigh. "What happens now that you're signed on?"

"I'm just going to observe for a while. I'd appreciate another twenty-four hours, so I can get a feel for your routines, your interactions. After that, I'll come up with some suggestions." She gave Derek a quick look—gauging his reaction? "And then I'll implement them."

"What kind of suggestions?" Slater asked.

"Last night you guys mentioned the adrenaline rush you experience after a show. I'll come up with alternatives to expending all that energy."

"There's no alternative to fucking, sweetheart."

The only give-away that he'd pissed her off came from the way her gaze dropped to the table. Taking a breath, she shifted, turning her back on Emmie and Slater, making her close in on him. It was all kinds of weird the way she could make him feel this rush of intimacy with her. "I need you to do something for me, Derek."

Damn, that voice. All soft and kind. It killed him. Dug right into the roots of his anger and yanked. "Just talk, okay? Don't use your psychotherapist voice with me."

She ignored him. "I need you to wipe out all your expectations about me, get rid of the resentment. You're the leader of this band. You might all be the same age, equally talented, whatever, but you're clearly the leader. So if you're not on board, if you're treating me like you can barely tolerate me, you're going to undermine my efforts. And none of this will work."

"Not my problem, babe. You do your job, I'll do mine."

Emmie gasped, but Violet didn't even glance at her, just held his gaze, keeping him locked on to her.

"If you don't want me here, I'm happy to leave. I've got other things I'd like to do."

"Derek," Emmie said, a warning in her tone.

Still, Violet ignored her. "But if you'd like my help, if you want to see if I can turn things around, then I'll give you a hundred percent. And in return, I need the same level of commitment from you."

"You're questioning my level of commitment?" He looked at Slater and Emmie. "I give a hundred fucking percent to this band. No one's as invested as I am in its success. But playing games with you? Sorry, not interested. Like I said, you do your thing. I'll do mine. Anything else we need to talk about, sweetheart?"

She rested a hand gently on his forearm. "I'm going to say this once nicely, okay? Don't call me terms of endearment like that. You're not Humphrey Bogart, this isn't the fifties, and I'm not some tart who's dying to give you a blow job."

Derek just stared at her. How did she deliver such a hard-ass punch with that sweet expression?

"It's condescending and patronizing," she said. "You don't need to put me in my place. I'm quite clear what my role is, and it's not catering to your ego. I have one purpose here, and that's to help. I'm not your commanding officer. You don't have to take my suggestions. But while we *are* working together, I'll need you to address me in a respectful manner. Okay?"

"Fucking hell." He pulled out of the booth, yanked open the fridge, and reached for a cold bottle of water. *Two weeks* into their first tour. This should be the best time of his life. Headlining festivals up and down the Eastern Seaboard with his band? *Come on.*

What the fuck happened?

He heard them talking behind him, but he tuned them out.

He didn't need anyone to tell him what course they were on. He saw where they were headed if they didn't get their shit together. And there wasn't a chance in hell he'd prove his father right. This band would not blow up because of partying and nymphs and rock star behavior.

No, he didn't need a babysitter. But truthfully? It *wasn't* working.

He twisted off the cap and downed half the bottle.

It wouldn't hurt to have someone looking out for the bullshit stuff—the drugs, drinking, and partying. It'd give him a chance to have a little fun himself.

He thought of Gen, how he should've been able to have time alone with her last night. He *should* be having fun—not just handling things.

Soft laughter drew his attention back to the trio at the table. As he stood before them, all their eyes turned to him, and he said, "Okay."

Violet's features warmed and lightened. "Okay."

Standing to the side of the stage, where she had a clear view of both the band and the audience, Violet watched the sea of ecstatic faces. Gazes pinned on the lead singer, the crowd screamed, danced, and sang along to the final song of the night.

She completely understood why the women called him Slater-fucking-Vaughn. It wasn't about his outrageously good looks or his incredibly hard body. It was the accessibility, the humility. He just came across as a really nice guy, who happened to rock a pair of jeans like a model.

Weirdly, though, while Slater commanded the attention with his stage presence and deeply emotional singing, her gaze always seemed to wander back to the bass player.

An intense bundle of energy locked into a rock-hard body, Derek didn't show off or try to draw attention to himself. Instead, he got lost in the music, sometimes closing his eyes, his head moving like he was reading the beat in the air. His passion drew her in, made her fixate on him.

Just then, as if sensing her interest, he opened his eyes and looked right at her. Awareness exploded in her chest, sending a shower of fiery sparks throughout her body.

Oh, brother. In his worn jeans that molded the hard muscles of his thighs and ass and his big black boots, he was pure, hot *man*.

With a screech of instruments, the song came to an abrupt end. The audience went crazy, rushing the stage and screaming. Ben tossed his drumsticks into the crowd, Derek hefted his guitar over his head with one hand and pumped it a few times, while Slater shouted, "We fuckin' love you guys," before leaving the stage.

The guys brushed past, not even noticing her. She could see the wildness in their eyes, the sweat on their skin, the savage smiles. They were amped up, just as Derek had described.

Forcing herself into work mode, she joined their entourage, trailing behind them, keeping her sights on Pete. So many people hugged them, shook their hands, it was hard to see more intimate interactions—like who was handing him a snack-sized baggie.

"First time backstage?"

She whipped around to face Derek. With a white hand towel, he mopped his face. *My God, he's gorgeous.* Towering over her with an almost feral energy, his worn black T-shirt clung to his broad shoulders and thick arms. A tribal tattoo banding around his right biceps only heightened his rugged appeal.

"Oh, no. My clients get all kinds of invitations. I've been to every kind of show or event you can think of."

"You don't seem pleased. Didn't like the show?"

She gazed into amber eyes that studied her with unnerving intensity. Where Slater had movie star good looks and charisma, Derek had a rougher, earthier vibe. Scruffy chin whiskers, tats, and an aura of pure sexuality gave him an edge that made her just a little uncomfortable.

Not that she thought of him sexually, but if she did, she'd think of him as hard, demanding, and *completely* uninhibited.

Why did that get her excited? She'd never been with anyone like that before.

Okay, not thinking about Derek Valencia in that context.

"I loved the show. You guys are terrific. It's just . . ." She gestured to the backstage frenzy. "It's hard to keep an eye on three guys in all this chaos."

He leaned in close, and she saw his nostrils flare. Was he sniffing her?

"Son?" A man appeared beside him, clapping him on the back. Tall with manic eyes, he wore a short-sleeved linen shirt men his age typically wore loosely over slacks to cover their bellies.

Derek flinched. A flash of stark fear quickly hardened into anger. "Dad? What're you doing here?"

So this was Eddie Valencia. The jazz legend looked nothing like the images she'd found on Google. Seemed he hadn't been photographed in many years.

"Now, why the hell would you be surprised your old man showed up at one of your gigs?" He gestured to the younger man beside him. "You've heard of Buck O'Reilly? Buck, my son, Derek Valencia."

The younger man tucked his long, lank hair behind his ear with one hand while the other reached for Derek's. "You bet. Been trying for a while to get him on the show."

Derek gestured to her. "Dad, Buck, this is Violet Davis."

Oh, nuts. She hadn't had a chance to talk to the guys about her role in their lives. Including her fake name. Usually, she posed as a girlfriend to avoid embarrassment for the client, but in the case of five guys, she could always be a record company representative. She should've talked to them about it already, but everything had moved so quickly.

"So nice to meet you." She shook both their hands, surprised at the swipe of Eddie's thumb over the back of hers. Unnerved, she focused on Buck. "What show is that?"

"Ever hear of *Artists Unplugged*?" Eddie asked.

"Of course." Violet smiled.

"That's Buck's cable show. All the big players do it." Under that genial persona, Violet saw a hardness as he looked at his son. Like he was taunting him.

Derek met his dad's focused expression with one of his own. "We spent nearly a year in the studio and now we're on tour. Been a busy time." He paused. "You remember what that was like, right, Dad?"

Tension pulled the group taut. Without even thinking, she reached for his hand, gave it a squeeze. He had to know not to throw down publicly with his own dad.

"You're damn right I remember." Eddie bellowed out a laugh. "My guys, man, we'd hole up in the studio day and night. Didn't give a damn about albums or tours or dating models. None of that shit. All we wanted to do was jam. For us, it was all about the music. But these are different times, right, Buck?"

Derek stiffened, and Violet could not believe a father could treat his own son this way. She pressed closer to him, wanting him to know she was right there with him.

"Where do you record your shows?" she asked, more to break the tension than to hear the answer.

The hipster seemed relieved. "New York. I've got a small studio in the West Village. I also do a blog. Hey, you guys mind if I get a picture of you? Father and son?" He whipped out his phone. In a flash, Eddie had his arm around his son. The picture was taken with Derek looking awkward and uncomfortable. Nothing like the strong, commanding man he was.

"Fuck," Derek muttered under his breath. She gave his hand another squeeze. She'd fix it.

"How about I get a shot of the three of you? Wouldn't that be fun for your blog?" She reached for the phone, and Buck handed it over. "Great." As they arranged themselves, Violet pretended not to know how to work the camera. She quickly opened the gallery. "Oh, darnit. I think I deleted that one." She glanced up at Derek, horrified to see his desperate, haunted expression. He completely hated this moment with his dad. "Okay, let's try this again. Smile."

She locked her gaze with Derek's, letting him know she'd wait as long as it took for him to settle into his cool bass player persona.

The moment he did, she pressed the button. "Got it." As she handed the phone back, she reached for Derek's arm. "We really should get going. You've got press to do."

"So what's it going to take to get you on Buck's show?" his dad said. "You're not afraid of performing without your band, are you?"

"Jesus, Dad, don't make an ass of yourself. I don't have anything to be afraid of. We've got a different festival or gig every night of the week. I'll do the show when things settle down."

"Sure thing. Looking forward to it." Buck seemed uncomfortable with the battle between father and son.

"I'm sure you've got plenty of talent under all that . . ." Eddie made a sweeping gesture from Derek's biker boots to his chin-length dark blond hair. His laughter died down as he gave Buck a serious expression. "You really should give my son a chance. Underneath all the noise, he's got some talent. Hell, he's my son. Some of it has to have rubbed off, right?"

Oh, hell, no. This man was not getting away with this crap. Violet smiled at Buck. "Didn't you love that article in *Rolling Stone* when Michael Kramer compared Derek to Les Claypool and Paul McCartney? Oh, my God, made me so proud of him. He said Derek's got the 'deeply melodic, flawless bass of Paul McCartney, along with the ability to funk things up with Les Claypool's signature slap bass sound.'" She made sure she radiated pure pride.

"Yeah, I read that. That was awesome." Buck clapped Derek on the shoulder. "Love to get you in the studio, man. Let everyone hear what you've got."

"Definitely," Derek began. "I'll be in touch."

"Won't we be in New York next week?" Violet asked him.

"Uh-oh," his dad said. "Isn't that where your publicist lives? Does she know you took up with this one?" Eddie lifted his brows in a show of feigned surprise to Buck. "Hey, here's one for your blog. Breaking news. Derek's got yet another new girlfriend."

Anger tightened Derek's features, and his body went rigid. "Dad—"

But before he could speak, Violet took one step forward. "It's so sweet how closely you follow your son's career in the press. You guys should get together when we're in New York, though, so you can catch up with him personally."

She gripped Derek's hand tightly. For just a few seconds, their gazes locked, and the whole world shut down. She could see his anger—a live, seething force inside him—settle down, feel his muscles relax. For that one moment, she felt like his lifeline.

A droplet of sweat trickled down the side of his face, and she gently wiped it away with her fingers. She willed him to keep his focus on her—and not let that snake of a dad get to him.

"Anyhow," she said to Buck. "Why don't you give us some dates and times, and we'll get back to you. He'll be pretty inundated with press in the city, but we'll try and squeeze it in. Sound good?"

Buck smiled. "Sounds great." He shook Derek's hand. "I'll be in touch." He nodded to Eddie and Violet before taking off.

Violet turned to Eddie. "Mr. Valencia, it's so great to finally meet you. Strangely, everything I've heard about you is true." She squeezed Derek's hand. "Ready to go?"

The white noise of the rumbling engine should've lulled her overactive mind to sleep, but thoughts kept charging through, jolting her, keeping her wide awake. Strange bus, strange people, weird and very strange new world.

Usually, she could sleep anywhere. She'd had to.

In her first foster home, after her grandma died, Violet had shared a bed with three other little kids. Squished together, they slept like puppies in a basket. She didn't remember much from the early days—she'd only been six—but she did remember the sticky heat, the tangle of sweaty limbs, and the mix of scents in that first bed. Nothing bad, really. Mostly spaghetti sauce, baby shampoo, and the laundered scent of cotton pajamas.

Her sharpest memory was the loneliness, the fear. When her grandma died, the sorrow had spilled through her like water, a constant, seeping, unstoppable flow. It saturated her tissue, until she carried the weight of it from house to house, along with the worn and tattered book of poetry her grandma had given her. She'd missed her grandma fiercely.

Not that she remembered much, of course. She'd been too young. Just the lovely, quiet routine they'd had. After her postal route, her grandma would pick her up from an old lady's house—a house she remembered smelled oddly of nail polish remover, no idea why—and take her home to their tiny little house on a busy street in Sound Beach, Long Island.

As she'd fix them a simple dinner, her grandma would talk to her about the dogs that had barked at her that day or the curious man who'd peer at her through the curtains each morning. And then—her favorite part—after they ate, they'd go outside to the tiny backyard and water the flowers, as Grandma told more stories. A whole backyard filled with wildflowers.

Boots clomped on the metal stairs, and her body went on alert. Her senses sharpened, tracking the movements.

The curtain pulled back, hands pressed down on the mattress, and a big body heaved itself into the tiny bunk. Though she'd only met him two days ago, she already recognized his shape and scent, so it didn't alarm her when Derek crashed into the tiny space.

"I didn't think that couch would work for you," she said quietly.

"Kept sliding off." His gruff voice sent a shot of awareness through her.

"I'm sorry." She kicked off the blanket.

"Where you going?"

She welcomed the wall of heat against her side, considering how cold the bus was with the constant flow of air conditioning. "I'll sleep there. You need your sleep more than I do."

His arm banded around her waist, tugging her back down. "You're right. So go to sleep."

"I'm not sleeping in this bunk with you."

"You're not sleeping in the lounge either."

"I'm not as big as you. I won't slide off as easily."

He was quiet for a moment. "That's not the only problem with the lounge."

Was he talking about the decadence that went on in there? They hadn't let any nymphs on the bus since Violet had joined them. "Don't worry about me. You can't imagine the places I've slept."

She started to climb over him, but his hand clamped down on her thigh. *Oh.* Why did his big hand on her skin feel so good? She'd never dated a forceful guy before. Had always chosen guys who let her take the lead.

"Slater's room is right next door. The walls are thin."

"If you think Slater's loud, you should—" A soft moan floated up the stairs. Heat burst inside her chest as she realized what he meant. "Ah." How awkward was that? Did Emmie know she could be heard throughout the bus?

Even in the darkness, she could see the flash of white teeth from his grin. "Yeah."

"Well, when they're done, I'll go."

"You'll never sleep. Abe's got talk radio going on all night. It's how he stays awake."

Why bother fighting? They'd be up in a few hours anyway, and Derek needed rest to play the festival in Virginia Beach.

"Well, we won't be sleeping on the bus as much from now on."

"Yeah? How's that?"

"We'll switch over to hotel suites whenever possible. I can make things more comfortable for you guys with a kitchen and actual bedrooms."

"That means driving during the day instead of all night."

"You'll be getting better sleep, so you can actually work during the day on the bus. Without distractions. Isn't that the fun stuff for you guys, making music?"

He studied her a moment, and she couldn't imagine what he was thinking. Maybe she presumed too much? He exhaled. "Yeah, that's the fun stuff."

He seemed so tired. She'd let him get to sleep. Just as she started to turn over, his arm hooked around her waist. "You protected me tonight."

"Your dad—"

"You don't need to do that."

"I know." As intimidating as he was with all his badass intensity, she had to admit the almost immediate intimacy he assumed between them utterly thrilled her.

"The only reason I let you is because I didn't want to lose it in front of Buck."

"And that's the only reason I did it. Has he always been like that?"

"No."

"Oh, that's good. I couldn't imagine growing up with a dad like that." Not that she could imagine growing up with a dad at all.

"When I was a kid, he was way more direct about it." His hand flew up, his palm right in her face. "This is the view of my dad I remember most."

Oh. It hadn't even happened to her, but she felt the stinging slap of rejection. How *awful*. She caught the offending hand, lowered it between them and held it tightly. No matter how powerful and in command he appeared, she read pain and vulnerability in those eyes. And he only confirmed it when he didn't pull away.

"You know what I remember?" Usually, Derek was passionate, full of energy. But when he talked about his dad, he flattened out.

She gently shook her head, keenly aware of his pain. The blond scruff around his mouth accentuated the sexiest pair of lips she'd ever seen. Were they fuller than most? Or did she notice them more because of the beard framing them?

"My dad had a studio in the basement. He always kept it locked. And, you know, we lived in the suburbs. There was no reason to keep it locked. Except to keep *me* out. So it became like the Holy-fucking-Grail to me."

"Of course."

"And when his dudes came over, I'd follow them around like a puppy. Not in the studio, of course. I wasn't allowed in there. But I remember this one time, the guys came upstairs and they left the door open. I snuck in there, and it was, like, surreal, you know? All those instruments. Owned and played by guys I revered. So I started just wailing on my dad's sax. And let me tell you, no one touched the great Eddie Valencia's sax. And then I beat the skins, had a blast. Eventually, the guys walked in. And they all just watched me. But in a cool way, and it egged me on. They smiled at me, like I was all right. And then my dad busts in and, you know, he'd never make himself look bad in front of anyone, so instead of yelling at me, he goes, 'Well, shit, buddy, you better keep up your grades in school. You're gonna need it.'"

Violet couldn't stand it. She hitched up on an elbow. "He's such a jerk."

"Yeah." Whatever hint of emotion had burned through cooled. "It was a long time ago. My point is that I've dealt with him my whole life. I don't need anyone running interference. It's between me and my dad."

"Not on my watch."

He studied her for a long moment. It was dark enough she didn't think he could see how upset she'd gotten. But then one side of his mouth hitched up. "You gonna be my champion?" He said it like he didn't believe it.

Shoving aside her completely inappropriate attraction,

she dropped back into professional mode. "My job is to minimize the stressors so that you can focus on your work. Everything I do is to help you screen out the noise so you can make the magic. Usually, the noise is drugs and alcohol, which it is for Ben, Cooper, and Pete. But for you? It's your dad. He's the noise in your head."

"Used to be. Not anymore." He closed his eyes. "Don't worry about it. Let's get to sleep."

On her back, she stared into the darkness, her body buzzing with disgust at what that man had done to his little boy.

Still on his side, one hand under his head, he watched her. "What're you thinking?"

"Sorry, I should go. You'll never sleep with a stranger in your bed."

"I'll sleep after you answer the question. What're you thinking?"

But she didn't want to bring up his dad again. So she brought up the other thing that'd been bugging her. "I'm thinking I caused you some trouble tonight." An article had shown up on Beatz, outing her as Derek's new love interest—implying that he hadn't bothered to break up with Gen first. Fortunately, they didn't have a photo of her to go with it.

"How's that?"

"With your girlfriend. I didn't mean for Buck to jump to that conclusion."

"That's on my dad."

"No, I kept touching you."

"Couldn't keep your hands off me."

She smiled. "I know. What's the *matter* with me?"

"I'm fuckin' irresistible." Something sparked in his eyes, and the rush of intimacy ignited something in her heart, making it beat harder, faster. Okay, this was not good. They shouldn't be connecting on this level. "Yeah, okay, Mr. Irresistible. The point is that the media got hold of it. Is Gen upset?"

He let out a hard laugh, and she covered his mouth with her hand. They didn't need to wake anyone up. "You're worried about Gen's feelings? Don't bother. Our relationship is nothing like how the media portrays us. Besides, like I said, that one's on my dad. Buck wouldn't have said anything about it. My dad probably told every reporter he saw."

"Well, tonight, for the first time ever, I was almost glad I didn't have a dad."

"What?"

She smiled. "Yours is awful."

He laughed softly. "Yeah, he is. But he hasn't been in my life in a long time. You never knew your dad?"

She shook her head.

"No stepdad?"

She drew in a breath. Normally, she'd never share her real life, but since he was Emmie's brother, he'd find out anyway. "I grew up in foster care."

His eyebrows shot up. "Your whole life?"

"My mom was an addict. She dropped me off at my grandma's when I was two. My grandma died four years later. After that, yeah, foster care."

"You must've had some damn good families if you came out like this."

"Like what?"

"All elegant and sophisticated. Someone took good care of you."

"Actually, I took care of them. I learned pretty quickly how to keep myself safe."

"Took care of who, exactly?" His features darkened.

She didn't like his suspicion. She'd worked hard to live a clean life. "The other *kids*."

He softened. "Ah. I wondered how you became a minder. Didn't think there was a major for that in college."

"I didn't go to college."

"No way. No *fucking* way."

Was that admiration she saw on his features? "Why does that surprise you?"

"Your vocabulary, your intelligence. You're polished. No way you didn't go to college."

"As soon as you turn eighteen, you're out of the program. It's not like there's a locker jammed with savings for us. There's no transition team or anything."

"So what did you do?"

"I became a nanny." She thought of Francesca, the

woman who'd changed her whole life by making a simple call. "Before I turned eighteen, I worked in a day care for one of the fancy beach clubs in the Hamptons. One of the women I met there hooked me up with my first nanny job. And then *that* woman's husband liked how I handled the kids, not to mention his crazy wife, so he hired me to mind one of his workers who had a substance abuse problem." She smiled. "And a business was born."

"You're kind of amazing."

The way he looked at her lit a fuse inside her. Her whole body heated and hummed. "Just scrappy. Like you."

"Naw. You've just pretty much humbled my ass. I won't be whining like a bitch about my dad anymore."

She liked him. Not that way, of course, but she didn't think she'd mind spending time with him. Which made her think of his girlfriend. "I can fix this, you know. In most of my jobs, I play the role of my client's girlfriend. But we don't have to do that in this situation. I mean, I can be Pete's girlfriend, if you want, since I do have to keep an eye on him."

He narrowed his gaze at her.

Guess he didn't like that idea. "Or a record company executive. Whatever you guys want. I just don't want to cause problems for you and Gen."

He practically glowered at her. "I already told you she's not gonna give a shit. And you're not going to be anyone else's girlfriend. Just leave it as it is."

"I'm not sure you understand what it means to have me pose as your girlfriend. I'll be with you all the time. I'll be . . . you know, touching you. Making it look believable. Trust me, Gen's not going to like what she sees." He remained still, quiet, and it made her uncomfortable. "We're going to be together a lot." All the time.

"Gen won't see you as a threat."

Heat shot up her neck, burning like a rash. She wasn't suggesting a woman like Genevieve Babineaux would feel threatened by *her*, specifically. More that no woman wants to see her boyfriend with some woman hanging on him, even if she knows it's only pretend.

A finger tipped her chin. "You can't be a threat, believe me."

Mortification burned a path from her neck to the tips of her ears. Her mind blanked out, but she wouldn't let him see his successful kill shot. She turned to stone. "I'll take care of it in the morning."

He clamped a hand on her hip, preventing her from flipping over. He practically yanked her back toward him. "No, you won't. You'll leave it as it is."

She would not let him hurt her. She barely even knew him. What an idiot to let herself develop feelings for a client. *Obviously* she wasn't his type. He'd dated two supermodels before hooking up with Genevieve Babineaux. *Of course* she wasn't his type.

"Besides, she's not my girlfriend."

"Well, whatever you call it in your world, she's the woman you're sleeping with at the moment. I don't want to embarrass her. I'll take care of it tomorrow. Now, if you'll excuse me, I'm sure your sister's gone to sleep by now." She swung a leg over him to get out of the bunk, but he blocked her with his body.

His fingers touched her chin. "I hurt your feelings."

In spite of the cold air circulating on the bus, her skin felt clammy. Perspiration beaded over her lip. "This is a job. I have no feelings."

"I don't know what I said, but I'm sorry."

"That's such a stupid thing to say. If you don't know what you said, then you can't *be* sorry. Let me go."

"No. You're going to wake everyone up. Just get back in bed and let's go to sleep."

"I'm not sleeping with you. It's unprofessional."

"You're my girlfriend. It's not unprofessional."

"I'm your *fake* girlfriend in public. There's no one around but you and me."

"And me," a voice from below said, all sleepy and rough.

"Go back to sleep, Coop," Derek said. He gave her a look that said, *See, you woke him up.*

"Then shut the fuck up," Coop said.

His fingers tightened on her chin. "Lay down." He tugged her, so she fell over him, lengthwise. Seeking purchase, her hand came up and brushed across something hard and long and thick. When he grunted and pulled his knees up, she knew she'd touched his erection.

"I'm so sorry." She quickly scrambled off him, but he only dragged her to his other side, trapping her between his big body and the wall.

He leaned into her, whispering in her ear, "If you can keep your hands off my dick, I might let you sleep here."

She couldn't help the snuffling laughter that came out of her, so she turned her face into his pillow.

"You'll never get to sleep in the lounge, not with that talk radio going all night long. Okay?"

She got a hold of herself, and gave him a short nod. Then, she turned away from him, curling up and folding her hands under her chin.

After several moments of silence, during which she used her relaxation exercises to calm down, she felt his heat near her face. "You look adorable like that."

Her foot kicked out, jamming him in the thigh.

"Ow."

"Go to sleep."

"Fine." He hovered over her. "But I *am* sorry I hurt your feelings."

She turned to look up at him, seeing the genuine worry in his eyes. "We're going to forget all about feelings, okay? We work together. Now, good night, Derek."

He didn't answer, and she didn't know what he was thinking.

But then she heard him exhale, then shift closer to her, one arm banding around her waist and pulling her in close.

SIX

Hot water slid over his body, and Derek lowered his head. The music still coursed through him, making his fingers twitch. And when he closed his eyes, he saw the fans screaming, arms in the air, as though the guys were offering food to a starving mob instead of tunes.

He let the water pummel his head, his neck, his shoulders, as he fought back the shame of having a minder. Of Irwin thinking he needed a minder. That he couldn't handle the band.

Worse, he didn't think he *could* handle the band. During the tour with Piper, he'd come up with the idea of the contract. And it had worked for a while. The guys had finished out the tour with no drugs and way less booze. But then they'd moved to New York City to record the album, and things started changing. Initially, nervous about pleasing the producer and Irwin, the guys had gone back to the rental in Brooklyn each night and fallen asleep. But over time, they'd started accepting invitations from the record company people, going out to clubs, staying out later and later. He'd thought they'd be okay, since Irwin had assigned them his assistant, Bax.

Derek had breathed a little easier, knowing they were

under Bax's watch. The guy had the extreme good luck to work for the hottest A&R guy in the business. It was in his best interest to keep Irwin happy—and that meant keeping his bands in line.

Still, Derek had taken it upon himself to make sure everyone showed up to the studio on time. Performed to the best of their ability. And when things had started to get out of hand—like Pete being too fucked up to play his part some days—he'd tossed the guys into a cab and taken them to a tattoo shop in Greenwich Village. They'd gotten inked, gotten back on the same page, and kicked some ass in the studio. They got it. Partying and decadence killed the music. Ended careers. They weren't going to fall into that rabbit hole. The tats were constant, permanent reminders.

He'd thought they were good. And now, they were unraveling all over again.

And it felt like shit that Irwin thought they needed a minder to keep them focused on their damn job.

Shutting off the water, he stepped out of the communal shower and grabbed his towel.

Well, fuck, how *did* you control the behavior of five guys? Four of your closest friends?

He couldn't. And now they'd find out if Violet could.

"**Fucking** *bowling*?" Pete scowled as he took in the crowded bowling alley.

"You'll love it." Violet grabbed her shoes from the clerk. "Thank you." Her radiant smile made the kid blush. She took off, leaving Derek in a cloud of the light, floral perfume that he'd come to associate with her soft body tucked up against him.

Not good. Not good at all.

"Why am I bowling instead of getting laid?" Pete asked Derek. "I'm a rock star, not a plumber."

Plumber? When had Pete become such a snob? Sure, his parents were both doctors, but Pete hadn't even gone to college. After spending middle school beating off in his closet with a stack of *Playboy* magazines, he'd landed a gig in a garage band. He and Slater had found his name on a corkboard in the first club they'd played during their junior year of college.

"Because our babysitter thinks it's a healthier way to let off steam." Coop had his hands on his hips, checking out the patrons. "We could still get laid." He did a chin lift toward a group of high school girls wearing skimpy clothes and thick eyeliner.

"They've got *braces*." Derek didn't want to bowl either, but what could he do? Undermine her first effort to find them healthier alternatives to working off their post-show highs? "Come on, get your shoes." He didn't think she could understand the level of adrenaline punching through their system after a gig. Nor why having sex with three women at once would take the edge off for these guys better than tossing a big ball down a lane.

As he headed toward his friends, Slater came up to him, looking all stern and pissed off. "You invited them *here*?" He tipped his head toward the door. "Your boy just walked in."

Derek spotted one of the reporters he often texted when he thought the band could use some good PR. "Yeah, I did. It's a good thing."

"Really? We're *bowling*. Last time you tipped them off because of the celebrities who came to the show. What's the excuse this time?"

"Gets our name out there."

"Why do you need this shit?"

When his friend's voice softened, when the anger turned into genuine curiosity, Derek calmed down. "Every time my dad says shit about me, it turns the spotlight on the band. Makes people look at us the wrong way."

Slater rubbed his chin, looking thoughtful. "Yeah, okay. I can see that."

"Matt'll get a few shots of our good, wholesome fun, post 'em, and Eddie Valencia's ugly shit'll be spun into what a neat bunch of guys we really are. And bonus, Irwin sees we're doing healthy shit."

Slater nodded, bumped his fist into Derek's upper arm. "Got it. Sorry. I just . . . I hate this shit."

Emmie came up just then, throwing her arms around Slater's neck. "You ready for me to blow a rack?"

Slater sputtered. "What?"

She laughed. "It's a bowling term Ben just taught me. It means a solid strike hit. I'm a git me one of those. Come on, let's do this."

She dragged him off to their lane, which had attracted more than a few hangers-on. Good, it would generate even more buzz.

As Derek approached, he watched Violet sitting in a chair, leaning forward, tying her shoes. When she sat up, her dark shiny hair swung back, settling around her, all silky and smooth. She caught him watching, and her features broke into a smile so genuine his breath caught in his throat.

He dropped his shoes, sank into a chair, and kicked off his boots. His pulse beat too fast. What the fuck was his problem? Another pretty girl. So what? He had to get a hold of himself around her.

"So is this what you normally dress like?" he heard Emmie ask her.

"Oh, you wouldn't want me dressing like me. I don't think anyone would buy Derek dating a girl in shorts and a T-shirt, no makeup, and her hair fresh from a shower. No, this is for my role with you guys."

"Well, I like it. That's a really pretty dress."

Derek couldn't help taking in the white sundress with bright red strawberries toppling all over it. The top part hugged her spectacular breasts, and then it opened into a swingy skirt. She looked something between a farm girl and a sex kitten. And it made him hard.

"Thanks." She lowered her voice, leaned closer to his sister. "I had to really think about it. Derek doesn't hang around nymphs, so I had to kill that look. And since he only dates supermodels and women like Gen, I knew I couldn't even begin to go there. No outfit can make me look like his type."

His head snapped up. He stared at her, last night finally making sense. He'd hurt her worse than he'd thought.

"So I had to come up with something that would seem believable. You know, why would he trade a sexpot like Gen for a regular woman like Violet Davis? It's not as easy as you think to fit into these roles."

She had it all wrong. He was such a dick.

"Hm." Slater nudged him. "What *would* an actual girlfriend of Derek Valencia look like? I'm not sure even he knows, since he's never given anyone a chance."

Derek looked away from his teasing expression. He grabbed Violet's arm. "Come here."

"Derek," he heard Emmie call, but he didn't care. "We're about to start, where are you going?"

He ignored his sister, towing Violet back near the vending machines.

"What're you doing?" Violet yanked her arm free.

With a hand at either side of her head, he pinned her to the wall. "You took it the wrong way. Last night, when I said you weren't a threat to Gen." His gaze trailed down her very hot body, down to the red-tipped toes peeking out of the sandals. Then, he let it crawl back up, unable to stop himself from taking in the luscious cleavage in the V-neck of her dress.

When he captured her gaze, her eyes widened, and her pretty pink tongue came out and licked her lips. "Okay."

"You thought I meant you couldn't compare to Gen. But you got it wrong."

"I don't care." Her tone sounded completely together, but her eyes showed something else entirely. "Remember what I said? No feelings. We work together. I was just trying to look somewhat believable as your girlfriend."

"Gen's not even in your league. I've never met anyone like you before. You're so fucking real." He didn't know how to describe her, but the way she held her breath, waiting, made him want to try. "A hundred shiny people can be in the room, but you're the one I'm drawn to. Because you're all calm and cool, like there's nothing you can't handle. And yet you're sweet and kind." The opposite of Gen. "But underneath . . . Christ. You're fierce. And that makes you about a thousand times sexier than she could ever be."

Standing this close, thighs touching, he felt the tremble run through her. "Okay. It's fine."

"No, it's not. I hurt your feelings last night."

"You can't hurt my feelings if I don't have them. You're my client."

"Oh, I hurt your feelings. And I'm telling you I'm sorry.

I never thought I had a type before, but that's because I've never met anyone like you."

Her lips parted, her features softening, and color spread across her cheeks. *Oh, damn.*

His gaze lowered to her cleavage again, and when she drew in a sharp breath, her breasts rose. Lust gripped his spine and his balls. "Fuck, Violet."

"Don't do this. We have to get back out there." She pushed off the wall, her breasts pressing against his chest through his thin gray T-shirt.

Just as he started to step away from her, he caught movement in his peripheral vision. He recognized the reporter's red flannel shirt. Derek set his hands on her waist, holding her in place.

She took in a sharp breath. "You have to stop . . . possessing me like this. It makes me uncomfortable."

"Good uncomfortable or bad uncomfortable?" He didn't need an answer. He could see it. The heat burning in her eyes only lit a match to his own desire. He lowered his mouth to hers.

When she flinched, when he saw her expression turn angry, he said, "There's a reporter over there. Can I please kiss you? Just for the shot?"

"I don't kiss clients." But her gaze lowered to his mouth, and her expression turned outright hungry.

"You've never wanted to kiss a client before."

"It's one of my rules. No kissing clients."

"Tonight, just this once . . . break a rule. For me."

"Easy for you to say. You have no rules."

"I don't need rules. Neither do you. Kiss me."

"No. It's unprofessional." Her breathing turned shallow, and her breasts quivered.

"Violet, please? Please fucking kiss me."

"No."

His semi had turned so hard he had to press it against her stomach for relief. Her eyes widened, and she sucked in a breath.

"Derek," she breathed. "Don't do this."

"Okay, how about this?" He set his hands on her waist, lowered his mouth to her ear. "Can I do this?"

"I guess so."

"And this?" He licked the shell of her ear.

Her hands fisted in his shirt and her body shuddered. "You jerk." But he could hear her laughter.

"Is this unprofessional?" His hands skimmed up her rib cage, his thumbs brushing the undersides of her breasts.

"Yes, you ass. It's completely unprofessional." But she'd tipped her head to his shoulder and he could feel her body shake with laughter.

"What about this?" He tipped her chin up, so he could trail kisses along her soft, smooth cheek, her silky hair tickling his face. When he caught the corner of her mouth, she gasped.

Caressing the bare skin of her back, he felt it pebble underneath his fingertips.

She let out a shaky breath. "Stop, Derek. Seriously, that's enough."

If he moved, Matt would get a whole lot more than a romantic moment between lovers. He'd get something R-rated. Desire blazed deep inside, and he seriously needed to grind against her sweetly scented body. But he wouldn't do that to her.

"I mean it. He's gone. You don't have to do this anymore." Her hands left him, and she straightened, letting out a shaky breath.

And then she walked away, leaving him with a hard-on so painful he had to lock himself in a bathroom stall until it settled down.

Violet held back her laughter as everyone stared at the steaming casserole of grain and vegetables in the middle of the table.

It might as well have been sautéed roadkill for the looks on their faces. No one moved a muscle. They just stared.

"Well." Slater clapped his hands together. "I'm going for it." He plunged the serving spoon into the dish and brought some to Emmie's plate.

"Thanks." Violet saw how hard her friend tried to keep a pleasant expression. It wasn't working. "What is it exactly?"

"It's not as bad as it looks. And I'll admit it doesn't look as appetizing as, say, a bucket from the Colonel. But it's just quinoa, spinach, garlic, onions, and sweet peppers. It's actually pretty tasty."

Slater served himself, then passed the spoon to Cooper on his right. Cooper shook his head. Slater offered it to Derek, who spooned himself a small portion.

Spreading his napkin across his lap, Slater said, "So, the pills." He gestured to the tiny paper cups she'd placed in front of each of them.

"Right. Well, it's a little different for each of you. I noticed that Ben occasionally sneaks a cigarette—"

"What? No. I—shit. Hardly ever."

"Ben, I don't care what you do. But since you do *sometimes* smoke—and it's usually right before a show, I figured I'd try some lobelia with you, plus some kava pills to calm your nerves but not make you lethargic. We'll just give it a try, see if it doesn't curb your nicotine cravings and alleviate some of your anxiety. If it doesn't, we'll try something else. Why not, right?"

The table remained silent. Ben and Cooper scowled, but Pete looked mutinous, ready to upturn the table and storm out of the suite.

"Why the fuck not?" Derek knocked back the whole cup into his mouth and swallowed them with the fresh lemonade she'd made. He smacked his lips when he'd finished.

Violet couldn't help smiling at his willingness to play along. Most of her clients fought every step of the way—sometimes for weeks. These guys were pretty decent.

Picking up Cooper's cup, she took out the large white pill. "Everyone gets this one. It's a multivitamin." She pulled out two others. "And I've given everyone milk thistle and dandelion for your livers."

Cooper tossed his napkin on the table. "Jesus. We're not alcoholics."

"Of course not. But the amount of alcohol you *do* consume is definitely more than your livers can handle, so while we're scaling back, why not help it heal a little? Can't hurt."

When Derek offered the serving spoon to Pete, he batted it away. It clanged against the CorningWare plate.

"Fuck this shit." The keyboardist pushed his chair back and stomped off to his bedroom, slamming the door so hard the framed artwork on the wall rattled.

"Sorry about that," Emmie said.

"Oh, please. Don't even worry about it." She drank some lemonade. "You guys are easy compared to most of my clients."

"This is so fucked up," Cooper said. "No offense, but it's not like we're out of control."

A knock on the door got Ben on his feet and racing to open it.

Slater chewed, swallowed, then drank some lemonade. "It's not bad."

"I like it." Emmie looked at Derek and Cooper. "You should try it."

Neither said a word.

"Now that's what I'm talking about." Ben came back to the table with two boxes of pizza.

"Pizza's here," Cooper shouted toward the bedroom.

Pete came out, headed into the kitchen, and grabbed some beers. He slammed them down on the table.

Tension filled the room. Emmie looked uncomfortable, like she needed to do something. But there was nothing she—or anyone—could do. It took time. Violet wasn't worried. She watched as the guys tore open the pizza boxes, twisted the caps off the beers, and dug into their dinner.

"Are you as cool inside as you look on the outside?" Derek reached for a slice of pizza. "Because nothing seems to faze you. Not even Pete's stanky dreads."

Emmie nearly snorted lemonade out her nose. Everyone laughed.

"Fuck you, asshole," Pete said. "I like it, and the chicks love it. And it's a hell of a lot better than what I used to have, right, Em?"

Violet noticed the look of affection in Pete's gaze as he regarded Emmie. A pang of envy struck her—these guys were so tight. No matter their troubles, they really liked each other. They were better than a family because they'd *chosen* each other.

She looked at Derek, laughing at something Cooper

said. That night in the bowling alley? She'd wanted so badly to let him in. Feel the stroke of his tongue in her mouth. Have him pour that energy, that *passion* into her. She wanted to know what it would feel like to have his possessive hands all over her body.

God, she'd bet he would just consume her. Nothing hesitant or careful—he'd just take what he wanted from her body. *Yes.* A tremor of excitement rippled down her spine, and the shock to her chest made her sit forward.

She had to stop thinking about him this way. He was a *client.*

Look at her getting carried away with things she couldn't have. Getting attached to Derek, this band? They saw her as an intruder, someone forced upon them. And as soon as they could be rid of her, they'd gladly see her gone.

"That's some nasty shit." Pete flicked a spoonful of quinoa across the table, nailing Cooper in the chest.

"Hey, asswipe." Laughing, Cooper got up and grabbed the spoon out of his hand, ready to scoop out his own ammo.

Before he could, Derek rose. "Knock it off."

Eyes practically bulging out of his head, veins and tendons popping from his neck, Pete grabbed a handful of quinoa and hurled it at Derek.

He ducked, and the mess splattered on the carpet. "What the fuck's the matter with you?"

Derek shot Violet an apologetic look, but she made sure not to reveal any emotion. She didn't care if they didn't like the dish, but Pete's behavior—his agitation—led her to believe he was deeper into his addiction than anyone thought.

"What's the *matter*?" Pete shoved back from the table, headed into the kitchen. "*She's* the matter. This whole fucking thing is bullshit." He grabbed another beer from the refrigerator and came back to the table. Popping the cap, he overturned it into the casserole. "I'm not eating this shit, and I don't want to fucking bowl. I want to rock, and I want to rock hard."

"Sit down, Pete." Slater had a hard look in his eye.

She couldn't be the only one to notice his jittery, anxious behavior. Or his dilated pupils.

"I don't want to sit down. I should still be sleeping

because it's not even noon." He shot Ben and Cooper a challenging look. "And don't pretend you don't agree with me. You're not on board with this crap any more than I am."

Derek slammed his glass on the table. "Okay, this shit stops now." He tossed his napkin on his plate. "Sit the fuck down. We're having a meeting."

Pete sat, but he gave off the attitude of a rebellious teenager.

"Whether you like quinoa or bowling isn't the point. The point is that we're going to blow ourselves up if we don't get our shit together. We *are* partying too hard."

"Fine, I won't party so hard, but I don't have to do what she tells me to."

Emmie and Slater had incredulous looks on their faces, like they couldn't believe this was their friend.

"You're right," Violet said. "You don't." Everyone watched her. "I have no power over you. If you want my help, great. Happy to do what I can for you. If you don't . . . frankly, the success or failure of this band has no effect on me." She shrugged.

"The success or failure of this band hasn't got dick to do with a pile of steaming horseshit," Pete said. "Or your stupid ass herbal pills that'll just make my piss stink."

"The steaming pile of horseshit is quinoa. And since you've got sound check in an hour, I figured it'd be the best source of energy for you guys. Unlike that slice of pizza, quinoa's a perfect protein, rich with iron and lysine and amino acids. You'll get—"

"A good shit," Ben said.

She laughed. "*That* you can count on. While this," she said, pointing to the pizza box, "is made of white flour, salt, and fat. It'll make you lethargic. Which of these is going to give you the energy to perform tonight?"

"There's nothing wrong with our performances," Pete said.

"Let me ask you something. What do you want?" Her gaze moved around the table, stopping on each one of the band members.

No one responded. She waited.

Slater cleared his throat, wiped his mouth with the napkin. "I want to make great music."

Violet smiled at him, appreciating his total willingness to make things work with her. "Great, because you already do. What else do you want?"

He looked to Emmie. "I want my girl to feel safe. I want her happy."

A knot formed in Violet's throat. God, the way Slater looked at Emmie. The way he constantly needed to touch her. She couldn't even imagine having that kind of intense, all-consuming love. To be the center of someone's world? To be wanted so fiercely?

She used to wonder if she was capable of it, but now? After being around these two, so crazy passionate for each other?

She absolutely yearned for it.

Derek brushed hair off her shoulder. "You okay?"

She nodded, not wanting them to see her lose her composure. "Well, Slater." Her voice came out funny, so she cleared her throat. "You're a lucky man. Seems you've got everything you want." She turned to Derek. "What do you want?"

"Since I'm not whipped like that sorry sumbitch, I'll tell it like it is. I want to go gold. By the end of this tour, I want to go gold."

"Fuckin' A, man." Pete slapped the table so hard the lemonade sloshed in the glasses.

"And then what? After this album goes gold, then what?"

"Then it goes platinum. And then double platinum." Derek smiled.

"And after that? Once this album has run its course?"

"Then we do it again with another one."

"So that's really all you want out of life? To sell records?"

He thumbed his lower lip, looking a little uncomfortable. He stared unseeing at his plate. His gaze swung up to hers abruptly, igniting sparklers in her chest. "Respect." He spoke quietly, making her feel as if they were the only two in the room. "I want to know I'm good." He swallowed. "Really good."

She couldn't believe this intensely proud man had

opened up to her. Her heart expanded, and she put all the warmth she felt for him into her smile. "Thank you."

The way he held her gaze so intensely . . . God, it just thrilled and unnerved her. It wasn't just his world that was foreign to her, it was *him*, his raw, unbridled masculinity, and yet she felt this powerful connection to him. It made no sense, but she *loved* it.

Stop it. Just stop getting carried away. This is nothing but business.

"Yeah, well, I just want to play fuckin' music." Pete snatched another slice of pizza, the peppers and sausage toppling off. "Which we're doing."

"You are doing it, Pete. But how long will you get to *keep* doing it? What about Irwin? Does your success hinge on whether you keep him as your A&R representative?"

Cooper eyed her over his bottle. Ben stopped chewing.

"We can be successful without Irwin." Pete dropped back into his seat with a twist to another bottle top. "Our music is fuckin' great."

"Well, if everyone agrees with that, then I'm not needed. I suggest you have a band meeting and figure out what you want. No offense to you guys, but I'm used to minding one client at a time. Usually that client needs me in order to keep his job, so he'll play along. But if you don't need Irwin, and you have no interest in trying new ways of doing things, then let me go. I have other work I could be doing."

"You're not going anywhere," Derek said. The room went quiet, the tension thickened. "I want Irwin. Our music was good, but Irwin made it great. And not only that, but if he doesn't want to work with us, we're fucked. Tainted. I'm not sure about all this shit." He lifted a paper cup and shook it. "But damn straight I'll give it a go." He looked down at this plate with a somber expression. "Whatever it takes to get us back on track."

He looked up, held Slater's gaze. His friend nodded, the two of them locked in agreement.

"I also like the new schedule," Derek said. "Most days on the road, I feel like shit, and I don't get anything done. When was the last time we wrote a song? More than a year ago? So, yeah, I'm down to try some new ideas." He seemed to perk up. "Definitely." He looked to the others.

"Me, too," Slater said.

"Fuckin' pussies," Pete said.

"You guys should discuss this privately. You need to be on the same page." Violet started to get up. "I'll give you some time."

"You're not leaving." Derek reached for her arm, his grip sliding from her wrist to her fingers.

"I'm not on board." Cooper reached for another slice. "Sorry, but we're doing just fine without you."

"Then why did Irwin wash his hands of you?" she asked.

Ben swallowed. "We got him back."

"And if I pack up my bags and go back to the city, will you still have Irwin?"

"No," Derek shouted. "Jesus, guys. What's the problem? So we're in a hotel. So we're eating this stuff. What's the big fucking deal?"

"Guys, I'm not going to force you to do anything. It doesn't hurt my feelings if you don't eat my quinoa. I'm still going to make healthy food whether or not you eat it because it's my job. My job is to make you feel so good that you get up on the stage without the use of greenies or cocaine."

"We're not druggies," Cooper said. "Jesus Christ."

"But you do use drugs." Violet didn't back down. "I've seen you." She motioned to the three of them, Pete, Cooper, and Ben. "You might not want me here but have the self-respect to tell the truth."

Ben and Cooper looked chastised. Pete just took a huge bite of the pizza and washed it down with a swallow of beer.

"Am I wrong that your lifestyle is unsustainable? After a gig, you're too wired to fall asleep. So you party hard, release a lot of sexual energy, and then need help getting to sleep. Then, you sleep late, spend the day hungover, and yet you need to find the energy to get back onstage and wow the crowd? Am I wrong about that cycle?"

"You're not wrong." Slater said. "And it's not sustainable."

"Well, I can help you fall asleep without Ambien or Valium or whatever else you've been taking. Look, I'm not judging. I've only been here a couple days, and I see how hard it is. It's exhausting to find the energy to perform like you do every night. But I can also see how you're going to burn out if you keep doing this. And I'm guessing that's what Irwin sees. He does this for a living. He can see the trajectory. If all you want is to rock stadiums and get laid, then by all means continue what you're doing. Bax clearly encourages the lifestyle."

"No, no," Emmie said. "I know it looks that way, but Bax has a really hard job. He's got to keep the band *and* Irwin happy at the same time."

Violet wanted to say something more about her suspicions but now wasn't the time. She needed to get some resolution to the problem at hand. "Listen, if you want to make a career out of this and not burn out early, then why not try some of my suggestions? What do you have to lose?"

"I want to get laid," Pete said, knee jackhammering. "I can't bring girls back to the hotel, not with you and Emmie here."

"You also don't have to come back to the hotel until one. I'm not trying to cut you off from nymphs. But the priority is your performance, and you can't give your all when you're run-down and tired. Balance, that's what I go for. Can you get laid after a show? You bet. Can you have all-night orgies? Not on my watch. But other than that? Talk to me, tell me what you want. You don't want quinoa, I'll make something else. The point is we work together to figure out the best way to balance it all."

"Can you imagine Jimmy Rogers living like this?" Cooper asked.

"Jimmy who?" Violet said.

Derek cut her a surprised look and then smiled. Of course she knew the former Paradox singer. She also knew he'd blown himself up.

"No, and that's why he burned out," Slater said. "You want to go over the list of bands that fell apart over drugs? Of rock stars that OD'd?"

"Guys, Irwin wants to work with you because he thinks you're phenomenal," Emmie said. "There's no one better in the industry to help you realize your potential."

"I want that." The intensity on Derek's expression caught Violet by surprise.

She didn't think for a second they'd vote her off the bus. She was too valuable to them.

No, them getting rid of her wasn't her concern. What struck her was that *she* didn't want to leave *them*.

She didn't get attached to her clients. She became fond of them, sure. But this . . .

She cut a glance to Derek, her heart beating double-time.

No, *this* had never happened before.

SEVEN

Violet stood with her back against the plate glass window of the old school gym. Seventies rock played on the speakers, and the place smelled like a hamper of dirty socks.

Processing the information she'd just gotten, she thought of Derek's question the other day. He wanted to know if she was as composed inside as she was outside. Basically, he wanted to know if she felt anything. Most people who'd spent time with her asked the same question. Right then, talking to Francesca about the news she'd been anticipating, she had an answer.

She felt *everything*. She just didn't show it.

And right then, she felt fear. Pure, unadulterated fear.

But no one looking at her would guess it. Because she shut down. Just flipped the sign over to *Closed*.

"What, um, what did you do?" Violet forced the words out of her throat. Because she needed to know, and she couldn't just stand there like a stone statue.

"I just went outside, asked how I could help her," Francesca said.

Violet could picture the realtor checking out her property—her kitten heels sinking into the moist earth, features scrunching in disgust at the rotted wood of her porch, the moss growing on the roof shingles, the dusty, ancient bales of hay crowding the barn.

And she could hear the woman's assessment. *Teardown*.

Every muscle in her body clenched at the thought of Jed watching the wrecking ball take down the home that had raised generations of Walkers. Could the amount of laughter spilled, tears shed, fights waged inside that house even be measured? Babies had been born, board games tossed in frustration, endless meals eaten, dirty footprints tracked onto the wood floor, vases shattered as kids chased one another through the many rooms. Lives lived, still breathing within the walls.

But, of course, she'd known this day would come. Jedidiah's kids wouldn't just abandon the property. "What did she say?"

"She said she'd been engaged to sell the place."

"Right. Of course. I expected this." Violet drew in a tight breath, twisting a strand of hair around a finger. She watched the guys in the ring learning the boxing stance. Emmie was right there with them, in her Spandex gym shorts and tank top. She looked adorable with her arms up, facing big, muscled Slater Vaughn.

"I told her the property wasn't for sale," Francesca said. "I told her about your agreement with the owner. I even asked if she wanted to see the contract, but she said she didn't care. She had a contract with the owner's adult children to sell the property, so that's what she's going to do. She said she'd email me the contact for their lawyer."

"Okay." She turned to face the window. "Will you forward it to me?"

"Let me take care of it, my love. It's easier for me to fax the contract. You're somewhere in Virginia right now, and you've got enough on your plate. Other than presenting the contract, there's nothing we can do right now."

"Should we hire our own attorney?" Why was she saying *we*? This problem was hers. Alone.

"Why don't we hold off for now? They might be perfectly happy with the contract, considering they get paid for the land."

"Eventually. I suspect they want the money now."

"Let's not invent scenarios. Let's go about our lives and handle each challenge as it comes up. We've got a lot going for us in support of the contract. It's not like Jed suffered from dementia. Anyone in the nursing home would attest to the fact he was of sound mind and body up to the moment he passed."

"But what if—" A big wall of heat behind her had her swinging around to find Derek standing beside her, all fierce warrior. His intensity sent a bolt of electricity winging through her body. Automatically, she gave him her placid work smile.

But he wasn't having it. "You all right?" Sweat dripped down his face, and it was just so overwhelming that he bothered to care.

"Fine. You better get back in the ring. Don't want to miss anything."

But he didn't go. He folded his arms over his chest, braced his legs apart. Letting her know he wasn't going anywhere.

"Francesca, I should go. My *client* needs my attention." She turned away from him, lowered her voice. "So you'll take care of it?"

"I'll fax the napkin with a simple letter explaining who you are and how you met Mr. Walker."

"Thank you. Thank you so much." The idea that she could lose it—the little spot of land she hoped to call home one day—made her stomach hurt. And God, Jed. He could've sold the land before moving into the nursing home, obviously, but he'd held on to it. Wanting to pass it on to someone who loved it just as much as he did. His kids clearly didn't.

But she did.

"Could you also add that he *wanted* me to own the land? Just say that he loved to look out his window and see miles and miles of wildflowers. It made him happy." Long after he could no longer work his own land, he'd still gaze out that window, as if seeing the way it had once been. She saw how it had killed him to see those fallow fields, overgrown with weeds.

And the day she'd come out there with bags of wild-flower seeds, his whole face had lit up. He'd loved the idea—but even better? He'd lived to see the results. Not two years later, she'd watched him sit on his screened-in porch and enjoy the endless fields of flowers. He'd been so happy.

"Don't worry, sweetheart," Francesca said. "I know the story. I'm going to tell those damn attorneys that you started planting wildflowers because you couldn't stand to see him so unhappy. And that you've now turned it into a profitable business, just as he'd hoped. I've got this, V. No one's going to take it away from you."

"I hope you're right. Thank you, Francesca."

"Always."

She disconnected, closing her eyes and seeing her flowers swaying in an ocean-scented breeze.

A big hand squeezed her shoulder, urging her to turn toward him. "What's going on?"

"Oh, nothing. I've got it under control."

"Don't bullshit me."

She looked to the ring, where the guys were still doing their footwork. "You don't want to miss your first lesson."

He tipped her chin to him. "I don't care about my damn lesson. I want to know what's gotten you upset."

"It's nothing to do with you or the band."

"No shit? You know, I actually suspected you had a life outside of us. Now tell me."

It was the leader in him. He couldn't help himself. But whatever, she'd give him a brief description. "Okay, well, a realtor visited my property today. She wants to put it on the market. It's a long story, but it's going to be fine. My friend lives there, and she's going to take care of everything."

Derek sat down on a chair, completely overwhelming it with his big body, hard muscles, and intense energy. He patted the seat next to him.

She laughed. "Why do you care?"

He took her hand, gave it a tug, and she relented, falling into the seat beside him. "See, that's just weird. It's a good thing that I care. What kind of world do you live in that people don't care what happens to you?"

"The foster care world?"

Pain flashed across his features. "Well, you're in my world now. So tell me what's going on."

She couldn't deny the zing of happiness that shot through her. She liked that he cared. And she believed that he actually did. "You remember that day care job I had in East Hampton?"

He nodded, wiping a trickle of sweat off his temple.

"Every year we took the kids on a trip to Jed's farm. They got to feed the animals, ride a pony, eat grapes right off the vine, and then we'd take them down to the beach for a picnic and swim. They loved it. Even after I stopped working at the club, I'd visit Jed. But he got too old to work the land, and that kind of broke him. I asked about his kids, but he just waved them off. Said they had no interest. So one day I asked if I could seed the land with wildflowers. And he let me. For the next couple of years, that's what he got to see when he looked out this window. Acres and acres of wildflowers."

Derek swallowed, gripping her knee. "That's nice."

"Before he moved into a nursing home, he asked if I wanted the land. I couldn't afford it, of course, so we came up with a lease-to-own plan. After he passed away, well, I mean, I've pretty much been waiting for his family to come and try to take it away from me."

"You have a contract?"

"Of course."

"So what's the problem?"

She exhaled. "It's not official."

"Meaning?"

"Derek?" Ben called. "Come on. Dude, we're gonna learn about jabs."

Derek help up a finger, and Ben jogged back to the group. Immediately, he trained that sharp gaze back on her, surprising her when he reached a finger to push a lock of hair away from her mouth. "So?"

"We signed a napkin."

"A napkin?"

"He was old-fashioned, a handshake kind of man. I was twenty-one, and I knew I had to have more than his word. He just laughed at me, grabbed a napkin out of the basket, and wrote down our agreement. Then we each signed it."

"Could still be legal."

"I looked it up. Real estate deals need to be notarized."

"Do you have an attorney?"

"I thought I'd wait and see their response to the contract."

"Is this going to keep you up at night?"

She nodded.

"Then let's get you lawyered up."

"No, no, that's the last thing you need to think about. I shouldn't have said anything."

"Why not?"

"Because . . . it's my problem. And besides it might not even be a problem. My friend's going to fax the contract to the family's attorney. Maybe they'll let it go. It's not like they've ever shown any interest in the property in all the years I've known Jed."

"Where is it?"

"The land? Long Island."

He seemed impatient. "Where on Long Island?"

"It's called Eden's Landing, near Greenport. It's on the North Fork."

He nodded. "They'll be interested."

"It's nothing like the Hamptons or Montauk, obviously."

"Lot of vineyards out there. And it's still land they could sell. You need an attorney."

"Yeah, I think you're right. It *will* eat away at me."

He pulled out his phone and started texting right away. When he finished, he shoved it back in the hidden pocket of his gym shorts. "Done."

"You texted an attorney?"

"I texted my mom. We're from Westchester. She knows plenty of people. She'll get it done."

"Thank you. You didn't have to do that. That was really sweet of you." She started back toward the ring. "I'm sure it's not that big a deal."

He caught her arm, stepped even closer into her space. "Hey. I've only ever seen your calm, cool, and collected face. Today's the first time you let it slip, so I *know* it's a big deal."

What could she say to that? She relaxed. Gave him her full attention. "It is. It's everything to me."

"Nobody's going to take your land, okay?" He ran a finger down her cheek, and she shivered. "Not on my watch."

She smiled. "Okay."

She wished it could be that simple.

Slater sat beside him on the couch, two reporters facing them. His T-shirt still damp from the show, Derek wanted a shower and a good, hard fuck.

No boxing ring or bowling alley would do.

Neither would enduring yet another interview. *But we don't always get what we want, do we?*

". . . working with Irwin. It's been a great tour, great experience."

He zoned out of Slater's conversation, grateful his friend did most of the talking, because his attention was focused on Violet. She had a way of discreetly keeping tabs on Pete that fascinated him.

Ha. Kidding. Truthfully, he kept watching the way the dress tightened over her breasts every time she turned sideways to slide between groups of people. The way her mouth formed a nice round O as she drank from a water bottle. And then the way she'd lick her pretty lips after.

Yeah, he wanted to fuck hard. He should call Gen. Get her out here.

Except he didn't want Gen. He wasn't hard for Gen.

He wanted the faintly floral-scented woman who slept in his bed each night.

Correction. He slept in *her* bed because he was a total pussy. Now that they were staying in hotels, he'd let Emmie and Slater have their own room. Ben, Cooper, and Pete shared another, and he'd given Violet the third, leaving him with the pull-out couch. Perfect setup, right? So what did he do? After everyone went to bed, when the suite went dead quiet, he slipped under her sheets. Held her sweet body against his all night long.

Like an asshole. Because all it did was torture him.

Slater nudged him, bringing him back to the interview.

"Sorry, what?"

"That's okay." The woman smiled. "I asked what this

means to you guys, sharing a stage with U2 and Kings of Leon?"

The next night they'd play in DC. Opening for two of the biggest bands in the world. How the hell had that happened? "It's cool. We're looking forward to it."

"What about your dad?" her colleague asked. "You gonna get him up onstage with you?"

"Now, why would he do that?" Violet said. He didn't even know she'd joined them. She squeezed herself between him and the edge of the couch. "Eddie's a jazz musician, for goodness' sake. I don't think he'd know what to do with Blue Fire's brand of rock."

"Oh, come on, father and son, rocking the stadium?" the douche said. "I know your dad's down for it."

"Really?" Violet's hand smoothed up and down his thigh with the kind of pressure that made him think of sex. If she kept it up, he wouldn't be able to fight the hard-on he'd been struggling with the last forty minutes.

"Yep. Talked to him myself."

She turned to Derek. "What's Eddie working on anyway? He seems to be getting a lot of press lately. Is he in the studio or touring or something?" When she looked at him like that, the whole world faded away. She had a way of focusing on him so completely, it was like no one else existed.

Until he remembered he had two reporters waiting for an answer. "Not that I know of."

"Huh, then why's he all over the press?" She shrugged her shoulders like she didn't much care what Eddie Valencia was doing.

Slater chuckled. His closest friend knew what Violet was doing. And Derek loved her for it. His fingers wove between hers, pressing into his thigh. To his surprise, she turned her hand over, locking their fingers together.

His heart gave a powerful thump.

"So any more questions?" Slater asked.

"Just one." The woman had a glint in her eye as she motioned between Derek and Violet. "So this is new. What happened with Genevieve Babineaux?"

He was used to rude questions, rarely let it faze him. What did he care? But this one involved Violet. Not okay.

Releasing her hand, he wrapped his arm around her shoulders and tugged her tightly against him. He kissed her soft cheek, inhaling her unique and beautiful scent. "Sorry, sweetheart. They can be rude sometimes."

The woman reporter laughed. "Not trying to be rude, tiger. Just trying to keep up with your dating life."

"So if that's all you've got, we should get going." Slater got up, reaching to shake hands with the reporters.

"Hang on," the guy said. "One picture?"

Slater had already walked off, so Derek used it to his advantage. Gesturing to his friend, he said, "Next time, I guess."

"No, I meant of you two."

"Hey, band's fair game, but leave her out of it." But before Derek could finish his sentence, Violet was already shifting onto his lap. She wrapped her arms loosely around his neck, tilted her head against his, and her ass squirmed on his thigh, like she was getting comfortable.

A current of electricity pulsed beneath his skin. He had to ball his hand into a fist to keep from planting his face into the softness of her breasts and tasting her nipples right through the cotton material of her dress.

When she cupped his cheek, pressing a kiss at his temple, that fist uncurled and settled on her bare thigh, sliding under the fabric. He went rigid from the sensation of warm, smooth skin. *Jesus fuck*, she felt good.

He heard a click, and it startled him. He had no idea what image they'd gotten, but he figured he'd had a pretty depraved look on his face since he'd been thinking about sucking her tits.

Oh, fuck. He should not be thinking about sucking Violet's tits. She would so not be down with that.

"Thanks so much," the reporter said. "This'll go live in about an hour or so."

"Great, thanks."

Violet started to get off his lap, but he held her firmly. She gave him a questioning look, but he just closed his eyes and let out a slow, tight breath. Honestly, his reaction to this woman made no sense. He hooked up with women who seduced, who wore their sexuality front and center, like a calling card. Women who grabbed his dick or sucked on his earlobe to let him know exactly what they wanted.

And they didn't want dinner and a movie.

But this one? She wasn't trying to seduce him. She actually believed he wouldn't find a woman like her attractive. But she was wrong. Maybe she wasn't sexually aggressive, but she was . . . sweet. So fucking sweet. And fierce. And protective. And . . . yeah. He was in so much trouble.

"You ready to go?" she said softly. "Booked you a gym and everything."

He didn't want to expend his energy in footwork. He wanted to strip off her clothes, suck her nipple into his mouth, and thrust into her slick heat. That was seriously all he wanted in the whole damn world.

When he still didn't release her, she sat back a little. "I've got a question for you." She cupped his cheek, lifting his face to hers. Her mouth was a breath away from his. "Instead of cooking up all this publicity to cover the horrible things your dad says about you, why not just do Buck's show? Show the world your talent so you never have to worry again if anyone believes a word your dad says. Isn't that the obvious solution?"

What hit him like a roundhouse kick to the solar plexus was her absolute belief in him. She had no doubt whatsoever he had the talent. And that all he had to do was expose it. But the truth was, the truth he'd never utter even if they took a flame to his balls, is that he *didn't* know if he had it. Talent. How did someone know something like that?

Slater had one of the best voices in rock history. Some critic said it best when he said Slater's gift came from the "ecstasy of surrender he inspires." Fuck, if someone said something like that about him, he'd . . . well, he'd be done. No, seriously. Done. That was really all he wanted. It wasn't the money, the fame, the nymphs. It was just *knowing* he was good. Truly, brilliantly talented.

Her thumb caressed his jaw. "What's the worst thing that could happen if you did it?"

Holding her gaze, confiding in her and only her, he said, "I could suck."

That thumb brushed over his bottom lip, sending a flare

of heat and light soaring through him. "And what would be the best thing?"

He shrugged, not willing to say it out loud. "It'd go well."

She didn't say a word, just kept her fingers sifting through the hair at the back of his neck. When he didn't give her more, she arched a brow.

He laughed. "Fine. I could be recognized in the industry."

"A Grammy?"

"No." What the fuck, right? *Just say it.* "I could make the Ledger List." He watched her expression—maybe she'd never heard of it. Maybe she had, and she thought he was full of himself. He was twenty-eight, a month into his second tour. Who was he to think he could make the Ledger List at this point?

"Well, then, I guess it's going to take a lot of courage to make it happen. You have to decide if it's worth the risk."

Glad she got it—the *risk* of doing the show—instead of dismissing it, he also got what she was saying. And she was right. It all came down to whether or not he had the balls to expose himself.

She was also right in that it would shut down his dad for good. No one would listen to him anymore.

Including Derek.

Everyone crowded into the van, ready to head to the gym. Except Pete. Where the hell was he?

"Dammit." Derek started to ask if anyone had seen him but noticed Violet striding back into the venue. "Wait," he called; she didn't. He jumped out of the van and ran to catch up with her.

She threw open the door and headed down the long, windowless hall.

"Violet." A hand on her shoulder got her to slow down. "I'll get him. You just go back to the van."

"That's okay." She peeked inside the first room they came across, before closing the door and carrying on down the hall.

He really didn't want her finding Pete, not when Derek

had a pretty good idea what the keyboard player was doing. "V, come on. You don't need to see this."

"Actually, I do. I need to see who he's with and what he's doing, otherwise I can't help him." She opened another door, but the farther down the hallway they got, the louder the music coming from one particular room. People streamed in and out of it. Closing the door, she set her sights on the action ahead.

"Fuck," he muttered.

"Don't worry. There isn't much I haven't seen."

So she thought. She hadn't been in the music industry long enough to fully understand the depravity. Underneath the bass pounding through the walls, other sounds rose, carried, and sharpened his protective instincts.

The sounds of sex.

He stepped in front of her. "Wait here. Let me get him."

"Derek, whether or not I want to see Pete snorting coke and having sex with multiple women is irrelevant. I need to see who he's with. I need to see who's supplying the drugs. Have *you* figured it out yet?"

His guts tightened at the implication. "No, I haven't. It could be anyone. It could be different people at each venue."

"It's the same baggie full of the same drugs every week. It's one person. And we need to find out who it is and get him away from the band." And then she softened. "I appreciate you looking out for me, but what I'd really like is for you to go in there with me and help get Pete out. Then, when he's sober, I need you to talk to him."

"I will."

"No, really talk to him. He's deeper into drugs than you guys want to believe. I need you to consider the possibility that he might need to take a break from touring."

"No." *What?* He wasn't some drug addict. "I'll talk to him, but I'm not kicking him out."

"I didn't say to kick him out. I'm suggesting you get him the help he needs."

"He's not that far gone."

"Derek, he is. He didn't just start using on this tour."

"'Scuse me," some guy said, stepping around Derek to get into the room. Derek used the interruption to think. He couldn't deny the erratic behavior he'd seen in the studio. They'd attributed it to booze and staying out too late. "No. I think he's been doing it longer than that." They hadn't really accepted Pete had a drug problem.

"Then he can't stop just because you ask him to. You're not talking to Pete. You're talking to the drugs. He needs help."

He nodded curtly. "I'll talk to him."

"There are a lot of alternatives. After Madison Square Garden, you've got a few days off. Put him in a detox program. It'll clear his head long enough for you guys to have a conversation. With real consequences if he chooses to use again."

"Yeah, I can do that." In the meantime, he knew he could get through to Pete. He wouldn't have to kick him out of the band—Derek wouldn't let it get that far.

They heard a thump, and then someone screamed. Derek burst into the room to find Pete dancing on a table, trying to hump some girl. His hands moved wildly at her jeans, trying to peel them off her body, his hips pumping and thrusting so hard she fell off the table, landing in a knot of people. Violet rushed to the girl, while Derek headed for the table.

"Jesus, Pete." Derek grabbed him around the waist and pulled him off. He checked on Violet, who talked to the girl gently, making sure she was okay. It looked like she hadn't gotten hurt.

Wild-eyed and crazy, Pete took a swing. Derek easily ducked.

"What the fuck, man?" He had to get Pete out of there, but not until he knew the girl was okay. He shot a look to Violet, who nodded. Everyone was all right.

He motioned to the door, letting her know he was heading out. Then, he practically carried Pete out of the room. "You're starting to freak me the fuck out."

"What? I was getting some action, man. What's your problem?"

"You knocked her off a table. You're out of control."

"Fuck you. I'm having fun. You ruined it. You're always ruining my fun. Pussy."

Violet was right. Talking to him in this condition would do no good. He needed to get out of the stadium without being seen by the paps. He shot a quick text to Slater. Go to the gym without us. Meet you at hotel later.

"Where we going?" Pete tried to twist out of his hold. "I wanna get laid."

"Not tonight."

"Yeah, tonight. Every night. That's the whole point." His head tipped back and he growled. "Christ. I'm fuckin' horny as hell."

A heavy sadness fell over Derek. He hated seeing Pete this messed up.

He got Violet's point. It *was* getting worse. And he couldn't risk Pete hurting someone.

But he knew Pete. He knew his insecurities. Knew how badly he wanted to be in the band, on this journey with them.

So, fuck, Derek had to get through to him. Kicking him out of the band wasn't an option. Getting him help, yeah, obviously, but when? He'd like to put it off until the end of the tour, if possible. He had to find a way to get through to him, because deep down he knew Pete wanted to be in the band more than he wanted to get wasted.

He just had to get him sober enough to remind him.

EIGHT

"Hey, man." Derek peered into the bathroom, filled with steam, and found Pete leaning against the sink, head hung. "We need to talk."

His friend didn't turn around, didn't look at him through the foggy mirror. He just exhaled and said, "Yeah."

"Come into the living room. Everyone's gone to sleep."

Derek made a stop to the kitchen first, eyeing a cold beer, but then he thought about Pete and realized he didn't want to go there. Instead, he grabbed the pitcher of lemonade and poured two glasses.

Pete made no eye contact as he quietly shut the bedroom door behind him and joined Derek on the couch. Dreadlocks tied back, shirtless and in navy gym shorts, his friend looked tired and wan. He reached for the glass Derek offered. "Thanks, man."

"So, tonight."

Pete barely acknowledged him.

"We were all in the van, heading to the gym. Had to go back in and find you."

"I'm not here to *box*." He eyed him meaningfully. "Are you?"

Derek shrugged. He got it. "No." He thought about it some more. "No, I'm not here to box. But you know what? She's right about something. We party all night, sleep most of the day, then hit sound check and do it all over again."

"So?"

"So is that what we're in this for?"

Pete didn't answer.

"We're not . . . it's not actually *fun*."

Pete shrugged, draining his glass. "It is for me."

"How about that girl tonight?"

His friend gave him a hard look. "What? Nothing happened."

Derek shifted onto the coffee table, so he could face him. "Thing is, I saw you, man. You weren't there. You were so high you didn't even know you were trying to fuck a chick on a table."

"Nobody got hurt." When he exhaled, his body slumped forward. "Yeah, okay, I'll ease off. I get it. She wins."

"This isn't about Violet."

"Are you fucking her?"

Anger welled so fast and hard, Derek nearly went dizzy with it. "No, I'm not *fucking* her. And don't talk about her like that. You're . . . Jesus, Pete. What's happened to you?" He got up, scraped a hand through his hair. "I don't even know who I'm talking to right now. This isn't you, man." He strode to the window. How the hell did he get through to him? What were the magic words? "She's the *solution*, Pete. *We* caused the problem. We almost lost Irwin. She's here to help. And she *is* helping. Come on, I'm actually waking up in the morning and wanting to write. I haven't written shit in a year."

"I'm sorry. Okay? I'm fuckin' sorry."

Derek turned to his friend. "I'm worried about you."

"Yeah. I know."

"Can we talk about it? Figure out a way for you to have fun but keep it under control?"

Pete scratched the side of his head roughly. "I can tell you what you want to hear right now. That I'm fucking up, and that I won't do it again. But when I'm in the situation, when I'm surrounded by chicks and people who want to party with me . . ." He closed his eyes.

"Is there someone in particular who wants to party with you? We could eliminate the temptation, you know."

"Are you serious? If you eliminate the temptation, we wind up on the prairie. In a tent. Nothing but cows for miles."

Derek smiled. He understood. There were very few good people in this industry. Even fewer who had the artists' best interests in mind. "There's no one in particular supplying you with drugs?"

Derek didn't miss the way Pete's gaze cut away. "No. You know how it is. Everyone's got something. Everywhere I turn, someone's offering me something."

"Yeah, but the greenies? The Ambien? Who's giving you that baggie?"

Pete sharpened. "You've seen that?"

Derek stayed still.

"You going through my shit?"

"Yeah, man. Had to. And I'll keep doing it until you get straight."

"That's fucked up." His body tensed, like he wanted to bolt. But to his credit, Pete stayed put on the couch. "Fuck. I get shit from everyone. But those ones? I put those aside 'cause I use them the most. That's on me, man. I do that."

"No one's giving it to you?"

"No. No one's giving it to me."

"You'd tell me, right? For the sake of the band? You'd tell me if someone was supplying you with drugs?"

Pete had a wary look in his eyes. He tapped his fingers on his knees, features pinched in concentration. Then, his gaze swung back to Derek. "Yeah, I'd tell you."

Derek turned his forearm outward, and Pete looked at the Hand of Eris ink. "We agreed to be smart about this shit. We'd have fun, but we wouldn't ever take it to the edge." He paused. "You're there, buddy. You're taking it to the edge."

"Yeah, I know."

"So you'll stop?"

Pete looked down at his hands. He didn't say anything for the longest time, and Derek wondered if he'd have to make a threat. He didn't want to do it, but he would. If Pete wasn't willing to give up the partying, he'd have to pull him off the tour.

But then Pete blew out a breath, looking defeated. "I'll stop."

Thank fucking Christ.

Pete got up and grabbed him in a tight hug, fists punching his back. And then he went to his bedroom and shut the door. Derek stood there, relieved, but also uncertain. *Could* Pete give it up so easily?

Derek would have to make changes. Just for a while, break the pattern, get Pete's head clear. No more partying after a show. Not even for an hour. Straight to the gym or bowling alley or whatever Violet had planned.

After the rush of the encounter died down, his thoughts turned to the woman in the bed on the other side of the wall.

It was getting dangerous. Sharing the same bed, pretending to be a couple. It was becoming too real. He'd started finding reasons to be with her in public just to feel her fingers linked with his. Her hands in his hair.

Tonight, when he'd touched her bare thigh . . . the sensations flooded him.

He wasn't used to being so close to a woman and not fucking her. Except . . . that didn't ring true. That wasn't the issue.

This is different. It wasn't the same kind of raw, purely sexual drive he had to be with Gen. It was . . . intense. And incredibly sexy. He *liked* it. He liked her.

Too much. He pulled the blanket and pillow out of the hall closet by the door, but even as he headed back to the couch to make up the bed, his body knew where it needed to be.

And it sure as hell wasn't there.

The moment he opened the door, he knew she was awake. The sheets rustled, and she turned to face him, hitching up on an elbow. "You talk to him?" Her soft voice made his skin pebble.

He nodded, wanting nothing more than to be near her. The pull was inexorable. He threw back the blanket, slid under those cool sheets, and it took everything in him to keep from scooping her into his arms.

He couldn't figure out this draw, this need to be near

her. To breathe in her unique scent. He pressed his nose to her hair. "What is that smell?"

"You like it?"

"Yeah."

He could see her smile, her hand flat on the white sheet. "It's wildflower perfume. I make it myself."

"You make perfume?"

"It's very rudimentary. I'm not going to sell it anytime soon. I've got to figure out how to make the scent last longer."

"Sell it?" He shifted closer to her, gaze fixed on her sexy mouth.

"Those wildflowers I planted for Jed? I'm trying to find ways to use them in products so I can live on the farm full-time. Live off the land, just like Jed wanted."

"That's . . ." He had to clear his throat. He thought she was probably the most interesting woman he'd ever met. It was like without role models, she'd had the freedom to completely invent her life. "You really want to live on a farm?"

"You haven't seen it. It's the most beautiful place in the world."

Yeah, but a farm? At the tip of Long Island? That was damn remote. "What flowers do you put in this perfume?"

"The most fragrant ones. Sweet pea, four-o'clocks. Roses."

"Sweet pea, huh?"

She nodded, her lips curling into the sexiest smile. "I named my farm after the four-o'clocks."

"I like it." *Four O'Clock Farm.* "What other products?" A lock of hair spilled across her cheek, and he reached for it, brushing it back. It slipped through his fingers like silk.

"Right now we sell tea to several gourmet shops around Long Island and a few in the city. And we're doing pretty well with it. We're also developing soap, honey, and stationery."

"How do you make stationery with flowers?"

"Oh, Mimi, a friend of mine, makes her own paper, and she uses the petals to create a scene. It's really beautiful." She pulled back a little, studying him. "Why're you looking at me like that?"

"Because you're fucking amazing. I mean, look at you. You just do it. Make your life happen. You don't wait for anything or anyone. Everyone thinks we're so cool 'cause we're in a band, but you're the creative one. Everything about your life is creative. It's awesome. You're awesome."

"Oh. Well."

"Do you get lonely?" She had no family. He rarely saw her on a personal call. He thought of himself, surrounded by four band members—they were inseparable. Not to mention Emmie, who'd always been a big part of his life. Add in the record company and roadies and engineers and nymphs . . . he was never alone.

"Yes," she whispered.

He might never be alone, but he sure as shit didn't have this closeness with anyone. This intimacy. That was what drew him to her. When he was with Violet, he didn't feel lonely. He felt whole. Alive. Happy.

He tipped her chin up. "Do you have a boyfriend?"

She shook her head.

"You're not seeing anyone?" He needed the clarification.

"It's impossible to have a relationship when I'm on the road most of the year."

He smiled. "I can relate."

"That's why you have Gen."

"I don't have Gen. I use Gen." When her features pinched in disgust, he added, "And she uses me. I'm a man, V. I have needs."

"And since you don't avail yourself of nymphs . . ."

"Exactly."

"Why don't you?"

"They're scary. They'll fuck anything. I don't know, it just doesn't interest me."

"What does interest you?"

"You." He shrugged, completely unapologetic about it. He saw it now. He got it. And he wasn't about to play games.

"We . . . that's not going to happen." She started to get up, and he realized his fatal error. She'd never let him sleep beside her again if she thought he wanted to fuck her.

"I know that." He pulled her back down. Not a chance would he let her get away. He'd just have to rein it in. For now. "You asked me a question, and I answered. I'll always give you the truth. You do interest me. I've never met anyone like you before. And I like you."

She threw back the covers. "Derek, look, this isn't my world. I'm not some girl you can have casual sex with."

"I know that. Jesus. I'm not . . . I don't want to fuck things up with us. I know we're not . . . you're not . . ." He rolled to his back. "Fuck. Why do I say whatever comes to mind?"

"Because you're an artist. You can get away with it." She was all tense and stiff now, and he hated that he'd done that to her. He didn't hate telling her the truth, but he hated her reaction.

He grabbed her arm. "Don't go. I'm not going to make any moves. I just . . ."

"Look, it's not your fault. What else would you think when I let you in my bed every night? It's just . . . I've never . . . I've never had this kind of closeness before. And I *like* it." She let out a shaky breath. "I like it too much. But it's selfish of me. Of course you want more." And then her eyes went wide. "God, do the others know you sleep in here?"

"You know they don't." He tugged her back onto the bed, waited until she settled under the covers, head on the pillow. "I make up the couch every night, and I don't come in until they're asleep. And you, Christ, you get up at ungodly hours. Why the hell do you get up so early?"

"I've never needed much sleep."

Meaning, she'd never gotten much sleep, living in foster homes where child care fell on her shoulders. "Obviously."

"Plus, how do you think the magic happens? I do my grocery shopping, schedule our activities, all that stuff in the early morning, when you guys are sleeping."

"I didn't know that." He brushed a thumb across that delectable mouth. "So, yeah, no one knows."

"Why *do* you sleep here? I mean, if not to have sex with me?"

"Those pull-out couches are hell on my back." He gave her a smile because she already knew the answer. The way he held her in his arms all night *was* the answer.

"I told you I'd sleep on the couch. I can sleep anywhere. A pull-out couch is a luxury compared to the places I've slept."

"I think you know I'm not letting you sleep on a couch while I get the king-size bed."

The lines between her eyes spoke of the tension within her.

He couldn't resist stroking them with a finger. "I like sleeping with you." He leaned closer. "Never slept better in my life. Must be that wildflower perfume."

She closed her eyes and for one moment pressed her forehead to his. But then she seemed to snap out of it, and she withdrew. "Um, okay, so you talked to Pete?"

And just like that the wall went up, and they were back to business. He'd let her get away with it. For now. "Yeah. He gets it."

"You sure? Most of the time they say that to shut us up."

"No, he does. We're going to come straight to the bus after shows. No more partying."

"That's a good idea. It'll make it much easier to see where he's getting his stuff."

"He's not going to do drugs anymore."

She gave him a challenging look.

"He's not. We talked about it. He knows he's out of control."

"It's not that easy, Derek. Please believe me. Don't ease up on him."

"I won't." *I won't let you down.* "I can let Slater handle more of the interviews, and I'll stick by his side."

"If we all tag-team each other, we should be able to keep an eye on him."

Her smile detonated a fiery bolt of pleasure in his chest. But then she licked her lips, looking away. "I probably shouldn't say this until I'm sure—but I think it's Bax who's giving Pete the drugs."

"Bax isn't going to risk his job by supplying drugs to Irwin's bands."

"But you'll watch, right? You'll be aware of him?"

"Okay." His thumb stroked her cheek, while the rest of his hand slid into her hair. He needed to kiss that mouth, needed to feel her body wrapped up with his.

With a sigh, she relaxed. "Thank you."

With other women, he kissed them as a prompt. It was the starting gun to the games about to be played. But with Violet . . . Derek wanted to *kiss* her. He wanted that sexy mouth like nothing he'd ever wanted before. Wanted the thrill of that first meeting of tongues, that first sigh of surrender.

He couldn't kiss her, but he had to touch her. Setting his hand on her hip, he said, "Okay?"

"Okay," she whispered. And then she closed her eyes. He shifted closer to her, sliding his hand to her back. He waited, hoping she'd let go.

Finally, she inched closer, set her head in the crook of his arm and sighed. And fuck did he love the way she relaxed into him.

What the hell? He'd never *cuddled* with a woman in his life. Why this one? The one who wanted nothing to do with his world, who was just passing through.

Why her?

"So here we are." Slater sat down beside him, the steam rising from his coffee mug in a lazy swirl.

Other than Violet, no one got up this early, so Derek was surprised to see his friend. It was a good thing he always went back to the couch as soon as she woke up, or Slater would've found it empty this morning.

"Here we are." A thrill shot through him. Tonight's concert would be unlike any they'd played before.

His friend lifted his mug, tipped it against Derek's glass of orange juice. "You worried?"

"Ha." Worried? The Fourth of July on the Mall festival attracted several hundred thousand fans. The biggest names in the industry played. That meant every entertainment outlet would be there. The whole world would be watching. "Nah. It's cool."

They held a gaze before bursting out laughing. After a few moments, Slater settled down. "I hope I don't shit my pants up there."

"What's your biggest fear?"

"About tonight?" Rubbing the back of his neck, Slater let out a breath.

Derek nodded.

His friend gazed into his mug. "Looking out into an

audience that's bored shitless. Finding them talking to each other or texting. Waiting for Bono to get on stage."

"Oh, man, that would suck." He started to laugh, until he considered how real that fear might be to him. "Gotta tell you, that's never happened before. Doubt it's gonna happen tonight. We've got real fans, man. We do."

"Yeah, but we never opened for U2 or Kings of Leon."

"True, true."

Something crossed Slater's features, something dark. "Sucks that my dad can't be here, you know?"

Ah, now they got to it, what was really bugging him. Slater's dad had thrown all his energy into turning his son into the rock star he could never be, and he'd died before Slater had achieved it. That would suck.

"It does," Derek said. "But he'd be so fuckin' proud of you."

Slater shifted, like the idea of it made him uncomfortable. "Yeah?"

"Yeah. You're killin' it. Livin' what he could only dream about." Derek nodded with confidence. "He'd be damn proud of you."

His friend stretched his legs out under the table. "I guess so."

"When you're up on that stage tonight, he'll be watching, punching his fist in the air, running back and forth and shouting to anyone up there who'll listen, 'That's my boy.'"

Slater blinked a few times, looked away. "Yeah. I could see that."

Soft footfalls coming from the bedroom made Derek's skin tingle. Fresh from the shower, hair wet, wearing shorts and a T-shirt, Violet headed into the kitchen. She smiled softly at them. "You guys are up early."

"Yeah," Slater said. "Couldn't sleep."

Derek sat mute, stunned at how beautiful she looked in the morning, her face younger without the makeup, her complexion smooth and clear. She opened the refrigerator, started pulling out eggs and cheese.

Slater leaned closer to him. "So what's up with you two?"

He shrugged. "Nothing." He kept his voice low, but she

seemed oblivious as she cracked eggs, fired up the stove, and hummed quietly as she prepared breakfast.

His friend, who knew him better than anyone, just waited.

"Hell. I don't know. I mean, nothing's happening. I'm not . . . *fuck*." He sucked in a breath. "Nothing *can* happen. I like her. I like her a lot. But . . ."

"But what?"

"But she's not in my world." He watched her answer her phone, tuck it between her shoulder and ear. A gentle smile warmed her features. She was so fucking beautiful. "I'm not gonna just fuck her."

"No, you're not."

"Yeah, so, then nothing's happening. She's only with us another month, maybe two. Then she goes back to her world, and I stay in mine. Nothing *can* happen."

"But it is happening. Anyone can see it. For both of you."

He cut a look into the kitchen, locked eyes with her, and heat poured through him. "Come on, man. I can't . . . I don't even want that."

"Want what? A girlfriend?"

Now, he just felt itchy and uncomfortable. "I can't want someone who doesn't want me back. I can't do that . . . wanting bullshit."

He picked up his glass, rocked it, the orange juice sliding from one side to the other. He'd had a lifetime of it with his dad. Wanting to be around him and constantly being pushed away . . . Yeah, done with it.

Besides, he knew what worked for him. Women like Gen. Who wanted the same thing he did.

"You know, I met a lot of girls before Emmie," Slater said. "And every one of them made it easy for me to say I didn't want a relationship. But then . . ." He blew out a breath. "When you meet *her, your* girl? Everything changes. All those excuses go right out the window. Because no matter how much I didn't think she fit into my life, how hard I figured a long-distance relationship would be, none of that shit mattered, because I'd found her. And nothing, I mean nothing, was going to stop me from hanging on to my girl. The one that's *mine*." He stared thoughtfully into his mug. "When you find her, you don't even question it."

Derek watched Violet, and heat spread through him. Did he want her? Hell, yeah. But so what? He respected her too much to make her his tour fuck buddy. And what more could he offer her at this point?

Not a damn thing.

She'd been on yachts and private jets, met politicians and celebrities. She'd dined in the most exclusive restaurants in the world. In some ways, she thought she'd seen it all.

But she'd never walked the red carpet.

The stretch limo pulled to the curb, the doors opened, and the world exploded into flashing lights and screaming fans.

Violet grabbed her clutch, wondering how she was going to keep an eye on the guys at an event like this one. Fortunately, they'd talked and agreed on a game plan. No hard liquor, 2 a.m. curfew, and they'd each take turns keeping an eye on Pete.

One at a time, the guys got out of the limo, Slater clutching Emmie's hand the whole time. Violet dropped her phone into her clutch, giving the band a moment to themselves in the spotlight.

"You ready?"

She looked up to find Derek leaning into the limo. Why did that make her so ridiculously happy?

She'd expected him to be with the others, enjoying his special moment. Instead, he'd waited for her.

She caught his hand and slid out to join him. As she stood, he leaned into her. "You're my girlfriend." His lips brushed high up her cheek, close to her ear. "You have to be with me."

A thrill zipped down her spine. "Well, if I *have* to."

He smiled, holding her gaze, blocking out the whole crazy world. Then he led her along the red carpet.

NINE

Once inside the building, they followed the others to the bank of elevators. Everyone on a high from an amazing show on the Mall in Washington DC, they crowded into the waiting car, their energy way too tumultuous for the small space. Derek led her to a corner, wrapping his arms around her and pulling her in close, her back to his front. He nuzzled her ear. "You okay?"

She leaned her head against his shoulder. "There's no press in here, you know."

"Violet." The way he said her name, almost chastising, definitely teasing, made her want to turn in his arms and give in to what he was offering. "Don't you know I'll take any excuse to touch you?"

She really shouldn't let him, not with everyone watching. What would they think of her? It would be awful if it got back to Irwin.

"Man, that was incredible." Pete bounced on his toes.

"Best show ever, guys," Emmie said. "Your throat okay?" She gazed up at Slater with concern.

"Fine." He smiled. "Perfect." And then he flashed his movie star smile Violet's way. "Thanks for the tea."

"You're welcome. I hope it works." She'd had Francesca

send her honey from their apiary. Mixing it with ginger juice and some herbs soothed vocal cords.

"You got that stuff for me?" And it wasn't lost on her how much Pete's attitude toward her had changed. She appreciated that he was trying.

"I had it sent to the hotel in New York." He worried about carpal tunnel syndrome, so she'd ordered him some ruta. Some arnica and hyperiam, too. But she wouldn't give him anything until he'd seen a doctor, so she'd made an appointment for him in the city.

The car landed with a lurch, and Derek's arms tightened around her. "Stick with me?"

Honestly? There was nowhere she'd rather be. Unfortunately, she had to work. "You go have fun. Just keep your phone handy."

His features shut down. She hated the way she did that to him—killed all that happy, vibrant energy. But what could she do? He was her *client*.

The moment they stepped onto the roof, the press, fans, and industry executives surrounded them. Hundreds of people—all VIPs—crowded the huge rooftop in downtown DC for the private party thrown by U2 to celebrate the festival they'd just played.

Candles flickered on every surface—café, buffet, and bar tables—and strings of little white lights caught on all the divots, sequins, and piercings worn by the guests. Shrieks of laughter, the roar of conversation, made the atmosphere animated and electric. It was unlike anything she'd ever seen before.

"Oh, shit, look, it's Michael Stipe," Ben said. "Come with me?"

"Let's hit the bar first," Cooper said.

"Don't want to miss him," Ben said, taking off. "Later."

Pete and Cooper headed toward the packed bar.

"I'll go get us a table," Slater murmured to Emmie. "You guys going to join us?"

"You go on," Violet said. "I have to keep an eye on Pete."

They both looked at Derek, who reached for Violet's elbow. "We'll catch up with you later."

The couple headed off, but Violet didn't miss the way

Emmie glanced down to where their bodies touched, confusion marring her pretty features. Violet stepped away from him, almost giving him a shove.

"You go with them. Have fun."

But he only smiled and caught her hand in his. "You're my girlfriend. We stick together." He nodded toward the flashing lights of photographers grabbing shots of all the celebrities.

She could not believe how easily she gave in to him. She'd never had a problem with boundaries before, but with Derek? He made it extremely difficult for her to turn him down.

And really, why would she let an opportunity to play his girlfriend pass her by? She stepped into him, her arms reaching around his neck, when she heard a feminine voice.

"Mm-mm-*mm*." Genevieve Babineaux sashayed over to them, arms thrown wide to embrace both of them at once. A quick assessing gaze of Violet was followed up with a stroke of her hand down Derek's chest right to his waistband. She tugged him toward her. "You are such a sexy beast. I've missed you."

He jerked back, obviously irritated with her. "Gen, this is Violet Davis."

"Yes, of course. Lovely to meet you."

Forced to take a step back, Violet shook her hand. "Nice to meet you, too."

In a cloud of expensive perfume, the woman swept right in front of her and slid her hands up Derek's shirt. "Before I get caught up in work, I have to give you this." And then she pulled a hotel key card out of her clutch. She slid it in his back pocket, giving his ass a squeeze. "I've got a room for us."

"Knock it off, Gen. You know I'm with Violet tonight." He took her by the wrists, pulling her away from his body.

A rush of prickly energy burned through her, making her realize she was jealous of Derek's *girlfriend*. What stupid game was she playing? Letting this sexy, gorgeous, completely wonderful man sleep in her bed every night? He wasn't hers. He never would be.

He'd never leave this crazy, decadent life, and she'd never join him in it.

Oh, my God. He doesn't want you to join him in it, you

nut. He wanted to have sex. That was it. He was a wildly passionate man who loved women, loved *sex.* And if she spread her legs for him, he'd dive right in. And then move on to the next woman he got a hard-on for.

It was just so confusing because he looked at her like he was one frayed thread away from snapping and just freaking *taking* her. The man touched her like he couldn't keep his hands off her. He held her so tightly all through the night she felt completely and totally possessed.

She'd never felt so wanted, so desired, in her life. And God help her she could *not* find it in herself to turn him away.

Maybe she needed this reminder that he had an actual girlfriend. That he was just a man with big sexual needs. And she was the available female body close enough to rub up against.

Thank God she hadn't compromised her integrity for him. Imagine if she'd given in to her intense need to touch him back, to kiss him, and relieve the ache she felt every time he touched her.

"I've got work to do," Violet said. "I'll give you two some much-needed time alone."

"You're not going without me." A minute ago, he'd been relaxed. Now, his jaw muscle strained. "I'll catch up with you later, Gen. We've got to keep an eye on Pete."

"That's *her* job. Let her do it." She hooked her arm through his, pressed her breasts into him. "You've got a job, too. I've got about a dozen interviews set up for you guys. Now, where's Slater?" She scanned the area, found him at a small table nearly hidden by potted plants. "Okay, seriously? He thinks this is sexy time for him and his little love muffin?" Grabbing Derek's hand, she said, "Let's go."

"Hang on." He reached for Violet. "She's my girlfriend, remember? She's coming with me."

Gen took Violet in, from the black sparkly stilettos to her deep purple full-skirted dress with the plunging neckline. "I'm not sure what look you're going for, but the public's buying it so who cares, right?"

Violet was well practiced at hiding hurt, pain, and mortification, so she could only hope her habits didn't fail her in this moment.

"What're you talking about?" Derek checked Violet out again, looking confused. "She looks beautiful."

Gen rolled her eyes. "Of course she's attractive. No one would believe for a second you'd be with a dog. She just doesn't look like someone you'd go for. Come on, sex god, put the pieces together. Me, Adriana, Lisa Van Owen?" And then she tossed a careless nod toward Violet.

He tightened his arm around Violet's waist. "I think she's the most beautiful woman in the room."

Gen looked stunned, studying his face carefully. "What is this?" She stepped closer, her finger wagging between them. "You're not sleeping with him, are you?"

Violet rolled her eyes, not letting either of them see how sharply the woman's arrows had pierced her skin. "Okay, I'm going to leave you two to do your thing, and I'm going to do mine."

"See? She gets it. It's just business, baby. That's all we're about. And she *wants* to know if her look isn't working, am I right?" But the woman didn't wait for an answer. "She's got the femme fatale dress, but Park Avenue shoes and hair. Derek doesn't do Park Avenue." Gen leaned in, tugged the bodice of Violet's dress down so that her breasts nearly popped out. "Swipe some red lipstick on." She shoved both hands into Violet's hair and messed with it before Violet could pull away. "Fix her hair. She's got to look fuckable if we want the public to believe you'd be with her."

"Jesus, Gen." Derek stepped between the two. "Keep your hands off her."

"I'm your publicist. It's my job to make sure she looks like your girlfriend and not a sober companion. Do you want it to get out, who she really is?"

Violet had had enough. "Excuse me."

She broke away from them, heading for the bar. Except, she really didn't want to run into anyone at the moment. She wasn't that good of an actress. Maybe she'd head to the bathroom, pull herself together.

But before she could get far, Derek grabbed her, tucked her under his arm. "I'm sorry about that."

"I'm going to the ladies' room. Would you please order me a San Pellegrino with a slice of lime?"

"Don't let her upset you."

"Don't let her upset me? Are you kidding me?" She pulled away, needing distance, and took a deep breath. "She's such a *bitch*."

"Fuck, I'm so sorry."

"It's fine. It's not your fault. We don't have time for this right now. You have press to do, and I have to find Pete. Just go back to her and do your job."

His arm slipped around her waist, and he slammed her up against him. "Not going to do that, V. Not until we get something straight, because I don't want you hurting even for a minute. You're ten times the woman Gen will ever be. You're *everything*. Strong, beautiful, smart, kind. You're fucking perfect. So don't let a cold, manipulative woman undermine you."

She smiled, her heart beating thickly. He kept giving her these glimmers of something unique and exciting, something utterly breathtaking. A potential for a kind of passion she craved.

She felt it again in that moment, as their chests pressed so closely, his gaze penetrating so deeply. When he did that, he made it hard to remember that this was just who he was. An intense, passionate guy.

It wasn't about her. He had Gen.

And she had a job to do.

And she never compromised herself on a job.

Lipstick tube in hand, Violet stood to the side, waiting to catch a glimpse of herself in the mirror of the crowded bathroom. Funny thing about women like Gen. They didn't make random comments—they knew a competitor's soft spot and went right for it.

How could she tell where Violet hurt? She knew she covered her emotions well—hid herself in thoughtfully prepared costumes. No one saw her real self.

Growing up in foster care, she'd never minded hand-me-downs, had never cared if the kids teased her for her dirty, ill-fitting clothes because she knew she'd never be in one school for long. Foremost on her mind had been managing the situation once she got home. So the kids could make fun of her, ignore her, and she barely noticed. Her mind was on where she'd get food, how she'd avoid angry hands, and finding places she could hide when things got bad.

And they always got bad. In her experience, good, kind, decent people didn't take in orphaned kids. They adopted. People who used unwanted kids for cash were a different breed altogether.

So, clothing? Teasing from other kids? Didn't make a dent. It wasn't until her first job, the one Francesca had gotten for her as a nanny for Teresa Blackwell, socialite wife of Hunter Blackwell, managing director of the Blackwell Fund, that the pain of not fitting in all those years had surfaced.

Teresa had dressed her. No nanny of hers would wear cheap, ill-fitting clothes. The woman shopped literally every day. And on each outing, she'd bring home the most luxurious, stylish clothing Violet had ever seen.

And the makeover drove it home—how those children throughout her childhood had seen her.

And right then, after combing her fingers through her hair to smooth out the mess Gen had made, as she assessed herself in the mirror in the dark bathroom, crammed with club-goers in sparkling body-hugging dresses and six-inch stilettos, cleavage everywhere, she understood how Genevieve saw her.

She never wore clothes that revealed her figure. She didn't choose clothes that made her stand out in any way. In her world, not only did being invisible work, but deemphasizing her sexuality kept her safe.

She'd never even thought about looking sexy for a guy. Until tonight, this moment, when Gen made her feel sexless and bland. For the first time, she wanted to be sexy. For *Derek* to find her sexy.

Until she remembered what he'd said.

You're beautiful and smart and kind and just fucking perfect.

She would never be Genevieve Babineaux. God, she didn't want to be.

She wanted to be the woman Derek saw. Which, of course, she already was.

And wasn't that the revelation?

Dropping her lipstick into her clutch, she smiled and headed out of the bathroom.

For the next couple of hours, Violet moved through the crowd, watching the guys in action. Mostly, Ben sat in small groups, having intense discussions, while Pete was all over the place, bouncing from one group to the next, hitting on women everywhere.

What he didn't understand was that these women weren't nymphs. Not only didn't they show interest in him, they gave off almost hostile vibes. He didn't seem to notice or care. She suspected he was high. Well, no, she didn't suspect at all. He was wasted. But so far his behavior wasn't out of control, so she'd let him be.

Occasionally, she'd glance toward the table where Derek, Slater, and Gen chatted with reporters. She couldn't lie—she got a jolt every time Derek's gaze collided with hers. He watched her. A lot.

Reaching for a fresh seltzer and lime on the bar, Violet felt arms belt around her waist, and a familiar scent filled her senses. "Dance with me."

God, he felt good. Those strong arms, that silky hair sliding across her cheek. She wanted to turn in his arms and just hold him. "Shouldn't you be working?"

"Slater can do the rest of the interviews."

She gestured to Pete. "He's high."

"I know." He tipped his head toward Ben and Cooper. "But they're watching him."

She'd been so preoccupied with Pete she hadn't noticed the way their gazes flicked over to him every so often. It warmed her, knowing they were all in this with her.

"The place is crawling with press. You need to be my girlfriend. Dance with me, make out with me. Show the world you're my girl."

A sharp sting of awareness burned in her chest. She'd never been anyone's girl. She could have—she knew that. She could've been Randall's. But she always took too long, waiting for something. Sparks? Trust? Something that never came. Well, either it never came or she talked herself out of it.

He lowered his face into her neck, breathed her in. "You want to know why I sleep in your bed?"

She held her breath, waiting.

"All day long, you're vigilant. You're the consummate professional, calm, in command. But at night? You soften in my arms." He swayed with her, still holding her from behind. "You relax into me, and I love it. I love being with you. I could stay awake all night just to be with the Violet I get under the covers. Now, I want Violet on the dance floor." His hands pressed into her stomach, and he kissed the corner of her mouth. "Dance with me."

See? See what he does? The man was so dangerous. No wonder she couldn't turn him away. Had anyone in her life ever made her feel this good about herself?

Screw it. For this one night, what could it hurt? He was right, the media was everywhere, and she was supposed to be his girlfriend. So she drew in a deep breath and turned in his arms. He led her to the dance floor, belted his arms around her waist, and held her close.

She tucked her head against his chest and sank into him. And he gave her just what she wanted—a tight, intimate hold.

She hadn't known what safety was until she'd stepped in his arms. Never in her life had she felt she could really, fully relax. *Until him.*

"All right?"

She answered by snuggling in even closer.

His hands pressed at the small of her back. "My sweet V. You feel so good."

She gazed up at him, sifting her fingers through the hair at the back of his neck. "You overwhelm me."

"That's probably a good thing."

She laughed. "That's never a good thing."

"With you it is. I'll bet you push away all the guys. And they want you so much, they'll do anything to have you, so they back off, give you time. What they don't realize is during that time? You're coming up with excuses why you don't want them or can't have them. So I think you need a guy like me."

"A pushy bastard?"

"A guy who sees right through you. Right into here." He placed his palm on her heart, the heel of his hand touching her breasts. "You need me, Violet." His teasing smile fell away as his features seized. Fear flickered in his eyes before he closed them and muttered, "Shit." And then he brought her close, so close she could feel his heart thundering, his body heating up.

"Derek?" What just happened? What changed his mood?

But he fisted a hand in her hair, tilted her head back, and gave her a look filled with hot, churning need. And, oh God, was he going to kiss her? Blood roared in her ears because she . . . she couldn't kiss him. He couldn't kiss her.

But he didn't. He just tipped his forehead against hers.

"Fuckin' Slater," he breathed. "It *is* you."

The music pulsed in his veins, bodies slammed into him, but the only thing he could process was this woman in his arms and the fact that she was his.

Something happened when they were together. When he was with her, his heart opened up so wide he actually felt things.

What he understood in that moment was that neither of them would willingly open up their hearts. Not when her mom had given her up, her grandmother had died, and one foster home after another had let her go. Not when his dad had fucked with him his whole life.

Neither would willingly trust anyone again.

Until they'd found each other. Christ, he'd found *her*.

She pulled back. "You should be with Gen."

Her voice tore through his thoughts, dunked his heart into icy cold water. The rejection stung—made his heart slam shut like a fist.

But she saw it, he could tell. She knew what she'd done to him. Her fingers dug into his arms, and her brow creased in concern. She brought her hand up to scrape the hair off his forehead.

"You've got her key card. She wants to spend the night with you. Isn't that what you want?"

"You know what I want."

She wrapped her arms around his neck and swayed with him, screening out the beat and the people thrashing around them. He wanted so badly to grab her ass, pull her up tight against him. Instead, he planted his hands right at the top of those gorgeous globes, his fingers digging into her flesh as he forced himself to go against his every instinct to make this woman his.

"Where's Pete?" She looked up at him.

But he clutched her close, not ready to lose her yet. "Stay. Just . . . fucking stay with me."

Those big hazel eyes gazed at him, and he could see it all right there. She wanted him, too. Her clear complexion gleamed with perspiration. Damp tendrils of hair stuck to her forehead. And she looked sexier than any woman he'd ever seen.

Gen appeared just then, giving him her seductive smile. She pushed her hand in between them, gripping his shirt. "About that room I mentioned . . ."

He caught the fleeting look of dismay on Violet's features, and Gen took a step between them.

"Damn, you're one hell of an actress," Gen said to Violet. "I love it. You're definitely worth what they're paying you. Now go on and take care of the other guys, while I take care of *my* guy."

"No." Derek held on to Violet, unwilling to break the moment. "I'm dancing with V."

"It's fine," Violet said. "I have work to do." And with that, she turned and disappeared into the crowd.

"Finally. Now I've got you all to myself." Gen stepped close, giving him a seductive smile.

He caught her arms before they wrapped around his neck. "We have to talk."

Violet didn't see Pete anywhere.

She'd kept tabs on the other guys, and she didn't want to bother Cooper and Ben, who were deep in conversation with the guys from U2. Not yet anyhow. So she did another tour of the rooftop before heading to the bartender.

"What can I getcha?" the dashing older man asked.

"Are there VIP rooms here?"

"With this crowd?" He gave a chin nod. "You bet. Go back to the elevators. You'll see an exit sign. Take those stairs down a flight. That whole floor's reserved for tonight's party."

"Great, thank you."

"Too late to reserve one now, though, so unless you've got an invitation, you won't be gettin' in."

"I'm looking for someone."

"Then you talk to Angie. Hang on." He pulled a beer, handed it off to someone, then made a gin and tonic. Coming back to her, he reached for the bar phone. "Who you lookin' for?" he asked, holding the phone between his ear and his shoulder.

"He's with Blue Fire."

"Record company?"

"Amoeba."

She waited as he turned away from her, talking on the phone.

When he hung up, he said, "Room 1345."

"You're awesome. Thank you so much." Dropping a ten onto the bar, she headed into the building. Hopefully, she'd find Pete there. If he was with people from the record company, he couldn't get into too much trouble.

"Everything okay?"

She swung around to find Ben and Cooper heading her way. Relief flooded her. It was silly. She could do this alone, obviously. But just knowing they were in it with her . . . it just felt good. She drew in a breath, pulled herself together. "I'm looking for Pete."

Ben tensed. "He's not out here?"

She shook her head, pushing the door open. "But I might know where he is."

Derek pounded on the door, so wired he was ready to shoulder it open.

"Jesus, man." Slater edged in front of him, sliding in his key card and pushing it open.

He found Ben and Cooper sitting at the table. Ben's fingers tapped a frenetic beat.

"Where's Violet?"

Ben swung around. "In her room."

"What happened?"

"It's okay, man, it's cool."

"Bullshit. Why did Violet have to bring Pete back to the hotel?"

"He was having some fun in the VIP rooms," Ben said. Oh, fuck. What had she seen?

"He was in the bathroom." Cooper shook his head, confirming how bad it'd been. "Violet, man, she's got balls of steel. She looked everywhere for him. Then she heard these sounds from the bathroom. It was locked, so she called us over. Had us pound the fuck out of that door until someone opened it. She's serious as shit."

"I told her to let me go in," Ben said.

As he should have. "What happened?"

"Derek." He felt Emmie's hand on his arm. "She's okay. I talked to her. She's fine."

"They were doing lines."

"Fuck. He did blow?"

"I don't think he had the chance to," Ben said. "Violet found him pretty quick."

"Where is he now?"

Ben jerked a thumb over his shoulder. "Bedroom. Pissed."

"Guys," Emmie said. "You know this has to stop."

Standing behind her with his hands on her hips, Slater whispered in her ear. She leaned back into him and nodded. "I'll leave you guys to talk about it."

But instead of heading into her room, she headed into Violet's.

"Where you going?" Was there a reason she needed to check on Violet? Fuck, he needed to see her.

"I want to find out when we get the results back."

"What results?"

"She had him drug-tested."

Good for her. "Let me talk to her." Derek started for the room, but Slater blocked him.

"No, you need to be here. We need to work this out. As a band."

He understood but watched as Emmie lightly knocked, ear to the door, then stepped inside. Derek couldn't believe Pete was this out of control. "What did she see?"

Cooper looked away, thumbing his lower lip.

Ben let out a breath. "I guess they were all naked. When she got in there, they were, you know . . ."

"Fucking," Cooper said. "She walked in on him with a bunch of girls."

"Shit."

"She handled it like a pro," Coop said. "I mean it. She took everyone's phones, checked for pictures."

He caught the look that passed between Cooper and Ben. "What? Just say it?"

Ben suddenly looked weary. "He was getting a blow job. From Mike Caldwell's girlfriend."

Derek's gaze shot to Slater. Shit. That was bad.

"Violet got him out before anything really happened." Ben looked apologetic.

"But like I said, she made sure there were no pictures. We're good. It's all good." Cooper didn't look like he believed it.

They didn't need the kind of press that would come if someone from Blue Fire was caught screwing the longtime girlfriend of one of the most famous rockers in the world. But there was no point in talking to Pete about it just then. Not when he was so high.

"Pete's pissed," Ben said. "That's why he's in his room. He was yelling at Violet, telling her he wants to ditch Irwin. Says we don't need him."

"'Fuckin' A&R guys'll be lining up to sign us,'" Cooper said in Pete's higher voice. "'We're fuckin' superstars, man.'"

"We're nothing," Slater said quietly. "We just started out. The only reason we were at that party tonight was because of Irwin. The only reason we got to play the festival was because of him. And it won't go down well if he finds out one of us was fucking Mike's girl."

Motion out the corner of his eye had him turning to find Violet peeking out of the bedroom. "Everything okay?"

Derek hurried over to her. "You all right?"

"Hey, man, sorry Pete went off on you like that," Cooper said.

"It's called grandiosity." She moved past him. "I don't need the test results to come back to know he did coke tonight. It makes them feel invincible, special. It's one of the characteristics of an addict."

"He's not an addict," Cooper said. "He's just getting carried away. This is new to us."

"This might be new to you two, but it isn't new to him."

Derek watched both Ben and Cooper look away, clearly embarrassed.

"I don't know you guys well, but I'm willing to bet you two don't have addictive personalities. At this point, you can probably walk away. But Pete can't. He needs help."

An unbearable heaviness weighed down on him, and Derek knew his friends felt it, too.

"I'll leave you guys to talk about it. But just know, it's only going to get worse." She gave them a gentle smile. "I'm going to shower and go to bed. Unless you guys need me?"

"No," Slater said. "You're right. Everything you said is right."

Emmie gave a weak smile to the guys and headed into her bedroom.

Once the women were behind closed doors, the guys just stood there for several moments.

"What do we do?" Cooper asked quietly.

"We drug-test him every day." *Dammit, Pete.* Why'd he have to take it so far? And how did Derek get through to him? "And the first time we see it in his system, he goes to rehab."

"And if he won't go? Then what?" Cooper asked.

Derek didn't appreciate the challenge in Cooper's voice. Like he *wanted* this? "What do you think, man? Then he's out of the band."

"You're taking it too far," Cooper said. "It's too soon."

"So how far are we willing to take it, Coop? What has

to go wrong before you think it's time for us to do something? Because I say we're hitting pretty close to that line."

Cooper shoved the chair in front of him. "You don't get to make these decisions. Who made you the boss of this fucking band?"

Anger rose in him like a hairy beast. "*You* did. All of you did. By not stepping up, you made *me* the boss."

TEN

He knew she didn't want anyone to know about them sleeping in the same bed, so he waited until the guys went off to their rooms. But it was killing him not to talk to her, make sure she was okay. He hated what she'd gone through tonight, and that he hadn't been there for her.

By the time he'd set up the pull-out couch, he couldn't take it anymore. He knocked on her door, but he couldn't wait, so he pushed into the room, closing the door behind him. She was just coming out of the bathroom. Face scrubbed clean of makeup, hair loose around her shoulders, and wearing thin cotton pajama shorts and a tank top that pulled tight across her breasts.

She was gorgeous and sweet and kind, and he wanted her more than he'd ever wanted anything in his life. He strode across the room, stopping inches from her.

He stroked the back of his hand across her smooth cheek. "You okay?"

She nodded, lips parted, looking like she was barely breathing.

"I'm sorry I wasn't there for you."

"You're allowed to spend time with your girlfriend. This is my job."

"Cut it out. Just stop it. Stop making me say it. She's not my girlfriend." She got him so riled up when she threw that bullshit in his face. "I told her that tonight."

"You told her what exactly?"

"That we're not seeing each other anymore. And that I don't like how she treated you."

"She treated me like I'm the minder of this band."

"But you're more than that to me, and you know it."

"Don't do this," she whispered, looking away.

He couldn't stand it. He just couldn't stand to see her hurting and hanging on so tightly to her control. "Do what? Fall for you? It's too late."

"Don't make me feel things I can't have." She pushed away from him. "I'm tired. It's been a long night. I'm going to bed."

Fuck. What could he say to that? He let her go, shutting himself in the bathroom to get ready for bed.

Brushing his teeth, he looked at his reflection. His instinct was to claim his woman. But he knew her well enough to know it wouldn't work with her. He had to give her time. Heading back out, he found she'd left a lamp on for him.

He drew back the covers, climbed in beside her, wanting to run his hands all over that gorgeous body, take what he knew they both wanted.

Until he saw her expression, all soft, guileless, and welcoming. The one she gave him every night. His heart pounded, the tips of his fingers tingling with the heady desire to touch her skin.

"Violet," he said as his arm draped around her waist, his palm opening on her back, his nose nuzzling into her neck. She smelled so fucking good.

As usual, she kept her hands pressed together at her collarbone. She smiled at him meaningfully.

"What?" he asked.

"You played the biggest show of your life, and you didn't even check reviews."

No, he hadn't. "Got distracted with all that Pete shit."

"You could check them now."

And leave her? "Wild, horny virgins could break into this room and I wouldn't leave. The fire alarm could go off and I'd stay right here."

"Don't say things like that."

Her breathy tone spiraled through him and wrapped around his dick. He inched closer to her, slid his hand down to her ass and gave it a squeeze. "Violet." Those big brown eyes gazed at him with heat and longing. Her chest rose and fell and her lips parted. Oh, fuck. He was a goner. He leaned forward, letting her scent wash over him, and he pressed his mouth to hers.

She sighed, her hand coming to his nape and clutching a fistful of hair.

He pressed closer, kissing her, his body alive and throbbing. The moment his tongue licked into her mouth and touched hers, his body flared with heat and desire. He gripped her ass, drawing her right up against him. Desire pulsed in his dick, making him so hard it hurt.

Closing his eyes, he sank into her, losing himself in the sensuous slide of tongues, the feel of her ass in his palm, and her sweet gasps.

And then she pressed a hand to his chest, tearing her mouth from his.

Stunned, he stared at her, his body still charging forward in its need to be with his woman. She covered her mouth with the back of her hand, her eyes wide and full of fear.

Just the sight of that palm in his face sent a cold chill through him.

He took in a deep breath, needing to calm himself down. "Don't push me away."

"Well, God, Derek, I obviously don't want to. Do you think this is easy for me?"

He couldn't tell if the tremor rocking through him was anger or need. "It should be easy. Look at us, for Christ's sake. Look at us." He gripped her harder, giving her a little shake. How could she push him away when they had so much fire between them?

"I want this, Derek. I want you. But I can't . . . we can't do this."

Her tone didn't match the yearning and blatant desire in her eyes, in the press of her lower body against his. "The fuck we can't."

"Even if I could be the kind of woman who lets herself have a passionate fling—and God, believe me, right now I wish more than anything that I could—it doesn't change the fact that I work for Irwin. I *can't* get involved with you."

"Of course you can. He'll never know."

Whatever he said banked the fire in her eyes. "He'll know. And even if he doesn't, I will. I'm sorry, but I can't do it. This is my job, my career. My reputation. I don't have anything to fall back on if I lose it. Nothing."

"I don't know how you can say that after that kiss."

She shook her head with a desperate expression. "You have no idea."

"Give me an idea, because I can't . . . Fuck, you can't mean this."

He knew he'd pushed her too far when she gazed up at him with so much pain in her eyes he wanted to punch himself in the face.

But then she reached for him, wrapping her arms around his neck, drawing him up close, and she whispered in his ear. "I didn't even know what I was missing until I found you. You make me feel all the things I never thought I could feel. I don't want you *as much* as you want me."

He flinched, his instinct to push her away. But he fucking couldn't.

"I want you so much more. You'll never know what it means to me to want someone the way I want you. To feel the way I feel. I just . . . I didn't even think it was possible."

Oh, fuck. She was killing him. "Then be with me." He kissed her again, long and slow and deep. "Fucking be with me."

Fingers tangling in his hair, she opened her mouth to him, tangled her tongue with his, but it wasn't the same. It almost felt like . . . good-bye.

And then she pushed away, letting go of him. "I understand if you don't want to sleep here anymore."

He rolled onto his back. *Christ.* His dick hurt, and the pressure was fucking killing him. So he got out of bed, unwilling to look at her, and shut himself in the bathroom. Turning on the hot water, he stepped into the shower and under the spray, lowering his head.

She wanted him more than he wanted her, but they couldn't be together.

He had no idea what to do with that information. Logically, he understood. He didn't want to ruin her reputation, make it impossible for her to get another gig. Obviously.

So was he supposed to give up? Walk away?

Everything in him rebelled against the thought. Because it was too damn late for that.

He was in.

The next morning, after brushing her teeth, Violet dressed in yoga pants and a tank top. She came out of the bathroom to find Derek at the desk, reading the computer screen. With each step she took, she felt the pull, the electric energy arcing between them.

He'd surprised her last night by coming back into bed with her after his shower. By wrapping an arm around her, lifting her head onto his chest, and falling asleep.

She wanted him. With everything in her, she wanted him.

Everything but the one tiny hold she had on her self-preservation. She couldn't blow up her career. Not for a guy who wanted her just for now. She didn't question their strange but intense connection—but she also knew she could never compromise her reputation, her career, for a short-term affair.

And even he would have to admit it couldn't last beyond the tour. Just look at his track record. Three months seemed to be his limit.

As she approached, he turned, looking relieved to see her. She touched his shoulder tentatively, and when his features softened, she stroked down to the middle of his back.

"Didn't anyone ever tell you not to read your own reviews?" She peered at the article.

"Hey, last night you told me to."

"No, I was just surprised you hadn't already done it."

He reached for her hand, brought it to his chest, and pressed it to his heart. "They're fucking great. Unbelievable." He gazed up at her with an evil glint. "Want to see something?"

"If it involves unzipping anything, then no, thank you."

He burst out laughing. "You're nasty."

"Only in your imagination."

He turned intense, pushing the chair back and tugging on her until she toppled into his lap. "Please tell me you can't see into my imagination. That would be bad. Really bad."

"You got something to show me or what?"

She started to get up. After all, someone could walk right in. But he tightened his hold around her waist. And, God, how was she supposed to resist the way this man claimed her? She couldn't. Just for this moment, then, she'd allow herself to have it. Savor it. She loved the feel of his big, powerful body, loved the grip he had on her. If she could, she'd never leave the safety and warmth of his arms.

She watched the screen as he scrolled through pictures of the party the night before. He clicked on one of them. Enlarged it, so it filled the screen.

Little white lights made blurry streaks in the background. In the foreground, the two of them were locked in an embrace. All around them couples danced, heads thrown back in laughter, arms captured mid-stroke, glimpses of white teeth and wild eyes.

But *them*. Good God, them. Their bodies pressed tightly together, gazing into each other's eyes, the yearning, the unchecked lust . . . it was palpable. Visceral. Her blood slowed.

That's me. Happiness filled her like light. She had no idea she could be that woman.

"That's . . . wow." She swiveled around to look at him. "We're hot."

His fingers dug into her thigh. Under her ass, she felt him hardening, lengthening.

For one second, she let herself go, squirmed on his erection, but when he hissed in a breath, when his hips pressed up, and sensation streaked through her, she got up. "I've got to go."

"Where?" He didn't sound happy.

"I'm meeting Bax for breakfast."

"Bax? Why?"

"Remember I told you I think he's the supplier? Well, he was in the VIP room last night with Pete. He's *always* with Pete. Was he around when you were in the studio?"

Derek got up, looking away with a thoughtful expression. Then, he nodded. "Yes."

"Did you ever see him giving Pete anything?"

"No. Never. And I can't imagine it. Working with Irwin . . . it's a premium gig, you know?"

"This is a way of life for him. I doubt he sees anything wrong with it."

He jammed his hands into his pockets. "This is so fucked up."

"I know, but we'll take care of it. We'll fix it."

"You always get a happy ending?"

"So far." She started to go, when he reached for her hand. Clasping it, he tugged her closer.

Her body responded, liquid heat softening her bones, desire pounding in her blood. That look in his eyes . . . *God.* "Derek—"

But before she could finish her sentence, his mouth closed over hers, and he swept the thoughts right out of her head with the sweetest, softest, most intimate kiss she'd ever had.

She'd thought him to be primal, rough, animalistic, but this kiss . . . God, his hands on her hips, his mouth so gentle and sweet and hot. He took his time, savoring her. Her legs went weak, her pulse kicking so hard she went dizzy.

And then his fingers slid into the waistband of her pants, skimming down until he held her ass firmly in his hands and squeezed, jerking her up against him.

"Oh," she gasped, completely swept away as hot desire rolled through her. His tongue demanded more from her. She couldn't resist, couldn't fight the fall into this big, strong man who took care of everyone—of *her.*

She moaned, so boneless she nearly collapsed, but his hands pulled out of her pants and he reached down to her bottom, cupped her, lifted her. Her legs automatically belted around his hips.

"Oh, fuck, V." His breath was hot on her neck as his fingers flexed into her flesh. He sucked an earlobe into his hot mouth. "I want you. I want you so much."

"God, Derek." Her hips thrust forward, her legs tightening. When she met his hard erection, lust detonated in her core and she ground against him, her hands grabbing his hair, pulling, her mouth needing more and more of his hungry kisses. Oh, God, she couldn't get enough, couldn't get close enough. "Derek." She cried out so loudly, she snapped right out of it, came back to herself. "Oh, God. I . . ." What had she done? She wiped her mouth, straightened her yoga pants. "I . . . Dammit. I have to meet Bax. He's waiting for me."

He dropped his head on her shoulder. "Violet." His tone so reverent, so gentle, she couldn't reconcile it with the man she'd come to know. Was he this way with Gen? His models?

He brought his mouth back to hers, gave her chaste kisses. "After the meeting, I'm taking you away. Just the two of us."

"You've got a show today."

"That's right. At the fairgrounds. We'll meet the band for sound check."

She pulled away from him. "I don't know if that's a good idea. My job is to mind the band. I shouldn't . . ."

"You shouldn't what? Do something for yourself? Besides, good news. I'm with the band." He gave her a devilish grin. "And the guys won't mind. They'll want you to have some fun, believe me. They feel like shit for what we've put you through."

"You haven't put me through anything. This is my job. It's what I do."

"And not once on a job has anyone done something nice just for you?"

"They're not supposed to." She headed to the closet, pulled a pretty silk tunic over her tank top, and slipped her feet into black flats. "I have to go."

"Give me a second to shut down my computer."

"Why?"

"I'm coming with you." He shifted the mouse, clicked out of the windows on his screen, and shut the laptop.

"You don't have to do that."

He reached for her hand, brought it to his mouth, and placed a kiss in the center of her palm. "But I want to."

They came out of the bedroom to find Slater and Emmie talking quietly in the kitchen.

"Where you off to?" Slater set his coffee mug down.

"Meeting Bax." Violet looked toward Derek, wanting to

lean against him, touch his arm, anything to be *with* him. "He's coming with me."

"You still think Bax is the supplier?" Slater asked.

"I will so kick his ass if he is," Emmie said. "What a lousy thing to do."

Cooper came out of his bedroom, wearing running shorts. "Hey, do we have time to hit the boxing gym before we head to the park?"

Violet wanted to pump a fist in the air. Cooper was a good guy; she'd known that from the beginning. But he'd offered her a lot of resistance, making it easier for Ben and Pete to follow suit.

"We've got sound check at three," Emmie began.

"More than enough time," Derek said.

Tonight they played the Maryland State Fair. And after the private party the night before, she figured the guys would rather sleep in. "I didn't book us gym time, though," Violet said. "I figured you guys would stay out late last night and want to sleep in."

"That's cool. I'll just hit the hotel gym." Cooper looked to the others. "You guys want to come with me?"

"Can't," Derek said.

Cooper looked between them. "What's going on?"

"We're going to talk to Bax."

Violet watched his features carefully. He froze, but then, the longer he looked at Derek, the more resigned he became. That's when she knew.

"Has Bax ever given you drugs?" She gave him a chance to come clean.

But his eyes never left Derek, resolve burning in them. "You're right. We do leave all the business shit to you, always have. I guess you were willing to do it . . . I don't know. It didn't occur to me to step in. Well, it did. But I guess I didn't want to. I wanted to have fun."

Derek nodded carefully.

And then Cooper looked at her. "Yeah, he did. It started when we were in the city. He got us whatever we wanted."

"Why'd you lie, man?" Derek asked. "We've got a fuck-ing problem here, Coop. You shouldn't have lied."

"Honestly, it didn't seem like a big deal. I thought you

guys were making more out of it than there was. But yeah, I fucked up." And then he seemed to shake off his guilt. "Ben and I were talking and we don't want to be, like, the kids in the band. You know? You and Slater are the mom and dad, and we're the assholes in the backseat distracting the driver."

She smiled at that surprisingly insightful description.

"We're gonna step up. Clean up our act." He gestured to the bedroom. "He's talking to Pete right now." He cleared his throat. "I'm sorry. We both are."

Derek stood still, looking like he was barely breathing. "Thanks, man. That means a lot to me." He gave a quick nod, looked away.

Cooper started for the door. "You want me to hang around? Talk to Bax with you?"

Violet should've been in the lobby ten minutes ago. "Let me get down there. I don't want to keep him waiting. You guys can decide how you want to handle things."

"No," Derek said. "Ask him to come up here."

"You can't put him on the spot," Slater said. "He won't talk."

"If he thinks he's talking to Violet alone, he will," Derek said. "We'll wait in the bedroom, see how he reacts. Time to put this shit to bed."

"Agreed."

"I don't need to play games," Violet said. "I'll get the truth from him."

"I know you will." Derek's smile told her all she needed to know about his opinion of her. His admiration. She didn't think anyone had ever made her feel as good about herself as he did. "I want to listen in, make sure things stay cool."

As long as they stayed hidden. "Okay." She texted the record executive, asked him to come up to the room.

Within five minutes, the rest of them had gone into her bedroom, leaving the door open. She let Bax in, his shaggy hair hanging in his eyes, his belt buckled so tightly his little belly hung over it.

"Hey." He seemed nervous, coming in and looking around. "Everyone at the gym?"

"Hey, Bax. Thanks for coming up. Do you want something to drink?"

"Sure. What d'you got?"

"Only water. We're checking out soon, so we cleared out the fridge already."

"Water's fine. So what's up? What's going on?"

She headed to the kitchen, reached for a clean glass, and filled it with cold water from the sink. "I think you know the problems we're having with Pete."

He let out a frustrated breath. "No, I don't. I mean, yeah, I get you didn't like what you saw last night, but he didn't do anything wrong. Maybe you shouldn't come to the parties. Give the guys some time alone. It kind of sucks that you're making them feel bad for having some fun."

She handed him the glass. "Pete doesn't look like he's having much fun to me. He seems manic. I think he's got too many chemicals in his system, and it's making him a little crazy."

"Okay." His fingers tightened on the glass. "So what do you want from me? I mean, no offense, but last night you didn't walk in on him shooting up or anything. You walked in on him fucking. Nothing wrong with that. Maybe you shouldn't judge him so bad just because he likes to fuck girls."

"I'm not sure he understood who he was fucking, you know? If he'd known it was Mike's girlfriend, would it have still been fun? Would Irwin think that was fun? Honestly, Bax, I don't think Pete knows what he's doing. He's kind of all over the place."

"Oh, Christ. Listen to you. You're in the wrong business. This is rock and roll, sweetheart. This is how we do things. You honestly think if Mike's girl's hooking up with Pete Larson that she's not fucking anything with a hard dick?"

"I don't care who she's with as long as it isn't someone in Blue Fire. But I can always confirm it with Irwin."

"*Fuck*." He tipped his head back, shaking his head. "Look, I get that you did a good job with Caroline, but that girl's a fuckin' psycho slut. These guys, come on, these guys are great. *Irwin* thinks they're great. They worked their asses off in the studio for nearly a year. So why shouldn't they have fun on the road?" He leaned into her. "They're rock stars, sweetheart. This is what rock stars do."

"You do realize Irwin doesn't want them doing drugs."

"What the hell do you know about Irwin? Just because you got his skanky daughter in line doesn't mean you know shit about him. I work with him every day—I know what he wants. And he wants these guys happy. You don't take rock stars on the road and give them *curfews*, make them eat spinach, and do *yoga*. Fuck, if that's the way we did things, who'd want to be a fucking musician?"

"I think you're playing a very dangerous game. Right now you think you're controlling the amount of substances they take. You think you've got a handle on the situation. And maybe with Ben and Cooper you're right. But you're wrong with Pete. He's spiraling out of control, and I'm telling you not to give him any more drugs."

"Listen here, sweetheart, you don't tell me any-fucking-thing, got that? I'll give them whatever they ask me for because they're grown-ups and get to make their own decisions."

"Pete's *addicted*, Bax. You're giving an addict drugs. You went way past letting him make his own decisions. You've become dangerous to him and everyone in the band."

"Fuck you, bitch." With a flick of his wrist, he doused her in cold water.

Derek rushed out of the bedroom. "Motherfucker, did you touch her? Did you fucking touch her?" He twisted Bax's arm behind his back, bringing the smaller man to his knees, and then he reached for a dish towel and handed it to her. "Are you okay? Did he touch you?"

She shook her head as she patted herself dry. The other guys joined them in the kitchen, everyone talking at once.

Slater pulled Bax away, and Derek reached for her, cupping her cheeks and lifting her face to him. "You okay?"

She nodded, blinking, trembling with shock. "Of course. It's just a little water." And then she realized they were all watching, and she pulled away from him with a soft laugh. "Let me just go change." Before she left them, she looked to Emmie. "You want to call Irwin?"

"You bet I do." She pulled out her phone. "I got it from here."

ELEVEN

The moment the sound engineer finished with Derek, he set his bass down. From his place on the stage he scanned the outdoor venue for Violet. He hadn't seen her since they'd started sound check.

The lighting engineer played with the lights, Slater squatted near the front of the stage to chat up some fans, and Ben set up his drum kit.

"Stand back, I'm gonna shred your face off," Cooper said into the mic, and he started strumming.

After they'd fired Bax and sent him on his way, Derek had gotten to spend the day alone with Violet at the state fair. He'd had the best time. Seriously, corny as shit, but watching Violet's face light up on the Ferris wheel, petting the pigs, or eating her first fried Oreo, had made him happier than just about anything he could ever remember.

She'd never gotten to be a kid. She'd never even *tasted* cotton candy. He'd won her a huge stuffed animal, made out with her during a milking demonstration, and held her hand on a rickety wooden roller coaster.

Happiness buzzed through him, so glad he'd taken the time to give her some fun away from the stress of her job with the band.

And then he spotted her, sitting in the back row, the huge orange and white stuffed cat on the seat next to her. Twisting a lock of hair in a finger, she had her shoulders slumped, cell phone in her hand.

Derek jumped off the stage.

"Dude, where you going?" Slater called.

"Be right back." He took off down the center aisle. The closer he came, the more he recognized fear in her eyes.

"Hey, what's going on?" Sitting beside her, he reached for her hand.

"It's nothing." She popped up, like she was ready to jump back into work mode.

"Nuh-uh." He gripped her hips, pulling her onto his lap, and then belted his arms around her.

Right away, she gave in to him, her body relaxing around him. Her scent drifted into his senses, and he held her close. "Talk to me."

"You remember the realtor who came to my farm?"

He nodded, stroking her silky hair.

"So my friend Francesca faxed my contract to the Walkers' attorney. We just heard back today. He said they think I took advantage of an old man. That the price he offered me is well below market value. They're going to contest it."

"Wait, did you call the attorney I got you?"

She shook her head. "She works in the same firm as a man I know. I didn't want to . . . I wanted to wait, see if they'd accept my contract. I mean, I knew it was a long shot, but I wanted to wait."

"It's the biggest firm in the city. Is your guy in property law?"

She shook her head.

"Then I doubt he'll find out."

She gave him a look. "He's not my guy."

"But I'll bet he wanted to be."

She smiled, shook her head. "I never went out with him, if that's what you're thinking."

But he could tell from her smile the guy wanted more. "He wanted you."

"Derek."

"Fine. You'll call her now, right? My mom's worked with her before. She's expecting your call."

"I'll call."

"So they think you took advantage, huh?"

"Yeah, but I didn't. He stayed sharp all the way until the end. You can ask anyone at the nursing home. His body weakened, but his mind never did. He *wanted* me to have that land. And I've never missed a payment. I've always paid more when I had the money. I would never take advantage of Jed. He was like a grandfather to me."

"Hey, look at me. No one who knows you would think you took advantage of anyone. You're the most honest, direct, and forthright person I've ever met. You're fucking amazing, V."

"Then why do you keep trying to get in my pants?"

He stilled. She was right. She was absolutely right.

Burying his face in her sweetly scented neck, he blew out a breath. "Because I want you."

She touched his chin, lifting his mouth to hers. And for the first time she kissed him, hot and full of want. "And I want you, too. But boinking you for a few weeks on the road would only make me feel cheap and then lonely and used when I leave you guys behind. You don't want that for me, do you?"

"No." But why did she have to leave them behind?

Reverb screeched, and they both turned to the stage. Cooper was laughing his head off, and Slater covered his ears.

"I have to get back up there." He kissed her cheek. "Call that attorney. We'll take care of it. We'll take care of everything."

The reporter lurched forward at the mention of Steve Bailey's fretless bass. "He was the runner-up bass player of the year in '94 and '96, man."

Derek appreciated the guy's enthusiasm. With Bax out of the picture, everyone felt more comfortable partying in the hotel room. So after the gig, they'd brought Vince and some of the other roadies, people from the record company, and a few select reporters back with them.

Violet sat on Derek's lap, her fingers sifting through his hair. He gripped her upper thigh, and it took all he had not to let it slide up her smooth skin to find the Promised Land.

"Yeah, but you know why he started playing a fretless bass, right?" Derek asked the reporter. This guy was good. He didn't ask stupid questions, and he clearly had a passion for music.

"Actually, I don't know." He smiled, looking eager for more details.

"He ran over his fretted bass with his Toyota when he was fourteen."

The reporter laughed. "That's great. Good story. Well, you've mastered it, man, you're as good as Bailey himself."

"I don't know about that, but we don't like effects. We like to make our own sound, you know? Plus, I really like the larger shift in pitch."

The guy nodded. "Cool, cool. So, uh, let me ask you one more question. I guess everyone's kind of wondering the same thing, but I'm not sure anyone's just come right out with it. So I'm going to take my shot."

Hopefully, he wouldn't ask about the rise to fame or what it felt like to have a guy with movie star good looks fronting the band. He hated shit like that. Everyone asked the same douche questions. Whatever, he had pat answers for all of them.

"Your dad said recently—"

Dread squeezed the base of his spine. What the hell had Eddie said now? Violet's hand tightened around the back of his neck, her fingers caressing his skin. Delicately, she rubbed the rim of his earlobe.

"Is this cool?" the guy said, making Derek realize he hadn't hidden his reaction.

"I don't . . ." He was going to say he didn't want to talk about his dad, but that would only draw more attention to the situation. "I don't care. Ask away."

"Okay, well, in the last *Rolling Stone*, your dad said he was self-taught and believed that the true musician didn't take hours of formal lessons. A true musician got lost in the music and taught himself just because he couldn't do anything *but* play. He said this generation—and by that I think he clearly means *you*—isn't like that. This generation doesn't care about the music. It just wants fame. He's made a lot of references to tattoos and model girlfriends and out-of-control partying. I know you've heard all this shit before, but I don't think anyone's ever asked you flat out how it makes you feel. I mean, it's your *dad*. But maybe he's not referring to you. Maybe you guys sit down for Sunday night dinner every week and talk about the same things. Maybe you agree that this generation's all flash and no substance. But, you know, you've got the tattoos and you've had the model girlfriends with the big public blow-outs." He looked to Violet. "Sorry."

"Oh, no, don't be sorry." She flashed him a big smile. Then she turned to Derek and said—as if they were the only two people in the room, "Wasn't your dad a jazz virtuoso?"

Derek nodded, not sure where she was going with this.

"That's what I thought. Well, a man who's known world-wide as a jazz virtuoso isn't going to trade that reputation in for bitter-guy-who-bad-mouths-his-own-son, right? So, of course he doesn't mean it the way you're suggesting." She rolled her eyes. "You guys have to stop looking for sensational angles. He's a guy. Guys give each other shit. No way would he damage his own reputation like that."

Both Derek and the reporter stared at her. A rush of affection flooded him so hard, it pushed out all thought from his mind. And then he looked at the reporter, and the two of them burst out laughing.

"Can I quote you on that?" he asked her.

Her arm went around him, and she hugged Derek close, pressing those delectable breasts to his cheek. "It's up to my man."

Her man. Desire roared through him. The slightest turn of his head and he'd sink his face into that cleavage. Fuck, he needed her. "I think she said it perfectly."

After they shook hands, another reporter came up.

"Hey, can I have a few minutes?" the woman asked.

Oh, hell, no. "Sorry, maybe another time?" He needed to be alone with his girl. *Now.* He stood up, grabbing Violet's hand.

The girl looked disappointed. "How about I email you some questions?"

"Absolutely. Get a hold of Genevieve Babineaux, and she'll send your questions to me."

He steered through the crowded living area, heading to the stereo to lower the volume. Then, he towed her into the bedroom and bolted the door.

"What are you doing?"

"This." Cupping her face, he kissed her. He was wild about this girl. His tongue licked into her mouth, and his hips locked with hers.

She jerked back from him.

Not a chance would she push him away. "Violet."

Her gaze drifted to his mouth, making his dick throb. Oh, fuck, there was nothing on this earth that was going to keep him from touching her. He wanted her with a ferocity that rendered him mindless. He cupped the back of her head as he took that sweet mouth of hers.

She leaned into him, her mouth opening just enough to give him a hint of all the dark, hot passion inside. When her hands slid into his back pockets and she squeezed his ass lustily, she cut off the oxygen from his lungs.

He couldn't speak. His body vibrated with need. And when her hips kicked forward, pressing hard against him, any restraint he might have had flew out in a dizzying rush. And then he was kissing her, unleashing all that urgent, wicked passion.

She tasted like iced tea, she smelled like wildflowers on a hot summer day, and when her hands pushed under his T-shirt and touched his skin, he burst into flames.

"Violet." Even her name made him wild. It conjured up so much beauty and peace and the fiercest desire he'd ever known. "I want you. Oh, fuck, I want you."

Her fingers curled, nails digging into his skin. She hitched a leg over his hip, aligning their bodies. He pressed hard, grinding against her core, his dick pulsing.

He had to touch her, just had to. His hand slid under her dress, and once he hit bare, warm flesh, he nearly jumped out of his skin. Gripping her ass, he lifted her. Her legs wrapped around his waist, her hands clutched the back of his head.

Depositing her on the bed, his body covered her, and his hand skimmed up her soft, smooth skin, only to fight against the waistband of her dress. Dammit, he needed to touch her breasts.

"Take this off." He didn't even recognize his strangled voice.

"Derek."

But she didn't stop him from reaching underneath her and finding the zipper. She sat up, and he peeled the dress off her. His pulse accelerated when he saw the lush mounds of her breasts barely contained within pale pink lace. Reaching behind her, his lips skimmed her cheeks as he unhooked the bra, lowered the straps, and tossed it aside.

The moment his mouth covered that beaded nipple, she gasped, her hand going around the back of his head and holding him in place. He lowered himself on top of her again, plunging his jeans-covered erection between her thighs, his need fueled by her moans and urgent exhalations. He slid his hand under the elastic band of her panties, one finger slipping into her curls, touching the slick heat of her. Oh, damn, she was wet and so ready for him.

She *wanted* him.

And then he found her sensitive nub and stroked it. Rearing back, she clutched his head to her breast. "Oh, God."

He licked the other nipple, tongue pulling hard, and her hips rocked in rhythm with his finger. He wanted more. He wanted so much more—*fuck* she felt so good. It was killing him, making him wild, but he couldn't risk her pushing him away. Couldn't bear it.

"Derek." Her neck arched, her fingers curled into fists.

Oh, fuck, did he need more. He slid his fingers inside her tight channel, his thumb rubbing faster, tighter circles on her clit. Her hips left the mattress as she bucked hard. He pulled back, needing to watch her features seize in perfect ecstasy.

Her eyelids drifted closed, her mouth opened, and she moaned his name. And then her whole body convulsed as she cried out. Hips rocking slowly, she settled back down, rolled her head toward him.

He didn't even get a moment to enjoy her pleasure

before fear got a hold of her. As soon as that awful moment of reality hit, he covered her mouth with a kiss, his cock so painfully hard he thought he'd die without release.

Relief rushed him when she returned the passion of his kiss. When her mouth opened, her body turned toward him, her hand gripped a handful of his hair. Lost in everything Violet, he moved on top of her, thrusting his hips and grinding his cock against her.

She arched off the mattress, releasing a cry, and then suddenly everything changed.

She pushed him away, scrambling off the bed. "Oh, God. Oh, dammit." Jamming both hands in her hair, she spun away from him. "*God.* What am I *doing*?"

His cock more than hurt. The pain was unbearable. He couldn't even speak, couldn't look at her.

"Derek. We can't do this. I can't—this is my job. My *career.*"

"Fuck, Violet." He rolled out of bed. *"Fuck."*

Her gaze shot to the door, obviously worried the others would hear them. They couldn't, of course. The music was too loud. And anyway, he couldn't think past the horrendous pain of blue balls.

"Derek, I'm sorry. I never should've—"

"Stop." He couldn't hear it. She looked tormented, standing there in nothing but her pink lace panties. And she just looked so gorgeous, her cheeks flushed, her hair wild. "Just . . . fucking stop." He couldn't get a handle on the pain. "I'll leave you alone. Okay? Believe me, I'll leave you the fuck alone."

"Derek." Her voice was a tortured whisper.

"Give me a minute, okay? Just . . . go get ready for bed or something."

The moment she was gone, he grabbed his phone out of his pocket. Punching in the number, he tilted his head back. What the fuck had he been thinking? She'd told him no from the beginning. He'd pushed and pushed, like some overeager teenage boy.

Why hadn't he left her alone? She'd told him it could never happen, but he kept pushing and pushing, demanding more from her than she was willing to give.

And he got it. Got that she had no backup in her life. No education. That her reputation was her only means of employment. And if it got out that she'd slept with her client, her reputation would take a huge hit.

He got it. But he'd kept pushing anyway because he was a selfish fuck. Like she'd said, he had no rules.

But she did. She lived by her rules. It was how she survived.

She'd told him she couldn't compromise her integrity, but what had he done?

Compromised her fucking integrity. So any hope he'd had of having an actual relationship with her, he'd just ruined. Fucking destroyed.

Because he was a selfish, impulsive prick.

The call went to voice mail, and he actually felt relief. He shouldn't even be making this call. It was stupid. She wasn't who he wanted.

But she was who he could have.

Then he heard Gen's smoky, sultry voice, and he snapped out of it. She wanted him the same way he wanted her. No rejection, no emotions, no fucking blue balls.

The message ended, and he heard the beep. He hung up. He didn't want to talk. So he texted instead. In NJ tomorrow night. Come to the show.

He disconnected and got the hell out of her room.

Violet didn't want to leave the bathroom. Standing naked and wet in front of a steam-covered mirror, her body still trembled from his outburst.

Of course she knew what her rejection felt like to him. It was his dad all over again. He'd been so honest, so pure-hearted with her. He was a passionate and intense man, and she just kept shutting him down.

She'd lost him for good. She'd felt it, had seen it in his eyes. He couldn't take it anymore.

She'd played with him. For her own selfish desires, she'd let him kiss her, touch her.

He was a man, and she was a girl whose emotional maturity hadn't developed along with the physical. Sure, she played the role of an adult, but she'd been so fixated on survival, she'd never really developed herself as a woman. She hadn't had those years of exploration.

And she'd loved how she felt in his arms, so she'd let him do it, when she should've remained firm all along.

I wish I could be more encouraging, but it's unlikely she'll ever have normal relationships.

Her knees gave out, and she snatched the towel off the rack, wrapping it around herself before sitting on the toilet seat lid.

When she closed her eyes, she was right back in that host's bedroom—any of them; all of them—wrapping the soft cotton hoodie around her grandma's poetry book, tucking each of the butter yellow patent leather shoes into a sleeve. Stuffing the sweatshirt into her worn ladybug backpack and then making that terrible, frightening walk across the host's house to the front door and into the waiting arms of the social worker.

That's what this loss felt like. That strangling sense of fear. Of being let go again, heading into another unknown. Only this time it was so much sharper because she'd lost something that mattered. And not just for its familiarity, but because it was profoundly important. Deep in her bones she knew what she had with Derek was irreplaceable.

And she'd discarded it.

Worse, he hated her. That look in his eyes—he'd wanted her gone.

And she didn't blame him. What a tease. Kissing him, letting him touch her like that.

Giving nothing in return.

She blew out a breath, forced the fear and self-doubt out of her mind. Yes, she'd messed up. Badly. Oh, God, *so* badly. But she was a professional. This was a job. She had to go back out there and work.

Maybe they wouldn't need her anymore, now that Bax was out of the picture. Pete had done great last night. He didn't have the same energy, but she suspected, with the encouragement of his friends, if he could get through the next several uncomfortable days, he'd come out the other side. He could be fine.

And then she'd be out of a job.

She'd go back to her farm. She closed her eyes, envisioning the acres of bright color, undulating in a brisk ocean breeze.

But it didn't flood her with joy. Because she'd lost Derek.

And that was unbearable.

When she finally came out of the bathroom, his absence hit her as distinctly as if he'd cleared the room of all the furniture, curtains, and carpet. But a strong scent filled the air, and she noticed the tray in front of the table by the window. With a white tablecloth and silver domed plates, it had to be room service. He'd ordered dinner for her?

Or, no, maybe he'd ordered dinner for them, but then she'd gone and ruined it by teasing him mercilessly. She'd let him touch her, but she hadn't done anything for him.

She hated herself.

Lifting the silver dome, she found a chicken and pasta dish. A single napkin and place setting.

No, he'd done this *after* she'd rejected him.

Where was he? She wanted to throw herself into his arms, apologize for pushing him away. She wanted to let go and just let him love her.

Oh, God, she wanted him back.

What was the *matter* with her?

Tucked into the banquette seat, alone on the bus, while the band finished their set, Violet's world crashed around her.

"It's an eviction notice," Francesca said.

She drew her knees to her chest, lowered her head, and closed her eyes. "They can't do that."

"No, they can't. And it's a good thing you hired that attorney because she agrees." She was thankful for Francesca's easy tone. It soothed the fear pounding in her veins.

"She said that?"

"She said they're trying to scare you. They have to prove you took advantage of Jed first, which, of course, they can't do."

But what if they could? "You read about stupid rulings in the paper all the time. Every day there's some judge somewhere that gives three million dollars to a lady who spills hot coffee in her lap."

"Everyone who knew Jed knew how sharp he was to the end. You've got the people of Eden's Landing, everyone at the nursing home, his doctor. They're not going to find one person who'll say he was losing his marbles because he simply wasn't."

Violet straightened. "You're right." And it's not like she'd let them take her farm. Not without a fight. "Do I need to come out there? We're in New Jersey, so I'm not even two and a half hours away. Is there anything I can do?"

"I'd love to have you come out here, but not for that reason. There's not a thing you can do. It's in the attorney's hands right now. This will work out. It's all in your favor. They're the ones who have to prove something that just isn't true."

"You're right." She thought about her farm, the pure peace she felt on it. "I hate that his own kids don't get what the land meant to him. That they could sell it for the money and then not care that it's turned into a subdivision. He would hate that, Francesca. He'd hate it."

"It won't happen. You don't need to worry about this. You know what I'm going to do? I'm going to send you a picture of Mimi's stationery. You're going to love what she's been doing."

"I'd love to see it. Good for you for getting her to come out there."

"Yes, well, only between interviews. You know how determined she is."

"I do."

"She doesn't know it yet, but she belongs in a more creative world."

"She'll figure it out. You know she will."

"I just want her to figure it out before she goes too far down the wrong path."

A text came in. "I'd better go. Show's probably over. We'll talk soon."

Fear seized her chest. An *eviction* notice. God.

She opened Emmie's text. Show's about to end. ☺

Violet had avoided Derek all day. She'd never even thanked him for the dinner he'd ordered her. She'd asked Emmie to let her know when the show ended—she didn't need to watch him onstage, where he became a completely different man than the one she saw in the green room and around the media. The way he sank into the music, lost himself in the groove, was about the sexiest thing she'd ever seen.

Why did a man who loved music so deeply spend so much time on things that drew him away from it?

Not her concern anymore. She'd made sure of that.

Time to meet the guys backstage.

TWELVE

Violet stood behind a speaker, watching the fans go wild, throwing underwear on the stage—and, oh, yes, at Derek, too, not just Slater.

God, what had she done? Anger, frustration rose up in her. It hurt so badly to know she'd had him—all that intensity focused on her—but she'd pushed him away.

She'd had a man whose gaze set off sirens in her body. A man who seemed to look into her soul and say, *Mine.*

And she'd thrown it away.

She looked at him, at his hot, hard rocker body and gorgeous face, and wanted to beat herself senseless.

"Here they come," Emmie said beside her.

Violet turned to look at her, but her gaze zipped right past her friend and landed on Genevieve Babineaux.

A wrenching pain gripped her chest. She hadn't known Gen was coming to this show.

Dressed in skintight jeans, black leather stiletto boots, and a corset-style top that showcased her breasts, she had her sights trained on Derek. Her wine-stained lips and heavily made-up eyes made her look like she was alone with her lover in a bedroom.

He must've called her. Asked her to come because he

couldn't take it anymore. The sexual frustration had to have been killing him.

Of course he had. She'd driven him to that. To calling the woman who could satisfy him.

God, she had only herself to blame. She wanted to disappear, run and hide somewhere.

But she had nowhere to go. Nowhere to hide. She had to stand there and take the hurt she'd created.

And, no, it made no difference that she knew she'd done the right thing in pushing him away. For the sake of her career.

Not to her heart anyway.

As the guys came off the stage, the roadies rushed forward to handle load-out. All around her, the hangers-on mobilized. All except Emmie, who held back, waiting. Slater zeroed right in on her, backing her into the wall and kissing the hell out of her. When the two came up for air, she held his head in her hands, tipped her forehead to his, and they talked quietly, just the two of them, locked in an intimacy Violet ached for.

She couldn't have that. The nature of her job, the nature of *her*. She was just so damn locked down. How did she fix it? If she closed her business, found a steady job on Long Island, commuting distance to the farm, she'd have no excuses not to have a relationship.

But would she feel for someone else what she felt for Derek?

She'd never met anyone like him before.

Oh, stop it. *Stop torturing yourself.* She forced herself to look away from the couple and get back to work.

But in searching for Pete, her gaze landed on *him*. A head taller than anyone else around him, Derek couldn't be missed.

He made his way toward Gen, who crooked a finger, reeling him in, her silky chestnut hair covering one of her bedroom eyes.

But just before he reached her, his gaze slid over and met Violet's.

Violet froze. All the noise and movement vanished, leaving her caught in the horrible memory of their last moment together. When she'd pushed him away for the last time. When he'd told her he couldn't take it anymore.

Gen leaned into his side, her hand on his chest. Together, they chatted in a small group, everyone laughing, everyone excited.

Except Derek, who looked miserable. She was an idiot. She couldn't have him, yet she made him feel guilty for being with someone who wanted exactly what he offered. God, she was a selfish fool.

She quickly turned to go, throwing herself back into work mode. She needed to pay attention to Pete. Keep him away from temptation. Moving through the crowd, she couldn't shake the feel of Derek's gaze burning into her. She chanced a look back at him, found him heading toward her.

Gen caught his hand, jerked him back to face her. She pressed herself to his front, while both hands came around and squeezed his ass. He pried her arms off him, twisted away, and came after Violet.

She let him, even though her heart thundered in her ears and her legs felt weak and shaky. She stood there and let him come up to her, even though she couldn't bear to hear his explanation for inviting Gen. For needing Gen. She would let him get it off his chest, so they could get back to working together.

She had no choice. *This is my job. My livelihood.* And, no, it didn't help to keep reminding herself. Not at all.

He reached her but didn't speak.

Her blood slowed, her world narrowed to the two of them. She reached for her cool composure, but when he was this close, she just couldn't find it. She fell into *them.*

"Did you invite her to the show tonight?" *Not fair.* She shouldn't have asked him.

He nodded.

Of course she'd known that already, but having him confirm it . . . it just sliced deeper into the open wound.

"What did you want me to do? You don't want me."

She blinked back stinging tears. *Oh, my God, I want you more than I've ever wanted anything in my life.*

"Look, V, this is all my fault. You never flirted, you never threw yourself at me. It's me. I pushed too hard." He looked away, sighing. "I don't want to compromise your integrity. I don't. I'm sorry if . . ." He gestured, stirring air. "I shouldn't have called her. I was hurt and frustrated . . . and I'm a selfish prick. I am. This is all on me."

"You don't have to apologize. You didn't do anything wrong. Things got out of hand. We got, you know, carried away. Of course you called her. You should be with her."

"I should be with Gen?"

It sounded so wrong, she couldn't even answer. Just gazed up into angry, searching eyes.

He stood there, waiting, jaw muscle working furiously. "You want me to fuck Gen tonight? Is that what you want?"

God, no. Of course not. But what could she say? *She* couldn't have sex with him.

It hurt to breathe. She didn't fit inside her skin. Nothing felt right, nothing.

This was a job. Derek was a client. He was at the beginning of his career. A career that would keep him on the road and in the studio. While she would be on her farm. So even if she could get past her rule of not getting involved with clients, even if she could cast aside her sense of business ethics, she still didn't see a future for them. At all.

Okay, this was better. Clearer. She forced air into her lungs, felt her head clear just a little. She lifted a hand to his jaw. "I want you to be happy. Honestly, that's all I want."

"And what if it's you that makes me happy?"

The shock of his words to her heart made her nerves sting. *You make me happy, too.* The man was relentless, and she *loved* it. Needed it. She wanted to throw herself into his arms and beg him not to give up on her.

But she couldn't do that. "I wish it could be that simple." Unfortunately, it wasn't.

So, ignoring the viselike grip on her heart, she forced herself to turn and walk away.

The moment she heard the elevator ding and male voices approach the suite, Violet poured the chicken broth into the pot and turned the burner on.

A key card in the door had her shoving the seasoned steaks under the broiler.

"Pete here?" Ben asked as they came in.

Not what she wanted to hear. "He's supposed to be with you." When she'd left the arena, she'd made sure he was in their care.

"Shit," Cooper said, looking worried. "Let me text Derek."

"Better leave Derek alone." She wished she hadn't sounded so bitter, but God. Knowing what he was doing with Gen just then . . . it made her sick to her stomach.

"Maybe Pete's with him," Ben said.

"No, he's not." She shut off the flame under the pan of mushrooms and onions, gave it a final stir, and then whacked the spatula against the side of the pan to remove the pieces stuck to it. *Way to act calm and natural.*

"Gen's in town," Cooper said quietly.

"Sorry." Ben flashed her an apologetic look.

She could not believe she was making the guys uncomfortable. She rolled her eyes. "There's nothing happening between me and Derek. Do we like each other? Yes. But we're not . . . together. In any way. Never have been. I wouldn't do that. This is my job."

When Cooper's brows rose, and Ben broke out in a smile, Violet realized she might've been protesting too hard. "Oh, cut it out. I said I like him. But he should be with Gen. That's the kind of woman he likes. And I'll be . . . I won't be with you guys much longer."

Without a word, Ben came right up to her, wrapped her in his arms, and patted her back. Then he pulled away and inhaled deeply. "Steak?"

She nodded.

"Fuckin' A." He reached into the pan and snatched some mushrooms. She batted his hand away, but not before he'd dropped them into his mouth. "You're the best."

"Why don't you guys see if you can find Pete?" She wished they hadn't lost track of him, but they probably figured he was fine now that Bax was out of the picture. *Wrong.*

"You worried?" Ben asked.

"He was totally sober last time I saw him," Cooper said. Waiting for the broth to come to a boil, she sprinkled salt into the pot. "He's not sober, Cooper. If he were still sober, he'd be with you. So I think you need to get everyone involved in finding him."

"I'm texting Derek."

He won't answer. Derek had invited Gen, so he'd likely gotten them a separate room.

She had to let it go. It was done. She'd made her decision—the right one—and now she was fully back in work mode.

No more sleepovers with Derek.

A terrible thought seized her chest. Would they continue to pose as a couple? That would mean she'd have to hold his hand, sit on his lap, continue the charade that had once thrilled her and would now absolutely destroy her. No, no. Of course not. The press would love the fact he'd dumped her and gone back to Gen.

Oh, God. *Stop.* Focus on Pete.

Voices murmured outside the door, female laughter. And then everyone turned to watch Slater and Emmie come in.

"You seen Pete?" Ben asked.

The peaceful contentment slid off their faces. "No. When was the last time you saw him?" Slater asked.

"He was with us in the green room, and then when we were gonna head back here, we couldn't find him anywhere. We figured he'd already come back."

"I thought Violet said you guys were watching him?" Emmie rested her hands on the kitchen counter. "She only came back to the hotel because he was with you."

They both looked chastised.

"You *guys*," Emmie said.

"Who've you contacted so far?" Slater whipped his phone out of his back pocket.

"I just texted Derek," Ben said.

"Should we head back to the amphitheater?" Emmie asked.

Slater shook his head. "Let's get everyone on the case. I'm texting Vince."

"I'll get some of the other roadies," Cooper said.

As the guys texted, Emmie gave her a smile. "Smells good."

"Thanks. They wanted steaks, so I made a salad and

polenta to go with them." She reached for Emmie's hand. "Don't worry, Em. It's always like this. They always take a few steps back. It's okay."

Slater's phone buzzed and he opened the text. "Yep. Vince says he's with him on the roadie bus."

"Fucker," Ben said. "Should've told us."

The broth boiled, and Violet added the polenta, stirring constantly. "You might want to make sure Vince brings Pete back to the hotel himself. He shouldn't trust him to come here on his own."

"On it." Slater focused on the keypad, his hair falling into his eyes. He was such a strikingly gorgeous man, but it was the way he loved Emmie that had Violet softening every time she was around him. He glanced up, stowing his phone in his back pocket. "Okay, it's all good." He gave his girl a soft smile. "I'm going to shower before we eat." Then he looked to Violet. "How much time do I have?"

"I'm flipping the steaks soon. So twelve, fifteen minutes?"

A slow, wickedly sexy grin spread across his features as he looked at his girl. "I can work with that."

Emmie couldn't hide her smile as hard as she seemed to be trying.

"You guys are disgusting," Cooper said.

"I really didn't need to know what's going down in that shower," Ben said as the two headed off to their bedroom.

Half an hour later, Slater checked his phone and then dug back into his steak. "Derek's here."

Dread slammed her like a fist. No way could she just sit there while he sauntered in, having been satisfied in every way by the hot, sexy, and completely uninhibited Genevieve Babineaux. God, no. She got up from the table and brought her plate to the sink. It wasn't like she'd eaten anything anyway. No, her stomach had been squeezed as tightly as a rubberband ball.

The moment she heard the door open, she stuck her head in the refrigerator.

Nice. Super mature.

"Fuck Gen, you look like sex on a stick."

"Aw, aren't you sweet, Coop."

"Sex on a stick?" Ben said. "Maybe that's why you don't get girls like Gen."

"And maybe one day you'll know the difference between a girl and a woman," Coop said. "And then you won't be stuck with your hand the rest of your life."

The guys laughed. Violet squeezed her eyes shut against the pain. She wanted to lock herself in the bedroom, hide in the shower stall, and beat her head against the tile. Instead, she'd have to sit with them. Watch Gen play with his hair while she sat on his lap until Pete finally got back to the suite.

She wanted to be with him. On his lap, his hand tucked between her thighs. And, oh, God, she'd never get to feel that again.

Only knowing she'd made the right choice got her face out of that refrigerator. Imagining Irwin finding out she'd slept with a band member straightened her spine.

Word getting out that she'd had sex with a client would kill her business. And then what would she have? She'd never earn enough working as a clerk in a shop to pay her lease.

With her head cleared, she turned to the sink. Rinsed out her dish and propped it in the dishwasher. She went to her happy place, where the sun beat down on her pretty flowers and an ocean breeze stirred them into a sprightly dance.

"Hey." She felt the heat of his big body at her back.

Oh, hell. She could do this. She had to do this. It was her *job*. Taking in a deep breath, she stilled herself, making herself go quiet inside. She turned to face him.

But the moment she looked into his eyes, saw her pain reflected back, she had nothing left inside to draw from. No reserves. She just felt like collapsing. And she couldn't fake it.

"Please excuse me." She tried to step around him, but his hand came up and stopped her.

He stood a little too close, watched her a little too . . . carefully. "What's up with Pete?"

"Not sure. Vince said he'd get him back here, but we haven't heard from him in a while. Slater's on it, so you should probably talk to him."

"I'm talking to *you*. It's your job to know where Pete is."

Well, that snapped her out of it. "I know that. I dropped the ball. We're taking care of it."

"That's not like you to drop the ball. How'd that happen?"

"I came back a few minutes ahead of the guys to get a start on dinner. I shouldn't have done that."

Derek's brows shot up. "No, you shouldn't have."

"But Slater found him with Vince, so he should be here soon." She tried again to shift away from him, but he stepped into her path.

"Is he shitfaced?"

"I don't know. We'll find out soon enough."

"It's past curfew."

"Yes, I know. I said I dropped the ball tonight. I'm sorry. It won't happen again." Resolve cleared her head. "Now, stop trying to intimidate me."

"I'm not intimidating you. I'm talking to you."

"Well, I don't have any answers. Let me talk to Slater about it." She looked up at him, pleading. He took short, choppy breaths, and he didn't budge. "Please?" she whispered.

"Hey, don't get my man all worked up." Gen sidled up to him, her hands caressing his chest. She was like a cat in heat, rubbing up on him.

"Gen," he said testily. "Can you give us a minute?"

And just like that, the woman dropped the whole sex kitten demeanor. "Let someone else deal with Pete, okay? You can have one night off. Isn't that why you called me?" And then her gaze slid to Violet. "Isn't this the only reason you're here?"

"Yes, it is." Violet forced her way around both of them and headed to the stove. "If you're hungry, there's some polenta and salad left. Help yourselves."

"Oh, I'm hungry all right." Gen threw her arms around Derek's neck and pressed her hips into him.

Something seemed to snap in him, because he lost all patience. Taking her by the shoulders, he led Gen to the master bedroom. He practically shoved the woman inside. Just before he went in, he turned to Violet. "Do you need anything from in here?"

Before you lock the door and bang Gen's brains out all night long?

So Violet got the couch tonight? That was fine. That was how it should've been all along. "Yes," she said quietly, before heading into the bedroom. She just would rather have gotten her belongings out before Gen had gone in there.

Heading for the bathroom to collect her toiletries, she kept a blank expression, unwilling to let the woman see her upset.

"Sorry he's such a shit." Gen grabbed a few liquor bottles from the mini fridge. She turned to her, all sexy and soft again. "He's sexually frustrated. But don't worry, I'll have him purring by morning."

Violet ignored her, her mind so filled with noise, her hands shaking so badly, she could barely accomplish her task. Making sure not to betray a hint of emotion, she gathered her face wash and perfume and stuffed them in her toiletry bag.

Plucking her sleep clothes off the chair, she shoved them in her suitcase and zipped it up. "Good night," she said as pleasantly as she could, wheeling her luggage out the door.

The guys were in the kitchen, cleaning, blasting music, so no one noticed her dragging the coffee table aside and removing the cushions from the pull-out couch. God, she wanted this night over.

What an idiot, falling for a client. Well, lesson learned. Pulling the blanket and pillow from the closet, she got to work making the bed.

He'd moved on, so she would, too. She'd think about her farm, her products.

And tomorrow she'd wake up with a whole new perspective.

What else could she do?

The click of the door jarred Violet awake. She sat up, squinting against the triangle of light that disappeared when the door shut. "Pete?"

His body slammed into the table, and he grunted. Violet's gaze slid to the clock. It wasn't quite two fifteen. Not that late.

"You okay?"

"I'm fuckin' great. Is that Vi-o-let?"

"Yeah. You going to bed?" She'd get him some water and ibuprofen. Fortunately, experience had taught her to go to bed fully clothed when dealing with her clients.

"Is that an invitation?" She could hear the energy in his voice. He wasn't going to sleep anytime soon.

She threw back the blanket, started to get up. "No, Pete. You seem a little angry."

"Angry?" He let out a bitter laugh. "Now, why would I be angry?" He tripped over her suitcase, which she'd left near the couch. Landed on his knees. "Ow. Fuck." He groaned.

She flipped on the lamp and then got out of bed. "Are you all right?"

He gave a maniacal laugh, his head tilting back.

"How about I get you some water?"

"Ah, that's so sweet, Vi-o-let. You're always so fucking sweet, right? That's what you like people to think, that you're sweet. But you're not really sweet. You're a fucking bitch. A destroying, lying, fucking bitch."

He looked totally wasted, and she suspected he'd swallowed yet another cocktail of pharmaceuticals. As she tried to move around him, he blocked her—not touching, just shifting his body in an attempt to intimidate.

She gave him a gentle smile. "I'm just getting you some water."

"I don't want water. I'm on tour with my band. You know how many years I fucking dreamed about this? And now I'm living it and you fucking come along and try to take away all the good shit. You think I'm doing this so I can go bowling? You think I want a curfew so I can get up early and go boxing? What *the fuck* do you think this is?"

Spittle flew from his mouth as he whispered harshly. Not loud enough to wake the guys.

"I want you to live your dream, Pete. I really do. But you

don't want your dream to end after this one tour, do you? From everything I've heard, Irwin has great plans for you."

He swayed, eyes hardening. "What the fuck do you know?"

"I know you're going to feel awful in the morning, so I'm going to get you some ibuprofen." She moved around him, but he grabbed her arm and jerked her. "Let me go, Pete."

"Don't fucking walk away from me. And don't fucking pull that pep talk shit with me. Your voice all low and gentle, like you're talking to a fucking mental patient. You don't know shit. You don't know fucking anything. You've turned them against me. They think I'm some fucking *addict*. I've known these guys *ten years*, and then you come along and make them hate me."

"Oh, my gosh, Pete, they don't hate you. They *love* you. This is tearing them apart. They'll do anything to help you."

He lurched to his feet, grabbing her sweater for support. "I don't need fucking help, you stupid bitch."

She yanked out of his hold and bolted away from him, but he stumbled forward, tackling her onto the bed. "Pete," she shouted when he landed on top of her.

The breath left her lungs, and her body went into fight mode. No one hurt her. *No one.* Her hips bucked hard, and she thrashed. "Get off me, you son of a bitch."

Feet pounded, lights flicked on, and soon everyone was in the room.

"Oh, my God," Emmie said.

But before anyone could even register what was going on, Derek threw Pete off the bed. His body hit the floor with a sickening thump.

Derek stood over him, his body shaking with anger. "What happened?" He whipped around to Violet. "Are you all right?"

She nodded, shaking with anger and fear.

"What the fuck did you do to her?" Derek bellowed.

Pete leapt to his feet, charged Derek. "You're going to side with her? With *her*?"

Derek cocked his arm and swung, dropping the wild-eyed man.

Emmie was on her knees, at Pete's side. "God, Pete, what is the matter with you?"

Derek spun back around to the bed, shoved his hands under her back, and lifted her into his arms. She could feel his heart pounding. "Tell me he didn't hurt you."

She drew the sweater across her chest. "I'm all right." Adrenaline still screamed through her veins.

He leaned back, looking deeply into her eyes.

Gen approached, watching, arms crossed over her stomach.

"Fuck." His eyes closed and his fingers pressed into her back. "I'm going to kill him. I'm going to fucking kill him."

"No, it's okay. He didn't hurt me."

Gen came up behind him, her hands sliding down his chest. "You okay, hon?"

Derek tore the woman's hands off him and got up roughly. "Cut the shit, Gen."

He turned back to Violet, leaving Gen wide-eyed. "That's it. We're done. You got a place for us to take him?"

She knew exactly what he meant. And she did know a great rehab facility for Pete in Manhattan, not even an hour away.

She nodded, knowing how hard this was for him.

She was proud of him for making the right choice.

The moment the elevator doors opened, Derek shot down the hall, surging ahead of the guys in his determination to get back to the suite and see her. *Fuck.* He should've listened to her. She did this shit for a living. She wouldn't have suggested rehab if she hadn't been able to foresee how things would do down.

He would never forget the look in her eyes with Pete on top of her. He still shook with rage that his friend had tried to . . . what? They'd both been wearing clothes, so what had Pete been doing on *top of her*? It didn't look sexual—Pete said it hadn't been—but he didn't know.

He was damn well about to find out. But really, goofball Pete? He couldn't imagine Pete hurting a woman.

Hurting *Violet.*

Sliding the key card in, he threw the door open.

The emptiness hit him as abruptly as if he'd walked straight into a wall.

Slater pushed past him. "Em?" He strode into the bedroom. "Fuck." And then rushed right out. "She's not here." He pulled out his phone, calling her for the hundredth time since they'd caught a cab to the rehab facility.

A familiar ringtone from the bedroom had Slater tossing his phone onto the couch.

Wherever they'd gone, the women had left quickly. The pillow still held the indentation of her head, the covers were still thrown back. Everything as she'd left it. Violet always straightened up her things—she didn't think it was housekeeping's job to pick up after her—so leaving the room in this state let him know she'd run.

He dialed her number yet again, but of course, the call went straight to voice mail. Was she feeling betrayed because she thought he'd been with Gen? Or did she feel he'd failed her? Hadn't gotten Pete the help he needed sooner?

Or, fuck, what if Pete *had* hurt her? It was killing him not to know.

She wouldn't take his call, so he shot her a quick text.
Slater's freaking out. Have Em call him.

Then he turned to the guys. "Pack up."

"I'm not going anywhere until I find out where Em is."

"We're going to her." And to Violet.

"Why wasn't Violet watching him last night?" Slater asked.

"It's not her fault," Ben said.

"She was," Cooper said at the same time. "But then she wanted to go to the hotel and get dinner started, and we wanted to stay a few minutes more."

"We told her to go ahead," Ben said. "Said we'd keep an eye on Pete."

"She didn't even leave a half hour before we did," Cooper said.

Derek didn't want to hear this shit. "This isn't anyone's fault. Assigning blame is a waste of time, considering we

have a shit load of problems to work out." Like their tour.
Like Irwin. And Violet. Dammit, why wouldn't she answer
her phone? Give him some idea how she was doing?

"We got rid of Bax," Cooper said. "I thought he'd be
okay."

"Look at us, man. Fucking look at us. We swore we
wouldn't become this." Slater thrust out his forearm. "I
meant this shit. Fuck. If this is how it's gonna be, then I
don't want it. I want to make fucking *music*. I don't want
shit like this. If you guys want all the bullshit, then we
should just end it right here, right now."

Derek's phone rang. Violet's caller ID. He handed his
phone to Slater. "It's for you."

Slater didn't even look, just punched the button and
snapped, "Em?" He dragged a hand through his hair.
"Where are you?"

After a pause, he blew out a breath. "I'm sorry." His
tone softened. "You're right. Where are you?"

"Come on, guys," Derek said to Ben and Cooper. "Pack
up. I'll tell Abe we're ready to roll." He just needed Slater
to find out where they were going.

"Why didn't you wait for me?" Slater said.

Derek mouthed, *Where are they?*

He mouthed, *Violet's place.* And then he snapped.
"Give me the address."

He pulled the phone away and stared at it. "She hung up
on me."

"Dude, chill." He took the phone. "You're yelling at her.
She's trying to take care of Violet, and you're going apeshit
on her."

Slater let out a defeated breath. "Get her back."

He punched V's speed dial and thrust the phone at his
friend.

"Em? Hey, I'm sorry." Everything in his friend relaxed
as he listened. "You did? Okay." And then he smiled. "You
did? You're amazing. I love the shit out of you. We're on
our way." With a smile that wasn't fading anytime soon, he
handed the phone back. "She arranged a rental car for us
through the hotel and had them program the address into
the GPS."

Derek's sister was amazing, but he didn't share Slater's ease. "How's V?"

"Em says she's fine. Not hurt, you know, physically. She just wanted to go home, to the farm."

Derek closed his eyes.

He hadn't been there for her. He'd thrown his little fucking tantrum, and look what had happened?

He needed to grow the fuck up. Pull his head out of his ass.

He needed to see her.

THIRTEEN

The four of them strode across the lobby. With his phone at his ear, waiting for Vince to answer, Derek tapped Cooper's arm with the back of his hand. "Get a printout of the directions from the front desk."

"Car's got GPS," Cooper said.

"And we're going to a farm on Long Island. I don't want any screw-ups."

Cooper nodded, throwing his duffel over his shoulder.

Ben and Slater stood beside him, both of them on their phones, texting.

"Derek?" Vince answered with a rough voice. "Dude, I'm so fucking sorry."

"You're fired."

Ben and Slater both looked up, like someone had jerked a string at the back of their necks.

"Dude, no way," the roadie said. "Don't do that. It wasn't my fault. He just wanted to party a little."

"You're right. It's not your fault. Whatever Pete did, whatever drugs he scored, that's not on you. That's on Pete. And it's on us for not keeping an eye on him. But you lied to us. You told Slater you had him with you."

"I did have him with me. But then I lost him, and I spent

half the night trying to find him. I swear, I looked fuckin' everywhere for him."

Vince was a good guy, but he'd failed them. He should've told them Pete had gone off with some girls. Partied in some bar.

"You're a great roadie, and we've counted on you more than anyone else on this tour, but you lied to us, man. I'm sorry, but if we don't have trust, we don't have shit."

He disconnected before the guy could respond.

"That was harsh," Ben said.

"No, he's right." Slater clapped Derek on the shoulder. "You did the right thing. Vince should've told us what happened, so we all could've gotten involved. It never should've come down to what happened last night. It scares me shitless to think what he could've done to Violet."

Derek held his friend's gaze and saw a deeper truth. "Or Emmie."

His shoulders sagged, but he didn't say anything. Didn't need to.

Cooper strode up to them, handing over the directions. Derek took them, reached for his bag.

"What now?" Ben asked.

"We go get the girls."

He hadn't talked to her in nearly eleven hours. Everything between them had gone to shit, and the fault lay entirely with him.

Hitting a red light, he pulled out his phone, texted her one more time. Just let me know you're OK.

But what would the words matter? She could keep telling him she bore no physical marks, but she wouldn't tell him how it'd felt to have a hundred-sixty-pound guy high as a kite pinning her to a bed.

His phone buzzed. Violet. *Finally.*

I'm fine.

Did he touch you?

Not like that. He was angry with me. It wasn't sexual, if that's what you've been thinking.

Fuck. He wished he'd known that. I'm sorry.

"Dude, let's go," Ben prompted from the backseat.

Derek looked up to see a green light. He checked the GPS. One mile to go.

They'd left the crazy traffic of Highway 495 nearly twenty minutes ago. The road had since narrowed to two lanes. The towns they'd passed were more rustic, historic, and much less populated. And now they'd hit farmland. Well, vineyards mostly.

The road climbed, giving them a view of asphalt and wide-open blue sky. And the moment they hit the top of the rise, the world exploded into endless fields of brightly colored flowers.

"Holy shit," he murmured. Violet's wildflowers.

"Jesus." Slater straightened, leaning forward to take in the spectacular view.

A frothy, gray-blue ocean lay sandwiched between acres of wildflowers and a robin's egg blue sky. "Unfuckingbelievable."

"I gotta take a piss." Cooper pulled on the back of Derek's seat. "We almost there?"

"You have reached your destination," the GPS said. "Your destination is on the right."

Violet lived here. She *lived* here.

"What's she doing on a farm?" Cooper said.

An old farmhouse, shaded by a massive copper beech tree, sat back a good distance from the road. He turned into the semicircular driveway. The house looked to be hundreds of years old and badly in need of repairs. Green moss grew all over the tar-shingled roof.

He didn't even have the car in park before Slater jumped out. He leapt up the porch stairs and knocked on the door. Arms folded, head down, his friend's body was taut with tension.

Derek got out of the car, breathing in the sweet scent of beach roses and taking in the quiet, peaceful farm. The door opened, and Derek's heart flew up into his throat. But it wasn't Violet. It was a stunning, voluptuous, dark-haired woman. "Hello." She gazed up at Slater, giving him a warm smile. "You must be Slater?"

"Yeah, hi. Slater Vaughn." Impatiently, he motioned at

the guys, who'd lined up behind him on the broad porch.
"This is Derek, Cooper, and Ben. Is Emmie here?"

"She's at the beach. Would you like me to show you how
to get there?"

Slater's hands flexed. "Yes." And then he let out a breath.
"Please."

The woman, older than he'd first thought, stepped out of
the house. "Do you see that break in the fields right there?"
She pointed across the street. A dirt path cut through a section of rosebushes, pink on one side, red on the other.
"Take that path, and you can't miss the beach. You just go
down the stairs and there it is."

"Thank you." Slater brushed past them, jumping off the
porch, gravel crunching under his boots on the driveway.

"Hey, I'm Derek." He offered his hand, and she clasped it.

"Francesca. Lovely to meet you."

"Is Violet here?" He hoped he didn't sound as impatient
as Slater had.

Francesca shook her head, looking worried. "She's in
the fields."

"Any idea where exactly?"

"No, sorry. She's weeding." The woman shook her head.
"She's been at it awhile, so it would make sense she'd be over
that way." She gestured to the southern part of the farm.

"Emmie?" Slater shouted.

Derek turned to see his sister coming up the dirt path,
her face lighting up when she saw her boyfriend.

Slater stepped into the road, right in the path of a pickup
truck. It honked, long and loud, swerving around him.

"Thanks," Derek said to the woman, and then jogged to
catch up with his insane band mate. "Hey, cool it. Everything's all right."

But Slater was focused on his girl.

Just as Emmie reached the road, Slater stepped out
again, holding up a hand to stop the traffic. An old pickup,
blasting some pop song, braked hard.

Emmie gave Slater an amused shake of her head as she
ran to greet him in the middle of the road. He swept her up
in his arms, kissing the ever-living shit out of her. Her legs
swung out, then slowly wrapped around his waist. After

whispering in her ear, he lowered her, and then got down on one knee.

"Oh, shit," Ben said.

"No fucking way." Cooper pushed closer. The three of them stood side by side along the edge of the road, watching.

The music shut off, and the passenger in the truck got out, leaving the door wide open. She aimed her camera phone.

Slater took Emmie's hands and kissed them. "I love you, angel. I love you more than anything, and I'm done fucking around. I want forever, and I want it now. Will you marry me?"

His sister let out a little cry, then sank down on her knees. "Jonny."

More people got out of cars, stacking up behind the pickup. More camera phones aimed at the couple.

Emmie cupped Slater's head and gave him the sweetest smile Derek had ever seen. "Of course I'll marry you."

Slater grabbed her, holding her so tight the sandals dangling from her fingers dropped onto the asphalt. "I fucking love you."

"I fucking love you, too." Tears glistened on her cheeks, and her smile spread across her whole face. He'd never seen his sister look so happy.

As soon as they got up, Slater took her hand, swiped up her sandals, and escorted her off the street. The witnesses clapped loudly before getting back into their trucks and taking off.

"Congratulations, man." Derek slapped his friend on the back.

"Fuck, yeah." Slater held Emmie tight to his side, practically shaking with happiness.

Derek held his sister's gaze, sharing her joy. And then he couldn't resist. He lurched forward, pulled her out of Slater's arms, and hugged her tightly. "Happy for you, Em."

"Happy for me, too." She turned to whisper in his ear. "Now, go get your girl. I don't know what the hell you were thinking bringing Gen back to the hotel room last night."

He was going to say that Violet didn't want to be his

girl, but he was done with that shit. "I fucked up." She did want to be his girl. She just didn't know how.

He'd show her.

A trickle of perspiration ran between her breasts, and Violet sat back on her heels to swipe the back of her gloved hand across her forehead. Van Morrison's "Into the Mystic" played softly from the truck, the hot July sun beat down on her back, and her arms ached from the constant yanking of the weeds. She'd been at it for hours, and as usual, all the noise in her head had quieted. She felt so much better.

Until she remembered she'd lost her job. And then she got all riled up again.

She had to stop thinking about it. She'd finish up out here, take a quick shower, and get on the phone. She'd line something up. Besides, she'd made a ton of money for one month. Usually, she used half to pay down the debt on the land and then divided the other half between savings and the farm account. For supplies, seeds, and renovations on the house.

This time, she'd hold on to it. She'd be fine until she lined up another job.

She hadn't slept with Derek, so she could get another job in the music industry.

Jason Becker sprang to mind. Not long ago the teenage phenom from New Jersey had girls around the world crying at his feet. Lately, though, he got more press for his drunkenness and partying than his pretty boy good looks and pop songs. She'd bet Irwin could get her in touch with his people.

Getting up from the soft quilt, she reached for her aluminum water bottle and surveyed her wildflowers.

Standing there, surrounded by nothing but sky and trees and flowers, she felt peace flutter over her like a silk scarf. She took in the bright baby blue eyes, their white centers making them look like birds with their heads thrown back in joyful song. The hot pink candytufts, the purple foxgloves, dangling off their stems like perfect bells. On the other side of the highway, she had her tea plants. The daisy-like chamomile, the mint leaves that always reminded her of her grandma's wrinkled hands, and the rows and rows of fragrant roses.

This is my happiness.

And working with a guy like Jason Becker? With his team of enablers? That would be a total nightmare. But she'd do it. If it meant she got to keep her farm, hell, yes, she'd do it.

The hair on the back of her neck shot up as a rush of sensation skittered down her spine. Movement out of the corner of her eye had her turning to find a figure striding across the fields.

Derek. Gaze trained on her, he headed her way, purposeful, focused, a man on a mission. The closer he got, the tighter her skin grew, the shallower her breathing. He looked . . . feral.

Her impulse was to run. The truck was a couple yards away, keys in the ignition. She didn't want to want this man, but with every stride toward her, her body opened for him. Heat flooded her, and everything feminine in her softened to welcome him.

He didn't say a word as he approached. Just bent, scooped her up, and held her tightly to him. His scent flooded her senses, that familiar mix of clean cotton, fresh soap, and Derek. Oh, how she yearned for this man.

She wanted to let go, sink into him—of course she did. But come on. He'd spent last night with Gen. He'd given up on her.

Irrational as it was—and it *was* irrational—she couldn't help feeling the sting of betrayal.

He nuzzled her ear. "You scared the shit out of me."

The dam burst wide open. All her affection for him came pouring out. He truly cared about her. "I'm okay."

He squeezed harder. "When I saw you on the bed . . ."

"He wasn't trying to hurt me. He was angry because he thinks I've turned you all against him."

"Violet." He imbued her name with reverence. "My sweet V." His face turned into her neck, and he inhaled. "I need to breathe you in. I need this. *Us.* Do you understand?"

She nodded, hesitant. He'd needed Gen the night before.

Did it matter if he'd used the other woman? She knew what they had between them, and she also knew how badly her rejection had hurt. So he'd turned to Gen. Was that so bad?

Her heart sank. Yeah, it was.

He pulled back, the look on his face so vulnerable, so *wanting*. And then he kissed her. Those beautiful, sensuous lips claimed hers, his tongue seeking, urging her to let him in. She wanted this—her body wanted this. But her mind screamed to push him away.

And so she did. She pushed at his shoulders, tore her mouth away.

God, he looked absolutely crushed. Destroyed.

She didn't want to destroy him, but come on. "God, Derek." Her voice came out shredded. "You were just with Gen."

"No, no. V, I didn't sleep with her. I didn't even touch her." Relief released the tension in his features. "She's not . . ."

"What?" *Please tell me you're mine.*

"You. I don't want her. I want you. Only you." He kissed her again. "I want you so much." He pressed soft kisses across her cheek, over her forehead, and down her nose. Tucking his face into her neck again, he opened his mouth over a sensitive spot, then licked. "I fucked up last night. I never should've called her. I was out of my mind. Wanting you but not being able to have you. But it's my fault. It's all on me. I was so fucking selfish, pushing you into something you didn't want. But even after I called Gen, I knew it wouldn't work. And I told her. I apologized. Because you're mine. And no one else will do."

She had a choice, right then. She could—

Oh, who was she kidding? She had no choice. She wanted him just as desperately. "Derek," she sighed as her mouth opened and their tongues met in a burst of sensation that kick-started the heart she'd neglected for so, so long.

She felt the surge of energy in his body as he tightened around her, and she let herself, go. Just let herself fall into him, into *them*.

"Oh, fuck, V." One hand slid down her back to grip her

ass. "Oh, *fuck*." He kissed her under the hot sun, the strains of Mazzy Star's "Fade into You" weaving around them. His hunger undid her, popped all the bindings from her heart, and she sank into him. The wet heat of his mouth, the urgent licks of his tongue. A shiver coursed through her.

Lowering her to the soft earth, his big, hard body came down on top of her, anchoring her to the ground. He cupped her chin to bring her mouth back to his as his tongue stroked inside, a knee pushing between her thighs.

"Wait."

She saw the desolation on his features, but she just reached for the quilt, started to drag it over.

"Oh, thank Christ." He lifted off her and flicked it open. They watched it billow to the ground. She scrambled onto it, laughing as she threw off her T-shirt and unbuttoned her shorts.

She could have him. Right here, in the middle of her wild-flowers. Then, every time she came out here she'd get that rush, that tightening, that glorious memory of when she'd let herself go, gave herself completely to this dazzling man.

He reached behind her back, unclasped her bra. Peeling it off and tossing it aside, he cupped her breasts. "You are so beautiful, V." His mouth covered her nipple, and the outrageous sensual heat made her body rise into his touch. His tongue licked so gently, heat poured through her, melting her.

She grabbed the back of his head, holding him in place. "I've never wanted anybody the way I want you."

His thumb flicked over a nipple, and he moved down her stomach, pressing open-mouthed kisses over her heated skin.

Tugging off her underpants, he tossed them. One finger delved between her folds, and he moaned, eyes closing. His hips thrust, his erection pressing into her hip.

Oh, my God. Sensation rode through her, so hard, so heady, she didn't know what to do with herself. The faintest ocean breeze fluttered across the flowers, offering a hint of cool on her blazing hot skin. Her fingers sifted through his silky hair, and she could hardly believe Derek Valencia had come for her. Was here, loving her like she was a feast.

His kisses sucked at her skin, each one placed hungrily, confessing his insatiable need. For *her*. The slide of his finger along her slick length made her bones turn liquid, desire streaming through her. When his finger circled her clit, a crack of pleasure hit with such intensity, a shudder rocked through her.

Nothing had ever felt so good.

"Fuck, V. Look at you." He shifted down between her legs, his shoulders nudging them apart. And then his tongue was on her, swirling deliciously around her sensitive nub. So good, so, so good. Her body turned hot, electric.

He loved her so ardently she wanted to cry. No one had ever wanted her this badly. Ever.

No, no, that wasn't it at all. That wasn't what had her in such a state. It was her. *She'd* never wanted anyone so badly, so wildly. Her body just opened for him in every way. He was pure, clean water, pouring into her every crevice and crack. Filling every hidden part of her.

Tension quickened, tightened. He slid one hand under her bottom, lifting her to his mouth, while the other glided up her stomach until it cupped a breast. He caressed it, flicking a thumb back and forth over her nipple, and when he gently pinched it, her hips shot up. Desire burst deep within, setting off electrical explosions.

She didn't think she could take any more. It was too intense. She needed to crest, to break, but it didn't end. All her senses engaged, and she felt everything. The lusty caress of his hand on her breast, the swirling lick of his tongue on her clit, the soft and frantic brush of his hair on her inner thighs. Oh, God, oh—

Every muscle in her body seized, the circuits in her mind shorted out, as she finally hit the peak and went soaring off the edge.

"Derek," she cried, holding his head tightly against her, rocking her hips, riding out the most intense orgasm of her life. And when she came back into her body, the aftereffects continued to pulse and spark through her veins. She blinked against the sunlight streaking through the limbs overhead. And then she exhaled.

Oh, God, that was *delicious*.

He kissed her inner thigh, then came back up to her and kissed her mouth.

She lifted his T-shirt, and he reached behind his neck and yanked it off. Then, he shrugged off his jeans, reaching into a pocket to pull out his wallet. He fished out a condom, then tossed the wallet aside.

Just as he tore the packet open, she took the condom from him, rising. "Let me." A new rush of desire hit her hard, making her hands tremble. "You don't know how badly I've wanted to see you. Touch you."

He shuddered, dropping his gaze to watch her hand grasp his erection. Just the feel of him, insanely hard and throbbing, gave her an aching hunger unlike anything she'd ever felt. She slid her hand along the length of him, and he stuttered out a rough exhalation.

"V."

"No, let me." Everything about this man was strong, powerful. He was intensely, uncompromisingly masculine. And she loved it. She had to taste him, so she lowered her mouth and licked him all around the head. He hissed out a breath, as her hands slid around to the back of his powerful thighs and drew him closer, her tongue and lips coasting all around his hard, smooth length. As soon as she got him nice and wet, she sucked him all the way to the back of her throat.

"Fuck, V. *Jesus*." His hands clamped around her head and his hips thrust, sending him deeper. "Sorry, shit, sorry."

She shook her head, she loved it. Loved how she excited him. Her tongue traced the vein underneath, then circled the head.

She loved the sounds he made, like he was out of control, loved the way his fingers curled into her hair. She sucked him hard, lodging him deeper into her throat, and he shouted, "Fuck."

He pulled out, snatched the condom from her, and then eased her onto her back. "I have to have you, V. *Have* to."

Clasping her hand in his, he brought it over her head as he stretched out over her, his erection gently prodding at her opening, slipping between her folds and sliding deliciously along her length. As if she wasn't ready enough for him, he continued his assault, striking her clit with each pass.

She moaned, hips undulating, as she reached for his bottom, grasped him, and pulled him tightly against her.

The moment he thrust inside, he let out the sexiest sigh she'd ever heard—like he'd finally made it home. And she was it. Happiness crashed over her. The intimacy with this man, it just overwhelmed her.

"I'm not going to last, V." His head reared back. "Oh, fuck, I'm not going to last."

She wanted the moment to last forever, the clear blue sky, the sweet scent of her wildflowers, the desperate thrust of his powerful hips—but she couldn't hold back the momentum, the barreling rush of desire. Something he did with his hips, the way he snapped them at just the right moment, made his pelvis scrape over her clit, lighting her up. He did it faster and faster, ratcheting her arousal so high and tight she couldn't breathe, couldn't think.

Her neck arched as her fingers fisted in the soft cotton blanket. And then her orgasm hit and held her in its relentless, euphoric grip. She pulled her hand out of his, and her arms came up around his back, her fingers digging into his skin. She needed him close, closer, as her feet braced on the ground and her hips rocked up hard, meeting his slamming thrusts.

He buried his face in her neck. "Violet. Oh, fuck." And then he surged into her, clamping his hands on her hips to hold her in place as he pounded into her. Losing his rhythm, their bodies slick and hot, he cried out with his release. His grip loosened, his thrusts slowly turned languid.

Easing out of her, he rolled onto his back, finding her hand and clasping it tightly in his. His other arm rested over his forehead and he turned to look at her. "I don't know what the hell that was, but can we do it again?"

She turned, too, holding on to his powerful bicep. "Yeah," she breathed. She just felt so good. So relaxed, so perfectly content.

He exhaled roughly, squeezed her hand. "Are we good?"

Oh. Her skin went from cooling down to chilled. Oh, God. She wanted to sit up, grab her clothes, *cover* herself. But some twisted sense of civility pinned her to the ground.

Were they *good*?

Did he mistake her for Gen?

She'd thought . . . God, she felt so confused. She'd thought she'd meant something to him. That he had feelings for her. But . . . is that where the whole sex god tag came from? That he could make women feel cherished? Make them think for those few moments they were the object of his feral desire?

He turned onto his side, his palm on her stomach.

Anger whipped through her, and she shoved his hand off. She did get up, then. And she reached for her bra.

"What happened? What'd I say?"

"What about me made you think I was in any way like Gen?"

He shot up, wide-eyed. "I don't. I'm not . . . What . . . What the hell just happened?"

"Are we *good*? Well, let's see." She stabbed an arm through her bra, shoving the strap up on her shoulder. "I won't cause problems for you, if that's what you mean. You can go about your business now that you've had your way with me."

A smile spread quickly across his ridiculously handsome features. And then he burst out laughing.

She reached past him for her T-shirt, but he snatched it. They played a tug-of-war with it, and it just sent her into a rage. Not only had he screwed her out of his system, but now he was laughing at her humiliation?

Oh, God, she hated him. "Give it to me." She yanked on it, but he wouldn't let go.

His arms came around her, his mouth trying to make contact with her cheek, but she squirmed away from him. His laughter faded, his arms tightened. He gripped her until she couldn't move. Heat poured through her, anger a burning fire in her gut.

"I didn't mean it like that. I meant, Are you upset? I've been pushing for something you didn't want to give, and then I just came out here and took it." She could feel his smile against her cheek. His fingers stroked her skin, but he didn't loosen his hold.

"You said, Are we good? Like you wanted to make sure I wouldn't pitch a fit now that we'd finally done the deed. I thought it meant you were hoping I'd behave like all your other women once you're done with them."

"I'm not done with you. How can I be done with you? We've just begun. I'm crazy about you, V. You know that."

The faintest breeze crossed her skin, and she felt herself cooling down. She supposed she did know that. "Can I have my shirt, please?"

He got up, reaching for his clothes. "I don't want to leave, but I've got to get back to the house. We're having a band meeting to figure out what to do next." Shirtless, wearing nothing but his jeans, he crouched before her, cupping her chin. "Hey. Are you okay?"

She was ruining it. Ruining this perfect moment she'd wanted to capture in a jar and preserve forever. She'd always vaguely hoped she wasn't as damaged as the social worker had implied, but in this moment she knew she was. Because who reacted like that after just making wild, passionate love in a field? He'd come to her, claimed her, and she'd freaked?

She didn't want to be this person. She wanted to be free, uninhibited. She wanted to abandon herself to passion.

She wanted to be normal.

God, then just freaking be normal. She let out a shaky breath and let go of her anxiety, let herself take in all the hunky gorgeousness of Derek Valencia. She smiled. "I'm better than okay." *Because I'm yours.*

Even if it was only for now.

FOURTEEN

When they entered the house through the back door, they found the band sitting around the big, rustic farm table. Violet couldn't miss their confused expressions as they all turned as one to watch them come in.

And, then, of course, it struck her. How she must look. Her hair, her clothes. She looked like she'd had sex in a field with their bass player.

She was *such* a slut. And one side of her mouth curled because she thoroughly enjoyed the feeling. Something deep inside of her awakened, took a leap into the air, and did a little cheerleader kick because she'd let herself go. She'd given herself over to passion.

"Oh, good, you're here," Emmie said. "Come sit down."

Derek headed for the table, but the moment she parted from him, intending to help Francesca at the kitchen counter, he tugged her to him, one hand wrapping around her back, settling above her ass. "Where you going?"

She gave him a smile, loving the way he always wanted her close. "I'm just going to make us some lunch. I doubt anyone's eaten."

"Sit with us. We gotta figure shit out."

"I know." She nudged him. "Go."

"You're part of this."

"No, I'm not." She wasn't about to interfere with band business, but he still didn't let go, just dragged her to the table.

Slater got up, pulling out a chair for her—as though she naturally belonged with them. "I feel like shit for what happened to you last night. Are you okay?"

"He didn't hurt me."

"Emmie told me, but I needed to hear it from you."

And a little bit more of what was buried deep inside her roused because he seemed to genuinely care. "He blamed me for turning you guys away from him. He was high, and he was angry, but he didn't hurt me."

"That was some scary shit," Cooper said.

"He doesn't like the changes I've made." She shrugged. "No one ever does."

"Yeah, but has anyone ever gotten rough with you?" Cooper asked.

"Sure. But in most situations there're bodyguards around. Honestly, it's all right. It didn't get far. How do you guys feel about putting him in rehab?"

Ben just shook his head. "He doesn't want to be there."

"They can't keep him," Cooper said.

"No, they can't." She couldn't say she was surprised, but it didn't bode well.

"It had to be done," Emmie said softly, her hand clasped with Slater's on his thigh. There was something different about them, but she couldn't define it. They were always so tight, but just then they seemed—soft, all rounded edges and flowing into each other.

"So what's going on?" Derek asked, one knee bouncing under the table. "You talk to Irwin?" Just then his phone buzzed. He picked it up, and she could see Gen's name on the screen. His brows pulled in as he opened the text.

He read the screen, growing increasingly agitated. "Wonderful."

Everyone's phone buzzed, and they all quickly opened their texts and started reading.

Emmie sucked in a breath. "Oh, no. This isn't good."

Violet got up, just as Francesca set the pitcher of

lemonade on the table. "Do we have enough bread to make sandwiches?"

"We do." Her friend squeezed her arm. "You okay?" she whispered.

"It's been a rough twenty-four hours."

Francesca gave her a sympathetic smile.

"Are you fucking kidding me?" Cooper said.

Violet glanced over to see Derek still reading. She recognized that look. He only got it when he was dealing with his dad. *What'd the jerk do now?*

"How did they find out?" Slater asked. "We just got him in there."

"We're the only ones who know," Ben said.

"I'd better call Irwin." Emmie got up. "Damn, I'd wanted to talk to you guys first, come up with a game plan."

"Well, hang on," Slater said. "We'll talk now. No matter what, we're more important than Irwin or record deals or any of this shit." He watched them reading their screens. "Guys, fuck the article. What're we gonna do? Call off the tour? Postpone it?"

Derek's expression . . . She sensed more going on than just anger over a journalist finding out about Pete. She wanted to go to him, but Emmie was there first. Hands on his shoulders, she peered down at his screen. "Don't let him get to you."

He sat rigidly, his mouth a tight line, his forehead a series of harsh lines. "Son of a bitch."

"He's an asshole," Slater said.

"No one respects what he says," Cooper said.

And that was it. Maybe the band wasn't her business, but Derek was. "What's going on? What does it say?" She squeezed Derek's shoulder. "Tell me."

Cooper showed her his phone. Violet startled at the blurry shot of Pete taken through the window of a cab. She skimmed the Beatz article until her gaze skidded on Eddie Valencia's name.

Am I surprised? No, I can't say I'm surprised. Look, you've either got the creative fire burning in your gut or you don't. Without that core of true talent, these flash-in-the-pan bands will fall apart. Of course they

will. You can't sustain success fueled by drugs, big
name producers, splashy headlines, and hype. I feel bad
for the kid, but hey, he had his fifteen minutes. That's
more than most people get.

In that moment, she didn't care about her job, her career,
or what anyone else thought. She leaned over Derek,
wrapped her arms around his neck, and kissed his cheek.
"He's got a very small dick."

Derek burst out laughing. Turning in his chair, he grabbed
her, his hands going under her legs, forcing her to straddle
him. In front of everyone, he kissed her. And then he pulled
back, scrubbed his face, and said, "Fuck it." One arm around
her, he faced the band. "Fuck him." He tossed his phone onto
the table. "We hire a temp keyboardist. Get back on tour."

"Hang on," Slater said. "We should talk about options.
I want to be sure we make the right decision for the right
reasons."

"Yeah, I mean, I want the record to go gold as much as
you," Cooper said. "But that can't be the reason we get
back on tour."

Violet felt Derek's body tense. She got off his lap and
faced them. "You know, Coop. I'm not sure what to make of
that comment. I've only been with you guys a little over a
month, but I've only ever seen Derek do what he felt was best
for the band. And, frankly, I think he's right. This isn't about
record sales. It's about preserving your contract, your reputation. I know you guys care about the band first, but this is a
business. And you do have to think about your future. If you
bail on this tour while Pete's in rehab, who'll ever work with
you again? Not when you can hire a replacement and get
right back at it. Derek's right. Get back out there and finish
the tour. Pete'll be there for the next album."

Silence gripped the room. She'd completely overstepped
her bounds as a minder. But Derek had enough people
attacking him. He needed support. Especially when their
inactivity forced all the business decisions onto him.

"I agree," Emmie said, breaking the tension.

Cooper gave Derek a chin nod. "Sorry, man. I didn't
mean it like that." He played with a spoon. "I just . . . Fuck,

I can't believe this is happening. I thought for sure he'd get his shit together."

Ben tilted his chair back, balancing on the back legs. "You're right, V. So Pete misses a few gigs. So what? He'll come out stronger, ready to handle his shit for the next tour."

She didn't miss the way Ben called her V. He'd never used a nickname with her before.

"Okay, so before I call Irwin," Emmie said. "How much time do we need? To audition some keyboard players, practice with them till they get the songs down? How soon before we can get you guys back on the road?"

"Wait, guys, before we talk about that, why don't we get Gen out here," Ben said. "Do some damage control."

Gen? She didn't mind having the band here, but Gen and all her posturing? This was Violet's home, her refuge. She didn't want Gen here.

"No," Derek said. "She doesn't need to come out here. We can have a conference call or Skype."

Thank you. She didn't want to let her personal feelings interfere with the important decisions they needed to make as a band, so she headed to the counter, pulling a big loaf of bread out of the paper bag from the bakery.

She heard a chair scrape back but kept her attention on the roasted chicken Francesca had taken out of the fridge. Should she make chicken salad sandwiches? The meat would go farther that way. She could add grapes—*oh.*

Hands gripped her hips, and that familiar scent washed over her as Derek nuzzled her neck. "You claimed me."

Heat spread up her neck. "What do you mean?"

"In front of the band. You claimed me. That was hot."

"They're not stupid. I'm sure they saw the weeds in my hair and grass stains on my butt." She tore lettuce leaves off the head.

His hands slid around her waist, and he pulled her back toward him. His body shuddered with laughter. "You don't have grass stains, but you do look well fucked."

She smiled, tilting her head against his shoulder. "Does that pass as a compliment in your world?"

"Fuck, yeah. And you can plan on me keeping you that way."

A sizzle of excitement shot through her, and she squeezed his arm.

And then he released her, returning to the group.

"Okay, one thing at a time," Emmie said. "First of all, Violet?"

Grabbing a towel, she wiped her hands and turned to them.

"Is there a hotel or a bed-and-breakfast close by?" She looked to the guys. "I guess we could go to the city."

Derek shot Violet a worried look that let her know exactly where he wanted to stay. She couldn't help smiling at him. "You don't need a hotel. If you can handle the quiet of the farm, you're all welcome to stay here." *Although, FYI, that invitation doesn't extend to former girlfriends.*

"I don't want to impose," Slater said. "Francesca?"

Her friend gave him a lovely smile, lifting the back of her hand to brush hair out of her eyes. "You're very welcome to stay."

"It's a big house," Violet said. "And there's a smaller in-law house out back. We've got plenty of room."

"We'll stay," Derek said.

"Don't be a baby," Ben said with a laugh. "I think you can live without her for a few days."

"But I don't want to." Derek sounded grumpy, and she found it adorable.

"Well, if it's okay with you, we'd love to stay," Emmie said. "Your farm is amazing. I've never seen anything like it, and we could use a little peace and quiet. Ben, could you please text Abe and ask him to bring the instruments?"

Ben looked to Violet. "So much for the quiet."

"The barn's wired, and it's set back from the house a little ways. We don't have animals anymore, so it's all yours."

"Are you serious?" Cooper said. "That would be awesome. We haven't played just for fun in a year." He gazed out the window over the sink. "This place is insane."

Her heart expanded, so pleased they appreciated it.

"He should bring the weights, too," Slater said.

Ben nodded, while texting.

"Okay, next." Emmie grabbed a pen and piece of note paper off the built-in desk. "I'll get on the phone with Irwin. Derek, can you set up a time to talk to Gen? Give me a chance to talk to Irwin—maybe an hour or so? Let's set up a conference call, spin our news the right way. Violet, do you have a computer we can use?"

"Of course. Come with me." She looked to Francesca to see if she could handle lunch by herself, and her friend nodded, *Of course*.

As much as she loved the peace and quiet of her farm, she did love the idea of the guys filling up the space with their music, their bawdy conversation, and their laughter.

And, of course, more sexy time with Derek.

Derek came back into the bedroom after a run along the beach to find his girl had kicked off the sheets.

A bolt of lust shot down his spine and fired up his dick. As he stood there, dumbstruck by her natural beauty and sensuality, she gave him a sleepy, satisfied smile. And the need to take her hit him hard and fierce.

He should leave her alone. He'd had her what? Three, four times the night before? But fuck him, he couldn't get enough of her.

Watching him, she sat up, her breasts bouncing as she got up on her knees, arms open to him.

He walked right into them and kissed her. Her arms slid up his back, cupping his shoulders, and she pressed him to her. The caress of her tongue, those beaded nipples on his bare chest, made him wild with want.

Tugging on his shorts, she said, "Off."

The moment he'd kicked them aside, she reached between them, her hand gliding up his cock, and he went hard as a pike.

He smoothed one hand up her back—the softest, smoothest skin he'd ever felt—and cupped her ass cheek with the other.

She lowered them both to the mattress, hips pitching forward, and she breathed his name.

Sensation broke across his skin, and everything in him tightened with want. Gripping her hips, he pulled her to him hard, sliding his dick between her legs, coating it with her warm honey.

"You make me crazy. Is it too much? Can I . . ."

"Yes," she whispered, shifting her legs to welcome him in.

Oh, hell. *Jesus*. He couldn't believe how good she made him feel. He gripped himself, watching as he nudged at her entrance, pushed inside her glistening folds. His skin pulled taut as a wave of pure desire swept over him.

She moaned, clutching his ass and driving him deep inside. Good God, he lit up. So tight, so hot, so fucking sexy. He pulled back and thrust into her, harder this time, and her slick arousal made him shudder.

Pressing closer to her, he cupped her breast and oh, fuck, the feel of that gorgeous fullness, the nipple beading in his palm, gave him an erotic rush that made him even harder.

"Derek," she cried, voice thick with desire.

No one turned him on like she did. No one. He hammered into her, losing his mind in all her soft skin, that tight, hot channel, and her desperate cries. Fingers digging into her hip, he held her right where he needed her, slamming into her, as she pushed right back into him. Her face turned into his neck as she moaned, hands still on his ass to keep him tight against her.

Completely unhinged, he couldn't slow down if he tried. Tension rose to an unbearable pitch, electricity shot down his spine, and with a shout he came in blinding, scalding bursts inside her. For a moment, he could barely catch his breath, so he remained deep within her, his cock still pulsing. And then he collapsed onto her, breathing in her pretty floral scent.

"I love the way you smell."

She sighed. "I love the way you touch me."

He rolled off her, wanting to enjoy a few more moments alone with her before he jumped into the insanity of his day.

She snuggled up to him, but she hadn't come. And he wanted her to feel as good as he did, so he nudged her onto her back, and then slid his fingers into her slick heat. Lazily, he stroked her hard little nub. Because he fucking loved watching her come.

"You make me feel *so* good," she said in a breathy moan.

Those spectacular breasts rocked with the motion of her hips, and he leaned over, licking a nipple. She gasped, gazing up at him with lust-drenched eyes.

"Derek." She scraped her fingernails across his scalp, sparking a trail of goose bumps across his skin. And then her eyelids drooped, closed, as her lips parted and her hips came off the mattress. "Oh, Derek." Her legs stretched out, her toes curled, and her whole body seized.

Yeah, he loved watching her come. "Gorgeous."

His finger continued swirling until she relaxed, opened her eyes, and gave him a wicked smile. "So good."

And then she sat up, looking horrified. "Oh, my God." Her hand went between her legs.

It hit him right then. He sat up on an elbow. "I'm sorry. Shit, V, I'm so sorry." What had he been thinking? "Are you on birth control?"

"Yes." But she didn't look any more at ease.

"Then we should be okay."

She scowled.

"I haven't been with anyone since I met you." And then it struck him. She thought he was this careless all the time. "Oh, no. Fuck, no. I've never gone bareback in my life."

Settling back down, she shook her head, let out a breath. "Sorry, that just . . . scared me."

"No, *I'm* sorry. I lose my mind around you."

He settled beside her. She reached for his arm, stroked his skin with her fingertips. "I'm not used to . . . you know."

"No, I don't know." This is what he loved. These moments alone with her, when she opened up to him.

"Getting swept away like that." She looked away. "It's scary and amazing at the same time."

"Scary because . . . ?"

"Because it's so good and I'm just . . . you know."

"I don't know."

She let out a huff of breath, obviously flustered. "Well, I mean, obviously, this is normal for you. You're a sexual man. You get swept away all the time. But for me . . . I mean, I just don't."

Flustered looked adorable on her. "You think this is normal for me?" And then he really got it, what she was thinking. So he hitched up on an elbow to look her in the eyes. "You think this is how it is with Gen or Adriana or any of the other women I've fucked before you?" He leaned into her, breathed her subtle fragrance, which set his blood churning again. "You're wrong. I never particularly liked them. Sex with them was fun and hot at first. But I didn't *crave* them. I didn't think about them every minute I wasn't with them. Hell, no. V. What we have . . . Jesus. Trust me, it's different. I didn't fuck you in that field." Which meant what exactly? He couldn't go there. "I'd hate it if I made you feel like I did."

"You didn't." She said it so quietly he almost didn't hear.

"Sorry?"

"You didn't. That's what's so scary. You make me feel special. You make me *feel*. And I didn't even know I could." She gave a contented exhalation.

"Could what?"

"You know . . . feel. This is a first for me."

"What do you mean, you don't feel?"

"Foster care and all that. Babies who don't get hugged, nurtured, they just . . . don't develop the right way. I can't feel things the way you do. I can't have normal relationships."

A heavy sadness pressed down on him. How in the world had she ever come to believe that? "That's bullshit. You feel something for me. I know you do."

"I do. That's what I'm saying. And you can't imagine what that means to me when I never thought I was capable of it."

Why did that make him feel like King fucking Kong? Like Superman? With rocket-fueled balls and wings and shit? "Listen, I don't know who told you that shit, but it's dead wrong."

He gazed out her gauze curtains to the sunny world outside. Sure, she might be fearful—what kid who got passed from one home to another wouldn't be? But she was nothing but caring and concerned. And in his arms? The way she responded to him? Yeah, she felt something.

"What's a normal relationship anyway? I certainly haven't had one, and I gotta guess my mom held me. But fuck it. This is good, V. We're good for each other." He rubbed the scruff on his chin, as he realized his words didn't mean a damn thing. Not if she believed this shit. And if she actually believed she couldn't love, couldn't have a normal relationship, what the hell did that mean for him? "I don't want to be alone in this, V."

The bed creaked, as she pushed him onto his back and straddled him. Clasping his hands, she held them by his ears. "You're not." She kissed him. "You're not alone in this."

He yanked his hands free so he could grab her hips. He fell into the softness of her mouth, the silky spill of her hair on his shoulders and chest. That sweet, sexy scent floated around him.

"Derek? You up?" Slater called.

"No."

Slater chuckled. "Come on, we're all in the kitchen. Francesca's made breakfast. We got shit to talk about."

The last thing he wanted to do was get out of this bed. But he had to. "I'm gonna grab a shower. Join me?"

She shook her head, giving him a soft smile. "You go on."

He didn't want to leave her alone to overthink things. She'd take those wrong ideas she had in her head and give them power they didn't deserve.

He just needed the time to show her that.

But hell. Time was the one thing he didn't have.

Derek couldn't remember when he'd had this much fun. When was the last time they'd jammed for the hell of it? As they unplugged and packed up their instruments, the guys headed out of the barn, eager to cool off in the ocean. As much as Derek wanted to join them, he needed to see Violet first. He missed her.

"What's up, man?" Slater said.

Derek looked up, realizing the other guys had left. He clipped the guitar case shut. "Nothing. Let's head out."

"This was good today. We needed it."

Derek nodded.

"We should do it more often. After the tour? We should hole up somewhere and just write." Slater gazed out of the barn, taking in the house, the huge weeping willow. "Maybe rent a place out here."

"She'll be on to the next job." But a warm feeling spread through him. He appreciated his friend looking out for him. They started out of the barn when Derek clapped him on the back. "So what's with the fuckin' sappy ballads?" A lot of what they'd worked on had been Slater's new material. "You're not going all Phil Collins on us, are you?"

His friend grinned broadly. "Hey, the ballads bring the girls in. I'm just doing my duty to the rest of the guys. They should thank me."

He noticed the way Slater didn't include him in that line of thought. Yeah, he guessed he pretty much wore his heart on his sleeve. Never had been much for playing it cool.

"What'd I say?" Slater asked as they stepped into the fading daylight.

"No, I'm just thinking about shit. Lot on my mind."

"Does it smell like flowers?"

"Yeah, pretty much."

Slater turned, stepped in front of him. "Listen, man. Don't waste your time on the reasons why it won't work. You just do it. You make it work. Don't fuck this up."

"Not *my* issue." It was different for Slater. His girl worked in the same industry, had the ability to tour with them.

"You love her?"

Derek shrugged. Too soon for that. But he did feel a bond, deep and powerful. "It's like you said, she makes it real." He had a chance to sound it out loud, so he went for it. "I don't think she trusts me."

"She say that?"

"Nah, but I know her. She thinks I basically hook up with the women I work with."

Slater didn't even hesitate. "You do."

"Doesn't everybody? How else do you meet women?"

"Yeah, but I see what she's saying. It's probably more than that, though. You dumped Gen pretty easily. She's probably afraid you'll do the same to her."

He hadn't thought about that. "I didn't *dump* Gen. We were never like that. We had fun when we were in the same city." Which he'd told Violet from the beginning. But he saw Slater's point. How would a woman like Violet understand the kind of arrangement he'd had with Gen? "Well, fuck me. How'm I supposed to show her it's different for me if she won't stick around long enough?"

"Dude, you're an intuitive guy. You size up a situation

pretty quickly and then you make a decision. She's not like that. She needs to think things through, consider the angles."

"If I let her consider anything, she'll walk. Nothing's in our favor. Soon as we find someone on the keys, we're back on tour. And then what? She's gonna think I'll move on to someone else, and she won't give me a chance to prove I won't."

"Then don't let her think. Show her how you feel and don't let up. You think it was easy for me and Em? You think she trusted me on the road, while she hung around an empty house in Austin? You *don't let up*." He blew out a frustrated breath. "Look at her." He gestured to the window of the laundry room, where Violet pulled an armful of clean clothes out of the dryer. "You think someone like her's going to come around again? You think she's replaceable?"

A clot of fear rose from his gut, lodging in his chest, making it hard to breathe. *No.* There was no one like Violet. No one who fit him so perfectly. "You think we can keep her as our minder?"

"No idea. But now's not the time to ask. Irwin's pretty disgusted."

"Yeah, we blew up pretty fast. A month into our first tour." If this tour was a test to see how they performed on the road, they'd failed. He couldn't see Irwin extending it.

"We also took care of the problem quickly, and we're back on track. Emmie says it's a good sign he's got some keyboardists for us. Says he doesn't want us wasting time auditioning assholes, so that means he's still invested."

"Jonny?" Emmie called from the back porch. "You guys want to picnic at the beach or eat here before we head down there?"

"Whatever's good for you," Slater said.

"You are so whipped." Derek shook his head, smiling. "I got this one." He called out to his sister, "No sand in my food. We'll eat first."

They headed to the house, fear and desire growing with each step he took closer to her. "I want her. I fucking want her."

"Yeah. Figured that one out." Slater touched his arm. "Then don't let up."

FIFTEEN

Beach grass rustled in the breeze, and the gentle crashing of waves made her feel more relaxed than she had in ages.

On a blanket, with the remains of dinner and discarded T-shirts strewn everywhere, Violet watched the guys chase after Derek, who held the football tucked close to his side. No one got near him as he raised the football in the air then slammed it to the sand. "Hell yeah!"

The guys continued after him, rushing him, knocking him onto his hip, and dog-piling on top of him.

Emmie, leaning forward in her beach chair, burst out laughing, clapping her hands. "Oh, my God, I haven't seen them like this in so long." She sat back. "This was the best day for them. Jamming in your barn, eating your incredible food, hanging out at the beach. God, did we need this."

"What about Irwin? And the tour?"

"He's more concerned with getting the guys back on track. And, not to make light of what's happening with Pete, but if it had to happen, it's good it happened locally because it was easy for us to find replacements for the guys at the two festivals they've missed so far."

"I'm glad to hear that. How long do you think you'll stay here?"

"Eager to get rid of us?"

"Not at all."

"It must be overwhelming for you, though. You're not used to so much . . . testosterone. We're a handful." She gestured to the blanket. "And a mess."

"Are you kidding? I love it." Theirs might be the first family she'd ever watched that truly loved and respected each other. Had fun together. And, well, stayed together because they didn't want to be anywhere else. "You're lucky."

Emmie looked over at her sharply. "I know. Even with this whole Pete thing, I think it just makes the four of them stronger, more sure of what they want. It's awful that this happened, but it's also a chance for them to regroup. This business is hard. The pressure, the attention. They never get a break. It's fast-paced and high stakes, and everyone wants something from them. So it's good for them to pull back a little and remember who they are and what they really want."

"I don't think Slater forgets for a second what he really wants." She chanced a look at Emmie. "Did you expect him to propose?"

Emmie laughed. "Right then? After he dropped Pete off at rehab? No. Not at all. I mean, I knew we'd get there eventually, of course, but it certainly hasn't been on my mind."

"I think I'd be wondering about it every minute of every day. Just, you know, needing to know if it's going to last or not."

"I know what you mean. I do. I'm a list maker. Organization keeps me sane. Not being able to control an outcome? Drives me crazy. But relationships are different. You can't control people. Especially their feelings."

"Then how do you do it?"

"Do what?"

"Just, you know, go all in. *Trust.* Your guy's on the road, surrounded by nymphs." She shrugged. "People are fickle. Their emotions change. You can't really count on anyone. Not really."

"Oh, Violet."

She didn't want to see the pitying expression. "Sorry, that's my foster care background peeking through."

Emmie's hand covered hers. "I wasn't feeling sorry for you. I was moved by your total honesty. Don't you think we all feel that way? We just don't articulate it quite as well." She sat back, gazed out at the ocean. "Of course I felt that way in the beginning with Slater. He'd never had a real relationship before me." She sighed. "Believe me, he was anything but a safe bet. And it did take me a while to find that trust you talk about. How *could* I trust him? Look at him."

They watched the guys wrestling, kicking up sand, laughing. Of course Slater stood out for his powerful build and breathtaking looks, but what Violet noticed about him most was the way he looked at his girlfriend. The way he treated her. Gah. It was just so . . . sexy.

"He's hot all right," Violet said, and Emmie laughed. "And he's got such presence."

"And he's been on the cover of *GQ* and girls push me aside to make a play for him." She looked contemplative. "So how did I know he was completely mine? I don't think there was a particular moment when something clicked, and I realized I could totally trust him. I think it was a decision to let go. To give it—*us*—a chance. And then over time, he just . . . We just worked. It gets stronger." Her features softened into a dreamy expression. "He shows me he loves me every day."

Derek leapt to his feet and grabbed Ben from behind. Force-walking him into the ocean, he got knee-deep before he hurled the drummer into the waves. He went back for Cooper, but when his friend saw his intention, he took off running. Slater blocked him, knocking him on his ass, and together he and Derek carried Cooper deep into the water and dumped him.

"I've never seen Derek like this before," Emmie said.

"Playful?" Her nerves started humming. Is that what she meant?

Or is she talking about me?

"No." She kept watching the guys. "He's never gone all soft for someone before."

Emmie always wore an aura of competence and inner strength, so when she spoke, people listened. Or maybe it was the profound sense of quiet she seemed to have inside her that made her so credible. So when she sat there watching the guys wrestle each other in the sea and said, "He's crazy about you," Violet shuddered.

Because it made her believe. "He's been crazy about a lot of women."

Emmie turned to her, no humor in her eyes. "Stop it."

Violet shot her a look, and Emmie just smiled, pointing at her. "I'm on to you. Look, you know he's had his fun. He's a guy. But, no, he hasn't been crazy for anyone before. Our mom's very . . . businesslike. She gets things done. She didn't give much affection. Or time. And you know about my dad, so you know Derek hasn't gotten anything good from him."

Violet nodded, not wanting to speak for fear of breaking this bubble of intimacy.

"So I don't think Derek expects much. He knows what he wants and he goes after it, but he doesn't expect rewards."

Violet pictured an eager-eyed boy—like so many of the ones she'd lived with and helped raise—wanting to please his parent, craving a simple look or a touch and never getting it. She could feel the pain of Derek's constant rejection from his parents because she'd seen it countless times. "What does that mean?"

"He knows how to take what he wants to make himself happy, but he doesn't expect anyone to mean anything to him, be there for him. *Love* him." She turned to her. "And the women he's hooked up with? It's like an arrangement. He gets what he wants, gives them what they want, and then it's done." She paused. "You've rocked his world."

"I'm just doing my job."

"Really? Is that what he is to you? Because if it is, we should stay somewhere else. There isn't a chance I'm going to let him open up to a woman for the first time only to have her treat him just like our dad."

"Emmie." Slater, knee-deep in the ocean, motioned for her.

She got up. "It's such a beautiful night. I think we'll

take a walk. Which way should we go?" Twilight covered the beach in pretty peaches and pinks.

"If you go that way, towards town, you'll hit the pier. There isn't much there, but if you're lucky, you'll catch Father Sam. He sells the best gelato you've ever had in your life."

"Father Sam?"

"He was a farmer, and when he couldn't farm anymore, he sold the land to a vintner. The new owner let him stay on in a cottage by the ocean. He's a legend around here. Seriously. What a character. After a life of hard work, he wasn't about to sit around or just, you know, visit people. So he started tinkering. Came up with this gelato, and it's actually amazing. He sets up a cart on the pier and hangs out talking to everyone and selling it."

"I love that. You want to come with us?"

She watched Derek come striding up the sand toward her. "Maybe we'll catch up with you."

How many times had she told Derek he was just a job to her? He was guileless and pure-hearted, so every time he bared himself to her, she'd essentially kicked sand into his open wound. As Emmie started to go, Violet couldn't stand it, so she called, "Em? He's more than that to me."

She smiled. "I know. I just wasn't sure if you knew yet."

"Well, I do." She sounded almost bitter. "I just . . . you guys are going back on tour again, and I've got the farm, and I'll have to take another job, so . . ."

"So?"

"So . . ." She gave her an impatient look. *So what can happen between us?*

"Can you imagine if I'd had that attitude with Slater?" She turned to find her man stalking toward her. He'd obviously had enough waiting for his woman. Emmie smiled, the confidence of a woman well loved. She looked back at Violet. "Can you *imagine*?"

Slater came up from behind, wrapping his hands around her waist, palms flattening on her stomach. He nuzzled her. "Walk with me?"

Emmie turned in his arms, wrapped her hands around his neck, and gazed up at him, blazing with affection. "You're the love of my life."

And then Slater-fucking-Vaughn, the rock god with the athlete's body and movie star face, gave a wobbly, vulnerable smile and leaned down to kiss his fiancée, his hands cupping her ass and squeezing.

"She's my sister, asshole," Derek said, coming up to them. "How'd you like it if I got nasty with your sister right in front of you?"

"Good news. I don't have a sister." Slater flashed a smile. "So it's all good."

"I can't believe you're not used to it yet," Violet said. As if the two of them ever kept their hands off each other.

"Guys, want to walk to the pier?" Emmie called to the other two, linking fingers with Slater.

Derek plopped down in the chair next to Violet's, then patted his lap. The others took off down to the shoreline.

"You're wet." But she smiled and climbed onto his lap anyway. "Ew, you're getting *me* wet." She tried to get off him, but he belted his arms around her and held her in place.

"Stay. I need a nurse. I got beat up out there."

"Oh, great, play the pity card with me."

He watched her for a moment, looking thoughtful. "Let's not play games at all."

"Okay," she said softly.

"Let's just be together." His grip tightened on her. "I want you."

Good gracious, when he looked at her like that he set her on fire. He kissed her, one hand gently cupping her jaw.

That mouth, that tongue. He kissed her like he couldn't live without this fusion between their bodies. And when he became needier, when his tongue sought hers and seduced it into an erotic dance, he reached for the back of her head and held her close, kissing her hungrily.

He pulled away, breathing heavily, his forehead pressed to hers. "Let me in, V. All the way in."

She thought about what Emmie had said, about making a choice. A conscious choice to give it a shot. Open her heart and go all in. She'd never done that before, but then she hadn't *felt* anything before. "I'm trying."

"You're so fucking beautiful, V. You've always been

beautiful. You're soft and sweet and strong and wise. But here? In your element? You're sexy and earthy and free. And I want you. I fucking want you all the time."

His erection hardened underneath her. She shifted over it restlessly.

Drawing in a sharp breath, he gazed into her eyes. "I *like* you."

"I like you, too." She did. So much.

"I want you on my lap and in my bed and by my side. I never wanted that before. I just wanted to fuck. But with other women, when they went away, I was . . . relieved. I'd rather hang with my friends than them. With you?" He pulled back, looking a little startled. "I want to be with you more than anyone else."

"I want to be with you, too," she whispered against his mouth.

And then his hand slid into her hair, gripping the back of her neck as he kissed her, and she let herself go completely. She wanted him, oh, how she wanted him. Her hands stroked over his broad shoulders, running down those thickly muscled arms. God, just the feel of his body made her burn for him.

His thumb skimmed her jaw, and oh, God, such tenderness from this big, intense guy made her feel cherished. A hot breeze fluttered over her skin as his mouth devoured hers. She thought she might melt into him.

When his fingers traced her collarbone, then lightly smoothed over the top of her breast, she arched into him. *Oh, yes, please. Touch me there.* She wanted . . . oh, God, she wanted so much. His hands everywhere, his mouth hot and open on her skin, she wanted all his attention and . . . and his *love*. She wanted all of him.

He reached into her bikini top, cupped her breast, and she arched into his hand. More, more, her body screamed for more of him. He cupped her, gently squeezing, like just the feel of her breast in his hand was driving him wild.

"More," she whispered against his mouth.

His other hand reached under her ass, a finger shifting the elastic of her bottom aside and stroking into her. She gasped, clutching her arms around his neck, overwhelmed with the sensual assault.

"Oh, God, Derek." The sound of the waves, the ocean-scented breeze, all dimmed, as her senses split open, sucking him in greedily. She was aware of every part of him, his mouth moving against hers, his finger gently stroking the slick length of her, barely brushing over her clit, and his hand urgently kneading her breast. The way he smelled like sun-warmed skin and a hint of salty ocean. The feel of his hair in her fingers. *Everything.*

She turned in his arms, shifting her legs so she straddled him. He untied her bikini top, tossed it aside, and gently pushed her back on his knees so he could see her. His mouth latched on to her nipple, and gone was the gentle exploration. In its place was pure hunger.

He tugged on her bottoms. She got up, kicking them aside, and got back on his lap. She shoved a hand into the waistband of his gym shorts and reached for him. God, the feel of his hot, hard length had her tightening her grip, sliding up and down to feel him pulse and surge into her hand. And then he tipped her onto her back, pressing his hard body over hers. The heat from the sand warmed right through the terry beach blanket.

His kisses turned wild as he lifted his hips and peeled off his gym shorts. And then he was there, his hard erection pressed to her stomach.

She wanted him inside. "Need you. Now."

He sucked her nipple into his mouth, tongue flicking, pulling hard, driving her wild. And then he lowered between her legs, a hand clamped on each thigh, spreading her open for him. He licked into her, focusing on her clit. She curled her fingers into his hair, her hips rocking, and she sank into the most obscene pleasure she'd ever felt.

When his hands cupped her ass, brought her right to his mouth, she lost her mind. She whispered his name, let it take off on a gust of wind, as she let go and closed her eyes, and gave herself over to him. Heat burned through her, melting her bones, igniting a fierce and wanton ache in her core that spread so wildly it made her body vibrate. His fingers flexed into the flesh of her ass, and he moaned as a hot wave of desire powered through her.

Her body tightened, fingertips and toes tingling, as the roar of her orgasm swept over her, sending her soaring into the twilight.

Before she even caught her breath, he'd reached under her back, cupped her shoulders, and thrust inside her. Oh, God, he just consumed her, the way he pounded into her so ferociously. It was wild and intense, and she'd never felt so connected to anyone or anything on this earth.

And she needed that. God, did she need it.

His hips pitched forward, and the scrape to her clit shocked her, making her cry out. The pleasure was so intense, she planted her feet on the blanket and thrust up into him, holding her hips right there so he could ram over it again and again. And then she was jerking, body twisting to get him deeper. Her second orgasm hit hard. Held her in an unrelenting clench.

Finally, it broke and she settled back down on the blanket. A torrent of emotion flooded her, as Derek's thrusts turned frantic. He'd lost all control, and she'd done that to him. She held on tightly, gave his thrusts right back, until he shouted his release, slamming into her with short, hard jerks.

When he slowed, he tucked into her neck. "Oh, fuck me."

She smoothed her hands on his damp back. He kissed her neck, her jaw, her cheek, her eyelid, her nose, and then her mouth. Plundering kisses that left no question in her mind how he felt about her.

"That was amazing," she said.

"If you call me a sex god, it's not going to go well."

She smiled. "Okay, but you do have some wicked good moves."

He lifted his head to look at her; he wasn't smiling. "I don't want to leave you."

She stiffened. Oh, God, were they planning on leaving already? She hadn't heard a specific date.

He tilted his head back and looked at her. "No, I mean now. I want to stay inside you." Gently, he pulled out of her, and she felt the loss of him right away. He flopped onto his back. "Get dressed in case someone comes by." He reached for her bikini, shook out the sand, and handed it to her.

Not like anyone would wander by this little cove, but she sat up to put the top on. "When do you leave?"

"Irwin doesn't care about the festivals. Too many bands on too many stages, so we won't be missed. He wants us to focus on the big show."

"Madison Square Garden?" He was holding something back, she could tell. She turned to him, caressed his chest. "So when does he want you in the city?"

He looked anxious. "He's got a keyboardist for us. He wants us to start working with him right away."

"Okay. In the city?" She didn't want to press, but he wasn't giving her a straight answer.

His hand covered hers. His other hand went under his head as he gazed at the stars. "Not sure. Irwin doesn't tell us much."

"Do you want him to come out here? Practice with the band in the barn?"

The most beautiful, peaceful smile curled his sensuous lips, and he turned to her, so they were face to face. "Yes. Would that be cool with you?"

She nodded. The idea of him leaving killed her.

"I'll talk to Emmie about it. I can't imagine it'll be a problem."

"You know, there's a great club in Westhampton, about thirty minutes from here. Live music Thursday through Sunday, and since it's right where all the cool kids hang out—East Hampton, Southampton—it's always hopping. You guys can try out your new music . . . and your new keyboardist."

"I like the way you think."

I like the way you look at me. And then she wondered why she hadn't said that out loud. He'd cut himself open for her, and she'd taken all he had to give. She needed to give some of herself back. The words formed on her tongue, but she couldn't let them out.

She thought again about what Emmie had said. How she'd never seen Derek like this before. Emmie would know. And she wanted to deserve this gift—of his passion. He needed someone who could be as open and loving with him as he was with her. God, she would do anything to be that person for him.

Well, it wasn't like she could back away at this point. She was in. For as long as she could have him, she was going to give it a go.

And that tiny ember of hope flared somewhere deep inside her. The social worker had been wrong because look at her now. Feeling so much, experiencing passion. Could passion lead to love? Maybe with the right man . . . Was Derek that man?

Her breathing quickened. She wanted that so much. She wanted *him*.

"What're you thinking about?" He brushed the hair off her face and tucked it behind her ears. "I love when you wear your hair like this. It's so fucking sexy."

She should tell him. Tell him how much she cared for him, what an amazing man he was. And she should tell him what worried her, that she feared she couldn't be the whole woman he so totally deserved.

He needed to hear good things from her—anyone would, but he needed it more, thanks to his dad, thanks to the way she'd kept pushing him away.

But the words got stuck in her throat. And in their place, she said, "Why did you get this one?" Her fingers stroked the tribal tattoo that encircled his bicep.

She was awful for missing an opportunity to return his honesty.

Worse, to miss an opportunity to make them closer. Because not only did she hurt him by withholding, she hurt herself, too. She kept herself from having the closeness with him she so desperately wanted.

He laughed uncomfortably. "I was eighteen. Slater and I decided to form a band. So we got drunk and went to a tattoo parlor. I asked for something *bad ass*."

"Why does that embarrass you?"

"Because I've grown up since then. Ink should mean something."

"What about the others?"

He shrugged, looked away. "I started dating the tattoo artist. She gave me most of them."

She swatted him. "Could you be any more predictable?" She laughed, but her heart squeezed. It was his pattern. That didn't mean what they shared wasn't real. It just meant . . . this is what he did. He hooked up with the women he worked with.

And that just sucked.

And she couldn't help feeling a little relieved she hadn't shared her heart with him.

Just in case.

Derek came out of the bathroom, skin still damp from a shower, and came to a stop when he took in Violet smoothing lotion onto her legs. All that dark hair shimmying with her movements, her sexy curves, Jesus, just the sight of her had his blood heating. When she looked up at him and smiled, he felt a crazy sense of energy shoot through him.

What *was* this? He quickened his steps and covered her body with his. Instead of laughing or pushing him away, she scraped her hands through his wet hair and welcomed his kiss.

"You smell good." He breathed her in, easing her down onto the mattress.

"You smell like me."

"Yeah, should've brought my shampoo in from the bus. Do you mind that it's parked out there?"

"Not at all. It gives us more room, especially if the new guy comes out here."

He shifted off her onto her side. "You need a bigger bed."

"Don't get me started. I have a list a mile long of all the things we need to have done here. If I even think about it, I hyperventilate."

"Speaking of ventilation, how about some air-conditioning?"

"The house is a hundred and fifty years old. You can't imagine what work needs to be done before we get to luxuries like air-conditioning. Besides . . ." She rolled to her side, those pretty fingers tracing the musical notes on his chest. "I like a natural breeze. We've got ocean on both sides of our little peninsula here. If you're very, very quiet, you can hear it."

"That's not what I want to hear."

"What *do* you want to hear?"

He lifted her tank top, exposing her full, round breasts, and then he licked a nipple. She moaned. "I want to hear that." His mouth closed over the hard little bead, and his tongue pulled hard.

"Oh, Derek."

"Definitely that." His finger slid under her thin cotton pajama shorts and into her slick heat. He swirled it around her clit, all the while licking her nipple to the same slow rhythm.

"Derek." She gasped, reaching for his hair, holding him in place. "Oh, God. It's . . . I'm so . . . it's so good."

He worshipped her breast, lavished her clit with attention, until she arched off the mattress. "Oh, my God." Body wracked with shudders, she clutched him tightly.

He waited until she calmed down some, before releasing her breast. "And that? That's what I want to hear most of all."

She stretched languidly. "That never happens to me."

"What doesn't?"

"With you, I just flare up. It's like I'm primed, and then you touch me and I go right up in flames. It's crazy." She sighed. "We're crazy."

"We're perfect."

Her finger traced the tattoo on his forearm. "Derek."

It felt so good, and his dick was so hard, he found it hard to speak. "Yeah."

"I got an email."

"Okay."

"From Buck O'Reilly."

His dick softened. "How'd he get your email address?"

"He didn't. He emailed someone at Amoeba, who forwarded it to me."

"Jerk's using you to get me on his show?"

"He's only got a couple of time slots left, so he was hoping I'd reserve one. He said he doesn't even care if you wind up having to cancel. He just wants to book you while you're in town."

"I'll think about it."

"Just . . . tell me what's stopping you. Instead of showing the world Johnny Depp onstage with you or the band bowling, show them *you*. Your talent. Give them a reason to take you seriously."

He jerked away from her, sat up. "I don't feed that shit to the media to get attention on *me*. I do it for the band. To sell tickets to shows. To sell records."

She sat up with him, all soft and sweet. She had one hand caressing his thigh, the other gripping the hair at the back of his neck. "Okay, but it *is* about you. You've said before it takes the attention off what your dad's saying about you."

"Right, so it doesn't affect the band."

"But you hate that people might believe him. He used to be a strong voice in the music community. What he says has impact. So when he makes disparaging remarks about you, it has to kill you that everyone will believe him. Do *you* believe him?"

"No." He paused. "I don't know."

"Irwin doesn't."

"You don't know what Irwin thinks. No one does."

"Of course we know what he thinks. He wouldn't have signed your band if he thought you were all flash and no substance. The band *is* you and Slater." She kissed right over his heart. "If you're worried people believe your dad, prove him wrong."

He shrugged. What if he couldn't prove them wrong? "I don't have to prove myself to anyone."

"Wouldn't you rather be called a virtuoso than a sex god?"

"Of course." But then she touched his face, made him look at her, and he just crashed. The heavy weight he carried in his chest just crashed. "I'm not a virtuoso. Do you know how rare that is? I might be good, but I'm not that good." *And if I go on the show, everyone will know that.*

"Derek." So much kindness in her voice. Such warmth and sweetness. "You're afraid you're not as good as your dad. You're afraid if you perform a solo gig, the truth will come out." She shifted so that she faced him, on her knees, leaning into him, all that hair brushing over his arms, his chest. "So do it to face that fear. Do it to let your dad go.

What he says, what he thinks, who he is, his talent? It doesn't affect you at all. You're you. And you're great. And by performing on Buck's show, you'll show yourself who *you* are. Not who your dad says you are."

She'd set something off in him. All this anxiety raced in his veins. He got off the bed, snatched his jeans off the back of a chair.

She got up on her knees. "Come back here."

He was breathing too hard, too much energy zinging around in him. He didn't need to prove himself to anyone. He had a career to manage. A record to sell. A band to get to the next level. "I don't have to prove anything. I have shit to do. I have to take care of my band."

But the soft look in Violet's eyes, her soft curves, and all that sexy fucking woman made his anxiety dissolve. She watched him expectantly.

"What?" He found it hard to be irritated with her when she looked at him like that, all soft and caring.

"Come here."

He loved when she got all forceful with him. He smiled, came back to the bed. She draped herself around him.

"I love that about you. That you take your career so seriously. You're a leader, and that's hot. But right now I'm talking about the other side of you. The artist. I'm wondering when you'll let that side shine through."

Her hands caressed his chest in slow sweeps. Her scent, her hair, everything about her surrounded him, invaded him, making him restless and hard.

"Doesn't matter."

"Tell me this then. Is your dad right? Are you more concerned with going gold than creating and playing music?"

What the *hell*? "You think I'm in it to be a rock star?"

"No one agrees with your dad. I'm asking about you. What's more important to *you*, the music or the fame?"

"I want to be good. Really good. Fame *means* I'm good."

"Does it? I can think of plenty of mediocre bands that had a lot of fame. Actors, too. I think you could go platinum a thousand times over and you still wouldn't feel good enough. You could be as famous as Mick Jagger, and you'd still be the little boy whose dad told him he was all flash and no substance."

Well, fuck. Talk about ringing true. That rang like a bell throughout his entire body.

She turned her face into his neck, kissing him lightly. "Derek?"

"Yeah."

"What will make you feel you're good enough?"

"You know the answer to that." He'd never told anyone but her. He cupped the back of her head and kissed her, poured all he felt for her into that kiss. As always, she responded to him—fuck, did she respond to him—and he tipped her back onto the mattress and pinned her down, sliding his tongue into her mouth. He was so fucking hard, he couldn't stand it.

She pulled her mouth away. "The Ledger List?"

He didn't bother answering, just sucked her earlobe into his mouth.

Her body tightened around him, nipples hardening against his chest. "How can you make that list, Derek?"

He blew out a breath of resignation. "You're fucking evil." She'd led him right into the mouth of the lion. She'd known what she was doing all along. "Buck fucking O'Reilly."

He could feel her smile against his cheek. "Then I think you should do it."

He dropped his head to the mattress. "What if I suck?"

"What if you're brilliant?" Her hand slid down his side, pushing between their bodies. He lifted up to give her room, and she grasped his throbbing dick. "Only one way to find out." She fisted him, sliding her hand up and down his shaft. "Hm, let me see." Letting him go, she cupped his balls, gave them a squeeze. "Yep, you've got the balls all right."

SIXTEEN

Violet awakened to pure quiet. A rare sound in her house lately.

No wall of heat against her back, she rolled over, taking in the empty space beside her.

This is what it's going to feel like when he leaves.

She'd never minded it before, of course. She'd always loved waking up to the peace and quiet of her farm. Now, though, she would have something to miss.

And she would. She'd miss him as surely as if she'd carved out a piece of her own heart and handed it to him to go in a doggie bag. Her pulse quickened, and her breathing turned shallow. The impulse to run hit her hard.

That was all she knew, really. Running. From one home to another, never making any attachments. Never even trying. Just knowing any day now, she'd move on.

But this time . . . this time she didn't have to run at all. She could try. Just go for it. Try and see if he meant what he said, if they really did have something special.

She threw back the covers, unable to lie still and worry over something she couldn't control. It wasn't like she could make someone love her, make Derek choose her. Either it worked—and her story ended up like Emmie and

Slater's—or it didn't—and he moved on to the next woman he worked with, breaking her heart.

But it wasn't like she could quit now. She'd gotten in too deeply. So all she could do was try.

At least I have a heart to break. That meant something, right?

After a quick shower, she headed down to the kitchen to find Francesca and Emmie at the table. A platter filled with crumbs, one croissant, and half a muffin sat off to the side. Mugs crowded the counter by the sink.

"Where is everyone?"

Francesca looked up. "Good morning, sleepyhead."

Violet looked to the clock on the stove to see it was nearly ten. "I never sleep this late."

"I'm glad you did. Your friends were up early, taking measurements. This one went around the property with them and made a big list." Francesca nodded to Emmie, giving her a warm smile. "I sent them into Riverhead, to the Home Depot." She looked worried. "I hate taking business away from Sal, but they needed a lot of things, and they don't have time to wait while Sal orders them."

"Wait, I don't understand. Are they building something? It's probably not a good idea because I don't actually own the land yet." A pinch of fear rattled her nerves. But she reminded herself she had a great lawyer and a strong case.

A big smile warmed Francesca's features. "No, honey, they're fixing things."

Violet's gaze shot to the faucet. "Really?" It was no longer dripping.

"The guys are pretty handy," Emmie said.

"Oh, God. The last thing they should do with their time is bother with my house."

"Don't even go there. There're plenty of hours in the day. They'll fix stuff, jam, write songs . . . believe me, I haven't seen them this happy in ages. There's something about this farm."

"I know." *It's magical.*

"Francesca was showing me your products." Emmie lifted the stationery. With wildflower petals, Mimi had made a picture of a svelte woman in a straw hat, carrying a picnic basket across a field and heading toward the beach.

"That's gorgeous." She looked up to Francesca, who beamed a proud smile.

"I love this." Emmie ran a finger over the pulpy paper.

"Isn't it lovely?" Francesca said. "My daughter makes it. I wish she'd do more of it. She'd be in her element out here."

"I think I could be, too," Emmie said. "And the guys? They're writing new material. I know how important this tour is, but I'm telling you, seeing them reconnect like this—to each other, to the creative part of their work—it's unbelievable." She ran a finger around the rim of her mug. "Last night, Jonny and I came back along the road instead of the beach, and we saw a property for sale. We're thinking about buying a house out here."

"Seriously?" Her heart pounded. "What about your place in Austin?"

"Slater only bought the house for the guys to live in while they tried to make a go of the band. Everything's changed now. We're getting married. We'll need our own place, and I'm just really loving it out here."

"You haven't seen winter," Francesca said.

"I'm from White Plains. I know all about winters in the Northeast. I actually like the change of seasons."

"But what about the band? Don't the two of you need to be near them?" Of course, she was only thinking of Derek, who lived in Austin when he wasn't touring or in the studio.

Her smile widened. "Come on, Violet. You know he'd move out here in a heartbeat. He's got no ties to Austin. Besides, Jonny's talking about building a state-of-the-art studio. Wouldn't that be amazing?"

It would. *God, it would.*

Could this be happening? Could she really have Derek Valencia?

"Guys, seriously, dinner's been ready for a while now," Emmie shouted into the barn.

Violet smiled at the way Slater instantly stopped what he was doing. He seemed to know how far he could push his woman, who'd been asking them to come in for at least twenty minutes. They'd been so into their jam they hadn't wanted to stop. But this time, Ben set down his drumsticks and said, "Francesca's making *biscuits*."

Violet got up off the old, dusty hay bales, and Derek held up a finger, asking her to wait. They shut down their amps, put their instruments away, and filed out of the barn.

Once everyone left, Derek dove onto her, tackling her. She laughed, welcoming him in her arms.

"I missed you," he said.

"I've been right here for the last half hour."

"I haven't been alone with you all day." He nuzzled her neck.

She loved the way he kissed her, overwhelming her with all that desire and need. He put his whole self into everything he did, including loving her. And when his hand slid beneath her linen shorts and panties and squeezed her bare ass, she stopped thinking at all.

Her hands glided up his back, curving around his shoulders to draw him more tightly to her. She loved the way he smelled, like fresh air and clean soap. She loved his powerful body, the grip of his hands that claimed her so possessively.

And he kissed like he never wanted to stop. Like kissing her was enough in itself.

Until it no longer was, and his hands jammed under her shirt so roughly, he popped a button off.

"We're not doing this in the barn." Although her body told him something else entirely, as her hands cupped the back of his head.

"I need you." He thrust his hips against her, his very hard erection pressing into her belly.

Desire churned, making her hot and hungry for him. She moaned from the assault of his hands, his deliciously sweeping tongue, and the insistent thrust of his hips. He had her shirt unbuttoned and shoved off her shoulders before she even knew it was happening.

She still had a hope of stopping things—anyone could come into the barn—until he jerked down the cup of her bra and his hot mouth covered her nipple. His tongue licked and swirled and then pulled hard.

"God." Reaching into his shorts, she grasped his hard length. "I want you in my mouth."

"Fuck, yes." He stood up, shucking off his shorts as he held out a hand and pulled her to her feet. "Take off your bra."

She shrugged the shirt off, unhooked the bra, and dropped it. His greedy hands cupped her breasts, sensuously squeezing them. She sank to her knees, licked him from the root to the head before sucking him deep into her mouth. He gasped, his hands threading through her hair, his hips gently rocking.

"Violet." Her name, spoken with such reverence, had never sounded so beautiful before. "Oh, fuck, V." His legs shook as he pumped faster, losing control. Her hands gripped the hard globes of his ass, as she took him even deeper into her mouth. And then he was chanting her name, fisting his hands in her hair, and thrusting hard enough to knock her off balance. But she held on to him, her body hot and restless for him.

"I'm coming. Oh, Jesus, V, I'm coming." He clamped his hands on either side of her head, holding her in place as he pumped in rough, unsteady strokes, releasing himself into her mouth. He moaned in ecstasy as he slowed and pulled out.

And then he dropped to his knees and held her, his face lowering into her hair. "My sweet V."

By the time they came out of the barn, twilight had fallen, so she didn't immediately recognize the figure striding toward them. Derek had his arm around her waist, holding her close, kissing her cheek. "After dinner, let's take a walk on the beach."

He gave her a smile, but it was in that exact moment that the crisp haircut, the light blue button-down, khakis, and boat shoes of the approaching man clicked into recognition. "Randall?"

The lawyer's gaze flitted between her and Derek, settling in a look of shock. "You have a boyfriend?"

She disentangled herself from Derek, thinking about the button missing from her shirt. "No, it's not—"

"No?" Derek snapped.

"No. God. I meant the last time I saw him"—she gestured to Randall—"I didn't have a boyfriend."

Randall's features hardened. "But you do now? You said you weren't looking to get involved with anyone. It's been, what? A few weeks and you're already with someone?" His arms came up in an apologetic gesture. "I'm sorry. I'm sorry. I guess . . . I'm just surprised."

"Who is this guy?" Derek asked.

"Derek Valencia, this is Randall Oppenheimer." She held on to his biceps. "I knew him through my last job."

"That's it? That's all I am?" She'd never seen Randall so worked up. "Some guy you knew through a job?" Beads of perspiration popped on his forehead, and the tendons in his neck strained.

"I can see why it didn't go any further." Derek slung an arm around her shoulder.

Ignoring Derek, he looked to her with a challenging expression. "So, should I call you Violet or Scarlet?" His tone and stance might've been aggressive, but underneath she saw the hurt.

Oh, brother. How did she explain the situation without compromising Joe Capriano? She had no idea. "How did you find out my real name?"

"Funny thing, I wanted to call you, but there wasn't a listing for Scarlet Davis. So I asked Joe."

"He told you?"

"Told me to look for Violet Davis. That's all he said. And I still can't figure out why you were dressed like a hooker the last time I saw you." Under his sarcastic tone she sensed genuine confusion.

Derek stepped in front of her. "I'm going to tell you one time, watch how you talk to her. Understand?"

"Everything okay out here?" Slater came out the back door. Cooper and Ben crowded behind him. All three made their way down the porch steps.

As ridiculous as the whole scene was, Violet could honestly say she'd never felt more protected in her entire life. All these big, badass guys had her back.

And it felt good. So good.

Her hand slid down Derek's arm to clasp his fingers. Really, she wanted to jump into his arms and have him hold her there forever.

"Who are these people?" Randall asked incredulously.

"They're my friends. What're you doing out here? How did you even find me?"

"*Find* you? Are you like a grifter or something? A con artist? Is that why you stood there with absolutely no emotion at your ex-boyfriend's engagement party?"

"Think I told you to watch how you talk to her." Derek came right up to him, his presence forcing Randall to step backward. Within seconds, all the guys stood to one side of him.

Randall just shook his head, letting out an uncomfortable laugh. "Can you get your boys here to back off?"

"You're not exactly making a good impression," she said.

"*I'm* not? I'm sorry, Violet—or is it Scarlet? Am I talking to the polished piece of ass I met on Joe's arm or the hooker in thigh-high boots?"

Derek threw a punch before anyone could stop him. Slater and the guys grabbed his arms and pulled him back before he could swing again.

"Whoa, whoa, dude," Ben said. "Chill out."

Reeling back, Randall straightened, looked at Derek with shock, and then rubbed his jaw, eyes wide. "Are you out of your fucking mind?"

"You called my girl a piece of ass." Derek looked angrier than she'd ever seen him. "Who the fuck do you think you are coming onto Violet's property and talking to her like that? You got something to say, you do it with respect."

"He's right, dude," Cooper said. "Uncool."

"Way uncool," Ben said. And then he jerked his chin toward the road. "That your Ferrari?"

"Ben," Slater said.

"Can we talk privately?" Randall asked her.

"Not a fucking chance," Derek said.

"He's not going to hurt me, Derek. You go in and eat. Let me hear him out, okay?"

Derek clearly didn't like her response. Breathing a little too heavily, he gave Randall a hard look. "You upset her, it won't go well for you."

"Jesus Christ," Randall said. "I can't believe this."

It wasn't like she'd dated him. She didn't owe him anything. Why was he this upset?

Derek got right up in his face. "Are we clear?" He snapped each word out.

Randall rolled his eyes, still rubbing his jaw. When Derek wouldn't back down, he nodded—vaguely.

The guys went back to the house, but while the others went inside, Derek pulled up an old wicker rocking chair on the back porch and sat down, facing them.

"Really? He's going to sit there and listen?"

"Looks like it. Why are you here?"

"Paula Rackson."

Oh, that. "I didn't think you'd find out. It's such a small case, and such a big firm."

"It's my father's firm. Your name came up in the Monday morning partner's meeting."

"I didn't want to go with your firm. Derek's mom gave me Paula's number. I need the help, so I called."

"Everything okay, V?" Francesca came around from the front of the house, wiping her hands on a kitchen towel. She obviously hadn't witnessed the pissing match.

"Francesca, this is Randall Oppenheimer."

Recognition lit her features. "Nice to meet you, Randall." She looked at Violet with a quirk of her brow.

"How do you do, Mrs. . . . Davis?"

"Romano," Violet clarified. "She's Francesca Romano."

He looked between the two then settled his displeased gaze on Violet. "So are you actually a Romano? Is Davis your married name?" He glanced at the porch.

"She's not my mom." He wasn't a bad guy. She decided to give him something. "I met her through a job. In fact, she's the one who got me started in my career."

His eyes narrowed.

"As a *nanny*. I started as a nanny."

"And you became?"

"I'm still in the role of caregiver. Just in a different capacity. There's nothing sexual or illegal about what I do."

His features softened, and she could tell he felt grateful for the truth offering. He seemed to relax.

"Would you like to stay for dinner, Randall?" Francesca called.

"He's not staying," Violet said.

"Okay, well, your dinner's getting cold."

"I'll be right in."

"Nice to meet you, Randall." Francesca went up the back porch stairs and spoke quietly with Derek. Then, hand on the screen door, she glanced at them before heading into the house.

"Why did you come out here?" It wasn't like she'd misled him. She'd never even flirted with him.

"I'm out for the weekend at my parent's place, but I also wanted to tell you that I'm going to take the case. I'll do it gratis, and in return I want the truth about you."

She couldn't help looking at Derek, who watched her carefully. "Why, Randall? We never even dated. Why do you care?"

"For three months I watched you on Joe's arm. You were . . . I swear, I just . . . you were perfect for me. All polished and reserved, yet incredibly sexy. Damn, I wanted you. But then I saw you one day in Chelsea Market. You didn't see me, but *fuck*, Scarlet—I mean, Violet. Sorry, Violet. Your hair was down, all straight and shiny. And you wore this . . . dress." He gestured to her chest, looking like he didn't have the words to describe what he'd seen. "Even before I realized it was you, I went all crazy inside. And then when I saw you at Joe's engagement party, and you were available, I thought, *Finally*. Here's my chance with her." He tipped his head back, running his hands through his hair. "And now you're with someone else? How did that happen?"

"I don't really know."

"Look at you." He shook his head, taking her in. "I come out here, and you're a whole different person. All relaxed and sexy. *This* woman is fucking hot."

Self-consciously, she touched her hair. Oh, God. She pulled a piece of hay out, discreetly dropping it to the ground. "I just . . ." She just what? Rolled around in the hay with Derek Valencia, bassist for Blue Fire? It sounded unreal just thinking it.

"No, you look amazing. Look at you. I've never seen

your hair like that, all wild and sexy. Even without makeup, you're a knockout. You look . . . you look gorgeous." He stepped closer to her. "Who are you?"

"I'm sorry, Randall. I'm with Derek now."

He let out a breath, gazing down at the ground. "Yeah." He looked up. "I'm still going to help you out with this case. And I won't charge you."

"But?"

"I'm not going to force you, but I hope you'll come to know me better and see I'm probably a hell of a lot better for you than that guy."

She looked at Derek, wound so tightly on that wicker chair, watching like a tiger waiting to spring.

In the long run, Randall probably was better for her, but what could she do when her body and soul cried out for Derek Valencia?

"Can we go somewhere?" he asked.

She gave him a doubtful look.

"Get a coffee?" His eyebrows rose. "To talk about the case, that's it."

"Sure. Let me just tell them where I'm going." She started off, but Randall reached for her.

Derek launched out of the chair.

She pushed him back. "Randall, give me a second to tell him where I'm going, okay? I'll meet you at the car."

She turned back to find Derek leaping off the porch railing. Call her a silly girl, but she couldn't deny loving his caveman ways.

And it wasn't lost on her that she maybe even needed it.

"That lick's insane."

Derek's fingers froze on his bass. He'd thought he was alone in the barn. When had Slater come in?

Pulling his worn notebook out of his back pocket, his friend sat down beside him. "Check it out." And then he began singing, using the backbeat Derek had just laid down.

It's the clatter of silverware on the table
It's the hum of quiet conversation

It's your sudden burst of laughter
That tells me I've come home

It's my laundry piled with yours
And your lipstick sitting beside my razor
Our shoes kicked off beside the door
Makes me feel like I'm home

Derek started playing again, and Slater reached for his
guitar, pulled it out of the case, and joined right in.

Sometimes at night
I hear you breathe
Your body pressed into mine
Restless, like you can't get close enough

You turn in my arms
Your hands on my skin
You whisper my name
And that's it, I get it

It's your blue sweater tossed on the couch
It's the hint of your perfume left on my pillow
It's waking up, your legs tangled with mine
Makes me know I'm home

Sometimes at night
I hear you breathe
Your body pressed into mine
Restless, like you can't get close enough

You turn in my arms
Your hands on my skin
You whisper my name
And that's it, I get it
I'm home

Derek rested his bass on his thighs, took in the expression on his friend's face, and just lowered his head. Emotion swamped him.

All his fucking life, he'd been on the run. His home life had sucked—his mom always working and his dad constantly pushing him away. The moment he could bail, he'd hit the road, heading for Texas not even a week after he'd graduated high school. Gig after gig after gig. Chick after chick after chick. He'd just barreled through life. Chasing one thing he thought he wanted after another. Just this bullet train to . . . where? Where did it end up?

Once he went platinum, once he became a household name . . . then what? What would come next? He'd never thought about it because he'd just been barreling along, the world around him a damn blur.

But he'd slammed hard into Violet Davis.

So fucking hard.

And everything felt different. Smelled different. Looked different. Everything *was* different.

Because he loved her.

He fucking loved her. And he couldn't imagine his life without her.

Violet was his home.

"I think we've got a song." Slater put his guitar away, shoved the notebook into his back pocket.

But Violet didn't want his life. The endless hours in the studio, doing press, months on the road. She wanted a quiet life on this little piece of land on the tip of Long Island.

She deserved the home and stability she'd never had. And he couldn't give that to her.

But Ferrari man could.

As they headed out of the barn, Slater locked up, and Derek's gaze lifted to the light on the second floor.

Violet. In the bathroom, getting ready for bed.

"You worried about the douche?"

"If Violet had wanted to date him, she would've dated him." Would that be true after he headed back on the road? When he wasn't physically in her life anymore?

"You're worried about the douche."

"Well, yeah. I mean, she's never had a home. Never had a family. She needs stability. *He* can give her that. What can I give her?"

"You're shitting me right now. You *have* to be shitting me." He tipped his head back. "Do I have to tell you what you give her that the douche can't?"

He didn't want to be a pussy. But if he had to be one, at least he could be one around Slater. "Yeah."

"Violet doesn't give a rat's ass about a Ferrari or a fancy law firm. She doesn't want to *summer* in some gated mansion in East Hampton. Stability doesn't mean a guy who can buy her shit and give her a couple of kids. Stability means the one guy who loves the shit out of her. It means knowing you've got the one person in the world who knows your crap, calls you on it, and still wakes up with you the next morning, every fuckin' morning, until the day you die." He pushed his shoulder. "You think you can do that?"

His gaze sought the light, watched her form move around, and his whole body answered in a rush of energy. "Fuck, yeah."

"Good. Because we're probably going to be neighbors."

Derek didn't understand.

Slater smiled. "Em wants to buy a place out here. She definitely wants to get married here."

She does? Why did that excite the hell out of him? "It is pretty cool."

"When was the last time we wrote material like this? For me, it's been a solid year. I don't know. The ocean, the land, the quiet. It clears the head. I can't get the lyrics down fast enough." He looked to the vast fields, covered in darkness. "I like it out here."

"V thinks we should play at a club in town."

"Try out our new shit?"

Derek nodded. "When the new guy gets here."

Slater nodded. "I'm down."

"Think we should invite Irwin?"

"Fuck, yeah. Our new stuff's the shit. Now *this* is why he signed us. Let's get this done."

Could he have it, though? Violet as his home? Because she sure as hell thought she couldn't have him. And he had no idea how to get her to see the obvious.

She already did.

SEVENTEEN

Moonlight shone through the lacy curtains, casting eerie shadows around the high-ceilinged living room. The blue velvet couch smelled a little moldy, and a spring dug into his back.

Derek wanted to be in her bed, his body wrapped up with hers, but he couldn't sleep. And he didn't want to keep her up with his restlessness.

Irwin had a keyboardist for them. They'd be back on tour in a few days.

Which was great—he'd still be on track to go gold by the end of summer. But what would happen with Violet?

Slater was fucking with his head, making him believe in things he might not be able to have. He made it sound so simple. You want her, you go get her.

But it didn't work like that. *Violet* didn't work like that. He didn't doubt she was the one for him. He didn't even doubt her feelings. She showed them to him every time she took him into her arms. She loved him so fucking hard. Let him in completely.

Physically.

Emotionally, that was a whole different story. To gain

her trust, dismantle her strange beliefs, he needed time. He needed a hell of a lot longer than a few days.

Not like he'd give up. But come on, the minute he got back on the road, Ferrari man would be "working" with her, trying to win her. How appealing would frat boy become when Derek was on the road and the press had shots of him half-naked with nymphs crawling all over him? They could turn any situation into a photo opportunity that made him look like he was fucking around.

A door creaked open. Awareness shot through him. Violet? Floorboards groaned. And then footfalls on the stairs.

Her bare, beautiful legs appeared, then the sexy swell of her hips in her little sleep shorts, her breasts bouncing in a tight white tank top. And then that spill of wavy dark hair. Their gazes caught, and sensation exploded deep inside him. His body hummed with her approach.

She didn't even hesitate, just settled on his lap, hands in his hair, mouth at his ear. "You didn't come to bed."

Her scent washed over him. He breathed her in, his arms going around her waist, his hands seeking the curve of her ass.

Christ, he was done for. "Couldn't sleep."

She touched him so gently, so soothingly, he couldn't contain all this want. So he gently sank his teeth into the tendon at her neck, arms tightening around her.

She clutched him. "I don't like sleeping without you."

He tipped his forehead against her collarbone. "Needed some space."

"No."

He pulled back, smiling at her. "No?"

"No space. Talk to me."

He let out a frustrated breath. "I'm falling so fucking hard for you."

Her fingers scraped through his hair, but she didn't say anything.

Fuck it. He was just gonna say it. "Ferrari man."

"Derek. We went for *coffee.* To talk about the case."

"He wants you."

"He doesn't even know me—he saw me as a socialite and a groupie in one night. I'm a mystery."

"I saw him. He *wants* you." Which wasn't even the point. All he really wanted to know was how much she wanted *him*. Enough to stick with him after he left?

"Okay, but I don't want him."

"Will you want him when I'm back on the road? In the studio for months at a time?"

She stilled. "What're you saying? God, Derek, I've gone twenty-five years without a serious boyfriend. Suddenly, I'm the type who'll go for a guy because he drives a nice car? Has a good job? I'll be with someone I don't have feelings for? I've done a damn good job of taking care of myself my entire life, but all of a sudden I need a *guy* to do it? Is that what you mean? I don't understand."

"Well, when you put it like that . . ." He smiled. "Okay, so I'm being an asshole." Tilting his head back till it hit the cushion, he closed his eyes. "This shit's new to me, too."

She leaned closer, stroking his hair. "I've never gotten this close to anyone else. Which is pretty amazing, considering we've only known each other five weeks."

He shifted lower on the couch, cradled her in his arms. Her hands played with the hair at the back of his neck, and she felt so good he wanted to stay in this moonlit room with her for-fucking-ever.

He slid a hand under the stretchy fabric of her tank, up all that soft, warm skin, and then he cupped her plump breast, giving it a gentle squeeze, and her eyelids fluttered closed. She sighed so sweetly, arching into his touch.

"You're so beautiful, V. Come on tour with me."

Her eyes opened. He could see her effort to concentrate as he caressed her breast, cupping the weight of it, enjoying the velvety skin, its heavy fullness.

"As your minder or your lover?" Eyes drowsy with lust, she shifted on him.

And there she went, dousing all his desire. "Both, either, I don't care. I just want you with me."

"You don't want to think about it, but *I* have to. If I'm your minder, we can't be lovers. It won't work. And I won't deceive Irwin." She squirmed on his lap, her fingers fisting in his T-shirt. "And I can't just be your *lover*. I can't give up my whole life to follow you on tour. I have bills to pay."

His fingers reached to her other nipple. She gasped as his hand scraped over both of them. Her thighs squeezed together. He knew exactly what she'd feel like between her legs when he did that, her honey flowing over his fingers.

"Derek." He fucking loved when she sounded needy like that. It made him wild.

But seriously, what the fuck were they doing? She wouldn't go on the road with him, so what did they have? A few more days together?

She had the power to crush him.

He pulled his hand out from her shirt. "You should go to bed, babe."

Her eyes narrowed, and she sat up, looking fierce.

He knew immediately what he'd done. He hadn't meant to fall back into that cavalier role she hated so much. But yeah, he had.

"Babe?"

He laughed, loving the way she got all fired up. "Okay, okay. I'm sorry. I'm a pissy little bitch." His hips thrust up, his erection grinding on her. "I'm so fucking frustrated." He drew her to him, found her mouth, both hands shoving under the elastic waistband of her shorts and gripping her ass.

Those gorgeous breasts pressed against his chest, her arms wound around his neck, and she rocked her hips over his aching dick.

"Oh, dammit, V. I want you so much. So fucking much."

Her mouth shut him up, her tongue seeking his. One hand found her breast again, and he squeezed, tweaking her nipple; the other slid deeper between her legs, found her drenched.

The fuck was he supposed to do when he had this woman in his arms, wanting him as badly as he wanted her? They couldn't be pen pals, for Christ's sake. Her breath in his ear, her hands in his hair, and her hips rocking with the rhythm of his fingers, made him wild with need.

He found her mouth, needing to connect with her, feel her everywhere around him. Stroking her clit, he felt her buck against him, heard her strangled cries, and he wanted in. Had to have her.

He reached to pull off her tank, but she clamped her elbows to her side.

"Someone might come downstairs."

"Every door, floorboard, and step in this house creaks. We'll hear them a mile away. I've got you. Believe me, I'm not sharing you with anybody."

Her arms relaxed, and she helped him pull off her top. Holy mother of God, she was so beautiful. He cupped both breasts, pushed them together, and sucked a nipple into his mouth. She thrust her chest out, hair spilling onto his thighs.

"Derek. Oh, my God."

And then she tipped forward, her hand reaching into his gym shorts. "Mine."

"Fuck, yes." He urged her up, so she got up on her knees, and he yanked down his shorts. "You own me, sweet V."

The moment his ass hit the cushion, her hand closed around him, stroked him firmly. She touched him like she loved his cock, and that drove him out of his mind. And then she guided him inside her. Slowly, with the slightest undulation of her hips, she sank down on him.

His eyes rolled back in his head as her slick heat fisted him. Nothing had ever felt as good as her body surrounding him.

Reaching for the wooden frame of the couch behind his head, she started riding him, hard and fast. Her silky hair slid over his cheeks, her breasts bounced between them, brushing his chin, and her tight sheath clamped around him, sensation spreading hot and thick through his body.

"Violet," he whispered, completely lost in her. Everything about her. It was all too much. He couldn't . . . oh, fuck, he wasn't going to last. "Fuck, baby, I'm gonna come." He reached between them, found her clit, and started rubbing her sweetness all over it.

She cried out, riding him even faster, her breath at his ear, urgent as she tried to quiet herself. And then she tightened around him, tucking into his neck and gasping his name.

He tumbled her back on the couch, a hand sliding under her ass, tilting her as he drove into her. He wanted her, only her. Desire burned in him, a reckless, frantic need for more. It wasn't enough. It was never fucking enough. He wanted her all the time, all the way.

"Sweet V, turn over. I gotta . . . oh, fuck, I gotta have you harder."

He pulled out, watching as she flipped onto her stomach, pushing her ass up in the air for him, and he gripped her hips, sliding deep. He watched her fingers curl into the throw pillow, drag it under her face. Watched her beautiful features turn crazy with lust, as her whimpers turned into cries, muted by the fabric.

He couldn't stop his brutal hammering. He just wanted in, all the way in, he wanted her so desperately. "Violet, fuck. Oh, fuck." The tingling in his spine burst into a fireball that streaked all the way up to his scalp as he exploded inside her.

Jesus, *fuck*, stars burst behind his eyes as his orgasm seized him so tightly he couldn't even catch his breath. Finally, he collapsed on top of her, rolling onto her side, both arms wrapping around her.

"I love you." He just lay there, panting, not even believing he'd said the words out loud.

Shit. He had no idea how she'd react, but her arm pushed out from between them, her fingers reaching for his cheek, stroking. "Derek," she whispered.

But she didn't say it with love. She said it with fear. Her touch was tentative, her muscles tense. As the silence grew, expanded, and took form between them, she pulled her arm back. And, Jesus Christ, she looked like she wanted to run, be anywhere but near him.

Well, fuck him. His skin chilled as he watched her wrestle the emotion right off her face.

Finally, she got up and gathered her clothes. Once dressed, she stood there awkwardly, uncomfortably. "You coming to bed?"

So that was it? That was her response to his fucking confession of love? He'd never said those words to anyone in his life. He loved his mom, he loved Emmie. But romantic love? *Fuck.* "New guy's coming. I feel like shit about Pete. I'm just . . . you know. I'll be up later."

He watched her walk away, and with each step the voice in his head grew louder to stop her. Half of him wanted to shake her, rattle some sense into her—he knew she had feelings for him; big fucking feelings—but the other half . . . Jesus, the other half felt her struggle as if it were his own. He knew she needed time. He couldn't force her, but dammit he wanted her to break through and just fucking love him back.

When she stopped at the foot of the stairs, reaching for the banister, his heart jumped into his throat. She turned to him, her vulnerability gutting him. Because he knew how hard it was for her to open up to him.

"I've never loved anybody before."

Fuck, he'd never heard that voice, all shaky and raw.

"And nobody's ever loved me. My grandma might have, but I don't remember. I remember the flowers in her backyard. I remember the books. I remember her tired feet. But I don't recall her saying, I love you. So I . . ." Her fingers caressed the wood. "I guess I'm not all that good at it."

She waited—gave him a moment to get off his ass and come get her. His heart pounded so hard it hurt.

She gave him a moment, but when he still didn't move, she turned and continued up the stairs.

He lasted all of twenty minutes. After staring at the old man's worn-out furniture, still too agitated to sleep, he got his ass up, snatched his gym shorts off the floor, tugged them on, and headed up the stairs.

Closing the door behind him, he pulled down his shorts, kicked them off, then climbed under the covers next to his girl. The minute he hit the sheets, she turned to him, arms opening, welcoming. He came up hard against her, cupping her chin and bringing her mouth to his. He poured all the passion he felt for her into that kiss. Maybe she couldn't say it, but he sure as hell could. "I love you."

She didn't say anything. Not a word.

And the funny thing? This time he didn't need her to.

She'd hurt him. *Oh, God.* Violet thunked her head on the table. This amazing, sexy, powerful, wonderful man had declared his love for her, and she hadn't said a thing. And then when she'd woken up that morning, she'd found him already gone. So, she hadn't even had a chance to talk to him.

Not that she knew what to say.

God, she couldn't get the look on his face out of her mind. She'd *hurt* him.

"They fixed the bathtub." Francesca came into the kitchen in a robe, her hair wrapped in a towel turban. "I just had a cool bath, and I feel so refreshed."

Violet's head popped up. "That's good."

Her bathtub, her kitchen sink, a part of the porch that had collapsed . . . Violet couldn't believe the work the guys had done in the couple of days since they'd gotten it into their heads to fix her house.

"The heat *is* awful," Emmie said, coming in from the covered porch with a laptop. "But you're lucky because you've got breezes going through the house all the time. Or maybe it's the trees shading it. I don't know, but it's cooler in the house, for sure."

Francesca pulled a mug down from the cabinet and poured herself some coffee, then joined them at the table.

"You smell like roses." Emmie looked up from the list she was making.

"Rose petals." Francesca closed her eyes, breathed in. "Isn't it divine?"

"It is."

"You know, I grew up with and married unimaginable wealth." Francesca stirred cream and sugar in her coffee. "But I never knew beauty until I moved out here. Creating our products, living on this spectacular piece of land . . ." She closed her eyes and sighed. "Heaven."

In spite of the early morning heat, Violet cupped her hands around the mug. She needed to fix this—but what could she do? He didn't want an apology from her—that would make it worse. She couldn't say the words back— she just couldn't, not yet. She needed time. But that was the whole point. He was *leaving*. They didn't have time

But damn him, he just kept pushing. She couldn't move this quickly. No, she'd never felt like this before, but *love*?

"Shame you all have to leave." Francesca tipped her head forward, unwrapping the towel from her head. Her dark hair tumbled down. She sat up and ran her fingers through it. "I've so enjoyed having you all out here. And not just for the bits of home improvement that've made our lives so much easier."

Violet remembered a time the woman wouldn't even let her husband see her without makeup and hair done.

Emmie gave a shy smile. "I have a big favor to ask you. I know it's short notice, and I know you don't know where you'll be in a month, but Jonny and I have our hearts set on getting married out here."

Hope jolted Violet's heart. "Really?" They'd be back. Derek would be back.

"We're interested in a property down the road, but since we haven't even put a bid on it yet, do you think . . . well, what would you say if we wanted to get married here? On Four O'Clock Farm?"

Francesca's face lit up, and Violet smiled. "We'd love it. We'd absolutely love it." But then just as quickly, reality shot through. *It's not mine.* "I mean, of course, I don't own it yet," she said in an altogether different voice. "And I'm not sure what will happen with the property."

Francesca neatly folded her damp towel. "Nothing will happen in a month. Right now it's up to Mr. Walker's children to prove the contract was forced on a man with dementia. That won't happen, but even so, the whole process will take longer than a month."

"I'll most likely be on a job," Violet began.

"But I'll be here," Francesca said. "And Violet will come home for the wedding."

"Of course." Thinking about the future scared the bejesus out of her. Would she still be with Derek?

"It's not too much trouble?"

"Trouble?" Francesca said. "Are you serious? Nothing would make me happier."

"We'd love to have you get married here," Violet said.

She reached for Emmie's hand, but Emmie lunged forward, sweeping her into her arms. "Thank you. Thank you so much."

An engine sputtered, then roared to life. All three women turned to look out the windows. The tractor came rumbling out of the shed, followed by Slater, Cooper, and Ben, all jumping around it like little boys, shouting and red-faced.

The engine shut off, Derek jumped to the ground, and the guys came running into the house. Suddenly, the quiet kitchen exploded with noise and vitality.

"They found the shed," Francesca called over her shoulder on her way out of the room.

"Got the tractor running, I see." Violet ran her gaze over Derek's grease-stained shorts and T-shirt.

He scooped her off the floor, set her on the counter. "Why didn't you tell us?"

She smiled. "Tell you what?" She searched his eyes for hurt but didn't see it.

"You gave us a *football*, V." Cooper scowled. "A fuckin' football. When you've got a whole shed full of shit."

"That stuff hasn't worked in years." Violet bit back her smile.

"Surfboard works," Ben said. "And I'm gonna use it."

"You found a surfboard?" Emmie asked.

"Couple of them." Slater stood behind her, lifting the hair off her neck and placing a kiss on her shoulder. "We hit the mother lode."

"ATVs, dirt bikes," Derek said. "Surfboards, bikes . . ." He shook his head, like he couldn't believe the treasure trove she'd kept hidden from him.

"That place is filled with fun stuff." Cooper grabbed a soda from the fridge. "I'm changing. Let's hit the waves."

"You don't know how to surf," Ben said.

"So? How hard can it be to learn?" Cooper turned to Violet. "Waves are for shit on that side, but what about the other side?"

"Oh, that's just a bay. The Peconic Bay. If you want waves, you have to go to the other fork."

"You don't have time for that," Emmie said.

"Fine, then I'm taking the dirt bike out."

"Got to get it running first." Derek's thumbs stroked her thighs.

He was okay. They were okay.

"You guys," Emmie said. "You've got a show tonight. The new guy'll be here in a couple of hours to go over the set. No one's getting the dirt bike running or learning how to surf."

"How 'bout we come back out here after the tour ends?" Derek asked them, keeping his gaze on her.

"I would love that." Emmie gave Slater a knowing look. "Especially since we have a wedding to plan."

Derek leaned in close. "See?" He kissed her on the mouth. "We can do this."

She cupped his cheeks, kissed his mouth. His generosity in loving her even when she couldn't say it back filled her with more hope than her body could stand.

When the song came to an end, the audience went wild. Violet, seated at a small table near the stage with Emmie and Francesca, couldn't take her eyes off Derek.

Even onstage, he led the band. It was a fascinating dynamic, the way the guys constantly shot him looks, and he responded with a nod or a slight shake of his head. Or he'd tap his foot, everyone watching to sync to the beat.

And the new material? It was sensational.

Slater lifted his shirt to wipe the perspiration off his brow. The girls went wild.

"Oh, my God, Slater-fucking-Vaughn," a girl shouted. "I want some of that."

"You are so fucking hot," another one shouted.

Catcalls went up, and the place exploded in laughter and shout-outs.

Emmie watched calmly. She didn't get possessive, didn't seem to need to let the crowd know Slater was hers. She just seemed to enjoy it all.

"We gonna play or what?" Derek asked, and the crowd finally quieted to hear the exchange.

Clutching his mic, Slater came to the front of the stage. "Hang on a sec. Wanna share my good news." He crouched, mic in his hand. "So you all know about my girl, right?"

The intensity pouring off him kept the crowd quiet, riveted.

"Yeah, so I did something a few days ago." He unleashed his devastating smile. "Haven't told anybody about it. Wanted to make sure my friends and family heard first. We're all friends here, right?"

The crowd burst into shouts, claps, and whistles.

"And friends keep secrets, so I know I can trust you with mine." He looked to Emmie, eyes blazing with love. "I convinced my girl to marry me."

"Noooooo," someone cried in a keening voice.

Raucous laughter filled the club, until some of the fans shushed and begged him to go on.

"Still gotta put a ring on her finger, but she said yes. My girl said yes."

This time the crowd exploded with clapping and good wishes. Violet couldn't keep the smile off her face.

"Yeah, so you know how I work shit out through my songs, right? So when my girl said yes, I had to write about it." He trained all that energy and love on Emmie, who literally squirmed in her seat. "This one's for you, angel."

Slater stood up, turned to Derek, and murmured something.

The ballad began with this achingly sweet melody, with Slater giving Emmie a look so filled with love every woman in that room had to feel it, long for it, and realize in that moment nothing but that kind of love would ever do.

Which made Violet look at Derek, because, God, she wanted him to look at her like that.

And he was. He *was*. Her heart thundered, and her blood pounded.

> *Sometimes at night*
> *I hear you breathe*
> *Your body pressed into mine*
> *Restless, like you can't get close enough*

She felt pinned in place. Couldn't move a single muscle. Slater might've been singing, but she felt those words in Derek's eyes.

> *You turn in my arms*
> *Your hands on my skin*
> *You whisper my name*
> *And that's it, I get it*

"Don't you dare let your fears hold you back." Francesca wrapped an arm around her.

Easier said than done. Violet leaned against her, unable to think, unable to take a full breath. "He's leaving." She didn't even know if Francesca heard her.

"The strong walk right through fear to get to the other side, where fools turn and walk away." Francesca gave her a hard look. "Don't be a fool."

I'm home

With the last note, Ben tossed his drumsticks, Derek lifted his guitar over his head and hefted it twice. The crowd roared, girls screamed, and boots stomped.

And then, "More, more, more, more." The chant was deafening.

Francesca pushed her gently away. "Go get him."

That was all the prodding she needed. She took off through the crowd, heading backstage.

So many people surrounded the guys, they got swallowed up. But Derek and Slater towered over everyone. Her guy saw her and pushed his way through, grabbed her, and lifted her off the ground.

She scraped the damp hair off his face. "They loved you."

"I don't care about them."

"You were amazing. The new songs are unbelievable."

He kissed her, carrying her down a dark hall. At the end, under a bright red exit sign, he pressed her to the wall and kissed her like he hadn't tasted her in years. Like he was starved for her. He slammed his hips up into her as his fingers dug into her ass.

"Come with me."

She knew he meant on tour, but she couldn't talk about it just then. Wouldn't ruin his night. So she stroked his hair, giving him her mouth and rocking her hips into his thick hard-on.

"I'm serious, V. Don't let it end. Come on tour with me." He growled deep in his throat and licked into her mouth.

"Dude, hey, asshole, get back out here," Ben said. "Irwin wants to talk to us."

Derek pulled away, not looking at his bandmate. Slowly, he set Violet down, never taking his arms from around her. His hand slid down her back, squeezing her ass through the thin cotton of her dress. Then, he inhaled, took her hand, and led them back to the club.

The guys stood around Irwin Ledger, with his black jeans, black T-shirt, black boots, and a thick head of salt and pepper hair. Handsome and lean, he had an aura about him. Something that kept people away. Not the arrogance of a movie star, but the intense concentration of a guy with extremely important things on his mind that no one dared interrupt.

Francesca came up to the group, handed her a pink drink with a bright red cherry in it.

Irwin's gaze shifted to Derek, coasted over Violet, and then slammed to a screeching halt on Francesca. His jaw slackened, his eyes glazed, and he lowered the hand that held his beer bottle.

Cupping her elbow, Derek introduced Violet. "Irwin, you remember Violet Davis?"

"Of course. Lovely to see you, Violet." The man swallowed, looking like a lost little boy, as he stared at Francesca.

"I'll meet you back at the house," Francesca said quietly.

"Irwin." Irwin stepped forward, into the heart of the group, holding his hand out to Francesca. "Irwin Ledger."

"Francesca Romano. So nice to meet you." Francesca had no idea who Irwin was—nor would she care. She offered her hand, and Irwin took it as though it were a precious artifact.

And then he looked down at their joined hands with a baffled expression. A moment later his features split wide open in a brilliant, unfettered smile. "Hello."

Emmie's eyebrows shot up to her hairline. Slater stared in amusement.

"I'll leave you to your business," Francesca said to the group.

"No," Irwin said.

Francesca stiffened. "Excuse me?"

"Right, business. A moment, please." He turned to the guys. "Sensational music. Haven't heard anything like it since the Smiths. Finish up this tour, take some time to pull together a record's worth of songs, and then you're going right back into the studio."

"Sounds good," Derek said.

Irwin motioned to the new keyboard player, a lanky fellow with long, stringy hair. Since he'd arrived at the farm that afternoon, he hadn't stopped fidgeting. Even then, in front of Irwin and his new band, his gaze ricocheted around the club. "Paul. Excellent performance. Thank you for coming out here tonight. Unfortunately, it's not a good fit for us, but Emmie will be sure to compensate you for your time."

The guy's jaw dropped, his features turned crimson. Agitation morphed into aggression. "What the fuck? I thought I got the gig."

Irwin shot Emmie a look. Some kind of silent communication went on that had Emmie looping her arm with Paul's and leading him away from the group.

He turned to Derek. "I've got just the guy for you. I can have him out in the next day or so to prepare for Madison Square Garden." And then he pressed his lips together, brow furrowing. "How's Pete?"

"He's okay," Derek said. "Getting the help he needs."

"Good, excellent." Irwin looked between Derek and Slater. "So, business done?"

Derek nodded. Slater seemed more focused on watching Emmie talk to the agitated keyboard player.

Irwin's demeanor changed, calmed, as he turned back to Francesca. "Sit with me?"

She seemed surprised. Knowing her friend had endured a twenty-year marriage to a business-obsessed husband, Violet suspected Francesca would hesitate to spend time with a commanding presence like Irwin.

"Don't be a fool," Violet said in her friend's ear.

Francesca gave her an indulgent smile. And then gave Irwin a nod. "Sure."

The moment Irwin left, the crowd swooped in, surrounding them, jockeying for attention.

But instead of indulging their fans as they usually did, the guys pulled in tighter. No one looked particularly happy.

"What the fuck just happened?" Cooper said.

"He hires a dude for the keys and fires him two seconds after the show?" Ben said.

"The guy was great." Cooper looked confused. "Irwin's a fucking scary dude, the way he makes decisions like that."

"Paul was high," Violet said.

"No, he wasn't," Ben said, surprised.

"He was?" Derek asked her.

"Slater-fucking-Vaughn, can I get your autograph?" A girl rammed herself into the band's circle.

"Give us a moment, okay?" Slater said, in his charming, sexy voice. And then he turned his back on her, effectively pushing her out.

"He couldn't concentrate on the conversation," Violet said. "And his pupils were dilated."

"His hands were shaking," Slater said.

"Bloodshot eyes," Ben said.

Violet just nodded.

"Too bad," Cooper said. "The guy was good. Hey, but Irwin likes the new stuff."

"It's fucking awesome," Ben said.

"Sorry Pete isn't here," Derek said.

The guys shared a quiet, somber moment.

"Derek, my man." Everyone turned to see Buck O'Reilly. "Great show. Fuckin' *unbelievable* show."

Buck popped the barrier, and all the fans rushed in, asking for autographs, touching the guys. It was mayhem, and Violet wanted out.

Until she heard Buck ask, "You ready to come on my show?"

Way to ruin his night. She stepped forward, ready to distract Buck, when Derek said, "You bet."

Buck's jaw dropped. "You serious, man?"

"Absolutely."

"Fuck. Really? That's awesome. When do you get into town?"

"Derek Valencia, oh, my God, will you sign me?" A buxom girl thrust a Sharpie in his hand and lifted her shredded tank top.

Derek gently lowered the girl's top. "Do you have a napkin or something?"

A trio of women slammed into Violet, knocking her off balance, but strong hands gripped her waist. She swung around to find Randall.

"Hey." He smiled warmly.

"Oh, hey." She righted herself, stepping away from Derek. "What're you doing here?"

"Heard about the show. I'm in town through the weekend."

She nodded. Just seeing him brought up all her anxiety about the farm. "Do you have any news?"

"I do. Do you want to go somewhere?"

God, yes. "Is it good?"

He shrugged. "At this stage, no news matters all that much. It'll come down to the judge who hears the case."

"I can't lose this farm, Randall."

"I know that." He touched her arm. "I know."

"It would kill me."

"Slater," a girl shrieked, throwing herself at him.

"Let's go somewhere quieter," Randall said.

Violet wanted nothing more than to get out of there, but she couldn't go without telling Derek. "Hang on. Let me just tell them."

She tried to press forward, but a girl elbowed her in the stomach and said, "Watch it, bitch."

The press of bodies, the noise level, all started to weigh on her. Dozens of girls surrounded Derek, hopping like Chihuahuas to get his attention. He wouldn't even notice if she left.

She pulled out her phone. Heading home. Leaving truck keys with Emmie.

Then she smiled at Randall, who cupped her elbow and led her out of the chaos.

EIGHTEEN

Derek had lost sight of Violet a while ago. Handing the pen back to a woman who had to be in her forties, he wended his way out of the pack and climbed a few steps toward the stage, looking for his girl. He saw Irwin and Francesca leaning toward each other over a small table, a single candle glowing between them. He saw his sister on Slater's lap in a corner of the club, talking to a couple of people. But he didn't see Violet.

Pulling out his phone, he found she'd sent a text. *Damn*. She'd left him. Of course she had. This wasn't her scene. He checked the time stamp, saw she'd texted a half hour ago.

He shot her a text. Are you home? On my way.

Skirting around the crowded dance floor, he made his way to Slater's table. "Hey."

The others at the table looked up at him. He'd rudely interrupted their conversation.

"Sorry." He focused on Slater and Emmie. "Just wanted to let you know I'm heading back to the house."

"Everything all right?" Slater asked.

"Violet left a little while ago. She must've taken a cab." Derek didn't miss the look that passed between him and Emmie.

Fortunately, his sister didn't fuck with him. Ever. "Randall was here."

Derek didn't like the hot rush of anger riding through him. "He took her home."

"Yeah, so I'm going. You guys coming?"

"Sure," Slater said. "It's late."

"And the new guy's coming first thing in the morning."

Derek didn't wait for them to say their good-byes. He took off to get Ben and Cooper.

Fucking frat boy.

Derek's hands flexed on the steering wheel of Violet's ancient pickup. The guys chattered on and on, excited about Irwin's response to their music—not to mention the fact he couldn't wait to get them back in the studio.

All Derek could think about was Randall taking advantage of the situation and escorting her out of the crowded club. Taking her home. A real hero.

He'd be back on tour in a couple days . . . and Randall would be right there for her, fighting to make sure she kept the farm.

But Derek wouldn't give the guy room to get in. He remembered what Slater had gone through with Emmie. He'd skip breakfast with the band or sightseeing, whatever, just to talk to her on the phone when the bus was empty. Skype with her, fly her out.

He'd do that with Violet. Wouldn't give her feelings a chance to cool.

Thing was, the situation was different. That's what kept spiraling through him. Emmie had worked in the business. She'd had the freedom to come on the road with them. Not so for Violet. She'd move on to the next job. Get consumed in a new role, a new life. They'd both be on the road for extended periods of time.

And worst of all, the idea he couldn't get out of his head was that Randall *was* the better guy for her. No matter what Slater said about unconditional love being the true stability, a musician's life didn't give Violet a husband who came home every night.

What could he offer other than a visit every couple of months?

Fuck. They had nothing in common. Their lives didn't intersect.

He should leave her alone. Leave her to the preppy lawyer.

The truck hit the top of the rise, and the sky opened up before him. A million stars glittering against a black backdrop. He turned into her gravel driveway, the yellow Ferrari parked right in the middle.

The fucker leaned against his car on the passenger side, arms folded over his chest, laughing at something she said. Derek jerked the gear shaft and threw open his door. He strode right to her. She kept her usual cool façade, not the least moved by the frustration that had to be rolling off him.

"Hey, guys." Emmie got out of the truck.

Doors slammed, boots crunched on gravel, greetings were exchanged. And Derek held her unflappable gaze. He wanted her to say something, feel something. To claim him, dammit.

But she showed nothing. Not a damn thing.

Fuck it. He strode past her and went into the house.

Alone in the barn, Derek strummed his guitar. Every time he closed his eyes, he saw her face. Her beautiful hazel eyes and that tender smile she only gave him.

There were two Violets. The warm, loving, sensual woman in his bed, and the cool professional.

He knew without a doubt he got the true woman—the heart of her—when they were under the covers. But the other one? The one with the armor up? That one told her heart to shut the fuck up so she could do her job the only way she knew how. It was how she survived.

He set the guitar in its case, hit the lights, and strode out of the barn.

Energy crackled through him, making his skin burn. Lights in the kitchen drew him up the back steps. Laughter, conversation . . . he could picture everyone high on tonight's success, imagine Slater and Emmie all tangled up together. And Violet reserved, feeling like an outsider.

Ah. That was it right there. *That* was the problem.

Why hadn't he seen it before? She'd spent her whole life looking in on other families, other groups of friends on the playground. Even her job had her pretending to be part of a client's life, before moving on to the next one.

Well, that was something he could fix. He needed to show her she was one of them, take away the distance she felt in her own mind. Like Emmie, she'd gotten into everyone's hearts. She'd become part of them. He just had to make her see it.

He passed through the laundry room, breathed in the lavender scent of her fabric softener.

It struck him how he'd never seen a single picture of her. In her bedroom, she didn't have posters or stuffed animals or anything chronicling her childhood, the mementos of a life lived. Jesus, that made him sad.

Her only "possessions," the things she hauled with her from place to place, were the memories of her four years with her grandmother. And, damn, he could see it so clearly, that little girl with dark hair and big eyes tucked in tightly against her grandma, reading books together.

This farm. This was the one place she belonged. She thought it was her home.

She was wrong. It was just a piece of land. *Derek* was her home.

The guys sat around the table, Emmie and Slater's hands clasped tightly, as Ben retold the story of a night they'd spent in the studio, working on the same song for twelve hours.

"Fuckin' Irwin comes in at . . . What was it? Four in the morning?" Ben said.

"Wide awake," Cooper said. "Like it was the middle of the day."

"He just shuts off the power, shuts the whole place down. Didn't say a word, man."

"We had to use our phones to find our way out."

"But he was right." Emmie participated as if she hadn't heard the story a hundred times. She was so patient with them. "He made you take a day off, and when he let you back in the studio, you guys nailed it. He knows what he's doing."

Derek came straight for Violet. She sat up as he neared her. He lost track of the conversation, couldn't see anything but the way Violet's chest rose and fell with each breath, the way the lights gleamed in her hair, spilling loosely around her shoulders.

"Hey, Derek," Emmie said. "You all right?"

But he'd locked on to his girl. Had to hold her, feel her against his body. As soon as he reached her chair, he leaned over, slid his hands under her ass, and scooped her into his arms.

"Derek," Emmie cried.

Violet's arms went around his shoulders, and she tucked her face into his neck, her breath warm on his skin.

"Hey, caveman, forget your club?" Cooper called.

"Let the poor guy get some," Ben said. "He's gonna be blue-ballin' for the next month."

Crossing the living room, his heavy steps making the vases and knickknacks rattle, he climbed the stairs, kicked open her door, and set her down on the bed.

He reached behind his neck and pulled off his T-shirt. "You went home with the douche."

Finally, a crack in the cool façade. "You were busy."

"I'm never too busy for you. Never. All you had to do was tell me you wanted to go home."

"You have to work. You have fans."

"Yeah, so? Check in with me. Don't just take off like that." He strode to the door, slammed it closed, and locked it. Then he came back to her. He unbuckled her sandals, tossed each one aside. His hands caressed her smooth calves, gliding up her thighs until he reached her panties. "Take these off."

She stood up and pulled them off. When he reached for the tie at the back of her neck, her hands closed around his wrists. "Derek." She sounded needy, restless, a lot turned on.

But that reserve in her eyes? The uncertainty only urged him on.

He'd fight through it. It was the only way to prove himself.

"You told me you don't know how to love, but you're wrong. You think there's some chapter in the book of life that you missed out on, but that's bullshit. Loving is just what we do. Just because you didn't have it growing up, doesn't mean you're destined to a life without it."

He peeled the cotton top down, exposing her breasts plumping out of a strapless bra. "Off."

As she reached behind her to unclasp the bra, he quickly tore off his clothes. Flicking the light switch, the room plunged into darkness. A wide shaft of moonlight cut across the room, falling right across her chest, bathing her in its milky light.

He covered her with his body, claiming that mouth that sent him reeling every single time. "Why'd you go home with him?"

"I'm worried about the farm. No matter how valid my contract, no matter what anyone says in my defense, I might get a judge who favors Jed's kids. I could lose it. I could lose everything."

"Not gonna happen. If we have to pool our cash together and buy the fucking place outright, you're not losing the farm. I promise you, V. You hear me? I promise you. You're not losing the farm."

Her fingers sifted through his hair, her hips shifted beneath him, making him even harder. "God, Derek, I . . ."

"You what?" *Fucking tell me already.*

"You overwhelm me. I can't think straight around you."

"I don't want you thinking. That's all you do is think. I want you in this with me."

And then her defenses crumbled, her body relaxing into the mattress. "I am."

She didn't seem happy about that, but he was. Damn happy.

"Get that macho smile off your face." She squeezed his bicep. "It's not a good thing."

"It's a fucking great thing." His knee nudged her legs apart. "Kiss me." He took her mouth, demanded a response from her tongue. "Give it all to me. Everything."

"You make me crazy. You make me lose my mind."

"*That's* where love is, V. Right there."

She jerked her mouth away from him. "Have you ever said it before, you know, that you love someone?" Her vulnerability split his heart wide open.

"Never."

"You *love* me?" Her pulse ticked in her neck, and he gazed into questioning eyes.

He knew his answer meant everything. So he waited. Waited for emotion to consume him, for his worries to dissipate and his feelings to rise, spread. And when it did, it released a stinging electricity in him. When he said it, she couldn't possibly doubt it. "Yeah, V. I love you."

Her smile unfurled slowly, softly, tenderly. "You're crazy." She gave him a look so imbued with love, it swept his remaining doubts away. "I . . ."

"I know."

"But . . ."

"You own my heart, sweet V. That's all that matters."

The guys came into the kitchen, laughing and jostling each other. Violet turned from the sink, where she'd been cracking eggs, and watched Derek break from the others and come right to her.

His hands went around her waist, his face into the curve of her neck. She breathed in the fresh air and sunbaked cotton that wafted off him, reveled in the strength of his hold. She loved that he *needed* to touch her.

"Good session?" she asked.

"Best music we've ever written. The new guy's all right."

"He's here?" She turned in his arms, curious to meet him.

Derek stepped back. "X, come meet my girl, Violet Davis."

Slater stepped aside and—oh, holy mother of God—the guy was huge. Tall and wide as a fullback, he looked like a badass biker with his shoulder-length dark hair, facial scruff, and a sexy wide mouth drawn into a wicked smile. The guy gave her a chin nod.

"Hey. Calix Bourbon." He gestured with both hands to the room around him. "So this is where the magic happens." Long lashes framed intense, dark eyes.

"Well? What do you think?" she asked him. "Think you can hang with these guys?"

"If it means I get to hang out on a wildflower farm with enchanted women, then hell yeah."

"Oh, we'll be hanging out here, all right," Slater said. "Emmie's meeting the inspector at the house today."

"You're serious about this?" Ben asked.

Slater nodded. "Gonna build a studio. Record out here."

"*If* we can find a producer who'll work with us on this sand bar on the tip of Long Island," Cooper said. But he didn't sound grumpy. "There are no hot chicks out here."

"Come to one of our bonfires." Calix's mouth cocked in a half smile. "I'll introduce you around."

"You live around here?" Violet asked.

"Marsapeague." When he got nothing but blank stares, he said, "South Fork. About half hour from here."

Derek's big arms came around her. "What can I do to help?"

"Can you grab the milk from the fridge?" Violet gestured to the thick slices of crusty whole grain bread she'd cut and laid out on the chopping block.

Emmie came up, watching them work. "French toast? Yum." She spun around to the guys. "Stuffed French toast, you guys."

"Fuckin' A," Ben said.

"That's awesome," Cooper said.

Emmie stepped back so Derek could set the jug of milk on the counter. "God, I love your food. I don't know where you even find bread like this."

"We've got a great bakery in town. I'll take you there. We'll get croissants for breakfast."

"Em, Violet?" Slater called. "Come here. You have to hear this beat we just put down."

"V'll be out in a minute." Derek turned serious. He looked almost troubled.

Emmie snatched a piece of bread before going out with the others, leaving them alone.

Fiddling with the crust on a slice of bread, he tossed it into the sink. "So you know I've got Buck's thing tomorrow, right?"

Violet set the whisk down and faced him, giving him all her attention. "You okay about it?"

He shrugged, looking uncomfortable. "Will you come with me?"

She looked away, heart squeezing. "I can't. I'm sorry." She loved that he wanted her there. Performing solo was such a source of fear for him. But she'd already made an appointment.

"Why not?"

She let out a shaky breath. "I'm meeting with a potential client."

"You didn't tell me."

"You know I have to take a job. I've put it off so I could spend this time with you, but now that you're leaving, I have to meet with clients and choose the next job."

He blew out a hard breath. "I'm not leaving *you*."

"I know that. But once you go back on tour, I have to get back to work, too."

He studied her for a moment as if he needed to figure out her motives. "What kind of client? Where will it take you?"

"Actually, it would keep me in the music industry. You know that pop star who's out of control?"

"Jason Becker?" She wasn't surprised at how shocked he sounded. It *was* a strange choice for her.

"He's heading off to Japan for the next leg of his tour, so I thought it would be the perfect opportunity for me to help him when he's out of the American media glare."

He looked frustrated, but he had to know she couldn't give up her career to wait for him. "You said you didn't want to work in the music industry. And that kid . . . Jesus, V, he's a mess."

"I know. But it would be for three months. And the pay . . ." She set her wrists on the counter. "I could pay for the farm outright, Derek." And never worry about being homeless again.

"So if you take this job, you'll go to Japan?"

Anxiety tightened her gut. "Yes." She drew in a tight breath.

"Don't take it."

"It would pay enough for me to *own* the farm."

"And what about us?"

"What about us, Derek? You're going on tour, remember?"

She could feel the heat radiating off his body. "Yeah, I'm going on tour for the next month. You're talking about going overseas for *three* months. We won't see each other, the time difference will fuck things up."

"Derek, I have to work. I have to take jobs when they come my way."

"You don't have to take this one."

"Are you serious? You're telling me not to take the job that'll enable me to own the farm outright? Come on, Derek. You can't ask me to give that up."

"There are other jobs. Don't you have other jobs to choose from?"

"It's not like that, Derek. I don't have an office and a website. There's no marketing department. My work is based on referrals. Besides, the money being offered is unlike anything I've earned before."

"Jesus, V. Do you care at all? You stand there so unemotional. Is everything just business to you? I don't get you at all. Do you *want* to end it right now? Do you want me to get on that fucking bus and never come back? Is that what you want?"

Her heart pounded so hard she could hear it in her ears. Her throat tightened into a hard knot, preventing words from escaping. She stood there, terrified, scared to death to lose him.

Scared, even more, to believe in him.

When she didn't answer, his features crumpled. She was destroying him. "Fucking say something."

She threw herself into his arms, and he held her so tightly he lifted her off the ground.

His mouth turned to her ear. "Fight for us, V."

"I don't know what to do."

He set her down. "You don't take a job that'll keep us apart for three months."

"But the farm . . . I can't lose it."

"But you can lose *me*?"

She looked at him, stunned. "You can't make me choose. That's a terrible thing to do."

"I'm not making you choose between me and the farm. You can take a different job."

She would do almost anything to keep him; of course she would. God, if she thought for a second she had a chance with him, that she could have a *life* with him, she'd give up just about anything. But he was going back on tour. Sure, he might stay in touch for weeks, maybe even a month or two. But his life would sweep him back out into the world. Women would come at him, woo him, seduce him. He was too intense, too passionate to hang on to a woman he saw occasionally. He needed full contact. He was a physical person.

And if she took the bet and lost . . . and then lost her farm, too? Her home. Her livelihood?

He closed his eyes, looking pained. "I knew it. I knew you'd pull away. Fuck, V, what do I have to do to make you see that I want us to be together? I'll do whatever it takes. We can make it work. I'll fly you out to shows."

Fear pierced her as vividly as stepping on a piece of broken glass. She jerked back from him. He didn't even realize he'd just dumped her in the same bin as all his other women. He'd treated her like Gen.

He called them when he needed to get laid. Oh, hell, no. She wasn't going to become that woman to him.

"Can you do me a favor, V? Can you postpone making a decision about this job until after Madison Square Garden? We've got three days off after it. Can you promise not to take a job—any job—until we talk some more? I can come back out here if you want, spend the three days with you. Will you hold off giving them an answer?"

"Sure." Whatever. She wasn't going to make a scene.

God, he wanted her to believe she was different, that they had something special—but hadn't Adriana thought that? Certainly Gen did. Derek could say whatever he wanted, but Gen was possessive around him. She definitely thought they were in a relationship.

This is what he does. He sweeps women away. She turned back to the counter, grabbed the bowl, and brought it to the stove. She transferred the saturated, dripping bread onto the butter-drenched griddle.

"Oh, my God, that smells so good," Emmie said as they all came back inside.

"What can I do?" Cooper asked.

"You want to get the orange juice?" Violet asked.

"Sure thing."

"I'll get plates," Emmie said.

The front door slammed hard, rattling windows.

"I'm telling you he's a fucking asshole, and I'm not going back," a familiar voice shouted from the foyer.

All conversation in the kitchen shut down. Heels clacked on wood flooring.

Violet turned to find Mimi Romano tossing her big black purse onto the table. Shaking with anger, she looked up, but her gaze slid right past Violet and her eyes widened. "Oh, shit." Her hand covered her mouth. "You've got company."

"Meems, what's wrong?" Violet went right to her, giving her a hug.

Mimi pulled away. "I finally get a job, a good one. And it turns out to be *completely* and *totally* full of shit. The guy who hired me? Turns out he's using me to get to my dad."

"What?"

"Yeah, I know. Big surprise, right? I'm the idiot who thought it would be different this time."

Her phone buzzed, and she scowled when she read the screen. "Oh, seriously, fuck a *duck*." Taking a breath, she answered in a totally different voice. "Hi, Dad. Yeah, sorry I didn't get back to you."

Violet shot a look to the others, wondering what the guys made of Mimi. The beauty standing before them in a charcoal gray pencil skirt and cream silk shirt didn't look like the kind of person who would swear like a sailor.

"Listen, I'm right in the middle of something, so can I call you back?" Her mouth snapped shut. Violet could hear her dad's loud voice through the receiver.

"No, I don't have another job to go to. Unless, of course, *you'll* finally hire me." She grimaced. "Oops, train's coming. I gotta go. I'll call you tonight." Mimi disconnected, tossing the phone on top of her bag. She looked up to see everyone staring at her. "Do not judge me. Yes, you heard me lie to my dad. But I am not going to listen to him go on and on about how I need real world experience before he lets me join the company. Blah blah blah. "

Violet stepped forward. "Mimi, I'd like you to meet the guys from Blue Fire."

Each one in turn reached out and shook her hand, then retreated.

And then Francesca came down the stairs. "Mimi? Sweetheart, what're you doing here?"

She gazed up at her mom. "I quit my job. And before you judge me, I had no choice. I mean, give me a freaking break already. I graduated from Cornell. I grew up in the business. I have great ideas. But does he care? No, he wants my dad to invest in his next chain of restaurants." She turned back to the guys, shrugging. "I'm totally screwed. No one will hire me on my own merits, and yet my dad won't hire me until I've worked for a few years. God, I'm sick to death of this."

"Can't you just put in the time?" Francesca said. "For goodness sake, Mimi, so what if he wants access to your father? Make the introduction and let your dad handle it from there."

"Okay, not even discussing this. You know how important it is to me to get hired on my own merit. But, fuck me, does *everyone* want me for my last name? You know what he said to me today? He said he really didn't see a future for me if I couldn't help him launch his next chain. In other words, unless I bring in Dad's money."

"Maybe your father would be interested." Francesca gave her daughter a meaningful look.

"Oh, my God. Do you hear a single thing I say? I'm not taking a job unless it's based on my own achievements. I interned with the Hazard Group three summers in a row. I know my stuff."

"Fine." Francesca glanced to the others. "We'll talk about this later. Have you eaten? How long are you here for, sweetheart?" Francesca ran her hands through Mimi's dark red curls.

"The whole freaking weekend. I want comfort food and blow-'em-up movies. I want to see body parts flying."

"Oh, Mimi, please," her mom said.

Mimi looked at the line of rockers. "Sorry about my outburst. I didn't know you guys were in the house."

"Come on, let's finish making breakfast." Emmie led everyone back into the kitchen.

Just as she turned to join them, Violet caught Derek heading up the stairs. Her body willed her to follow, but her mind couldn't stop playing back his words.

I'll fly you out to shows.

She believed he had the best intentions. She even believed he thought he loved her.

But she also knew he was a passionate man who got carried away.

And there wasn't a chance in hell she'd become the next Gen.

NINETEEN

Thunder rumbled in the distance, and rain pattered on the roof. Derek liked that Violet kept the windows open in her room, even if she had to lay out towels on the floor beneath them to absorb the splatter. The cool gusts felt good on his heated skin.

On this last night together, he wanted her all to himself. He'd run out of words to convince her, so he'd used his body. How did you keep someone who didn't want to be kept?

Pressed up against him, her head nestled into the crook of his arm, her silky hair in a tumble all over him. It was a restless sleep, so he kept his arm loosely around her, letting her know he was there—would always be there—but giving her the room to move as she needed.

Her palm opened on his chest, her fingers gently stroking. "Can't sleep?"

He didn't bother answering.

"I don't know if I'll take the Becker job." She went quiet. "I'm just going to talk to his people."

His arm tightened around her, and she turned onto her back, keeping a hand on his forearm. He kept his mouth shut. She didn't believe his words anyway.

"Derek?"

He squeezed her wrist in response.

"You're going to do great tomorrow."

Fuck, really? He pulled his arm out from under her, rolled on top of her. "You think I can't sleep because of Buck's show? Jesus, V. I can't sleep because this might be my last night with you."

"Aren't you coming back after Madison Square Garden?"

"Am I?" He studied her eyes, her mouth, the way she swallowed like it hurt. Looking for the truth. "Or will you be in Japan?"

"I don't know yet. But I'll do what I have to do. And don't look at me like that because it's the same for you."

"It isn't the same. You can take any job. I have to finish this tour." Hands on her head, he kissed her, teasing her tongue into play. When her hands came around his shoulders, clutched at his back, when her hips shifted ever so slightly toward him, he sighed, "Violet."

"We'll have our three days, okay? I won't make any decisions until we have our three days."

Three fucking days. He wanted so much more. When his rocking hips pushed harder, his dick pressed between her damp curls, giving him a hint of slickness. A rush of electricity flashed across his skin. "Oh, fuck." Jesus, he'd already loved her twice tonight.

Her thighs spread wider, her hips tilted, allowing him to sink more deeply into her heat. Christ, she felt so good. His beautiful, gentle, strong Violet. Lifting up on his arms so he could see her, he slid back and forth along her hot length, watching her breath hitch, her eyelids lower.

Lightning flashed through the room, and a crack of thunder preceded a rush of heavy rain.

Holding her gaze, the hair on his body rose, his skin tingled. She brought a hand between them, stroking the top of his dick. Holy fuck. Her gentle hand petting him, her slickness coating his sensitive underside. He quickened his pace, sinking deeper into the honeyed embrace of her channel. Every time he surged forward, her thumb made a swipe around his head, sending pleasure flashing through him.

He was going to come. Jesus, he was going to come so

hard. The look in her eyes told him she loved him, even if she didn't think she knew how. His arms trembled with the weight of his body; his ass muscles clenched. He didn't know if he could hold out much longer.

Her other hand went to his balls, and they tightened. The steady patter of rain, the gentle but firm stroke of her hand, the hot rush of desire as he glided through her, all sent him straight out of his mind.

Tension gripped his spine, blood roared in his ears, and he started panting, gasping. Jesus, he couldn't hold it in— the tension kept building—the pressure, the indescribable *pleasure*. He didn't want it ever to stop. He never wanted to be anywhere else but here, in this flower-scented room with her hands on him, their gazes locked.

"Oh, Jesus, V, I'm going to come." He knew he sounded surprised, but come on, just her hand stroking him, his dick sliding along her length? When he'd already come twice?

He shouted with a release that powered through him in a blinding, blazing roar of heat.

His arms shook, his muscles ached, and he still couldn't get enough of her. Slowing his thrusts, he pumped a few more times. Exhausted. Sated.

Bliss.

Collapsing onto her side, he held her tightly, burying his face in her neck. Tremors wracked his body.

"Not giving up, V," he said into her neck. "Never giving up."

Derek stood outside Buck's brownstone. Music from the studio merged with the dull buzz of a window unit air conditioner. He had to set his Fender case down to wipe his damp palm. Christ, the bowels of hell couldn't be hotter than Manhattan at the end of July.

Hand on the waist-high wrought iron gate, he hesitated, not ready to head down the stairs. Had to get his head on right for this show. He couldn't mess up. Too much at stake.

But fuck, *Violet*. Last night had been intense. He hadn't wanted to leave her bed, her bedroom, her house, her farm. Leaving her had felt like tearing muscle from bone.

He blew out a breath, wiping the sweat off his forehead. Here's what he knew. If she took a job overseas, their relationship would end. She needed to be physically connected to him or she'd drift away. She wouldn't trust his feelings—or her own—to hold true.

So he had to convince her to take a different job. A job that would keep her close to him. He shot off a text to his sister.

Don't want V taking this job that'll keep her overseas 3+ mos. Can you find her one that'll keep her closer to us? Can't lose her.

Trust his sister to get right back to him. Aren't you at Buck's? Get your head on right! Let me talk to Irwin. See you for sound check at 2, k?

He didn't need to say another word. His sister got him, and he had absolute faith in her. Shoving his phone into his pocket, his head cleared. The music drifting up to him came into clearer focus. Jazz. Great, a reminder of his dad before his big acoustic, televised gig.

Shake it off.

Unlatching the gate, he headed down the stairs into the ground floor studio of *Artists Unplugged*. He rang the bell, peering through the iron screen. Male laughter and deep voices carried over the loud jazz music.

"Come on in," someone shouted.

He stepped inside the windowless foyer. To his left was the studio—with lights hanging from the ceiling, microphones, and video cameras facing a couple of chairs. Straight ahead, a plain wooden staircase that led to the main floor, probably where Buck lived. He wandered down a short, dark hall then turned into the kitchen.

With a quick sweep of the room, he took in Buck, some scraggly-haired dudes, and . . . his *father*.

Fucking hell. "What're you doing here?" He had to keep a lid on it. No matter the energy roiling through him, picking up speed to the point he could hurl the refrigerator out the sliding glass doors, he had to rein it in.

"There's my boy." Eddie Valencia smiled warmly.

My boy? A horrible sensation rose from his chest, the wrenching pain of the boy who desperately wanted his dad to spend time with him, to acknowledge him, to just give him a smile. Any-fucking-thing other than the palm of his hand in his face, pushing him away.

His dad stood there as if this past year in the press—all the cracks and put-downs—had never happened. Somehow he could call his son a poseur in the press, but in front of Buck O'Reilly he was suddenly *my boy*?

Get a grip. Not the time or place for anger.

Buck looked concerned. He motioned to someone in the studio, and the music shut off.

"So what's the deal?" Derek said, unable to keep the sharpness out of his tone. "Did you double book?"

"Don't worry, you'll get your exposure, son." His dad chuckled.

My boy, my ass.

"Whose idea was this?" Derek needed to know who'd played him. If Buck had done this for ratings, Derek was out of there.

His dad clapped his shoulder. "It was my idea. Come on, father and son musicians. It's a great angle. Every show needs a hook. That's how you get ratings."

"We don't play the same kind of music. What's the point?"

"Hey, it's me." His dad moved toward him. "Don't be intimidated."

Intimidated? Derek's hand tightened on the guitar case handle.

"This isn't the sex god versus the virtuoso, for Christ's sake. Relax. It's father and son. Old generation and new. I'm the old school guy, on the Ledger List for ten years. You're just starting out. Come on, it's a great story."

Derek looked to Buck. "Was that your plan when you asked me to be on the show?"

The guy looked uneasy. "No."

"You want your first time on the show to go well, right?" His dad gave him this look like he was doing him a huge favor. Like he had to carve time out of an otherwise packed schedule, when in reality he hadn't performed or recorded in years. He'd only been interviewed because of his son's newfound fame.

Son of a bitch.

Derek cut a hard look to Buck, letting him know he felt sabotaged.

"It's your *dad*." He seemed bewildered as if he'd assumed Derek was in on it.

"This'll be great." Eddie clapped his hands together. "We haven't played together in years. You've been down in Texas, and I've been in the studio."

Ugly energy pounded through his veins. He needed to get out. Fuck it. He didn't have to do the show, not like this. He started to go, but then Violet filled the screen of his mind. He saw her face, felt her calm and gentle spirit. She'd asked him once if he'd ever talked to his dad. If he'd ever *communicated*, given his dad a chance to see how he was hurting his son. And he thought about all the situations she'd handled, never losing her cool, always winning people over to her perspective by being reasonable and keying into what *they* wanted.

"Can I talk to you a second, Dad?"

"Sure thing." He gestured to Buck. "You want to get the cameras rolling?"

"No," Derek snapped. Then he took a breath, filling his lungs, calming himself down. "I'd like a minute to talk to you off-camera. Alone."

"No problem." Buck motioned for the other guys to head into the studio.

Derek led the way through the sliding glass door and outside. A tiny triangle of dirt and brown grass, the backyard was littered with beer cans, cigarette butts, and some worn beach chairs.

"What's up?"

Christ, he wanted to get the hell out of there. But if he bolted, his dad would let it be known all over the press that his son didn't feel confident enough yet to play with the great Eddie Valencia.

But he knew himself. If he performed right then, he'd fuck up. Too much energy, too much anger.

He didn't know where to start, so he'd just go right to the heart of it. "You know my biggest memory, Dad?"

Eddie's gaze flicked inside, like he didn't want to eat

into his time on the show. "How about we talk about this later? Get a drink after we tape?"

"Dad, I'm playing Madison Square Garden tonight." *Thanks for paying attention.* "I don't have time for a drink. Besides, I'm not gonna tape until we talk."

His features hardened. Good-time Eddie had left the building. "Can you for once get your head out of your ass and be a professional? We've got an hour, that's it. This isn't the time—"

"*I* have an hour."

"What?"

"*We* don't have an hour, *I* do. This is my time slot. Buck invited me."

"And what're you going to do with your hour? Talk about your big-tittied girlfriend? The keyboard player who's in rehab? Or how about the supermodel who trashed the restaurant because she caught you boning a groupie?" Eddie leaned in close enough so Derek could see the deep grooves around his mouth, the heavy bags under his eyes. "I'm here to help you. So the world takes you seriously, since you're so set on playing the fool."

"You're helping me?" He was about to go apeshit over all the quotes Eddie had given to the press, but he felt the calming hand of Violet and he settled. Took a step back.

He started again. "My biggest memory is when I was nine years old. Chet Baroni—remember him? He came upstairs, looking for a glass of water. He saw me all pissed off, and he asked me what was wrong. I told him I wanted to be in the studio with you guys, but you wouldn't let me in. That you never let me in. And he asked if I knew how to play. I told him I was learning. I took him into my room and pulled out the guitar I'd bought at a garage sale—and he sat with me, teaching me fingerplay. It was . . ." Derek could not believe he was getting all choked up over something that had happened nearly twenty years ago.

"What's your point, Derek? Can you hurry it along so we can get inside and do what we came here to do?"

"My point is that Chet gave me something. It was small, and it might not seem like much, but it's the reason I'm here today. You wouldn't let me in the studio, wouldn't let me touch your instruments. But that day, Chet took the time to teach me something. And I'm telling you, man, I remember making the transition from noise to music. I swear, Dad, that was the moment I got it. It just clicked into place. I formed a band as soon as I hit middle school, and I never stopped playing and learning. So what I'm saying is I'm here today because of *me*. The only thing *you* ever did was fuck with me. And that includes my reputation. Do I invite publicity? Yeah, I do. But we live in a different age. It's all about social media. I'm working it. And if I fuck up here and there, well, hey, I'm learning. Just like I learned to play bass all by myself."

"Jesus, fuck, you were always such a whiny baby. It's a wonder you've made it this far. If you think you can blame me for your fuck-ups, think again. Everyone had shitty parents. The ones who wallow in that shit, sink. The ones who shake it off, rise to the top."

Talking with his dad, it was like shaking up a carbonated beverage, all that pressure building, threatening to explode. The only thing keeping him in check was knowing Buck waited for him, cameras ready to roll.

Derek nodded tersely. "You're absolutely right." It *was* time to shake his dad off.

And with that Derek went inside to do his acoustic gig for Buck O'Reilly.

Above the din of excited chatter, a voice rose. "Five minutes."

Derek watched while his bandmates turned away from whoever they were talking to and drew together, forming a tight, closed circle. For several tense seconds, no one spoke.

This moment had only ever been a vague dream. Come on, he was from New York. What kid in a garage band didn't dream about playing Madison Square Garden? But it had never seemed real.

But it was real. They were here. His band. His brothers. And Pete was missing it.

"I'm so proud of you guys." Emmie reached her hand into the center. They all joined in, a tower of hands.

"Madison Square Garden." She said it with the reverence it deserved.

"Shame Pete's not here," Ben said. But he looked to Calix with a smile. "But you're a fuckin' maestro, and we're glad to have you on board."

"Happy to be here."

Derek hadn't talked much to the new keyboardist, but he knew about Calix's impressive résumé. He'd have to find out later why a guy with his connections, his talent, didn't have a permanent place in a band.

"Guys?" someone called. "Show time."

An electrical charge jolted through their joined hands, and they all leaned in.

"Fuckin' A," Slater said.

"Let's do this," Derek said.

As they headed out of the room, Derek tagged Emmie. "You hear from Violet?"

Her features pulled tight. "No."

"She's coming, right? She wouldn't miss the show."

"Not a chance. She'll be here."

"Did you find her another gig?"

"I haven't even had a chance to talk to Irwin. But I will. After the show."

"You think she'll take the job? Leave the country for three months?"

Emmie drew in a slow, deep breath, lips pressed together. She knew exactly what he really meant. *Leave me.* "I think she'll do what she has to do. Just like you or I would do. And you can't blame her. It's not like you guys are married or anything."

"Oh, my God, *someone's* got marriage on the brain," a woman said, coming up to them.

"Oh, hey, Sam," Emmie said. "Derek, this is Sam Kramer. She's Dak Johnson's assistant."

"Nice to meet you," Derek said, needing to talk to Emmie alone.

"Dak's going to meet with you guys tomorrow," his sister said. "Talk about producing the next album."

"He's here tonight." Sam gave him a big, warm smile. "Pretty sure he's watching Buck's show right now. He and

Irwin are off somewhere with my laptop." The woman gave a shrug of her brow.

Oh, *fuck*. He did not need to hear that. He'd completely screwed up in Buck's studio. His dad had taken over—even interrupted Derek's jam to "teach him" something about fingering.

Jesus, he couldn't think about this shit right now. Couldn't picture Dak and Irwin grimacing as they watched a replay of this afternoon's shitshow.

"Gotta hit the stage." He gave Sam a lingering look, hoping she'd get the hint that he wanted time alone with his sister. She didn't. "Em, walk me out?"

"Derek, dude?" Cooper called from the doorway. "Let's go."

Fuck it. He had to go. He grabbed Emmie's shoulder. "Make sure Violet's here."

"I'll make sure she's right where you can see her." She looked worried about him.

"Thanks."

"Derek?" She stopped him.

Fuck. He had to calm down. "Yeah?"

"Focus, okay? Put everything else out of your head." Then, she reached for his hand. "Everything will work out, I promise. Just be here now."

He nodded, then turned away. Jogged out onto the stage, instantly hit by blinding lights and a roaring crowd.

He had to shut it all down. Shut out the image of Irwin watching his live performance right then. The memory of his dad sabotaging him in Buck's studio. Fuck it. He glanced to the side of the stage one last time, looking for Violet. Where the fuck was she? He needed her to calm his shit down. But he couldn't see anything through the glare of lights.

Wipe it clean. Focus on the music.

Show time.

Usually, he lost himself in the beat. He tuned into Ben's rhythm on the sticks, but tonight . . . he couldn't concentrate. It wasn't the heat from the blazing lights, it wasn't the crowd—not that they'd ever played a venue this size before—but still, he wasn't freaking out that it was Madison Square Garden.

He was freaking out because something was off with Violet. Emmie had brought her to the other side of the stage, closer to him. And he kept looking over where she stood, huddled with Emmie, Sam, and a few others. But where the others were loose, singing along, even dancing, Violet held herself still.

It made him think she'd taken the job with Jason Becker. Why else would she be so uptight?

Fuck. He lost the beat, had no idea where they were in the song. Quickly looking down to Ben's feet, he focused, got it back.

He wouldn't look at her again. Didn't need to see Violet all tense and worried.

Definitely didn't need to see Irwin and Dak talking intensely.

He knew they weren't talking about Derek's performance on *Artists Unplugged*. He wasn't a narcissist like his dad, so he knew the whole world wasn't thinking about his sucky acoustic gig.

But people *were* watching it. Right at that moment, thousands of fans, musicians, and industry professionals were watching him get flustered by his dad. Why hadn't he kicked his dad the hell out? He owed him nothing. He should've had the balls to kick him out.

Wait, *fuck*, he'd lost his place in the song again. He needed to shut his mind down completely, close his eyes, and block it all out.

Just as they neared the end of the song, their last one of the night, he opened his eyes, caught a flurry of movement offstage. Some tall, skinny guy—a kid—his hair short at the sides, one front section long enough to cover half his face— jumped on Violet's back, wrapped his arms around her neck.

Blood roared through him. He was ready to hurl his bass aside and tackle the fucker. Until he realized it was Jason Becker, surrounded by his entourage. A beefy guy who had to be a bodyguard, pulled the kid off her back. Violet smiled—that cool, professional smile.

And right then he knew he'd lost her. If the kid had

come to the show, she'd obviously decided to work with him.

Oh, hell fucking no. She was not going to Japan.

She was not going to drift away.

He had to talk to her—fuck that. Words didn't work with her. They bounced off her like Ping-Pong balls. He needed to *show* her.

The song ended, and Slater started to thank the audience, thank Imagine Dragons for giving them the opportunity to share the stage with them, but all that blood roaring in his veins, all the panic choking out his lungs, had Derek moving, dropping his Fender and rushing toward Slater. He grabbed the mic, thinking only one thing. He'd give her what his words couldn't make her believe.

Slater stepped back, surprised.

Derek saw nothing but a blur of faces, a blizzard of lights. "Thank you, New York!"

The crowd roared.

"Tonight was a dream come true for us. I'm from here, so you gotta know what it's like for me to play the Garden." Feet pounded, lighters flicked to life, and the audience went crazy.

He raised a hand to quiet them down. "This is definitely one of the greatest nights of my life, and there's only one thing that can top it. And that's saying something, considering we just opened for Imagine Dragons at Madison Square Garden."

The crowd went crazy.

Sweat trickled down his face, his back. He felt light-headed, sick to his stomach. But he didn't stop. "It's about a girl."

Women in the crowd shrieked. One voice rose above the others. "I'll be your girl."

He laughed. "Sorry, but I'm taken. Completely taken. Violet?" he called.

He watched as her curious expression turn horrified. People tried to push her out onto the stage, but she turned back, ducking between bodies.

"What're you doing, man?" he heard Slater say, but he ignored his friend. He had to see this through.

"Violet, baby? Come on out here. I need you with me." If only she understood how much. But she would now. Now, she'd finally get it.

She shook her head, waved her hands. Was she actually not going to come out onstage?

"Don't do this to her." Slater stood at his side, and Derek nearly shoved him away. Too much energy pumping through his system. Why wouldn't she come?

Sweat dripped into his eyes. He gave Emmie an imploring look. He needed her help, but his sister looked grim. Pissed, almost. What the fuck? He loved Violet. He wanted her. Fuck them if they didn't understand.

Finally, Jason Becker and some other guy took her by the shoulders and walked her a few feet onto the stage before giving her a push. Then they turned and left her there.

Slowly, she headed toward him. She looked scared. For one moment she glanced at the audience, shielded her eyes from the glare, and then quickly looked away.

"Right here, baby." He only wanted her eyes on his.

And when he got them, when she looked right at him, emotion exploded in his chest. This was his girl. She calmed him, centered him. Gave him the kind of attention, *affection*, he'd never had. The intensity he needed in a relationship. It's why he'd never had one before. No other woman got him on this level. No other woman saw him so deeply.

He loved her. He couldn't live without her, and he *knew* they were better together than they were apart. And the idea of leaving her in three days? Forget it.

He gave her a soft smile, and finally, finally, she smiled back. And just like that the lights, the noise, the heat, everything faded away, until it was just the two of them. Just how he liked it.

She reached his side, but she didn't look calm and centered. She looked freaked out. And that set his nerves on fire.

"Don't do this." She mouthed the words.

He wanted to shout, *Are you going to Japan with Jason Becker?* But he didn't bother. Jason and his entourage were here. They wouldn't be here if she'd turned down the job.

And he had to keep her in his life.

He got down on one knee. The crowd screamed, a couple of cameramen raced forward, kneeling along with him.

"Please," she said, and this time he could see the panic.

The cameras were on him. The crowd went wild. And all he knew was he had to seal the deal.

Holding the mic, he reached for her hand. "I love you." He gazed up at her. "I've spent my entire life on the run. And then you came along, and . . . Fuck, V, it ended right there. Everything I thought I was chasing ended in you. Violet, I swear there will never be anyone else for me. Be with me forever, V. Marry me?"

The audience gasped, and catcalls fired across the arena. One of the cameras angled closer. And through all of the chaos, his heart beat sure and strong, because he knew it was Violet for him. For life. He'd marry her right then if he could.

Violet tugged on his hand. He didn't want to get up, but he did. He just wanted to see her smile, fall into his arms. But she was standing there, looking anguished.

Finally, finally, she leaned into him. Oh, thank God. Her arms went loosely around his shoulders and she pressed into his neck. Was this a yes? She was saying yes?

The crowd thought so. The band started playing "Here Comes the Bride." Slater slapped him on his back. Everyone thought she'd said yes.

But she hadn't said a word.

And then . . .

"I can't," she said into his ear.

He jerked away from her. Had to see her face, look into her eyes. Her whole body trembled, and her face shone with perspiration. She took short, choppy breaths, but she didn't change her mind. She didn't say yes.

The floor slipped away, and he was in freefall. She cupped his chin, forced him to look at her. Her mouth moved, but he heard nothing. A stillness gripped the air around them. The crowd went dead silent. Slater stepped forward, took the mic, and started blabbing, shutting down the show. A hand gripped his shoulder, pulling him along.

He followed the band off the stage, losing sight of Violet. Which was good. He couldn't see her. Couldn't be around her.

She didn't want him.

Jesus. She actually didn't want him.

Violet pushed her way through the throng, no idea where she was going. She just needed to get away. *God*. She'd seen his face. She knew he hadn't heard a thing she'd said. He'd simply shut down.

"Babe, hold up." Jason Becker, the nineteen-year-old pop sensation, caught her around the waist, hauling her against his skinny chest.

"Not now, Jason." Blue Fire and its entourage had disappeared. She saw an endless stream of strangers, all of them laughing and talking like nothing had happened. Like she hadn't just destroyed the bass player.

"Hey, chill, man," the kid said. "Why you gotta be like that?"

She pushed at him, hard. He released his hold on her and stumbled. But, no worries, since his bodyguard was there to catch him.

"Bitch, what was that for?" Jason screamed, red-faced.

"You're high, you're drunk, and you're about to flush your career down the toilet."

He gave her a dopey smile. "It's all good."

"Nothing is good, all right? Nothing."

Frantic to get to Derek, she fought her way through the bodies, finally making it into the green room. Someone overturned a bottle of champagne on Slater's head. Emmie stood beside him, hands clapped over her mouth, eyes wide with excitement.

Ben lurched forward as someone drew him into a hug, and Cooper lifted his plastic champagne flute in the air, tipped his head back, and howled.

"Fucking gold, man," Ben shouted.

She couldn't see Derek anywhere. Hating to interrupt their celebration, she came right up to them. "I'm sorry . . ." Her mind had switched off. She couldn't think, couldn't get words together to form a sentence. She'd hurt him. She knew that, but what had he done? How could he have proposed to her? In front of thousands of people? What had he been thinking?

Emmie enfolded Violet in her arms. "I'm so sorry."

"Where is he?" She couldn't be held just then. She had to find him, talk to him. She'd destroyed him.

"Honey, I don't know. I've texted him to let him know the good news. Did you hear? The record went gold." Her excitement quickly dimmed when Violet couldn't form a smile on her numb face. "But he hasn't responded." She pulled back, stroking the damp hair off Violet's forehead.

Slater leaned into her. "You okay?"

"Am *I* okay?" She didn't understand why there were being so nice to her. She'd rejected Derek in front of thousands of people. In front of cameras. No doubt if they went online, they'd be able to watch every second of his humiliation. He would *hate* that.

"I don't know what he was thinking," Slater said. "He knows you better than that."

"His dad sabotaged him at Buck's today." Violet watched their expressions to see if they'd known that. They hadn't. "He got there thinking the show was about him, but his dad showed up. He filmed *his* episode with his dad. And I didn't go with him. I went to talk to a client instead. I wasn't there for him. And now . . ." She squeezed her eyes shut, until she felt Emmie's hands on hers.

"This isn't your fault," Slater said. "You can't blame yourself."

"It's not about blame. He thinks Buck's show didn't go well. You know what that means to him. In his mind, the whole world—*Irwin*—thinks he's everything his dad has ever said about him. He went on that stage thinking all those terrible thoughts. And wondering about me, if I was taking the job in Japan. God." She doubled over with the horror of it all. "Oh, God."

"Honey, I'm so sorry." Emmie rubbed her back.

"Where is he? I have to talk to him. He thinks I rejected him."

She saw the look that passed between them, and it twisted the knife she'd lodged into her own gut. "I didn't reject him."

"I know that, sweetie."

"Give him some time," Slater said. "Let him get his head straight."

"I don't want him in his head right now. His head is telling him terrible things. I want him with me. Right now, before it's too late. Before he talks himself out of us."

"He won't," Emmie said. "He loves you. My God, he proposed to you."

"He proposed to me so the publicity would cover the bad reviews he thinks he'll get for *Artists Unplugged*. That's what he does."

Emmie shook her head. "He loves you, Violet. Yes, I see your point about publicity, but his proposal was sincere. I know my brother. You think he turns that intensity on everyone, that he'll turn it on the next woman who comes along, but you're wrong. He's never cared about anyone the way he does you. He loves you."

"And I just rejected him in front of thousands of people." Her heart screamed in pain. "He thinks I don't love him. I have to find him."

"Let me call him." Slater whipped out his phone.

"Maybe he's at the hotel." Violet dragged her hands down her dress as she waited for Slater's call to go through.

After a few moments, he shook his head, pocketed his phone.

"I'm going to try the hotel." Violet started off, but then stopped. "If you hear from him, will you ask him to call me? Tell him I . . . I have to talk to him."

TWENTY

Violet raced across the lobby, only realizing when she pressed the button for the elevator that she didn't know his room number. He'd checked in without her, of course.

Because she'd chosen to meet with Jason Becker's people instead of supporting him at Buck's. She would never forget his expression when he'd asked her how she could so easily choose a job over him.

A stupid *job*.

Yes, her farm meant everything to her. But he'd been right. She could've taken another job. She just . . . God, she didn't make normal decisions.

The doors opened, but she just stood there, letting them close without her on board.

Oh, God. What had she done? If she could just get to him, be alone with him . . . she had to let him know she wasn't rejecting *him*. But . . . a public proposal? It just . . . No. It wasn't her. It wasn't *them*.

She wasn't rejecting him, just the proposal. Because he hadn't meant it.

Frantic, Violet shot a text to Emmie, asking for his room number.

Her phone chimed. Caller ID said Emmie Valencia. Violet quickly answered, heading to a private corner in the lobby.

"Emmie? Have you heard from him?"

"No, I haven't. But look, Violet, we love you, all of us do, and as much as I want to give you my brother's room number, I just can't. I hope you understand that I can't get between the two of you. I'm here for you, and I'm here for him, but I can't be the intermediary. I know how upset you are, and I'll listen to you and be here for you, but I can't take sides. Okay?"

Oh, God, this wasn't happening. She had to get to him now. "Emmie, God, please. I hurt him. I have to talk to him. He has to know . . ." Her back hit the wall and she closed her eyes, her body aching. She couldn't get his expression out of her mind. The phone slipped from her fingers.

"Violet? V? Are you there?" she heard Emmie call.

She scrambled to pick it up. "I'm . . . I'm here."

"I'll talk to him, I promise. I'll tell him you're sick over what happened."

But she disconnected because she could no longer speak, no longer hear anything but her own sobs.

I hate that I hurt you. I can't stand it. I miss you. Please talk to me.

Violet hit Send, then set the phone back on her nightstand. She rolled onto her back and stared up at the ceiling through a veil of tears. Her stomach muscles hurt from crying so hard. Her swollen eyes needed relief, but she hated closing them. When she did, she saw Derek's face the moment he realized she hadn't accepted his proposal. Panic beat a frantic tattoo on her heart. Why wouldn't he respond to her? Why wouldn't he talk to her?

She wanted to tell him she loved him but not in a text. But should she let another moment pass without him knowing?

She grabbed her phone back. Can we talk today? I'll come to your hotel. I miss you. I can't stand it.

Her door creaked open, and Mimi marched in. She plucked the phone out of Violet's hand, set a cup of steaming tea on the nightstand, and handed her a pill.

"Sit up." With a grip on her shoulder, she practically

hauled Violet to a sitting position, jammed a few pillows behind her, and dropped the pill in her hand.

Violet shook her head. She needed to keep her head clear in case he called or texted or came by. A jolt shot through her at the idea he might come out to the farm.

He loved her. He'd told her he loved her. His sister had said he'd never felt this way before.

"Enough." Mimi sat on the edge of the mattress. "Enough crying, enough beating yourself up. The fucker blindsided you." She wrapped an arm around her. "You did nothing wrong. Could you have been a ditzy groupie bitch and thrown yourself into his arms and said yes for the whole world to see? Yeah, but then he wouldn't have loved *you*. Because that's not you. The real you, the woman he loves? Said no to a lame-ass proposal in front of a zillion freaking fans."

"Me sucks. Me is *horrible*. I hate me. Me is this flat, dead, boring person." Tears welled and then poured down her cheeks as her body was once again overcome with racking sobs. "I hurt him. He said he loved me, Meems. And I didn't say it back. I'm a snail. I'm a blob. I dress all these different parts, but I'm not really anyone. The real me is nothing." She wasn't educated, she hadn't traveled—not on her own, and not to explore—she hadn't really lived. She had so little to offer a vibrant, passionate man like Derek.

But he'd loved her, and she'd come alive in his arms.

Mimi turned, tucking Violet's head against her chest. "No. No, no, no. He's impulsive, and you're cautious. Look, this guy comes out of nowhere. He knocks you down, sweeps you away, and then right when your future together is uncertain, he springs marriage on you. He's a selfish prick because he did it to keep you."

"He's not selfish."

"Bullshit. Did he know you were going to meet Jason?" She nodded.

"Did he see Jason with you backstage?"

She nodded, the sickly feeling of a hard, cold truth snaking its way down her spine, making her want to retch. "Yes."

"Then he thought you'd taken the job. And I'd bet my left tit he proposed so he could hang on to you."

"He shouldn't have had to feel he had to hang on to me.

I pulled away. Who does that? Who takes this amazing, beautiful gift and tosses it aside? Who does that?"

Mimi's hands tightened, holding her closer. "Oh, Violet. You're killing me here."

"I have to talk to him."

"Right now you have to sleep. Take this pill, drink this tea, and black out for a few hours, okay? I promise you this clusterfuck will be exactly how you left it when you wake up."

With trembling fingers, she took the pill and reached for the tea. As she cupped the hot mug, breathed in the lavender steam, she watched Mimi snag her phone and start typing.

"What're you doing?"

Mimi's brow furrowed in concentration as she tapped away, chipped red polish on her fingernails.

"Meems, what're you doing?" She tried to grab the phone, but Mimi whisked it out of reach and continued typing. "Are you writing him? No, don't do that." Hot tea splashed on her chest as she set her mug down and lunged for the phone. Only when Mimi hit Send did she toss the phone on Violet's lap.

With shaking fingers, she opened it.

Listen, you fucking fucker, you have destroyed my girl. She's crying her eyes out right now because you're too much of a pussy to talk to her. You're the asshole who thought it was a brilliant idea to spring a marriage proposal on her in front of a million strangers. Grow a pair and talk to her or you never deserved her in the first place.

Violet flung herself back onto the pillow. "Oh, my God, why did you do that?"

"What? Tell him the truth? Because it's not just about him. It's about you, too. And he's not the man for you if he doesn't get that."

"I've never seen her like this."

At the sound of Mimi's voice, Violet stopped, reaching for the banister. She wished Mimi hadn't given her a sleeping pill. It made her legs shaky, her mind fuzzy, and her mouth taste funny.

"You know what?" That was Francesca. "It's the best thing in the world for her. Her whole life she's been in survival mode, trying her best to hold everything together. She's never been allowed to be a kid, throw a tantrum, have her heart broken. She's just skimmed the surface of life."

She breathed in the aroma of freshly brewed coffee and imagined them drinking it on the covered porch. Her legs too weak to stand any longer, Violet sat on the top stair.

"That's great and all, but I can't stand to see her like this. I swear, I want to shove his balls in a nutcracker. Why isn't he getting back to her?"

What was he doing? Was he celebrating? Had he already forgotten about her? Worse, was he partying with Gen, erasing Violet's scent, her touch, her imprint on his life?

That would destroy her.

"He's a scaly bastard, that's what he is."

"My darling, he thought he was losing her. He acted rashly."

"You're excusing his behavior? I want to squeeze his nuts till they pop for what he's done to her. That's not how you treat Violet. That girl will give you her blood, her last granola bar. She'll give you—"

"But she won't give her whole heart. And that's what he wanted. Look at her history, sweetheart. Men fall madly in love with her. She's beautiful, nurturing, smart . . . she'll give you one hundred percent of her attention. She'll find all the good in you and help you draw it out. She'll give you the wildflowers and the sea . . . but she won't give you her heart. And that's what keeps them chasing her. She's a beautiful, elusive woman. But for Derek? He *loves* her. Anyone can see it. He loves Violet with his whole heart. And I'm not sure a guy like that knows what to do when the woman can't give it back."

But that wasn't fair. She didn't have a whole heart to give. Whole hearts were nurtured, developed. Every hug, every stroke, every loving look a baby got forged a whole heart.

She'd thought this time, with this man, what she had to give would be enough. It wasn't.

Oh, God. Violet got up, rushed into her room. She started to throw off her smelly clothes when she caught a glimpse of herself in the antique mirror on the dresser. She drew back in horror. Her left eye was bright red.

"Francesca! Francesca!" Panic reached such a pitch inside her head she thought she was going mad.

Feet trampled up the stairs. Francesca and Mimi raced into her room. She stood there in a bra and black leggings, fingers on her cheek, under the damaged eye. Francesca put a hand over heart, features crumpling in sorrow. Mimi threw her arms around her and hugged her tightly.

"My eye."

"I see that, sweetheart," Francesca said. "You burst a blood vessel, honey."

"Fix it, please. You have to fix it."

"Sweetheart, I'm so sorry, but I can't."

Mimi glanced over her shoulder. "Eye drops, Mom."

"Of course. Sure. I'll be right back."

"We'll take care of it. It'll be all right." Mimi rubbed circles on her back, but Violet needed to get ready.

"I need to shower."

"Yes, you do." Mimi pulled back. "Wait, why?"

"I'm going to the hotel. I'm going to see him."

"We don't know his room number."

"I can get it from someone. A roadie maybe. I'll get it. I have to see him."

"Maybe we should wait until he gets back to you?"

She shook her head. She'd been about to do something, but she couldn't remember what it was. Oh, right. Shower. She walked into the closet, stood there, staring blankly. Clothing. What should she wear?

"I'll get the shower started, okay?" Mimi paused, watching her, and then left her alone.

Violet looked at the row of dresses and shirts, touching the silks, the satins, the expensive wools. All clothing she'd bought for jobs. Anything she'd bought for herself was inexpensive, utilitarian. Shorts, leggings, T-shirts. Things to wear while working in the fields or running into town on an errand.

She couldn't wear a work outfit to see him. She couldn't

wear a *costume*, for God's sake. A cry escaped her throat, and she leaned back against the wall.

"Oh, God, V, what's wrong? What happened?" Mimi stood there, shaking her hands. "Please tell me what happened."

"I don't even know who I am. I mean, what do I wear? If I'm not on the job, what do I wear? I can't go to him in shorts and a T-shirt. I can't . . . what do I look like? In his eyes?"

"You look like the most beautiful girl in the world," Mimi said softly. "That's what you look like to him."

"Why do you say that?"

"Because I saw the way he looked at you. And, I swear to God, if someone ever looked at me the way Derek Valencia looks at you, I could seriously die a happy woman."

Agony wrenched through her entire body, and she fell to the hardwood floor.

"What did I say?" Mimi crouched in front of her. "Mom? Mom!" And then she leaned forward, scooping Violet into her arms. "What did I say? I don't know what I said."

The throbbing pain in her skull beat in time with the squeezing, pulsating hurt in her heart. "I lost him. I found the one person in the world who loves me, and I pushed him away. Oh, my God, what have I done?" Sobs wracked her overheated body. She thought she was going to die.

Francesca's cool hands touched her face, lifting her, smoothing tears away with her fingers. "You didn't lose him. What do you think, sweetheart? Love just evaporates like that?" Her friend got down on the floor, facing her, their knees bumping. "No, my sweet. I know you're scared. I know you're hurt. And it's okay to feel all of it. You can let it all out. All of it."

The way she emphasized *all* let Violet know her friend meant so much more than the loss of Derek.

Mimi got up, swung around to the row of horrible clothes. "I'll find you something to wear. We'll find just the thing, okay?"

And God, the look of concern on Mimi's face as she flicked through the clothing on her rack. Violet could see nothing worked.

Because Violet Davis didn't have a style. She didn't even have a name. "I'm not even who I am."

"What do you mean, sweetheart?" Francesca kept rubbing her fingers over Violet's cheeks, softly, gently.

"I'm not really Violet."

"I don't know what that means, honey."

"My birth certificate. I'm Baby Jane Doe. My mom was strung out when I was born. My grandma let me name myself. She had the prettiest violets all around her house, like a magical barrier keeping all the bad out. So I called myself Violet." Her head hurt too much to stay upright. It was so heavy she thought she might topple over.

Francesca's mouth trembled; tears filled her eyes. "I didn't know that."

"He doesn't know that either. I didn't tell him who I am. I need to tell him who I am. I need to tell him I love him."

"Okay. Okay, let's get you dressed." Mimi pulled some dresses off the hangers. "You get in the shower, and I'll have a few things for you to choose from, okay?"

The sobs dried up. The ache dulled. She stood up. "I don't really care what I wear. I hurt him. Just like his dad, I rejected him. That's the one thing he can't take, being pushed away." The need to get to him compelled her into the bathroom. She closed the door and stripped off her clothes. Walking through the billowing steam, she stepped into the hot water and closed her eyes, letting determination seep in, replacing the pain.

She'd get to him. She'd talk to him. She'd tell him she loved him.

And then everything would be all right.

Love doesn't just evaporate.

Thank you so much! Violet hit Send. She'd added the exclamation point only to cover for the absolute fear she felt as the elevator rode up to the twenty-first floor. She hoped the roadie didn't get in trouble for giving out Derek's hotel room to someone who no longer had access to it.

When the car landed, she touched the wall, fear turning

into full-blown panic. What if he wasn't there? What if he *was* there but with Gen?

Oh, God. Oh, *God*. She couldn't bear it. She just couldn't bear it.

Placing a hand over her heart, she stepped into the hallway, staring too long at the wall plate indicating which rooms she'd find to the left and those she'd find to the right. She saw the numbers but nothing registered. Her mind was on lockdown.

Three days, she hadn't heard from him. The three days they were supposed to spend together. Figuring things out.

He'd check out tomorrow, head back on the road, driving away from her. This whole bubble of time they'd shared together—six weeks—would be a memory, like all her other jobs.

Stop it. She'd made the decision to come here. She'd fight for him. For them.

Reading the wall plate again, she turned in the direction of his room.

On the train she'd looked through the texts she'd sent him. She'd made herself perfectly clear on all but one point.

She loved him. And really, nothing else mattered. So she'd tell him. And get him back. They just needed to talk.

Standing outside his door, she pressed an ear, listening. She heard the TV, nothing else.

She knocked, her stomach twisting, palms sweaty. Wiping them on the pretty pink and white sundress she'd chosen, she looked down at her patent leather pink wedges. She'd bought them for a job last summer. She'd always associate this outfit with that time on the yacht.

And so she needed a new wardrobe. Needed clothes that didn't tie to a job—just to her. Whoever she really was.

She knocked again, louder this time.

Finally, the door swung open. Derek stood in a towel wrapped around his waist, droplets of water on his muscled chest. His smile dulled. He looked a little too long at her left eye, and emotion whipped across his features. "What happened to you?" But as soon as the words were out, he turned expressionless.

"Will you talk to me, Derek, please?"

He stepped aside to let her in. "I thought you were someone else."

Opening the security latch, he propped the door open and then strode into the bedroom.

She followed him, looking around the suite for signs of a party, of women.

But she didn't see anything other than a room service tray, a pair of his big, black boots by the coffee table, and his Fender leaning against the couch.

He was ignoring her, going about his business, so she headed into the bedroom. *Please, God, let him be alone in there.* If she found Gen in there—getting ready? Naked in bed?

Oh, God.

"Derek."

He dropped his towel, digging into his suitcase for a pair of clean boxers. "What's up?"

"I hate that I hurt you."

He stepped into the boxers. "Got it. Read the texts. We're good."

"Please don't be like this."

"Like what?" He looked at her like she was some nymph he'd slept with the night before. Then, he grabbed his jeans and put them on.

"It took me by surprise. I don't—"

"I get it. My bad. Now we move on."

"I don't understand why you won't talk to me. If you loved me enough to propose to me, how do you just shut me out the very next day? How real could it have been?"

"That's what I always liked about you. Sharp as a tack."

His phone buzzed. He picked it up off the nightstand, read it, and smiled. Then he looked up at her. Total stranger. "We done?"

"No. Stop this. We need to talk about what happened. I thought we'd—"

"Babe, I've had a lifetime of rejection. Not interested in hearing yet another version of why."

"I'm not . . . I'm not rejecting you. I want us. I just . . . we're not ready for marriage."

Laughter heralded the arrival of his guests. "Yoo-hoo," a woman called.

"Let's get this party started," another said.

"Fuck me, do not put a shirt over that chest," a third one said, striding into the room and coming right up to him, running her hands all over his abs.

Violet watched three overly made up, underdressed women surround him.

"Not until I lick it all over." The woman licked a path from his nipple to his belly button.

The pain hit her full in the chest. A shrill noise screamed in her mind, and her heart curled into a tiny little ball of pain.

"Well, aren't you just a breath of sunshine?" one of the women said to her. "She work for you?"

"Not anymore." Derek's voice sounded different, not so cocky.

"Oh, my God, what happened to your eye?" another one asked.

Violet's hand automatically went to her cheek. Numbness seeped in, leaving her with a dull sense of emptiness.

He'd done it. He'd moved on. She was just another notch on the neck of his guitar.

All three of the women spoke over one another, vying for his attention. He laughed, turned on that charm and cockiness. He was gone. He'd left her completely.

"You wanna fuck around here first or you wanna meet up with everybody?" one of them asked.

"And miss the celebration?" Derek said, all full of energy and joviality. "I waited a long time to go gold. We're gonna party first. "

"Then let's do this shit." And the women headed out of the bedroom, one of them holding his hand.

He was going to walk out on her, leave her alone in his hotel room.

"Derek." *Screw him.*

He snapped around at her tone.

"I'm hurt, too. I don't have a dad in my life to keep the wound open and fresh, but if I don't always respond the way you want, it's because *I'm hurt, too.* I gave you more in the six weeks I've known you than I've ever given anyone else. My feelings go deeper, take longer to build, but when they take root, they last. That might not seem like a good thing to someone who wants everything from me all at once, but it's a good thing for someone who actually wants to *marry* me." She waited, gave him a chance to put his hurt aside, come back to her. To them.

But he stood there stonily.

"Come on." The woman tugged on his arm.

"Yeah, yeah." And then he turned away.

"So I was right after all. I'm no different than all the others." She pushed past him, past the women raiding his mini fridge, and out the door.

She forced her feet to move, feeling like her spirit had left her body.

Would he come after her? He'd come after her, right? He couldn't be that detached, that bloodless. She stepped into the elevator, nerves strung so tight they hummed. She pressed the button to keep the door open, waiting. But he didn't come. So she let go.

And the elevator doors closed.

As soon as she hit the lobby, she knew she couldn't take another step. Collapsing in the nearest chair, she pulled out her phone. She had to keep blinking away the tears in order to punch in the numbers.

Francesca answered on the first ring. "Violet?"

Emotion rushed her so hard, it burned like a rash on her skin. Her throat muscles tightened into a hard knot.

"Sweetheart?" She could hear Francesca talking quietly to Mimi in the background. "I don't know. She's not saying anything."

Mimi got on the phone. "Talk to me, V. What'd the fucker do?"

"Mimi?"

"I'm right here."

She'd never asked anyone for a favor in her life. Not once. She didn't lean on people. She didn't put them out in any way. But she literally could not move a muscle. Could not get her ass off this chair if the building were on fire. She needed her friends. "Come get me. Please?"

"Of course. Stay right where you are. We're on our way."

The phone dropped in her lap. She closed her eyes, imagining curling up into a little ball, hardening like a marble.

TWENTY-ONE

He'd gone twenty-eight years without her in his life, so why couldn't he stop thinking about her? Why did her scent still come to him as if she were in the room?

He'd known her all of six weeks.

Derek yanked back the shower curtain and stepped out of the stall, covering his face in a clean, white towel. Shittiest week of his life.

Should have been the best—his record had gone *gold*. Critics loved Blue Fire. Life couldn't be better.

A knock on the door jerked him out of his thoughts. He'd told the guys he didn't want to party with them. Just wanted to crash early after tonight's gig in Syracuse. If they'd come to lure him out, they could forget it.

Shoving his legs into jeans, he peered through the peephole.

Oh, shit.

He opened the door to the vision of Genevieve Babineaux. Dark hair gleaming and tumbling over her bare shoulders, she stood there with her red-glossed lips and strapless skintight dress, her tits mounding over the top.

"Hey, baby." She breezed in, her expensive scent floating in the air around her. "Ooh, this is just how I like you."

She ran her hands over his bare chest, then cupped the back of his neck and pressed a kiss to his mouth, her tongue flicking out.

Okay, this was good. *This is what I need.* He needed to go back to the man he was before Violet Davis.

Baby Jane Doe.

Why the fuck did Mimi keep torturing him? He didn't need to know details about the woman who sure as fuck didn't want him.

Didn't need the guilt she kept piling on.

But fuck, it charged him hard, knocking him flat on his ass. Because like everyone else in Violet's life, he'd left her. And why?

Because she hadn't wanted to discuss a future with him in front of twenty thousand people?

Fuck. He couldn't stand it. Couldn't stand what he'd done.

He would never forget her eye, the white turned a livid red. He'd made her cry so hard she'd burst a blood vessel.

Gen squeezed his biceps. "Mm, you smell so good. God, I've missed you."

He had to stop thinking about Violet. No matter her past, no matter the time they spent alone together, where he'd seen a side of her he suspected few people ever got to see, no matter any of it, she still wasn't going to open up for anyone. She couldn't.

He remembered Ferrari dude. That guy had been crazy about her. But she'd just stood there, all quiet and reserved. She didn't have it in her.

An image of Violet straddling him, their hands clasped at either side of his head as she rode him hard, hips swiveling, grinding, her head jerking back as she came with a wild cry of release.

She opened for him.

The heel of Gen's palm rubbed his dick. Instead of a shot of lust, instead of going rock hard, he felt a mild tingling. She just . . . wasn't his girl. He stepped back, let her in.

"I expected to see you out with the guys. When they told me you were staying in, I figured you could use some cheering up."

"Appreciate it, but not tonight. I'm just gonna crash."

She cocked her head. "Still licking your wounds? That's not like you at all."

Christ. He didn't want to deal with her shit. Ignoring her, he headed to the desk, where he'd left his water bottle.

"Derek, I could've spun this for you. I don't know why you let the whole world think she rejected you. I had a great story we could've run with. We could've milked this thing for weeks."

·"I don't want it going on for weeks. I need it to end. I need it all to go away."

"Oh, please. Since when do you let media attention go away? You work it. You build it to your advantage."

"Not at Violet's expense. She has a job, an identity, and if I let the press get to her, it'll ruin things for her."

"Ah, that's so sweet. Looking out for someone other than yourself. But she *rejected* you. So no need to be sweet anymore. Well, in any event, we can keep the story going by being quiet about it, too. We'll just show up at events together, keep everyone speculating about who you're with. That'll work just as well."

It would destroy Violet. Literally hit the target and blow up her heart. Her greatest fear realized, that she'd been just another chick in his string of short-lived, passionate relationships. He couldn't do that to her.

He already had.

His fucking heart. Would it ever stop aching?

He closed his eyes, letting the humiliation blaze across his nerves. Who springs a proposal on a girl he'd known six weeks? "Just gonna let the whole thing fade away." Just like the feelings he'd had for her.

Although not doing such a good job on that front.

"So you're just going to wallow in your room? You don't care about going gold? Making the list? Nothing?"

He sat on the edge of his bed, just wanting to be left alone. "Look, Gen, no offense, but I'm not in the mood for company tonight."

"Oh, for Christ's sake, you should be celebrating. Gloating. Shove it in your dad's face. I can help you do that, you know. In a way that won't make you look like the bad guy."

"Going gold doesn't mean shit to him. He's multi-platinum a dozen times over. It doesn't mean I've got talent."

"I'm not talking about . . ." She looked stunned. "You don't know, do you? What're you, living under a rock? Where's your phone?"

"Turned it off. I just want to go to sleep."

She cocked a hip, tipping her chin down. "Derek, babe, you made the *Ledger List*. It came out tonight."

She may as well have sprayed him with a fire hose. "What?"

Coming at him with her arms open, she wrapped herself around him, gripping his ass, and pulling him in against her. "You're on it, baby. You're the best rock bass player in the world."

Fuck. Oh, fuck. He pulled away from her, heading toward the window. Jesus Christ, he'd made the list? How was that possible? He'd sucked on *Artists Unplugged*. Let himself get rattled by his dad's constant interruptions.

He was too young, too new on the scene.

The *Ledger List*? He smiled, imagining Violet's expression. She wouldn't be jumping up and down; she wouldn't be gloating. It'd be a private moment between the two of them. She'd give him the time and space to let it really sink in.

He'd made the Ledger List.

Violet. He closed his eyes remembering the last text she'd sent him.

You swept me away, and despite my
reservations, I let go, let myself fall for you.
Tonight you showed me you're exactly who
I feared you were. Next time choose your
targets more carefully. Choose women you
won't destroy.

Soft hands slid around his waist, Gen's breasts pressed into his back.

Violet was gone. Over. And he was free. Free to be a rock star. His album had gone gold; he'd made the Ledger List. Everything he'd wanted, he'd earned.

He closed his eyes, the impact spreading through him. Jesus. *The Ledger List.* He had talent.

He should go out with his friends. Celebrate. Biggest moment of his life, and he was alone. Well, with Gen, but she didn't count.

Oh, fuck him. She didn't count. Adriana didn't count. He chose women who didn't count because they couldn't tear his fucking heart out the way Violet had.

But what *had* Violet done? She'd rejected his idiotic marriage proposal. She'd come back, tried to talk to him, and what had he done? Pretended to be banging three nymphs.

He was such an asshole.

Gen's hands caressed his bare skin, skimmed down into his unbuttoned jeans. "Mm. I missed you." Why did her *mm*'s irritate the shit out of him? Because they were fake. Everything about her was fake. He shrugged her off. "I'm gonna call Slater." He headed for the door, wanting her gone. He should be with his friends. Of anyone in the world, Emmie and Slater knew what this moment meant to him. The fucking *Ledger List.*

Except . . . Emmie and Slater might be able to *guess* what this moment meant because they'd known him so long. But Violet—she was the only person he'd ever talked to about it.

He opened the door, eager to get Gen out. "Thanks for stopping by." He turned, but Gen wasn't with him.

She stood at the window. Standing there bare ass naked, she licked her lips. Cupping her big breasts, she offered what he would've welcomed two months ago. "Come here, baby. Let me be your present for making the list. You can have me any way you want all night long."

"Gen." He knew he sounded as bored as he felt, and he didn't want to hurt her. "I'm sorry, sweetheart. I'm just not . . . I think I'm still tied up in someone else." Grabbing his phone, he turned it on, waited for it to boot up.

There was only one person he wanted to share this moment with. Could he call Violet, let her know? She'd be so excited for him.

Yeah, right.

You're exactly who I feared you were.

* * *

The guys stood around him, Emmie's hand on his shoulder, as Derek sat at the desk in his hotel room. The Beatz logo filled the screen of his laptop. The music faded, and then Cassandra Miller, the music blog's top reporter, smiled at the camera.

"And so it's out. What everyone who's anyone in the music industry waits for each fall. The Ledger List. Started by the most illustrious name of all, Irwin Ledger, it's a list of the world's best musicians in jazz and rock, voted on by a select group of the biggest players in the industry. Now, everyone's heard of Irwin Ledger, of course, but few have ever seen him. Why? Because the bastard gives no interviews. No matter what we offer him, how we bribe him, the twat rarely shows his face. Well, tonight, friends, we're about to pull back the curtain on that elusive wizard. Yes, I, Cassandra Miller, have scored the interview of the decade. Ladies and gentleman . . ."

A cartoon image of a green curtain opened to reveal Irwin, sitting there looking annoyed.

"Irwin Ledger," Cassandra said.

"Look at him," Ben said.

"Dude looks like he's sitting on spikes," Cooper said.

"Why'd he do the interview anyway?" Ben asked. "He never does shit like this."

"Shh." Emmie waved a hand.

"You never give interviews," Cassandra said. "So I have to start out by thanking you."

"Well, I didn't really have a choice now, did I? Beatz has boycotted Amoeba artists for the past year, so in order for my bands to get the exposure they've earned, you've *convinced* me to have this bloody little chat."

The camera zinged to Cassandra, and she gave a comical expression of being shocked, accompanied by sound effects. "You are *not* editing this out," she said to someone in the room. She burst out laughing.

"All righty, then. I've got you here, let's do this." She turned serious. "Normally, of course, we'd edit out a comment like that. But we're not going to, and I'll tell you why.

We are a cynical generation. We don't trust award shows or lists. We think everything's rigged or bought somehow. Well, I think you can see for yourself who Irwin is. He takes no shit, and he pulls no punches. He tells it like it is. So the Ledger List? It's the real deal. These truly are the best musicians in the world."

"Shall we get to it, then?" Irwin looked impatient.

"Yes, absolutely. The moment we've been waiting for has come. The list is out."

Irwin shrugged. "Not sure why so much is made out of a silly list."

"There's a hell of a lot of talented people out there. The market's flooded with musicians. Thanks to social media, new bands spring up every day. Weeding them out, sorting through them to find the true talent? That's important. That's meaningful. Tell us how the list came about?"

"Bunch of blokes going out for a pint after work each night, sitting around arguing about the best musicians. Someone started writing down our answers, and somehow, my list found its way to my boss at the time." Irwin shrugged. "For some reason my list became formalized. An annual expectation. It wound up in *Billboard*, *A&R*, the trade magazines of the time. Ridiculous, really."

"And you got promoted, and here you are twenty-seven years later, with a string of the most famous bands in the world to your credit. And now you've got Blue Fire, formerly known as Snatch."

Irwin winced; Cassandra laughed. "I'm going to guess you had a hand in changing their name. So let's start with the rockers. Specifically, the bass player. Talk to me about Eddie and Derek Valencia. It's interesting that you chose Derek, considering all the press his dad's got out there on him. Tell me the truth, did Eddie—a jazz virtuoso who stayed on your list for ten years—influence your decision at all?"

All humor left his eyes. "The man hasn't been relevant in years. How could he possibly influence anyone's decisions?"

Emmie's hand on Derek's shoulder squeezed. He smiled. *Hasn't been relevant in years.* Fuck, yeah. He laughed, and the band around his chest snapped, giving him room to breathe for the first time in . . . ages.

"You want to know why I chose Derek? 'Four O'Clock Farm.'"

Every time Derek thought of the song, he was taken right back to the barn, Violet on his lap on a bale of hay, arms wrapped around his neck. Fuck, he could still smell her sweet scent. Still picture the sea of wildflowers rippling in a warm breeze.

"Did you happen to catch him on *Artists Unplugged*?" Irwin continued. "I can't even tell you what they blabbered on about or what songs were played, until he did an acoustic version of that song. It's not out yet, so I can't offer you a copy, but when you get a chance, close your eyes and listen to it, really feel it. At first you'll hear Slater Vaughn's vocals—you have no choice. The kid's brilliant. You become a vessel for his feelings. That's why he took the spot for best rock vocals. The next thing you'll hear is a haunting melody that will make you weep. And if you don't believe me, come to their next show and look around the arena. You won't find a dry eye in the place. But let me tell you *why* that song is so haunting. Because of the bass. People think bass is nothing more than the background. Just the guy keeping time for the band. They're wrong. The bass gives the track its groove and rhythm. Derek is the rhythm of Blue Fire. He's the heart and soul of it. Slater's the voice, the lyricist, the face, but Derek's the heart."

The moment turned completely surreal. Derek didn't even think he was in his body.

Had Irwin Ledger said that to promote the label? The band? The only reason he was on the show was to get Amoeba back in their good graces, so maybe . . .

Jesus, listen to you. He was so full of shit. Irwin had said that Derek was the soul of Blue Fire. The *heart.* He'd chosen Derek out of all the bass players in the fucking world—and Derek was still questioning his own talent?

Emmie wrapped her arms around his neck, hugging him. "I'm so proud of you."

Slater cupped his shoulder, squeezed. Didn't say a word. Didn't need to. Derek felt it.

"Your dad's a has-been, dude," Ben said.

"Like V said, he's got a small dick," Cooper said. "So small he'd fuck his own kid over. You gotta get that."

"Get free of it, man," Ben said.

Derek popped out of his chair. "You want to grab some food?"

"I could eat," Ben said.

Slater slipped an arm around Emmie's waist. "Hungry?"

She nodded, and Derek grabbed his key card, following them out.

But the truth was he wasn't hungry. He was anxious. All he could think about was Violet.

And he didn't give a shit about eating.

He stopped. "Em?"

She turned toward him.

"I fucked up."

She smiled sadly, nodding. "Yeah, you did."

Ben and Cooper reached the elevator bay, punched the button.

"Have you talked to her?" he asked. "Is she all right?"

The smile turned to frustration. "I told you, I'm not getting involved."

"I know that. I'm just asking how she is." Fuck it. He had to just go for it. "I need to know where she is."

"Ask *her*."

"I don't think she wants to talk to me." The image of that nymph's hands all over his chest, licking him right in front of Violet ate away at him like acid.

What an asshole.

"No, I don't think she does."

"She thinks I slept with nymphs."

"Three nights after you proposed, you blew her off for a three-pack," Emmie said in an accusing tone.

"Bad move, dude," Cooper said from down the hall.

"I didn't do anything with them." Derek gave him a quelling look, then focused on Emmie. "Tell me where she is."

Emmie's gaze cut away. She bit her lower lip. "Chicago."

"Chicago? She didn't take the job with Jason Becker?"

"I don't think she's taken a job yet. As far as I know, she's still meeting with clients before she decides."

"So she's not in Japan?" Thank fuck. Relief swept through him so fast his knees went weak. "When will she be back?"

"No idea. I don't have her itinerary. I'm talking to her about the wedding, that's all."

Right, the wedding. Out in Eden's Landing. The ceremony would take place on the beach, the reception on Four O'Clock Farm. So no matter what, Derek would see her.

Not for another week. He needed to see her now. Spinning around, he marched back to his room, slid the key card in.

"Derek," Emmie called. "What are you doing?"

"I'm going to the farm."

"She's not at the farm."

"No, but maybe they'll tell me where she is. I have to talk to her."

"She's not . . . she's not going to just come back. Trust is hard for her. You broke it."

He looked at her, standing in the dimly lit hallway halfway between Derek's room and the elevators. "I hate that I hurt her." *Destroyed her.*

Jesus, he had to fix it. Erase the pain he'd caused. "Is it too late?"

Emmie let out an exasperated breath, her hands going up in a helpless gesture. "It's hard to say with Violet. But you'll never know if you don't try."

If New York in August was unbearably hot and humid, Chicago was like crawling into the devil's armpit. Violet strode quickly down Oak Street, dying to get to the comfort of her hotel room. Perspiration dripped down her back, making her silk shirt cling. She'd worn a light, swingy skirt to keep it loose, but nothing eased the stifling humidity.

Unused to heels after spending a few weeks on the farm, she wanted nothing more than to get to her air-conditioned hotel room and kick them off, strip, and take a cool shower.

Crossing the street to her hotel, she considered the three possible jobs she could take. Jason Becker would be the most difficult. Surrounded by enabling parents, security guards, hangers-on, all who wanted to keep him happy so they could share in his riches, he had absolutely no interest in cleaning up his act. He was too young to understand the fleetingness of fame or how quickly adulation turned to disgust. The same fans who turned him into a superstar would easily transfer all that affection onto the next It boy.

Finally, the revolving door in sight, Violet let go of the breath she'd been holding. Truthfully, she hadn't taken the Jason job because of Derek. She couldn't bear the idea of letting him go completely. Going overseas for three months, all the way across the world, would have cut him off for good.

The Chicago attorney would be a job like all the others she'd ever had. It paid well, and it didn't involve musicians. The third, another CEO like Joe Capriano, would keep her in the city. Back in Randall's world.

Randall. He was a really good guy. He'd been so supportive through this whole ordeal with the farm. More than anything, she appreciated his even-tempered nature. She could count on him.

As much as losing Derek hurt, she knew she wasn't cut out for someone with such a passionate nature. Mercurial, she'd discovered, didn't work for her.

She would never forget the week of pure hell she'd endured after he'd blown her off.

Never again.

The moment she entered the lobby, cold air enveloped her. Her skin tingled, then tightened as the perspiration dried. Only, as she strode toward the elevators, the tingling didn't stop. The hairs at the back of her neck sprung up.

Awareness gripped her. Out of her peripheral vision she noted the form of a man. She turned and saw him, and electricity swept through her.

Derek.

Her heart leapt into her throat, her blood raced.

Derek.

She froze, the weight of her bag digging into her shoulder.

"Violet." His broad shoulders stretching the fabric of a dark gray T-shirt, his thigh muscles prominent in the worn jeans, Derek approached her with urgency, like he was afraid she'd go up in smoke.

She wished she would. She didn't want to see him. Why was he here?

What *the hell* did he want?

Everything in him softened when he reached her. "Hey."

She forced herself to speak over the pounding of her heart. "Derek." She said it coolly. Good. "What are you doing here?"

"I need to talk to you."

He needed . . . *are you kidding me?* She didn't give a damn what *he* needed. "How did you know I was here?"

"I went to the farm. Talked to Mimi. V, please, can we talk somewhere? Let's go to your room."

"No, Derek, we can't talk somewhere." Was he serious? Just like that she'd take him to her room? "Please excuse me." *Go to hell.* She carried on toward the elevator.

He stepped in front of her. "No."

At the snap in his voice, people turned to look.

She wanted to curl into herself. For as much as she'd pulled herself together since her week in a twisted ball of misery, she realized in that moment how tenuous her hold on her inner strength really was. "Don't make a scene."

"I'm not making a scene. I just need to talk to you."

"I don't care what you need. I really don't." She took a breath, calming herself. Hitching her bag up her shoulder, she looked at this impulsive man who thought he could take whatever he wanted when he wanted.

God, he was gorgeous. From his bulging biceps to his battered black Converse high tops, he was a seething, roiling wall of pure masculinity.

And he'd nearly killed her. She had to remember that. "For every moment we shared over our six weeks together, do you know the one I see every single time I close my eyes?"

His shoulders slumped, and it looked like the life drained out of him. "I think so."

"How could you propose to me one night and then three nights later ignore me like some groupie you'd already forgotten?"

He winced. "I was fucked up." But then he straightened,

reanimating himself. "I didn't sleep with those women. I haven't been with anybody—how could I? I've missed you. V, I can't . . . I can't fucking live without you." He reached for her hand, but she jerked it back. He seemed surprised. "Sorry, I . . ." His eyes lit up from within, and he smiled. "Hey, I made the Ledger List."

A jolt of happiness traveled along her nerves, but she tamped it down. "That's wonderful. Congratulations."

"Yeah. It's pretty cool."

"So you got everything you wanted. I'm happy for you."

"I did, and it sucks. I'm miserable without you."

Oh, no. Oh, no, no, no, *no.* She was not going to get sucked back into that world with him again. Okay, she needed to get a hold of herself.

Mercurial. As much as she'd enjoyed the wake-up call to her heart he'd provided, she didn't have the temperament to endure his inconstant nature. Because as quickly as he'd turned his energy on her, he'd turn it off.

And now he was nothing but a former client. She would do well to remember that.

"Well, of course it doesn't make you happy." Oh, good. Her calm, professional tone had returned. *Thank God.*

He cocked his head, confused.

"The kind of happiness that comes from an award or a great review is fleeting. It doesn't scratch the itch. The only person who needs to think you're talented is *you.* No matter how many times your records go platinum, it'll never be enough. Until you believe in yourself, you'll always need more."

His gaze hardened. "Cut the shit, V."

"Excuse me?"

"Drop the act. I'm not your client anymore." He grabbed her arm and tugged her so hard, she slammed into his solid chest.

Oh, God, he smelled so familiar it made her ache. It threw her right back to their bodies pressed together in the dark of his bunk, the rumble of the bus's engine humming through her bones. She wanted his arms around her, wanted his kisses on the curve of her neck.

She wanted *them.*

He stood there, a wall of heat and energy. "I'm your man. And I'm here to get you back."

She shoved his chest, but he didn't budge. "Go to hell."

"Oh, I'm already there. Don't worry about that. Yeah, I fucked up. I get that. Your rejection on that stage hurt, and I acted like an immature jerk trying to shut you out. I'm a pussy, I get that. But I can't . . . it's not over, V. I need you. The way you touch me, the way you see me, the way you calm me the fuck down, V. I need you."

Damn, he was good. He was *so* good her brain scrambled to find a way to let him back into her life. Give him a second chance.

Like that would ever happen. "You need me *now*? Oh, okay. That's nice. But what about when I do something to hurt your feelings again, which I *will* do because I'm only human after all, then you won't need me anymore, right?" She shook her head. "Sorry, I'm afraid I'm not up for that kind of game."

"This isn't a game." He leaned toward her, grabbed her arms. "I love you."

People were watching them, but she couldn't stop. "*Love?* Are you kidding me? You don't love. You play this high drama *show* of love, but you don't *feel* love. That whole side of you was shut down when the little boy in you decided he'd had enough rejection from the dad he worshipped, the man he loved with his whole and trusting heart. *That* piece of you is locked and buried away. How do I know? Because you proved it to me. Not when you proposed as a publicity stunt—that I could get over. But when you didn't return a single one of my texts begging you to talk to me, when you ignored me so cruelly—you saw my eye, you knew how devastated I had to have been to wind up with a broken blood vessel. I could *not* have gotten into your heart if you could treat me the way you did in that hotel room. No, you don't love me. You want me to get up onstage with you and play out a few more high drama scenes before you move on to the next play thing. And I can assure you, that is *not* going to happen. Not with me."

God, everyone was watching them. How could she let herself get carried away like this? She needed to escape to the privacy of her room. "Good-bye, Derek."

He followed her, so close that with every swing of her arm she brushed up against his hard body. She reached for the button, but he caught her hand, brought it to his chest, right over his heart.

"You make me want to be a better man. You see me. And guess what, sweet V? I see you, too. You've got that damn professional face on again—I did that, I know—but I see the beating heart underneath. The passionate, sexy woman that only *I* bring out. We're good for each other. Don't walk away from me. Give me a chance."

A big part of her was ready to cave, to fall into his arms, because that woman he described? Yes, she was alive and breathing somewhere inside her. But Violet didn't want her to be. Because that woman knew too much pain. And she couldn't do it. She couldn't go there again. Not for anything.

So she looked behind her, scanning the lobby, making a big show of it. "Is this being taped? Am I going to find myself on every entertainment outlet in the morning?"

"What're you talking about? Of course not."

"I'm curious. What happened this time, Derek? What did your dad do to hurt you and make you go racing off to Chicago to stir up new drama for the press?"

He stepped forward, crowding her. "You think losing you wasn't lesson enough? Are you fucking kidding me? Yeah, I get what I did. I get it. I used the noise from the press to cover up my own fucking inadequacies. I get that. But believe me, I'm done with it. Because it cost me you."

"Wrong. Ignoring me, pushing me away, that's what cost you me. I never opened up to anybody before you. You taught me to never do it again."

He stood there, stunned, and she took advantage of the moment and stalked off to the elevator.

She pressed the button, stood with arms folded across her stomach.

He came up behind her. "I'm sorry. I'm so fucking sorry I hurt you."

She ignored him. There was nothing left to say.

"Are you taking this job? In Chicago?"

"I'm not sure which job I'll take, but it doesn't really matter. It doesn't concern you."

"I want it to. I came here to tell you how sorry I am. To tell you that I love you, and I want to be with you. And to ask you not to take a job without considering me first. I want you to take a job with me in mind. So we can be together."

She drew in a shaky breath. All the anger rushing out of her. "Well, I can't do that. I have to take the job that will bring in the most money so I don't lose my home." And then, more softly. "I can't lose my home."

"I can't lose you."

"You already did."

TWENTY-TWO

The front door slammed so hard the windows rattled.

"Mail." Mimi waved a handful of letters as she came into the kitchen.

Violet grabbed her keys and purse. "Anything good?"

Her friend slapped the pile on the kitchen table. "You're going out like that?"

Violet looked down at her outfit. Shorts, tank top, flip-flops. "What?"

"I thought we're going clothes shopping."

"Yeah, so?" Violet had dressed for easy access—pull off her tank, drop her shorts, kick off her shoes.

"So you look like you're going to clean the oven."

"I'm trying on dresses. Who cares what I'm wearing? Besides, it's like a hundred degrees out there."

"Fashion doesn't hinge on weather. Tell her, Mother."

Francesca came into the kitchen, immediately reaching for the mail. Pushing her glasses up the bridge of her nose, she flicked through the stack. "I think she looks comfortable on this unbearably hot day." She looked up with a smile to Violet. "Are we ready to go?"

"Yup." She flipped her keys around her finger, noticing when Francesca frowned at an envelope. "What?"

She handed the letter to Violet. "It's from the county, but it's addressed to Jedidiah Walker Irrevocable Trust."

"Let me see it." Mimi snatched it and tore it open.

"Easy, sweetheart," her mom said. "Don't want to rip it."

"Oh, I'm easy. Believe me, I'm easy." Mimi quickly scanned the documents. "Tax bill." A curious smile bloomed. "The tax bill for this property's been sent to an irrevocable trust. I'm guessing Old Man Walker didn't mention a trust to you?"

Violet shook her head, her nerves flaring. New information. Was it good news—or bad?

"And the lawyer didn't mention a trust either, so his kids likely don't know about it." Francesca tapped it against her hand. "Let's fax this to Randall, see what he can dig up."

Three hours later, Violet faced the mirror in a huge dressing room. Dresses hung off the bars on the wall. Since Francesca wasn't buying anything new for Emmie's wedding—she had a lifetime of fancy dresses to call on—and Mimi couldn't afford one, not until she got a job and started earning money, all of them were Violet's.

The one she wore didn't flatter her figure, and the *aubergine* color looked harsh against her pale skin. Also, the way the neckline cut halfway to her belly button made her boobs look indecent.

"What are you thinking about, my love?" Francesca asked. "You look so lost."

"I would never wear something like this."

In the mirror, Violet saw the look pass between the women. Yeah, her voice didn't come out strong, but hey, her days of breakdowns were over. "I'm just wondering what I would wear, you know? This is too revealing. But what would I like? I mean, what expresses me?"

"I don't know what you mean," Mimi said. "I just go with what I like. What looks good on me. I don't think about what *expresses* me."

"That's because you know who you are."

Mimi let out a bitter bark of laughter. "Oh, please. I'm the perfect Manhattan businesswoman."

Now it was Violet and Francesca's turn to share a quick look.

"What?" Mimi asked. "Like I don't know how hard I try to fit in my dad's world? I'm not that clueless. The point is, don't think about what expresses you. Because that's gonna change from day to day. Wear what you like, what gives you that zing. Nothing else matters."

Well, of *course*, other things mattered. She had to choose a dress that fit the occasion, matched the tone or theme of the event.

"What?" Mimi said. "Stop overthinking this. Just choose a dress that makes you zing and let's go. People to see, places to go, bee-atch."

Violet glanced at some of the other dresses. She had earth-woman, hippy dresses and polished, elegant ones. She had flirty, youthful ones, and she had nearly risqué ones.

"I just, you know, I don't know if I can pull off sexy."

Mimi stood up behind her and set her chin on Violet's shoulder. "You are incredibly sexy. You're also down to earth and elegant and beachy. You're all those things. That's why you choose the dress that feels right in this moment. And then you buy another dress when you're feeling different."

"Sweetheart, when do you most feel yourself?" Francesca asked.

Violet didn't even have to think. "When I'm with Derek." Their pained expressions made her look away. "It's okay. I can talk about him."

Derek continued to text her now and again.

Thinking about you.

Miss you.

Coming to the wedding?

And the worst. Please give me a chance.

And, God, the wedding? It would be torture to see him. Would he bring someone? It didn't seem likely that he'd continue to text her while seeing someone new. Yet pictures didn't lie. He'd been seen around with a woman named Sam on his arm. Nothing sexual or anything—

Oh, come on. Was she really thinking about him and who he might be dating?

She shut it down. She wouldn't think about him at all.

"So think about him looking at you at the wedding. What're you wearing? What makes you feel like the woman he sees?"

In the mirror, her gaze landed on the one dress that had made her heart beat a little faster.

Ah, the zing. *Got it.*

Even if she couldn't have him, she still wanted him to think she was beautiful. And that dress would do it.

A band of dusky purple-gray clouds buffeted the horizon. With the gentle lapping of waves, the heat of the day still warming the sand, Violet should've felt relaxed. She was home. Her closest friends in the world surrounded her. She had jobs to choose from. Everything was all right.

But she ached. And it wouldn't go away. No, she didn't want a mercurial man, but she wanted *Derek.* Everything in her cried out for him. It wasn't going away.

It should've passed by now.

"I thought I'd find you ladies down here."

The three of them turned as one to see Randall coming down the stairs to the beach. In his blue button-down and khakis, he looked handsome and clean-cut.

"Randall," Francesca said. "Come sit with us. We have way too much food."

Mimi lobbed a vine of grapes at him. He caught it one-handed and started popping them off the stem. "Delicious. Everything tastes better out here."

He kicked off his boat shoes and plopped down beside Violet, leaning into her. "I'm beginning to see the appeal."

She smiled, but she knew he was just humoring her. This place would never suit him. It was too far from the city to make it worth a weekend visit, and no matter what restorations they made on the house, it would never be the kind of place an Oppenheimer used for a retreat.

But did it matter? What if she let him in? What if she just tried? With Randall, she'd have peace, stability. She glanced at Francesca, head resting against the back of her beach chair, features completely relaxed as she held a glass of wine in one hand.

She'd have the exact life her friend had fled.

Charity balls, auctions, luncheons, vacations with Randall's friends on the yacht.

That life . . . it just wasn't her.

"What's that?" Mimi pointed to the large manila envelope he'd set down on the blanket.

"It's the golden ticket, ladies."

"What're you talking about?" Mimi sat up on her knees, hands pressed together. "Oh, my God, spill already."

But he only had eyes for Violet. He watched her with a knowing smile. "You want to hear my news?"

She barely nodded, her heart thumping in the cavern of her chest.

"Sorry, what was that?" he teased. "I couldn't hear you."

Mimi smacked her arm. "What is your problem?"

"Mimi," Francesca murmured. "Not everyone shows her feelings on her sleeve." She gave Randall a chastising look.

"Right." He sat up, brushing sand off his hands. "Okay, so." He paused. "They're dropping the suit. Land's yours as long as you can keep up your lease payments."

"They're accepting the purchase price?" Violet asked, still wary.

"Research shows it's fair market value for farmland in Eden's Landing. Jed wasn't doing you any favors."

"Ha." Mimi punched a fist in the air.

"So the trust?" Violet held her emotion in check, waiting for all the facts.

"Before he died, Old Man Walker set up an irrevocable trust for the land. No one can build on it, subdivide it, or use it for any purpose other than farming. In perpetuity."

Both hands went to cover her face. Her breathing turned shallow, and tears stung.

Francesca set her wineglass aside, went to her knees, and threw her arms around Violet. Mimi dog-piled, and the three of them toppled the chair over, Violet's head hitting the sand.

Laughing, Randall got up and put his hands on Mimi's waist. "Okay, okay, give my girl some room."

My girl. Did she want to be Randall's girl?

The women got off her, and Randall reached for her hand, pulling her up. Gently, he brushed sand off her cheek, off her shoulders, his gaze settling on her mouth. "The land is yours, Violet. All yours."

She bit down on her bottom lip hard enough to cause pain.

"Oh, for crying out loud," Mimi said. "Let it go already."

"You're home, sweetheart." Francesca gave her a warm smile.

Violet couldn't really see them through the sheen of tears, so she got up and took off down the beach.

She ran, stumbling in the rocky sand, making her way to the harder-packed shoreline. She had to get her head around this news.

She had a permanent home that no one could take from her.

She had a means to support herself on her land. Her products were already selling well, and her new ideas were so good she knew they'd do well, too.

She was safe, stable, secure.

Oh, my God, what's the matter with me? Why do I feel so freaking empty?

Why is it not enough?

Would she never feel full-up inside?

"What is the matter with you?" Mimi came up behind her. "You should be happy."

"You think I don't know that? You think I don't know my reactions aren't normal?"

Mimi rolled her eyes. "Oh, my God. You're not seriously hung up on what that old hag social worker said to your grandmother all those years ago, are you?"

"Of course I am."

"Violet."

"What?"

"You were *six years old*. The things you remember? A six-year-old wouldn't know words like that. That's, like, out of a textbook."

"I remember."

"Are you sure you remember her words so exactly?"

"Well . . . I mean, I did read them. In a child psych class I took in high school one semester." The impact of the words in that textbook had been like a gunshot blast to her heart. It had given form to the idea of what she'd heard at her grandma's house that morning.

Mimi wrapped her arms around her from behind. "You silly girl. You took some passage you read in a book and made it your truth. Those studies don't matter. The only thing that matters is what you actually feel. Did you love him?"

She nodded, tears brimming, spilling over. "Very much."

"Then forget some excerpt from some random study. It doesn't mean shit. Listen to your heart. Okay?"

She smiled. "Yeah. Okay."

"And is your heart wanting to do a happy dance right now?"

Her heart wanted to be with Derek, but she nodded. Because she was definitely happy with Randall's news.

Mimi grabbed her hand and led her back to the blanket, where Francesca and Randall waited for her. They'd packed up, and Francesca held the picnic basket in one hand and the blanket folded under an arm.

No, she didn't feel like doing a happy dance, but she knew Mimi was right about trusting her heart. She needed to let down her damn guard. So she walked right through it and into Randall's arms. "Thank you, Randall. Thank you so much."

His arms came right around her.

"See you up at the house." Mimi grabbed the beach chairs.

Randall gave the women a nod but never let go of Violet. "I didn't do much of anything. Jed had it all worked out for you. Unfortunately, his attorney spends July in Nantucket, so he wasn't around to let us know about the trust. You wouldn't have had to go through any of this if it had happened a month earlier or a month later. But it's done now."

She could see his soothing demeanor turn into something else—something hot and lustful. He wanted her. Slowly, he lowered his mouth to hers.

She had a second to push him away, let him know this wasn't what she wanted.

But she didn't take it.

Because he was kind and constant. Because she wanted to want him as much as he wanted her. She wanted a man whose heart she could count on.

So when his lips brushed over hers, she lifted her arms, hung them loosely around his neck, and waited. Waited for sensation to bloom on her skin, for desire to pound in her blood. Waited for her hips to shift restlessly, for need to carve her wide open.

"Violet," he whispered as he pressed harder and slid his tongue into her mouth.

But it didn't come. Because those feelings she waited for came from passion.

Passion didn't offer security. It died out. She could have that kind of relationship with Derek, but it would end in a fiery wreck.

Oh, wait. It already had.

She didn't do fiery. So she sank into Randall, tangling her tongue with his. And sure, little sparks flared up along her nerves. If she let herself go, she might come to enjoy his touch.

He was such a good guy.

Then he pulled back and said, "Is this okay?"

And for some reason, that just changed everything.

Because he always asked. He never took.

And God help her, but Violet wanted to be taken.

"What're you doing?" Mimi leaned against the doorway, watching her with concern.

"Packing." Violet stood in front of her dresser, staring into her underwear drawer, wondering how many pairs she should bring.

"You took a job?" Mimi dug into the suitcase, lifting a handful of neatly folded shirts. "When? Twenty minutes ago we were high-fiving each other over randy Randall's good news. And now you're packing?"

"Yep."

When Mimi sat on the edge of the mattress, the suitcase tipped. She lunged for it, saving it from toppling over. "You didn't even tell us. I thought things were going great with you and frat boy. I thought we'd have to wear earplugs while you guys banged the headboard into the wall. Instead we come home and the Ferrari's gone."

Violet picked up her clothes and straightened them. "I've got a car coming in half an hour, so I really need to think right now."

Passport. Oh, damn. Good thing she'd remembered. *Imagine forgetting something like that.*

"Instead of banging Randall, you're going to Chicago?"

"Japan."

"Mom." Mimi jumped up, strode to the bedroom door. "Mom!"

Feet pounded up the stairs. "What's the matter?" A barefoot Francesca entered the room wide-eyed, like she was expecting another broken blood vessel.

"She's going to Japan."

Violet turned to see the look of disappointment on their faces. "What? This job will pay off the lease, and I'll own the farm outright. Then I'll be done. I won't need to take any more jobs."

"Too much saliva?" Mimi asked. "Did he make a boob grab?"

"Randall has nothing to do with this."

"But shouldn't he? Don't you want to stop running?"

"I'm not running. I'm *working*. It's what we do when we don't have fathers to pay our bills until we find the perfect job."

Mimi flinched, rearing back. "That was a bitchy thing to say." Her features turned pink. "I don't . . ."

"Yeah, you do," Violet said. "But that's okay, and you're right. It was bitchy. I just had to turn away a really good man, and it sucked and I'm feeling ornery. I shouldn't have been a bitch but don't pretend you know what it's like to have no one. Literally no one. Every bite of food, every gallon of gas, every cup of water I use from the faucet, comes from me. My ability to produce an income."

"Sweetheart, you're okay," Francesca said. "You got good news tonight. You're going to be okay. There's no rush to pay off the debt."

Francesca had never wanted for a thing her entire life, so she couldn't begin to understand. And, yes, of course her friend had offered to buy the farm and set up a payment plan. Years ago. But Violet didn't operate like that. She'd do it herself. She *was* doing it.

"There's always a threat. For my peace of mind, I need to put this all behind me and own the farm outright. Then I'll settle down and start working it." She shot a glance to Mimi. "And I'll date."

"But not the frat boy?"

She shook her head. "He's just . . . not the man for me."

Violet knew from the sudden silence in the room that the mother-daughter team was communicating with their silent language of facial expressions. She also knew Mimi wouldn't be able to keep her mouth shut, so she wasn't the least surprised when Mimi said, "What happened exactly? You were playing tonsil hockey and then *bam*. You dumped him. What's up with that?"

"Nothing happened. He came to give me the news."

"Right, he drove two hours to the tip of Long Island to pass along two sentences he could've texted."

"Mimi, honey," her mom said soothingly.

"No, she's running, and I want to know why."

"I'm not running. I just told you what I'm doing." Sweat prickled under her arms, and she started flinging underpants into the suitcase. "I'm *working*. Did Randall come here for more? Yes, he would like more from me. He's a great guy. I like him very much. He's perfect. He's a perfect guy."

Great, now they looked at her like she'd lost it. Well, maybe she had. She wanted to flip her bed over, throw these stupid, ugly clothes out the window. They weren't her. Why was she packing clothes to make her look like Jason Becker's corporate attorney?

His entourage was so large it didn't matter what she wore. She'd be invisible. Disgusted, she reached into the suitcase and tossed her silk blouses and ugly skirts onto the floor.

"What are you doing?" Mimi shouted.

"I'm working with a nineteen-year-old spoiled brat. I don't need to look like his accountant."

Mimi bent over and picked up a deep pink cropped cashmere sweater. "An accountant would never wear this, but I'd totally wear it."

"Take it, it's yours."

"How can we help you, sweetheart? What kind of look are you going for?"

"I don't know. I've never worked for a nineteen-year-old spoiled brat on tour in Japan. Why would they even hire me for this job? It's not like I can get through to a kid who has too much money, too many handlers, and too much exposure to everything bad and not enough self-discipline and self-awareness to just simply say no, thank you."

"Oh, boy." Francesca sat on the edge of the bed. "Honey, you don't have to take this job."

"Stop saying that." She'd never raised her voice to her friends. Ever. But she felt like tearing off her clothes and streaking out into the night. The walls were coming down around her, nothing made sense, and she just had to keep marching along the same track she'd always walked on until she came back into her own skin. "No other job's going to pay me this kind of money."

"Oh, for Christ's sake, is no one going to speak the truth here?" Mimi got right in her face. "This isn't about a damn job." Mimi gave her a challenging look. "This is about Derek Valencia. *He's* why you sent Randall away."

Violet turned away so abruptly she heard the tendons in her neck crunch.

"Why can't you admit it? What's the big deal?"

"Of course he's why I sent Randall away. How am I supposed to go back to my life after him?"

"You love him."

"Of *course* I love him. Who wouldn't?"

"I sure as hell would. But he doesn't want me. He wants *you*." She reached for Violet's arm, rubbed it. "He wants you. But you turned him away."

Francesca leaped up. "Mimi."

"No, she has to face this shit. Not run from it. If you're gonna put on your damn running shoes, at least go run and get him."

"What's the point? God, Mimi. So, great, we can burn up the sheets a few more times before his interest in me fades and he moves on to the next woman who gets him all worked up?"

"Oh, I see. So he's just a fickle son of a bitch who follows his dick? 'Cause that's not the guy I met. The guy I met takes his work seriously. He's intense, and he's focused, and when he gives himself, he gives it all." She leaned into her face. "And he gave himself to you."

"You don't know him. It's all about the passion for him. Passion burns out. And then what will I have? I'll have given up everything and wound up with nothing."

"He's not your mom. He's not a drug addict."

Violet stood stone still. Stunned. "I know that. Of course he's not my mom. I didn't even know my mom."

"But you know *him*. In your gut, you know what you have is real, and that freaks you out. Because he could up and dump you just like your mom. Except, oh, right, Derek's not a junkie. And I'm sorry to tell you but love just doesn't offer any guarantees. But you need that guarantee, don't you? And without it, you'll what? Settle for the same bland, dull emotional life you've been living for the past twenty-something years? Now that you've had Derek, can you really stand one more day of your old life?"

"It's not my *old* life. It's my life. And I don't know what I want."

"Sure you do. Randall is stability and security, and you feel the same bland emotion with him you've felt all your life. And interestingly, you could have him, but you sent him away, didn't you?"

"Mimi, that's enough," Francesca said.

"No, actually, it's not enough. You're too careful with her, Mom. You're too careful with everyone. You don't just say it like it is."

"Okay, I'll say it just how it is." Francesca stepped between them, facing her daughter. "Back off. You can't bully people into doing what you want, feeling what you want them to feel. Haven't you learned that lesson enough times with your lovely group of friends?"

"You guys, stop. Don't fight over this. It's not your problem. I'll figure everything out, but for now I have to go. I can't miss my flight." She dropped to her knees, scooping up all the discarded clothing and shoving it into the suitcase.

"You leave, you lose Derek," Mimi said. "You get that,

right? You don't have to take this job. You've got choices. Choosing this job is your way of making sure you don't risk your heart. When you settle for a boring guy in a dull marriage, you can always reassure yourself that you tried passion once, you gave it a go, but it wasn't for you. But you'll always know the truth. You didn't have the balls to go for it, and your penance will be a life of blandness."

"Mimi," her mom said.

But Violet didn't want to hear another word. She zipped up her luggage and wheeled it out of the room.

TWENTY-THREE

Loud, shrieking laughter snatched her out of a deep sleep. Before she could think, she reached for the robe she kept handy and dropped her feet to the cold floor. Racing down the narrow hallway, she tackled the steep steps and spun around the corner to find the same scene she'd left an hour ago, when she'd finally gotten Jason into bed. Lights on, booze bottles everywhere—party interrupted.

The bus driver, who didn't speak a word of English, turned in his seat to look at her, features twisted in pure disgust as he pointed out the open door.

"Oh, shit," someone called, and then erupted in hysterical laughter.

"Nailed it," someone else shouted.

Violet dashed off the bus to find Jason and his entourage lobbing eggs off the overpass of a highway. Immediately, she spotted his dad, arm cocked as he aimed at a car whizzing by.

"Jason, get on the bus—now." Her harsh tone got everyone's attention. Where on earth had they found these groupies at three in the morning? She tried to block the girls from entering the bus, but Jason's dad came right up to her, towering over her, and gave her a menacing look.

"They're coming with us."

"No, they're not." She tried to back away from him, but he grabbed her arm and jerked it.

She stumbled back against the bus, and he rushed her. He stank of booze and pot. The bus hadn't smelled of pot, so she looked to the ground, found it littered with butts, both cigarette and weed. "You took your son outside to get high? And then you let him commit vandalism?"

"Listen, bitch. Kid needs to let off some steam. You can't keep him on this fucking retard regimen. He doesn't eat spinach, he doesn't want to get up at the crack of dawn and go to some fuckin' gym. He wants to blow off some steam, get it?" He motioned to the girls behind him, giggling and preening, as Jason tickled them.

"I told you the next time you called me a bitch, I'd talk to Keene." Not that Jason's manager cared. He wanted to keep his job and please the record company at the same time.

"So do it already. Who gives a fuck? Keene works for us."

"Us? Did you mean Jason? Because this is your son's career we're talking about. And he's not going to have one unless you let me help him. Look, I'm done with your interference. As soon as I get Jason back to bed, I'm going to make the call and tomorrow you're going back to New Jersey."

"Fuck you. He's my kid. I got his best interests." He gripped her arms, lifted her off the ground, and set her down against the concrete wall of the overpass. Turning, he smiled at the young girls and ushered them onto the bus.

As Violet stood there, rubbing the skin at her elbows that'd been scraped raw against the concrete, she closed her eyes and thought of her farm. Francesca in the cellar, filling the tea bags, the wildflowers drying overhead. Mimi on the covered porch, sunlight splashing over the pretty dried petals scattered all over the big picnic table, her forehead creased as she chose which color to place on her pulpy paper.

By taking these jobs, she was denying herself the very life she was fighting to claim.

How had she not seen that until now?

She thought of Derek, and her pulse soared. What was he doing right then? The tour had ended, so he was getting ready for Emmie's wedding.

The wedding at Four O'Clock Farm. Which she would

miss because of this stupid, pointless job. Trying to help a kid whose parents fought against her every step of the way.

She wanted a normal life, but she kept making choices that kept her from it. She wanted a normal relationship, but she pushed people away. This wasn't about some missing piece in her—a lack of affection in her mother's eyes. This was fear. Plain and simple. Fear informed her choices and kept her from having all the things she wanted.

Well, fuck that.

I'm going home.

Three weeks since he'd seen her. Three weeks of hell. Every night, every waking moment, he lived with a spike in his heart.

He'd fucked up.

His bare feet dug into the hot sand, and the sun burned the top of his head. As he waited for his sister to come down the stairs, he looked toward the canopy they'd constructed for the ceremony. Slater and Francesca, the officiant, chatted underneath the riot of wildflowers woven into the latticework. His friend looked calm and perfectly happy.

One thing he could say about Slater—when he'd found Emmie he'd never doubted, never looked back. He'd held on to her and never let go.

Derek had let go.

Why the *fuck* had he let go?

"You've got about six minutes to pull your head out of your arse before your sister shows up." Irwin came down the wooden steps in his white linen pants and sky blue Hawaiian shirt. He wore a lei—as they all did—of fragrant wildflowers. The Brit came up beside him.

"Yeah, yeah, I got it. Hey, I wanted to . . ." Did you thank someone who chose you as best bass player in the world? "Thank you for the honor of including me on the Ledger List. That . . . uh, that's pretty incredible."

"Did you ever wonder why your father lost his place on it?"

"No." He'd never even considered it. His dad had always just been this God, this larger than life icon. He'd never wondered why his career had, essentially, ended. *Interesting.*

"Because he stopped growing. It's quite common, actually. Talented artists who get their energy from the accolades, the nymphs, the applause. Not the music itself. They dry up."

Derek thought about that. It made sense, given the way Eddie had lived his life. The man had blown up his marriage to fuck groupies and party. The talent had stopped working with him because he'd lost his focus.

Oh, Jesus. Realization struck hard. He got it. He fucking got it. All those horrible comments his dad had made over the years hadn't had anything to do with Derek at all. They'd been about his father's own fears about losing his mojo, his reputation, his fame.

Flash over substance. That had been his *father's* fears for himself. It had nothing to do with Derek. Except that Derek had a fresh slate—a chance to do it right. And Eddie's was over.

Irwin leaned in, and Derek got a whiff of Francesca's expensive perfume on the man's shirt. "Feed the muse, not the wounded boy, and it'll all work out."

A collective gasp had them turning to the stairs. Emmie floated down in a simple pale pink dress, tight on top, then flowing out around her. Her bare feet peeked out, the toenails painted a bubble gum pink.

His sister looked radiant.

"And there's our girl," Irwin said, voice filled with warmth and pride.

His mom, draping Emmie's train over an arm as she followed behind, made a shooing motion. "Go on and get up there with Slater."

Derek took off. The closer he got to his friend, the more his mood turned. The way Slater and Emmie looked at each other, their utter certainty in their love for each other . . . it made everything snap into place.

Fuck fame, fuck his reputation, fuck all the gold or platinum records in the world. At the end of the day, at the end of his life, the only thing that mattered was his heart. Whom he'd loved, who'd loved him. The only thing that mattered was the woman who'd walked through life by his side.

The woman that slept in his bed.

And that woman sure as fuck was Violet.

No more dicking around. He'd let this go on long enough. Tomorrow he'd go get his girl. Wherever she was, whatever she was doing, he didn't care. He'd take her. Claim her.

Done.

Music started playing as Derek took his place beside Slater. Across from him, Ben played a beat on bongos, Cooper strummed an acoustic guitar, and Pete played a portable keyboard. Fucking Pete. He'd left rehab to come to the wedding, but they all knew he had no intention of going back. He didn't want to miss out on recording the new material. What could they do? They were happy to have him back, just . . . worried.

And then Calix started singing, and the world came to a screeching halt.

"What the hell?" Derek said, laughing.

"Dude has pipes," Slater said.

The groove was simple, sweet, the guys whistling between verses. "What is this?" He liked it. Liked it a lot. And it fit Emmie. Really fit her.

"'You Love Me,'" Slater said. "It's by Kimya Dawson. And it's perfect, so shut the fuck up."

"You gonna kiss your bride with that mouth?"

"Count on it."

Derek cupped Slater's shoulder. "Happy for you, man."

"Happy as fuck."

And then he turned to watch his sister walk toward her groom, the lyrics of the song slamming him in the gut. Too scared to let anybody close—fuck, yeah. They hit him right where he lived. He'd never gotten close to anyone either, but Violet? She'd gotten right in.

Right. In.

He'd known it that first night together, when he'd convinced her to sleep in the bunk that barely fit his own body, let alone both of theirs. But she'd stayed.

Because she'd felt it, too. He knew she did.

Perfect song.

Slater's gaze jerked up, causing everyone to turn toward the stairs. The music stopped.

Violet.

Oh, fuck. She'd come.

Violet. Her hair loose and wavy, she wore a lavender dress that was fitted on top and had a dark purple silk band under her breasts. She looked fucking gorgeous, and she looked right at him.

She froze when she saw everyone watching her. "Oh, I'm sorry. Go on, please. I'm so sorry."

His heart thundered, and his knees buckled.

"Oh, thank God," Francesca murmured.

"Yes," Slater said in a hiss.

"Please go on." When Violet reached the sand, she pulled off her heels.

Emmie shielded her eyes with her bouquet. "Are you kidding? We'll totally wait."

"I'm so sorry I'm late," Violet hustled toward them.

"Go get her." Slater elbowed him hard.

Derek took off, his bare feet kicking up sand. He caught his girl in his arms, lifted her, and held her close. Breathing in her sweet scent, a calm spread through his body, even as his nerves vibrated. "You came for the wedding."

She shook her head, tears spilling onto her cheeks. "I came for you. I don't want to miss one more minute with you. I'm a coward."

"You're here. That makes you the bravest girl in the world."

"I love you. I'm sorry I pushed you away."

"I love you. I love you more than anything. And that's never going to change."

"Derek, dude?" Slater called. "Not everything's about you, you know." Laughter broke the tension.

"Hang on." He swung around to his sister, looking for her okay. Emmie nodded, giving him a thumbs-up.

He dug into his pocket and pulled out a ring. "I was going to leave this on your pillow, but I'd much rather put it on your finger myself." The silver glittered in the sunlight.

Violet gasped when she saw the Hand of Eris symbol. "You . . . oh, I'm not . . . they might not like . . ."

"You're one of us. Have been all along." He slid it on her finger, kissing her cheek, loving her pretty floral scent.

"You can wear this until you're ready for a tattoo." And if she didn't want one on her forearm, he could think of plenty of places to ink her skin with the band's symbol.

"Tattoo?" She looked a little confused. "Those are permanent."

"Exactly."

"Oh, Derek," she sighed. She turned to him, got up on her toes, and cupped his chin. "I love you so much."

"I love you, too." He kissed her.

"I'd like to get a ring on *my* girl's finger, if you don't mind," Slater called.

"Em's not going anywhere," Derek shouted back, taking Violet's hand and heading back toward the impatient groom.

She tried to pull away, disappear among the guests, but he wouldn't release her. Clasping her hand, he kept her close as he took his place beside the groom.

"I'm so sorry, Slater." She raised their joined hands in explanation.

Slater just smiled. "Nowhere else you should be." And then he trained his gaze on his bride.

The music started up again, and Derek watched Irwin finish walking his sister toward the canopy. He took a moment to appreciate the absence of his father, knowing there wasn't a person at the ceremony who wanted him there, but also to let it really sink in that everyone present had gathered as a shield to *keep* his dad away. For Emmie, of course. But for Derek, too. And he appreciated this band of brothers that had now grown to include two irreplaceable women.

His sister couldn't keep the smile off her face as she locked gazes with Slater. The two of them sharing a secret as they always did. Only now Derek understood what that secret was.

This was what mattered. Everything else life threw at you was just shit you had to deal with. But this love? This woman? *This* was what made it all worthwhile. Slater was right. Finding the one who made things real made all the shit fall away.

After Irwin delivered the bride under the canopy, he kissed her cheek, murmured something in her ear that made Emmie throw herself into his arms. They hugged a good, long while before Irwin gently pulled her away. "Go on, now. Hurry and make it legal before nymphs start popping out of the sand and attach themselves to him like barnacles."

Everyone laughed, and Slater took a few steps forward, lifting his bride off the ground, planting a kiss on her mouth, and depositing her in front of Francesca.

More laughter. Derek couldn't help looking at Violet, squeezing her hand. Oh, fucking hell, he loved her. The sooner the ceremony ended, the sooner he could get her under the covers.

Derek couldn't help noticing Irwin's expression. Francesca's husky voice had the man squirming as she led the ceremony. For all the time Derek had known the guy, he'd never once seen him show interest in anything other than work. Watching him consume Francesca with his eyes made Derek smile.

"I know you've written your own vows, so . . . Slater," Francesca said, nodding toward him.

Eyes blazing with love, Slater captured Emmie's hands, kissed her fingers, then held them over his heart. "You're the love of my life. I give you my hand, my heart, my loyalty, my trust, and I hold your happiness higher than my own. I am yours, and you are mine."

Tears glittered in his sister's eyes. Derek heard a sniff, and he quickly turned to see Violet's features crumpling. He wiped her tears with his fingertips.

"You're the love of my life." Emmie gazed up at her man. She brought their joined hands to her heart. "I give you my hand, my heart, my loyalty, my trust, and I hold your happiness higher than my own. I am yours, and you are mine."

With a huge smile, Francesca said, "You may kiss the bride. Again."

Everyone laughed as Slater scooped his woman into his arms and kissed her.

"Ladies and gentlemen, I present to you Mr. and Mrs. Jonny and Emmie Vaughn."

Clapping and whistles filled the air.

"Now, let's celebrate," Francesca said.

TWENTY-FOUR

A warm hand cupped her breast, a mouth closed over her earlobe, gently sucking. Violet smiled. Could there be a better way to wake up each morning?

Her hips pitched back, right into Derek's very hard erection. He groaned, his fingers curling into her flesh, his palm rubbing her nipple. "Merry Christmas, my sweet V."

Overwhelmed with love, she turned in his arms, draping a leg over his hip and pulling him tight against her. "Merry Christmas."

He kissed her gently, stroking the hair off her face. "I love you."

"I love you so much." She kissed him, sinking into that hot, hungry mouth.

Over the sound of Otis Redding's "Merry Christmas, Baby" someone hollered. She thought they were calling for them.

Whoever it was could wait.

Violet curled herself more tightly around him. Her hand went to the back of his neck, caressing. He gripped her ass, squeezed the flesh, and deepened the kiss. God, she wanted him inside her so badly.

Feet tramped up the stairs. Fists pounded on the bedroom door.

"Guys?" Ben called. "You up?"

"Everybody's waiting." *Cooper.*

Dropping his head into the curve of her neck, Derek sighed. "Believe me, I'm *up.*"

He'd said it quietly, but when they snickered outside the door, she knew they'd heard.

"Come on," Ben said. "We're opening presents."

"In a minute," Derek called over his shoulder.

"You have the whole day to fuck around," Cooper said.

"And, V, you promised to make that stuffed French toast."

"I *said* a minute." And then he pushed her onto her back, turned the kiss more heated, more carnal, and her whole body burned with need. His hands roamed restlessly, pulling her to him, stroking, grabbing. Roughly pinching her nipple, he stroked down the length of her body until his fingers parted her curls.

Sensation soared through her. "Oh, God, Derek." Her hands gripped his tight ass and sealed him to her.

"Well, if it's just a minute, we'll wait right here," Cooper said.

Derek lowered his head in frustration. "Get out of here."

She could hear them cackling outside the door.

"Come on, you selfish prick," Cooper said. "Don't you want to see what I got you?"

"What's going on up there?" Emmie called. "What're they doing?"

"Derek said just a minute, and that was about thirty seconds ago," Ben said. "So they should be coming right about now."

Both guys hooted with laughter.

Violet smiled, caressing Derek's back. "Later?"

"Fuck." Derek closed his eyes, taking his time releasing her. Just as she started to roll away from him, he pulled her back, cupped her chin, and looked into her eyes. "As crazy as this day is going to be, I want to make sure we have some time alone together."

Heat flooded her. "Me, too."

He kissed her again. "I want today to be perfect for you."

She'd never had a real Christmas before. Not with a houseful of people. Not with a Christmas tree and stockings and a turkey to baste.

And she'd never had a boyfriend. Well, *boyfriend*. Derek was so much more than that. He was . . . her heart. He was part of her. She blinked back tears, and his expression turned concerned.

"Hey. You all right?"

"It's already perfect. Everything's perfect."

The doorknob rattled. "Okay, your minute's up, so we're just going to come in now," Cooper said.

"Would you fucking grow up?" Derek called, but they smiled at each other because he knew. He understood. They were part of something bigger now, a family, and they both loved it.

She loved him. She loved their life. And, good God, she wanted him. Reaching between them, she gripped his hard length and stroked it. Her skin tingled, all the way from her scalp to the soles of her feet. "Can we just finish real quick?"

His big hands grabbed her hips, shifting her back underneath him. That hungry look in his eyes made her crazy.

And then the door flew open. "Merry Christmas!"

Both guys ran into the room, throwing themselves onto the bed.

The mattress bounced as her arms went to cover her breasts.

"Get the fuck out of here," Derek shouted while reaching behind him to pull up the sheet. It engulfed them, and they shared a smile at their moment of privacy.

Scents from downstairs filled the room—cinnamon and pine, warm bread. Eartha Kitt's "Santa Baby" played on the stereo.

Both guys bounced on the bed, and Derek hurled a pillow at them.

Violet lowered an edge of the sheet. "We'll be right down. I promise."

And then Mimi came into the room with a steaming

mug of coffee in one hand and a glass of orange juice in the other. "All right, you morons, hit it. I've got this covered."

The guys rolled off the bed and headed out of the room. "Hurry up."

Mimi set the drinks on the nightstand. "Do you have any idea what it's like for me? Irwin's practically humping my mom in the kitchen, Emmie and Slater are doing unspeakable things to each other on the couch, and those two morons are shaking this one big present to see if it's a *Sports Illustrated* swimsuit model."

Violet sat up, forcing Derek off her. "They're shaking it?" She didn't want them ruining his present. "We're coming."

Mimi gave her a warm smile. "Maybe later you are, but right now you're putting on some clothes and coming downstairs."

The moment they entered the living room, the conversation and laughter stopped.

Irwin got up. "Before we open presents, may I have a word?"

Derek kissed Violet's cheek, then sat down on the couch.

"Sure. What's up?" She looked around at their faces, trying to judge if she was about to receive good news or bad.

"As you know, playtime's over for these silly arses. Time to get them into the studio."

They were leaving. They'd go wherever their producer wanted them to go.

But come on. She couldn't exactly complain. She'd had him to herself for nearly four months.

"Last time they toured, things didn't go so well. And frankly, I think you bring an element of structure to their lives they clearly need." He gestured to them. "They're all right on their own, of course, but really all bands should have someone like you. To give them, shall we say, healthy outlets for their energy. Keep them on a good track."

Emmie came forward. "What he's saying is Amoeba would like to hire you as their minder."

"I . . . what does that mean exactly?"

Slater stood behind his wife. "The studio's almost finished, so we'll be making the album out here."

"You will?" *Oh, my God, they're staying here?*

Derek nodded with a very satisfied smile.

Slater continued. "We could put the guys up in that B and B up the road—"

"No, they're fine here." She didn't want them leaving. Not when she'd grown so close to all of them.

Emmie's smile broadened. "And then after the record's done, we'd like you to come on tour with us."

Her gaze went straight to Derek's. His knowing smile filled her with happiness. "So I'd be the boss?" She nodded toward Derek. "Of him?"

Everyone laughed.

"Yes, you'd be the boss." Irwin smiled, taking his place beside Francesca.

Derek leaped up, grabbed her hand, and tugged her toward him. "You can be whatever you want to be."

"Now can we open presents?" Ben crouched in front of the nine-foot-tall Douglas fir taking up a corner of the living room. Glancing at Violet, he held her overflowing stocking in one hand. "I'm playing elf. Sit down. The rest of us already opened our stockings, so you work on this while we move on to the good stuff."

She smiled, sinking into the couch. They'd all spent a morning decorating the downstairs. Wreaths hung on the doors; garlands strung from the mantel and larger pieces of furniture. A huge basket of cinnamon-scented pinecones sat beside the fireplace, which now blazed with a crackling fire.

This was her home. Her family.

She almost had to pinch herself to make sure it was real.

Hoots and hollers drew her attention to the tree, where Cooper, Ben, and Slater tore open the hockey sticks and skates she and Derek had given them.

"So much for our little elf." Irwin got up, rooted around the presents, and returned with a rectangular package for Francesca.

Violet could practically feel her friend's anxiety. Given the shape of the box, what could she expect other than jewelry? And Irwin might not know about Francesca's past, how

her family and husband had only ever given her tennis brace-
lets, diamond earrings, and necklaces she didn't even wear.

Francesca slid her finger under the paper, careful not to
tear it. She took her time, which only reinforced Violet's
suspicions that her friend was worried.

And when she saw the big, velvet necklace box, her
smile looked forced. But then she opened it, and her features compressed. Tears sprang into her eyes, toppling over
and spilling down her cheeks. She turned into Irwin, hiding her face in his chocolate brown cardigan.

He wrapped an arm around her, holding her tightly.
Violet noticed Emmie's hands covering her mouth, her
forehead scrunched as she fought back tears.

The box fell to the floor, and Violet leaned forward to
pick it up. Setting it on the table, she noticed the map, the
Monopoly car, and a book entitled *1000 of the Weirdest
Sights to See Across the USA*.

Francesca had always dreamed of a road trip, where she
bought corn nuts at gas station convenience stores and visited the biggest ball of twine. No one had ever had the time
to do it with her.

Irwin was making the time.

Violet gazed up at Derek, and the look he gave her sent
a bolt of lightning from her chest down to her toes.

Ben appeared. He thrust a gift at Derek. "From V."

She looked at it and couldn't imagine how they'd gotten
swimsuit model from the shape.

But Derek got it right away. His eyes went wide. "What
did you do?" He ripped off the paper to reveal a Fender. She'd
asked the guys to rip out the frets, like he'd wanted, but they'd
told her to let him do it. Apparently, that was half the fun.

"A Fender?" He planted a kiss on her mouth. Holding
the guitar over his head, he shouted, "She got me a Fender."

Of course, everyone already knew about it, but Emmie
said, "That's so awesome."

"How'd you know I wanted one?" he asked her.

"In that interview with *Guitar Player* you said you'd
always wanted another Fender so you could rip out the frets
to get 'an authentic Jaco Pastorius tone.'"

A slow smile spread across his beautiful mouth. "You're

incredible." He set the guitar down and lifted her onto his lap. She wrapped her arms around his neck. "I love you so much."

He kissed her thoroughly, then pulled back. "Now, open up your stocking stuff."

Everyone went back to opening presents. In the craziness of it all, paper crinkling, voices murmuring, Violet sat quietly, hoping to remain invisible. She couldn't imagine what these guys had gotten her. It wasn't like she needed anything. She literally had everything she could ever want right there. Her home, her friends—family—and Derek.

But as she opened each present, her chest grew tighter. Tears burned the backs of her eyes. Each gift had a tag on it to let her know who'd given it to her. Ben had gotten her a bubble gum pink diary with crystals all over it. Cooper got her a Furby. She blinked back tears as she unwrapped the Barbie doll Francesca had gotten her. Then she opened the New Kids on the Block cassette tape from Mimi.

As tears streamed down her face, she realized the room had gone quiet. She looked up to find everyone watching her.

"Merry Christmas, sweetheart," Francesca said.

She fought the urge to curl into Derek and hide her emotions. But they'd done such a lovely thing—buying her all the gifts she'd never received as a child—that she couldn't do that to them. "You guys—" Her voice broke, so she cleared it. Derek hugged her tightly to him. "You guys are so great. Thank you." She waved the set of three Beanie Babies that Emmie had given her. "A girl at school used to stuff her backpack with them. She'd line them up along the wall in the cafeteria and play with them every day. I used to sit near her so I could watch." She held them to her chest. "I coveted them."

Smiles warmed their faces, and she started to look away. But then she didn't. She let the emotion wash over her, and she let them see it. How much she appreciated their thoughtfulness. Even though they'd turned blurry from the tears, she could feel their love. "Thank you."

But when she blinked away the tears, she saw they weren't just sitting there watching her. They were gathered around her. Slater and Coop held guitars. Ben knelt before the coffee table, hands flat on the surface, fingers tapping. Emmie, Mimi, and Francesca stood together off to the side.

And then someone handed Derek a guitar. He shifted away from her, facing her.

Her heart leapt into her throat. What was going on?

And just like that, they all started playing.

And Derek sang.

I thought I wanted gold
I thought I wanted fame
But I didn't
What I wanted
I couldn't name

I thought I wanted quick
I thought I wanted fast
But I didn't
What I needed
Was your love to last

And then the women joined in, harmonizing. *Oh, my God.* She had *no idea* they could sing.

Because I found you
And that was it
It was done
You and me
We are one

I love you
It's done
You and me
We are one

And then he set the guitar down and got on one knee, reaching for her hand.

Her heart pounded furiously. He held her gaze, the certainty she saw in his eyes stealing the breath from her lungs.

He pulled a red velvet box out of his pocket and set it on her knee. The women sat down on the couch.

It was just Derek singing now.

Do you love me, too?
Do you feel the same way?
Because if you do
Then I've got something to say

Marry me.
Marry me and make me whole.
Marry me.
Marry me and soothe my soul.

Say we'll be together, forever
Say you want this, too.
Say we're going to make it
Marry me, say I do.

Let me wake up with you every morning
Let me lie with you every night
Be the warmth inside my winter
Your smile, my internal light

The guys stopped playing. Setting down their instruments, they quietly filed out of the room, heading into the kitchen. The women followed.

Derek squeezed her hand. Then he opened the ring box and pulled out the most perfect antique yellow gold band with three pink sapphires.

"I love you. You're the only one for me. Marry me, V. Please?"

"God, yes. There's nothing else I could ever want in this whole world." She got down on her knees and threw herself into his arms.

Oh, my God. She hadn't thought it was possible for her—not just to love, but to feel whole, complete. Nothing was missing anymore. *Nothing.*

He tipped her chin and pressed the sweetest kiss on her mouth. But need swept through her in a rush, and she licked inside, kissing him with all the love she felt. His hands slid down her back to her bottom, squeezing lustily.

"V?" Ben called.

She smiled against her fiancé's mouth. "Yes?"

"You gonna start the French toast?"

"Are you fucking kidding me? I just proposed to my woman and you want her to fix food?"

"I'm hungry."

"Then eat."

"But she promised me stuffed French toast."

Derek tipped his forehead to hers, and they laughed quietly.

And in that moment she knew. She had it all.

She literally had it all.

Keep reading for an excerpt from the first
Rock Star Romance novel by Erika Kelly

YOU REALLY GOT ME

Now available from Berkley Sensation

"Oh, bollocks, *Emmie*!"

Emmie Valencia's boss hollered so loudly her teeth rattled. And there was a *wall* between them. She pressed the button on her intercom and said, "Be right there." He could be such a baby.

Seconds later, the office came alive with excited voices and laughter. Her coworkers hurried down the hall, heading for the foyer.

Frontierland was back from their tour. Which meant . . . *Alex.*

Her gut twisted hard. Briefly, she imagined ducking under her desk, maybe dashing to the mail room. But, of course, she wouldn't do that. She could face him. No big deal.

In fact, that's exactly what she *should* do. Talk to him as casually as she did the rest of the guys. She hated the way people looked at her whenever he came into the office. Besides, they'd ended it months ago.

One of the interns popped breathlessly into her office. "They're here." Her features flushed, she mouthed, "Flash," and pretended to fan herself. Then she darted down the hall.

Emmie smiled and shook her head. Even though they

worked with bands for a living, everyone got all goofy and fawning when the artists came in.

Except Emmie, of course. She'd grown up around musicians. She saw beneath the glitter to their tortured, attention-craving, twisted souls. Everyone wanted a piece of them, to be the one to get in, breach the barrier. To win their hearts. But she knew better. They didn't let anyone in. Not really. They drew people in with their dazzling charisma and then pushed them back when they got too close. Loving an artist *hurt*.

Obviously, she'd thought Alex would be different. They'd grown up together. Their parents were best friends. Silly girl. Musicians were musicians. She'd *known* that.

As she pulled papers from the printer, she heard, "Emmie!" in a far more upbeat tone than her boss's. She spun around to find the boys from Frontierland crowding into her office.

Crap, was Alex there?

She'd keep her cool. Treat him exactly the way she treated the other guys. No big deal. Because *he* was no big deal. Not after what he'd done to her. Lifelong friendship be damned.

"Great job, you guys," she said, as the drummer pulled her to him. They played an outrageous mix of rockabilly, country, and country rock, so they dressed like badass banditos in leather, vests, and straw cowboy hats. "Have you read the reviews yet?"

"Brenda doesn't make those fuckin' scrapbooks like you do, man." The keyboardist pushed through the others to give her a hug. He smelled of whiskey and patchouli.

"Why couldn't we score Irwin as our A&R guy?" another one asked.

She winced. Her boss wouldn't sign them because she'd been dating their bass player.

As the next guy leaned in for a hug, Emmie made a quick scan of their faces. No Alex. *Good.* But right when the rhythm guitarist belted his arms around her and lifted her off the floor, Emmie caught sight of him.

Alex Paulson, clad in black leather pants and a stretched-out white T-shirt, flirted with the new receptionist across the hallway. Emmie hated that he'd do it right in front of her, of course, but mostly she couldn't believe he thought so little of their relationship that he actually felt *comfortable* doing it. Like their time together hadn't really counted.

It had to her.

Flash, the lead singer, yanked her out of the other guy's arms and said, "There's my girl." Gorgeous in a rough way, Flash had gotten his nickname because in the middle of every show he asked the girls in the audience to "flash me your tits" so he could take a photo on his phone and post it on the band's website. Classy. "You gonna marry me yet?"

"I think I'd rather marry your fiancée. She's hot."

Just as his hand skimmed down her back heading for forbidden territory, she jerked her hips and pulled out of his embrace.

"You're no fun, Emmie Valencia."

A sharp pain sliced into her heart. Her gaze flicked over his shoulder to the office where Alex and the receptionist shared a quiet laugh. "So I've heard."

"Hey." Tilting his head, he gave her a concerned look. "I'm just playing with you."

"I know." She smiled, hoping to brush away the uncomfortable moment. God, she had to get ahold of herself.

"But if I can't get you to marry me, then can you at least get me one of those bags you got Irwin's kid?"

"You want me to score you the latest Hermès purse?"

"For my fiancée."

Emmie let out an exaggerated sigh. "What did you do this time?" She whipped her hand up. "Never mind. I don't want to hear. And you don't need me to do it—just get yourself on the list. Make a call like I did."

"Oh, come on. We're stuck with Brenda. She doesn't do shit for us. Besides, I don't have your connections. You make shit happen."

"Yes, for Irwin. And I don't *have* connections. I make them when I need to."

"I could make shit happen for you."

Their gazes caught. Behind his incessantly flirtatious vibe lived a shark of a businessman. "You offering me a job, Flash?"

A slow smile ate up his ruggedly handsome features. "Fuck, yeah."

"What kind of job?"

"What kind of job you want?"

Wasn't that just the question? She didn't want just a *job*. She wanted *inside*. Eight years on the periphery of the music industry as Irwin Ledger's personal assistant was enough. She needed to take that next obvious step to A&R coordinator—discovering bands, working with talent—and Flash couldn't help her with that. Only Irwin could.

"Flash?" his bandmate called. "Leave Em alone and get in here. Bob's waiting."

"We'll finish this convo later." Flash started to go.

"Hey, can you close the door behind you?" She didn't need to watch Alex flirting.

Unfortunately, Flash followed her gaze, got an eyeful of Alex and the receptionist, and then looked back at her with a hint of pity. He pointed a finger at her. "Golden rule, baby. Never get involved with the talent."

She smirked. "So we're *not* getting married?" So much for her resolve not to make people uncomfortable. "You know what? Leave it open. I haven't said hello to Alex yet."

He gave her an appreciative smile before taking off.

"Oh, for fuck's sake," her boss shouted. "Emmie?"

"Coming," she said into the intercom box.

"I can't imagine what's taking you so bloody long. I have a crisis, Emmie. Cri-sis."

She pressed the button. "Crisis as in you scuffed your favorite Bruno Magli chocolate suede loafers and they don't make them anymore so you need me to call the designer himself and get a pair custom-made? Or crisis as in the drummer from Wicked Beast fell off the wagon again and can't make the show tonight so I need to get to the hotel and get him sobered up?"

"You mock me. I count on you, and you mock me."

She smiled. "Two seconds." Grabbing her iPad, she spun around to the door . . . only to catch the receptionist pressing her body against Alex.

Oh, hell.

Memories slammed her. His hard chest, the spicy scent of his soap, the creak of his leather. How many times had she held him just like that?

Alex's hand wrapped around the woman's waist, pulling her tight against him. That moment of intimacy, the way Val conformed her body to his, the way her hands cupped the back of his neck, her features soft—it struck Emmie right in her core.

It was so intimate, so sensual. And it hurt. God, it hurt. Because she wasn't sexy like Val. She just . . . wasn't.

Tucking the iPad to her chest, she leaned back against the wall, out of sight. Why did she let him affect her? It wasn't like she missed him or even wanted him. He'd cheated on her.

The sex is fine. It's just not . . . you're not wild, you know? You service *me.*

She cringed remembering his words.

A guy wants more than that.

Oh, God. She couldn't bear the memories. She charged out of her office. Just as she turned into the hallway, she saw Alex capture Val's leg, his hand cupping her thigh, as he murmured against her mouth. Val curled around him, her expression sultry.

God. Emmie had never held him like that. Not with that kind of total abandon.

"Emmie?" Irwin shouted.

"I'm coming." Seeing Val be the woman Alex had wanted *her* to be, the kind of woman who melted around a man, who lost herself in sensation, well, it just made it hard to breathe.

The worst thing was that she'd never felt that kind of passion, that urgency. Not for any guy.

She stood there a moment longer, contemplating barging in and greeting Alex, letting the whole office know she was cool with him. Letting *him* know he didn't affect her anymore.

But then she realized something. She *wasn't* cool with him. She wasn't unaffected at all.

Because he flirted right under her nose with the receptionist.

And that was just a lousy thing to do.

Taking a deep breath, Emmie pushed off the wall and strode out into the hallway. She didn't even spare Alex a glance as she hurried into Irwin's office.

She came to a halt when she saw her boss's expression.

Lips drawn into a taut line, he held the phone to his ear. She walked right up to his ultramodern chair, which hung from the ceiling like a hammock, and he looked at her with utter relief. Immediately, his features turned slack, and he thrust the phone at her.

Placing it to her ear, she had about two seconds to get up to speed, not having the slightest idea who was on the line.

"He wants me to be there, Daddy. I'm, like, his muse. He said he for sure can't do his best work unless I'm there. Do you want this track to suck?"

"Caroline," Emmie said. "Who're we talking about?"

The girl exhaled roughly. "James. He wants me in the studio with him."

Honestly, Emmie did not have time to deal with this nonsense. "James is a drug addict, Caroline. Your dad had to drop him from the label because he couldn't fulfill his contract. Do you see why your dad wouldn't want you hanging out with James while he's out of the country?"

"So, what, I'm supposed to be all locked up because my dad's out of town? I'm an *adult.*"

"Not when your dad's paying your bills, including the lawyer he keeps on retainer for your *indiscretions.*"

"Oh, my God—"

"Last weekend the sound engineer got you so drunk you blacked out. Your dad and I spent seven hours racing around the city, out of our minds, trying to find you. You can't blame him if he's not comfortable giving you the run of Manhattan when he's not around."

"You don't even know what you're talking about. Rory didn't *get* me drunk. I thought I was drinking iced tea. I didn't know they were *Long Island* Iced Teas. That's not his fault. We were just hanging out. Besides, it's not like I'm going to be *alone.* You'll be here."

Tipping her head back, she blew out a breath. "Caroline. You know I'm going with your dad. Look, hanging out with James the drug addict is obviously out of the question, but let's come up with a few—"

"No, you're not."

"I'm not what?"

"Going with my dad."

"Of course I'm going with him." She glanced to Irwin, found him examining his cell phone, swinging in his chair. He didn't have a formal office, the kind with the big oak desk facing two guest chairs, a potted plant, and a filing cabinet. Why would he need a desk? No, he had a plush couch, a world-class sound system, a pinball machine, a dartboard, and a Picasso hanging on the wall.

Movement from the corner of her eye made her turn to the door. Alex stood in the threshold, a hint of remorse on his face. Her heart pounded, and her nerves tingled. But before he could take one step into the office, Irwin flew out of his chair, stalked to the door, and slammed it in her ex's face.

Emmie smiled.

Irwin stalked back to the chair, gripping the metal arm, and set it off rocking again.

"I'm not talking to either of you anymore," Caroline said. "I'm going into the studio with James because I'm his muse and he needs me. And if my dad doesn't like it, then you can just come with us and hang out in the lounge."

"I won't be able to come with you because I *am going to Australia*."

Irwin got up, leaving the leather and chrome chair swinging. He went to the built-in media center that took up one wall and got busy shuffling through his CDs.

"You're not going to Australia! Dad said. God, why are you being such a bitch?"

Emmie closed her eyes, taking a moment before responding. "And so ends my efforts to help you. Here's your dad." With that, she handed the phone back to Irwin. "Hold your ground. She shouldn't be anywhere near James Beckman."

He put the phone back to his ear. "What did you say that made your auntie Emmie hand me back the phone?" His gaze kicked up to Emmie's. "Nothing? Are you sure? She's usually so indulgent with us." His brow furrowed. "A bitch? Ah, well, then. I'm afraid you're on your own on this one, darling. Must go, my love. Kiss, kiss." He hung up on her. "Wretched child, isn't she?"

Emmie smiled, knowing how he adored his only kid. But the smile quickly faded. "So, Australia?"

"Yes, right. Slight change of plans." He ran his hand through his messy, floppy hair. Only the silver streaking through his dark hair made him look anything close to his forty-nine years.

"We're not going?"

"That would be a *total* change of plans. Slight means only one of us isn't going."

"Irwin. We leave tomorrow."

"Emmie, darling, I'm sorry, but I can't leave Caroline alone for six weeks. I'm going to need you to stay here."

Okay, wait. For months Emmie had planned this trip. Two weeks ago one of the producers had realized his passport had expired. She'd had to wave her wand, cast spells, and rub magic lamps in order to push his renewal through. She'd planned every detail down to the minute of their time there. Down to using MapQuest to find the coffee shops closest to the recording studios. She'd booked reservations, arranged delivery of industry periodicals to his hotels, and spent months researching and contacting up-and-coming bands.

Oh, and hang on. She'd spent last night *packing* for her boss. Yes, that meant handling his black silk boxers.

Not only that, but this trip meant more than assisting Irwin. She'd gotten him to agree to let her go off and discover some bands of her own. So she could finally get that promotion. But now, the day before departure, he was telling her she couldn't go. Because . . .

"Wait a minute. You want me to *babysit*?"

"Don't be ridiculous. Of course not. You're not changing nappies. You just need to look after her."

"You want me to babysit your daughter." She said it dully, lowering herself onto the plush leather couch. "I'm twenty-five years old, I've worked for you for eight years—" She flashed him a look. "Even as a high school intern I did more for you than your own secretary. And your best use for me is babysitting."

"You make it sound so trivial. This is my daughter we're talking about. And you're more like a mother to her than her own mother."

"I'm four years older than her. I'm not like her mother."

"No, you're better than her mother. And something's off with her."

Emmie narrowed her gaze.

"More so than usual. You heard her. She's all screechy." His phone buzzed, and he quickly answered it.

Coward.

She needed to get a handle on this situation. Heading to the window, she glanced out, pressing close to look down to the street twenty-seven floors below. If she focused on the steady stream of pedestrian traffic, the yellow cabs, the exhaust-spewing buses, she could tell herself he really was just looking out for his daughter. But she knew better. It was so much more than that.

Oh, hell, she couldn't hold it back. The unbearable pain of being shut out again rolled in and threatened to just *crush* her. God, it hurt.

She wanted in so badly. Why was it so elusive? All these feelings . . . God, it was her childhood all over again. Being shut out of her dad's world for not being creative enough, for not really *getting* him, had made her too sensitive to these slights. Because, truthfully? Artists didn't have a lock on creativity. She had it, too, just in other ways. The whole reason Irwin valued her as his assistant was for her ability to think outside the box. She'd proven herself an Amoeba a hundred times over. So why did he hold her back? Sure, he needed her in this role as his assistant. But she could do so much more.

She knew she was lucky to work for the top A&R guy in the business. At the best record company in the world. She didn't take it for granted, but she also knew it was time for more. If she actually stayed behind and babysat Caroline, she'd never break out of this role. At some point, she had to take the initiative and actually say no to one of his demands. She had to force him to see her in a more creative role, or she'd never have the chance to explore that side of herself. To unleash it.

Besides—*hello*?—he couldn't function without her, so how could he get through the next six weeks on the other side of the world?

She spun around, pointing a finger at him. "What are you going to do without me?"

He looked alert then. Most of the time he had a dozen very important ideas going on in his head all at once, so it was nearly impossible to gain his full attention.

Those sharp blue eyes pierced her, and she knew she had it then.

"Right," he said to the caller. "Emmie will get back to you later." He stowed his phone in the back pocket of his jeans. "I'm taking Bax with me."

Had she been standing on a trap door? Because the floor gave way, and she was in free fall. Baxter Reynolds had started as an intern five years ago. When Irwin hadn't shown any interest in promoting him, he'd attached himself to Bob, one of the other A&R guys.

And *now* Irwin was showing an interest in him? Instead of Emmie?

She didn't know what to say. "Bax?" How was *Bax* better than her?

His phone buzzed, but he ignored it as he came right up to her, close enough that she could smell the Christian Dior cologne she kept stocked for him. He brushed his hand down her arm. "I'm sorry, Em. As much as I need you with me, I can't leave Caroline alone."

"Where's her mother?"

"Well, that's the point, isn't it? I can't really count on Claire. But I *can* count on you."

See? When he did that, she caved. Irwin loved his daughter, and who else could he trust to look out for her? His entire family lived in England. Flighty, gorgeous, sexy Claire Murphy flitted around the world on a whim, barely touching down long enough to take care of anything but her most immediate and impulsive needs.

But Emmie needed more. She needed *in*. She couldn't stay his personal assistant forever. So what should she do? Of course, if Caroline were in any danger, Emmie would have to help. But the girl was twenty-one. And, sorry, but Emmie simply wasn't her mother or her big sister.

She didn't want to let Irwin down. But she was continuing to let herself down if she never took the next step—which meant taking charge of her own career.

She needed the promotion. "I'm not going to babysit Caroline, Irwin. You need me in Australia, and I need to go to Australia to see the bands I've been researching."

He let out a deep sigh. "Truth is, you've set everything up perfectly, as you always do. You've got my every moment organized and arranged to the point that I *don't* need you there."

"But you need Bax?"

"You've given me the list of bands to check out, along with the scheduled times to meet them. So, yes, I need Bax."

"I researched those bands."

"From the privacy of your office. Bax *lives* it, Emmie."

"You're saying I'm not good enough to be promoted?" She felt the sting of it, like he'd doused alcohol on a blister. *No, no, no.* That was bullcrap. She *was* good enough.

"I'm saying that I need you right where you are."

"And I need a career. Not just a job."

His phone buzzed again, and this time he checked the caller ID. "I have to take this."

"No. Please, Irwin. Not until we settle this."

"It *is* settled, Em." He said it gently. "I'm taking Bax." He punched the button on his phone. "Yes?"

"Then I quit."

Irwin's eyes flared. His features burned crimson.

She stood there, letting the words settle around her. The only sound was her own breathing, the only movement the wild and erratic beating of her heart.

Had she actually done it? Quit her coveted job?

"Wait, wait, hang on a moment," he said into the phone.

"I'm sorry, Irwin. I can't keep doing this. You have no intention of promoting me." *Standing on the periphery hurts too much.*

"You can't quit." He turned back to the phone. "Let me get back to you." Without waiting for a response, he hung up. "You can't quit." He looked utterly lost and baffled. "Why would you quit?"

"I'll find my replacement." She turned to go.

"Good God, Emmie. You cannot leave me."

"You've given me no choice."

"All right, just stop this. Stop it right now. I can't function without you, and you know that. You're threatening me. That's not a good way to get a promotion."

"It's not a threat. I told you I needed a career, and you told me you needed me right where I am. Fetching your Americanos and cajoling your landlord into letting you keep amphibians in your penthouse apartment isn't a career. I can't be your personal assistant the rest of my life. You get that, right? I've loved working for you, but it's supposed to be a stepping stone. You've just shown me it's a cage. I deserve more."

He had a strange expression, like he was listening to an incoming message from an ethereal source. "It's not right for you."

"What isn't?" He'd punched the accelerator on her pulse, making it rev so fast she went light-headed. *This is not happening.* He was *not* shutting her out of this world.

"A&R."

"I . . ." She found it hard to take a full breath. But he was wrong. Of course it was right for her. She pretty much did the job anyway. Maybe not discovering the bands, but . . . oh, God. She needed to breathe. *Deep breaths.* "That's ridiculous. I've been doing it for eight years."

"Em, look, I have to get to the studio. You simply can't quit. I won't allow it. We'll find a way to compromise, right? I want you to be happy."

"I'm not happy babysitting your daughter."

He winced. "Loud and clear."

"I need to know there's a place for me here other than going through your laundry room and drawers looking for a missing cashmere night sock."

Looking pained, he touched her arm, ignoring his buzzing phone. "Let's both think on it. Come up with a solution."

"Am I going to Australia with you tomorrow?"

"No."

She bit down hard on fear. It was scary as hell, but she had to do this.

"Emmie . . ."

She turned and walked out of the room.

ALSO AVAILABLE FROM ERIKA KELLY

Praise for *You Really Got Me*:

"Lovable characters and pulse-pounding chemistry
make this one of my favorite reads of the year!"
—*New York Times* bestselling author Laura Kaye

"Sexy, lyrical and electric with hot, romantic tension."
—*New York Times* bestselling author Lauren Blakely

erikakellybooks.com
facebook.com/erika.kelly.1293
penguin.com

M1641T0215

Discover Romance

berkleyjoveauthors.com

See what's coming up next from your favorite romance authors and explore all the latest Berkley, Jove, and Sensation selections.

See what's new

~

Find author appearances

~

Win fantastic prizes

~

Get reading recommendations

~

Chat with authors and other fans

~

Read interviews with authors you love

berkleyjoveauthors.com

M1G0610